A Whisper of Smoke

A Nove

By

Angela Hoke

For Grandma Sandy (Elsie),

whose real life was always more interesting than fiction

Part I

Chapter 1: Shit Fits and Dead People

Summer 1965

On the day of the camp-out that changed my life, I found my sister and brother playing psychic gypsy at the kitchen table. I paused in the doorway to watch.

Annabelle slapped both hands on the table, her silver bracelets ringing against the metal surface. "I see danger in your future," she said, as the polka-dot scarf tied around her head slipped down over her eyes. She shoved it back into place.

Hank plucked a cocklebur from his sock. "What kind of danger?" he asked. His wavy blond hair stuck out at odd angles, and I could smell his dirty-dog little boy smell from across the room.

Steam from the stove rose behind Annabelle as she consulted her crystal ball. "The kind that will change your life forever!" Mama had put mascara on her, and she had a big beauty mark painted above her lip.

Hank crossed his arms and raised an eyebrow. "You're not very good at this."

"Yes I am!" she snapped. "You will have a terrible accident in fifteen days!"

But Hank only snorted. "Fifteen days?"

Or maybe a year," she hissed. At this, she gestured dramatically, casting a dull reflection in the black surface of her "crystal ball."

Wait, black *surface?*

"Is that… Is that my Magic 8 Ball?" I asked, and she jumped at the sound of my voice.

Hank snatched it from the table before Annabelle could hide it, turning it over in his hand. "Neat," he said, shaking it vigorously. Annabelle bolted from the room, long chestnut curls and scarves flying.

I screamed in frustration. "Stay out of my things!"

Grabbing the ball from Hank, I stuffed it into my pillowcase with my other supplies – a flashlight and my red scarf, a couple of candles (though Calvin would probably nix those, call them a fire hazard), my prayer book and my new Ouija Board, still smelling of shellac and cardboard dust in its new Parker Brothers box. By the door, I set down my pillowcase with some force and turned, anxious to find Annabelle and make her pay. But before I could, my older sister Lorelei came in, reminding me that there were more important things to attend to – like getting the rest of the snacks together for Mabel's camp-out. I was looking forward to the festivities, with a bonfire and later a séance in the hayloft, and maybe a little ghost hunting in the woods.

Mama pranced in as we were finishing up, Annabelle scuttling in behind her. She scrambled up on a chair, out of arms' reach and not daring to look in my direction. I wanted to snatch her up and give her a little shake. But before I could do or say anything retaliatory, Mama grabbed me.

"Dance with me, darling Susanna," she said, spinning me in an under-arm turn. She was wearing a loudly-patterned apron over her bright blue top and crisp white cigarette pants, white Keds on her dancing feet. I thought she looked beautiful.

In spite of my lingering irritation, I laughed with her, but pulled away after one turn around the kitchen floor. Mama wasn't fazed – she twirled alone as she glided back to the stove. She hummed as she stirred, excited about the party she and Daddy were hosting which would be starting in an hour or so.

"You ready?" Lorelei asked me, as she packed away the last of our provisions.

Annabelle smacked her hand down on the table. "I want to go too!" I had already annoyed Lorelei by inviting Hank to come with us to the bonfire. Earlier, he'd knocked a spoon on the floor, slopping sauce, and Mama had very nearly lost her temper with him. Partially I'd invited him because I felt sorry for him, but I also didn't like the idea of leaving him alone with Mama when he'd already gotten under her skin. In any case, I hadn't planned on asking Annabelle too. I waited for Mama to insist that I do just that.

But Mama looked at Annabelle conspiratorially. "Belle, wouldn't you much rather spend your evening with me? Prince George is coming for tonight's festival, and we maidens must prepare the royal court."

"Good gosh!" Lorelei muttered, jerking the picnic basket off the counter and flinging her glorious (her opinion, not mine) long hair behind her. She was agitated, like she was itching to go. Uncle George was a jokester and always picking at us. I found it kind of endearing, but it pissed Lorelei off.

Annabelle bounced on her knees. "Think Uncle George will bring me a surprise?" Before anyone could answer, she lifted her chin and turned to Hank. "I can't come. I'm busy helping Mommy and you're not invited."

4

His shoulders drooped, just a little, enough so that I wanted to smack her. But I resisted and, instead, gathered up my pillowcase and sleeping bag, pushing Hank ahead of me out the door as I shouted good-byes over my shoulder. Lorelei followed, and I sighed with relief when she and Mama crossed paths without an altercation. Finally we were safely outside, heading towards Cora, Elton and Kathleen, who were playing twilight stickball next-door.

We lived on the outskirts of Louisville, at the shoreline that separated city and country. We straddled the two worlds, like a threshold between two dimensions. On one side was a city lane, with house after house lined up like box cars, extending until the distant hillside swallowed them up. I found it comforting how normal it seemed, with people doing what I imagined normal people did everywhere – efficient fathers like Mr. Wagner and Mr. Harris racing against the night, trying to mow one more row before it was too dark to see; rambunctious kids, like the Taylor twins, playing Swinging Statues through a maze of sheets while their mother, determined to hang clothes on the line, chased them away; older kids flying down roads to the faint whirring sound of bicycle wheels on pavement, or the soft click-click-click of baseball cards clothes-pinned to the spokes.

Those sights were comforting. But there was one place where I was completely content, and that was the Conner farm, with its acres of woods and fields, and all its unexplored mysteries. This was where magic happened, and I was drawn to it, like flies to honey. I'd always been, even before Calvin and Mabel became my best friends.

A Whisper of Smoke   *Angela Hoke*

5

Seeing us approach, Kathleen broke away from the game (Elton yelling *'Oh, come on!'* with evident frustration) and ran up to greet us. "Here you are, finally. We've been waiting forever for you." She bounced on the balls of her feet, twisting her body and swishing her blue and yellow sundress. Her dirty blond hair was falling out of her pony tail and she repeatedly swept it away in a compulsive salute as she stared at Hank. She eyed him like he was blackberry jam on toast and she wanted to gobble him up, but he didn't notice.

"We had to escape from prison," said Lorelei. But by then, Kathleen was no longer listening – Hank had taken off towards the others, and she chased after him yelling for him to wait up.

Mabel stood by the fire pit with her hands on her hips, wearing Calvin's old blue jeans rolled up to the knees and mismatched socks. She lugged one more hay bale into position around the circle and nodded in satisfaction before cheerfully waving to us. Over by the barn, Calvin wrestled firewood from a stingy rick. Besides his standard white t-shirt and jeans, he was wearing his new glasses – yet another of many recent changes that I found unsettling.

Calvin always acted a little bit like an old man, but I'd chalked it up to him being a boy that was, shall we say, "too big for his britches." Even though he was only fifteen, he talked about stripping tobacco, baling hay and bushel prices. But lately he had sprouted some new muscles, and they wound around his bones like kudzu. His leg hair had gone from sparse to substantial *(ick)*, and this new protuberance he called a goozle was just distracting the way it bobbed up and down his neck. I did my best to ignore these new developments, and even found myself irritated at his audacity, plunging into puberty so blatantly.

By the time I'd unloaded our supplies and helped Mabel finish with preparations, the sun had set and Calvin had a good fire going. Everyone raced to claim seats around the flames just as Mr. and Mrs. Conner came outside carrying the ingredients for S'mores. As we roasted marshmallows and pieced together chocolate and graham crackers, Mabel and Calvin told funny stories about each other until we were crying with laughter.

"Remember when you thought diaper rash cream was pomade, and you fixed your hair with it?" Mabel said, and I snorted RC out of my nose.

"Hey – it held its style. You just didn't appreciate my ingenuity," Calvin replied.

I was still sputtering giggles when Mr. Conner began speaking in his low voice, immediately quieting us. Taking us back over a hundred years, Mr. Conner told the tale of a sweet young slave girl named Jezzie, and how she had been tragically murdered right on that very farm. According to Mr. Conner, Jezzie was a kind soul, and even took care of the cruel master in his time of need. But the other slaves hated her for it and, during a terrible, dark thunderstorm, they beat her to death with human bones in a fit of rage. I was following him up to that point, as enthralled as everybody else. But the human bones as clubs part sounded a little far-fetched to me. Catching Calvin's attention, I mouthed to him, *"Is this real?"* He shrugged and looked away, a little too quickly.

Whether true or not, I shivered as the trees rustled with unrest.

"That's why Jezzie still haunts this farm," Mr. Conner was saying. "Yep, she's still in these parts. See, she's trying to find who would have betrayed and killed her like that. And on a warm night sometimes, a night like this one as a matter of fact, you can sometimes hear her calling out in the night. Wanting to know who did this to her."

Hank and Elton sat stock still next to each other on a hay bale, their knobby knees lined up like four baseballs on a bench. Cora burrowed into Mabel's side, and Kathleen was curled up on Mrs. Conner's lap. We all sat tense, like we were each straining to hear Jezzie moaning in the wind. Then, out of nowhere, we heard it.

"Whoooo! Whoooo!"

I nearly jumped out of my skin as several of the kids screamed. Mr. Conner broke into a wide grin as the barn owl that had been the source of our fright took flight from the open hayloft. As I watched its dark shadow, breathing deep to calm my own racing heart, it didn't escape my notice that Calvin was snorting at our expressions, annoyingly smug.

As the moon began to rise, Mrs. Conner gathered up the kids to head inside. She tried to talk Hank into staying the night with them, but it was Elton's pleading that finally won him over. Hank hesitated, looking uncertainly back towards our house. He was probably hoping that when they called Mama to ask if it was okay, she would say she missed him and order him to come straight home. But the reality was he wouldn't get any of Mama's attention tonight, not with the party going on. He would just end up putting himself to bed, all alone.

Hank ran over to give me an awkward hug (he knew I wouldn't let him off without one) and I patted the sweaty blond curls pasted to his head, then he waved to the others before following Elton to the house. I watched him go, hoping he'd have a good time, glad that he would be safe. Mr. Conner checked on the animals and made sure the pasture gates were locked before heading in. He called out good-night and then added, with a perfectly straight face, to watch out for spooks.

Angela Hoke   *A Whisper of Smoke*

I shivered with excitement tinged with fear, a feeling I loved. Our prospects for contacting spirits were looking promising, and I was ready to get started. I jumped up. "Let's do some ghost hunting," I said. Ghost hunting had become a favorite pastime of ours over recent weeks, and that was before the added allure of Jezzie and the murderous slaves.

Mabel was on board with that. "Goody!" she squealed, as she darted off to the barn for some flashlights. She quickly returned, but she'd only found two flashlights that worked, so two of us would be running blind.

"Give me one of those," Lorelei bossed. She took the big silver one, which left a smaller flashlight for someone else.

"I don't need one," said Calvin.

"Me neither," I said, not to be outdone. Mabel shrugged and flipped on the other light, and we were off.

According to the unofficial rules of ghost hunting, we were each to venture out into the woods surrounding the barn and look for ghosts, while at the same time looking for opportunities to scare each other. Calvin and I were the best at it. I had good night vision, and I wasn't scared of much. And he knew the woods better than anyone else.

I immediately took off towards the west. There was a trail there that wound around across a small creek, and doubled back towards the barn. I knew this trail almost as well as Calvin—I'd walked and played on it enough times. As I crept through the forest, I dodged big tree limbs that reached for me like earth's claws. I swatted at mosquitoes that bit at my neck and brushed aside brand new webs that would be rebuilt as soon as I passed. I moved quickly, intent on putting some distance between myself and Calvin, my ghost-hunting nemesis.

When I reached the creek, I listened for gurgling but there was none. It was dry, which was a blessing and a nuisance – a blessing because I could cross it quickly, and a nuisance because I didn't have the sound of running water to mask my movements. I leapt across, crouching when I landed, and paused to listen. I heard scores of frogs and crickets and, yes, some rustling twenty or so yards to my right. It could be some nocturnal animal—a raccoon or possum, but I had to be vigilant. Calvin was sneaky, and I couldn't afford to be caught unaware.

As stealthily as possible, I made my way slowly along the trail, performing a continuous sweeping scan of the foliage as I walked. Then I was entering a part of the trail that was covered by dense trees, where the moonlight was obstructed with such finality it was like someone flipped a switch. I paused just before entering that section, and I couldn't help thinking about the wicked witch's forest in *The Wizard of Oz*. It had that kind of ominous feel, as though it were not just dark but some kind of spatial vortex that consumed light. It was the kind of place where ghosts would linger. At that thought, the hair stood up on my arms and across my neck. My heartbeat sped up and thundered in my ears, even as I strained to listen more intently for unnatural presences.

For a moment, I was frozen by fear. But that was unacceptable. I couldn't stand the thought of Calvin coming upon me, seeing me scared stiff. He would never let me live that down. By force of will, I took a step into the void. Immediately, it was like I'd crossed into another world. There were no frogs singing or crickets chirping here, and even though I knew they continued their songs just a few yards away, they seemed miles distant. All of my nerve endings were alert, as every part of me reached out with its senses. It was the brief blast of cool air that really made my skin crawl, and I knew I was not alone.

Angela Hoke   *A Whisper of Smoke*

My instincts told me to run, but my feet were planted on the hard ground. I surveyed the dark shapes around me, my eyes wide and unblinking. Shadows flitted in my peripheral vision, and flapping rustled leaves above my head. Skittering noises to my left and right made me jumpy. And then I saw it. Something white, flickering between the trees – visible one second, then gone, then visible again.

"Jezzie?" I whispered, hoping that it was her and not one of her murderers. I forced myself to take a step forward. There it was again, off in the distance. At times it seemed to have a distinct human form, and I thought that I might be seeing my first real live ghost. I was thrilled and terrified all at once. I took another step, and searched again. There! It seemed closer this time, as it flashed between the trees.

Could this be real? Could I be on the brink of an encounter? I'd sensed the presence of sprits before, particularly during our séances. At times, I felt as though I shared a connection with them, like they were conveying their deepest desires and emotions through me. Calvin was convinced it was just my over-active imagination. Maybe so – I would concede to having a healthy imagination. But I liked to think it was something more, that I had perceptions the normal person did not.

I heard a sound to my right, and it was very close. I spun around, my heart pounding. Nothing. And if there was something, I'm not sure I would have seen it. It was just too dark.

"Is that you Jezzie?" I spoke softly, and the wind carried my words away.

I sensed the presence at my back a moment before it touched me. Fingers brushed my neck, and I lost it.

"Shit, shit, shit!" I screamed, and I started to run. Pounding feet followed me as I barreled through the trees. Lights and darks flitted all around, giving chase. Up ahead, I saw the break in the trees, and I prayed that I would reach it in time.

I didn't. Something clamped over my arm and jerked me to a stop. And I collided with a big, solid form.

"I got you!" Calvin said into my hair.

My chest was heaving with fear and adrenaline, when I noticed the wood smoke slash cow poop smell that I knew so well.

"Oh, you!" I said, punching at his chest. "You asshole." I punched him again.

"That's four cuss words in a row. Don't you need to do some Hail Marys or something?" I could feel his smirk in the dark. He was still holding my arm, and I shrugged it off. I glared at him, and as my eyes adjusted to the filtered moonlight that now came through, I could see his eyes shining in the night. I was so mad I could spit, and at the same time so relieved I wanted to hug him.

Of course, I wasn't about to follow through on the second impulse. Instead, without another word, I turned and stalked off, back towards the campfire. I could hear him coming after me.

"Aww, Sus. Don't be mad. You'd have done the same thing to me, if you found me talking to dead people in the middle of the woods."

I knew he was right, but I was too embarrassed to say so. Plus, I wasn't sure I could trust my voice not to shake.

Across the field, I saw Mabel bending over with her hands on her knees, as though she were panting from exertion. Lorelei was lounging on her hay bale once again, none the worse for wear. Her white shirt glowed, and I wondered briefly whether it was Lorelei that I'd seen in the woods. It seemed unlikely because I couldn't imagine my sister wandering at night through the part of the woods I'd just exited, particularly without her flashlight on. But was that really any more unlikely than the alternative? That I'd seen Jezzie?

"Susanna," Calvin said from behind me. Man, he was persistent. He grabbed my arm and pulled me to a stop. I refused to turn around and look at him, so he was forced to come about and stand in front of me. I glanced at Mabel and Lorelei to see whether they were watching, and it didn't appear that they'd seen us yet.

I glowered at him. "What?"

He looked me right in the eyes. "I'm sorry I scared you."

"You didn't," I said, turning my head.

"Hey." He reached up and touched my chin, turning my face towards his. I felt a jolt, and it made me uneasy. We didn't touch each other like that, ever. And as though he suddenly remembered that fact, he dropped his hand.

"I am really sorry." I looked at him and he seemed so earnest, I couldn't be mad. Plus, he was absolutely right – I would have done the same to him in a heartbeat, and reveled in it.

I took in his white t-shirt and had a thought. "Was that you?" I asked.

"Huh?"

"In the woods, running through the trees ahead of me."

"No, I was behind you. I'd just found you when you had your little "shit fit," so to speak."

I grabbed his shirt. "Are you lying to me? Don't lie to me."

"I'm not lying. I don't know what you saw, but it wasn't me."

I searched his face, but I didn't detect any deception. "Okay," I said slowly. I was turning around to walk back towards the fire, when I saw something white flash in the corner of my vision.

"There!" I said, pointing. He turned around to look, but it was gone, whatever it was. I stood still for a moment, searching, but I didn't see it again.

Shrugging, I turned back towards the fire and started walking. As we made our way back over to Mabel and Lorelei, I was secretly glad that Calvin was with me. I was feeling a little creeped out.

"Who screamed?" Mabel asked when she saw us.

Calvin looked at me, but he didn't say a word.

"I did," I said. "Calvin got me good." I glanced at him, expecting him to gloat, but he was stirring the fire with a stick.

"Well, you scared the crap out of me," said Mabel. "I came high-tailing it back to the fire."

"What are we going to do now?" Lorelei asked, like she was bored.

Chapter 2: Frenchy-Frenchy

"Truth or dare, Susanna," Lorelei was saying, but I barely heard her. I was still in shock over what she'd just been dared to do by Mabel, and how enthusiastically she'd complied. I wasn't quite sure how we'd ended up here, playing a game that's generally only played between girls. But yet here we were, and things had deteriorated quickly. Somehow, we'd graduated from the supernatural to the unnatural in a few short minutes.

Even before Mabel suggested playing *Truth or Dare* I was feeling unsettled. The ghost hunting, including its hair-raising climax, had gotten my adrenaline pumping, and I was having a hard time chasing away my jitters. I told myself it was because I'd had a heck of a scare, and that the strange encounter with Calvin, when he'd touched my face, had nothing to do with it. I almost believed it. But then Mabel veered us down a path that, in some ways, was even more frightening. And from the scared rabbit expression on Calvin's face, he seemed like he might have been regretting his decision to stick around.

The game had started off slowly, with everybody choosing "truth" and answering questions about who you would marry and have you ever kissed anybody before (the French kind, with tongues). Mabel and I each picked a famous person as our ideal husband. Calvin declined to answer on the basis that it was a stupid question. Lorelei was the only one that gave a real answer, but it was some boy that went to one of the Catholic

A Whisper of Smoke   *Angela Hoke*

high schools and none of us knew him. Then we progressed to questions about French kissing. I never got the question, thank goodness. My answer would have been embarrassing, especially after learning that Calvin spent seven minutes in heaven with Barbara Big-boobs and now was some kind of make-out king. The only truly uncomfortable moment so far came when Calvin admitted he'd sometimes seen Lorelei and me getting dressed in front of our window when it was dark outside. He assured us it was accidental, but I was still mortified. I guess I thought that since we couldn't see out through the screen, no one could see in.

Still, except for his obvious discomfort about his "accidental" spying, even Calvin had begun to visibly relax. But then it was Mabel's turn again, and when she asked Lorelei the big question, I could tell before Lorelei said a word that she would choose "dare." When she did, Mabel smiled slow and wide and my skin prickled.

"I dare you … to …" while she hesitated, Calvin gave us a mock drum roll. "I got it. Take your shirt off and run around the fire topless!"

The drum roll abruptly fizzled, and I gasped like a clumsy cymbal.

"Mabel, I think you've flipped your lid," Calvin sputtered, when he found his voice. But Lorelei thought it was a good dare, and the next thing I knew, she was peeling off her top, revealing her cross-your-heart white cotton bra. I expected her to stop there, but instead she reached around behind her back and began to unfasten the clasp. Lorelei was scared to walk through the woods at night without a flashlight, but apparently topless traipsing was no big deal.

As Lorelei undressed, Mabel's eyes widened and she shifted up on her knees. Calvin glanced at the sky, at the fire, towards his house – anywhere except at Lorelei. I barked at him to close his eyes.

Angela Hoke   *A Whisper of Smoke*

"It's okay, he doesn't have to," Lorelei said. But Calvin seemed grateful for some instruction, and he closed his eyes tightly, even shielding them with his hands. He'd barely covered them when Lorelei dropped the bra to the ground. Whooping like a wild Indian, she ran around the outside of the campfire. Mabel cheered while Lorelei's water balloon breasts pounded her ribcage.

In seconds, Lorelei was back at her seat. She pulled her top back over her head and told Calvin it was safe to look. He was hesitant to open his eyes, I could tell. But when he did, I looked at Calvin and he looked at me, both of us a little traumatized. Mabel and Lorelei, on the other hand, were grinning hugely. They'd found a common bond – an appreciation for outrageous personal expression. I personally thought we ought to stop before someone had to jump through the fire naked or tip cows blindfolded or something equally extreme, and I said so. Or better yet, we could search for the mysterious white ghost in the woods, a prospect that seemed infinitely less risky than playing this game with Mabel and Lorelei. But Lorelei wasn't about to let us quit.

"It's just getting good," she argued, and Mabel whole-heartedly agreed. That's when Lorelei turned to me, smiling slyly. "Truth or dare, Susanna."

Well, I knew what the answer had to be. I wasn't going to be a wimp, especially with Calvin there. I just hoped it wasn't anything too embarrassing.

"Dare." Even to my own ears, my voice was flatter than Sister Agatha reciting the multiplication tables.

Lorelei slapped her hands together and rubbed them back and forth.

A Whisper of Smoke   *Angela Hoke*

"I dare you to … "I waited, and the pause was excruciatingly long. Turned out, it wasn't long enough.

"French kiss Calvin!" she said. I hit my ear with my palm to clear it, because I was sure I hadn't heard right.

"Yes!" Mabel exclaimed, clapping her hands. "That's a great one."

Well, that was not what I was expecting. I just stared at her, my mouth hanging open stupidly. Calvin seemed not to know what to do, and he just looked from one crazy girl to the next. Finally, he looked at me. I didn't want to look at him, but I couldn't turn away either. So we just stared at each other, dumbfounded, sharing a moment of uncertainty.

"Susanna, you don't have to," he said to me, but instead of making me feel better, it kind of hurt my feelings.

"Oh, yes she does," Lorelei corrected. "She chose dare, and that's my dare. It's no worse than running around the campfire with your titties hanging out."

She had a point, there.

I took deep breaths to calm my nerves and cast a nervous glance at Calvin. I searched his face intently for any sign of disgust or dread, but I didn't see any. As I considered, I flashed back to earlier when he'd touched my face in the dark. And while it had surprised me, I decided it wasn't entirely unpleasant, being close to Calvin. I reached a decision – if I had to share a first kiss with someone, it might as well be with him.

"A dare's a dare," I shrugged, though my stomach fluttered.

Somehow I gathered the strength to move over to his hay bale. I sat down next to him and my bare legs brushed his jeans. Even through denim, he was warm as the fire.

Angela Hoke   *A Whisper of Smoke*

"Come on, smoochy, smoochy," Mabel goaded.

"Mabel," I said, turning to her. "I can't do this if you're going to say stupid things."

"Okay, I'll shut up." She pretended to zip her lips, lock them closed and throw away the key.

Looking back at Calvin, I faltered. He saw it and offered me a private smile that was meant to comfort me, but I was still terrified. This was much scarier than ghosts.

He hesitated for a moment, and when it was clear I had absolutely no idea what to do, he tilted his head to the side and moved in. I froze. All I could see were lips coming towards me, so I tried to focus on other parts of his face. I noticed he had an asymmetrical spray of whiskers across his upper lip, and that his nose was sunburned and peeling, revealing a pink patch of baby skin shaped like Texas.

The closer he came, the nearer I was to full-on panic. But then he was right there, a breath away. When I was sure there was no turning back, I closed my eyes and waited.

And his mouth was on mine. *Wow.* Immediately a rush of heat soared down through my middle all the way to places I usually don't talk about in polite company. I wasn't sitting outside under the stars any longer – I was in a dream and falling, drowning even. I flailed around for a bit, figuratively speaking, but after a moment, I started to get the hang of it. I liked that he smelled of beef jerky, and that his lips were slightly sticky, sweet as marshmallows.

This was actually very nice, I realized.

But he was only getting started. The next instant, he pressed his lips harder against mine and suddenly our mouths were open. That was surprising enough, but when his tongue touched the space between, I

A Whisper of Smoke   *Angela Hoke*

went over the moon and didn't come down. Colors flashed against my eyelids, quick, like the strobe effect of an old movie reel, and chills raced in and out of secret places even I didn't know I had.

He kissed and kissed me, and I could have let him keep kissing me forever. After a minute or twelve, my hands grew restless, itching to latch onto something. I was timid, but they had a mind of their own and I found myself reaching towards him. They settled on his shirt, where they rested lightly. I could sense his chest beneath the fabric, and I wanted to press my fingers against it, to feel whether it was firm and angular as I imagined. But I was too shy.

I'd had no idea that this was what kissing was like, but I really, really liked it. *We should have started doing it a long time ago!* I thought, and I suddenly realized that having a boy for a best friend was actually pretty brilliant.

I should have been more focused. While my brain was strategizing about how and when we could do this again, I didn't realize that the kiss was ending. When he broke it, he cut loose my tether and now I was floating away into the void. I was still somewhere else, and I didn't want to come back. But then that part was over too, and I *was* back – on a hay bale, listening to Mabel's giggles and the sound of crackling logs, shivering from a cool breeze.

I didn't want to, but I opened my eyes slowly, afraid of what I would see. But it was just Calvin, the same boy I'd known since forever. Except that he was looking at me very intently, and I was quite sure this was the first time we'd ever stared into each other's eyes like this. His were brown and beautiful as a doe's, by the way. I'd never noticed that before.

Angela Hoke   *A Whisper of Smoke*

"They did it! They actually did it!" Mabel yelped, bouncing on her knees. "I cannot believe it. You did the Frenchy-Frenchy with my brother!"

Mabel's excitement broke the spell, and we turned away from each other. Suddenly I was extremely embarrassed, and I could no longer look at him at all. It was beginning to seem unreal that just a couple of minutes ago, I was certain kissing was going to become our new favorite pastime.

By the time I stumbled back over to my hay bale, I noticed that Lorelei was eyeing us speculatively.

"What?" I snapped, anxious to regain my previous persona of unflappability.

Her eyes were trained on me. "Well? How was it?"

"Leave her alone," said Calvin, and I felt a rush of affection to hear him defend me.

"Maybe I was asking you," Lorelei replied. She turned her eyes on him. "Maybe I'd like a turn." I had been feeling a little dazed, but *this* got my attention. I looked at Calvin to see his reaction, and for a split second, I pictured him grinning at his amazing good fortune. When I actually did look at him, he looked stunned – his mouth worked, but no words came out.

"Oh, things are getting *really* crazy now," said Mabel, and in the next moment, Lorelei was crossing the short distance to Calvin. She sat next to him, grabbed the front of his shirt and crushed her lips against him.

My jaw dropped in disbelief, and my stomach flipped in an unpleasant way that was the opposite of what I'd experienced kissing Calvin. But then my shock faded and I really started to get pissed off.

Curling my hands into fists, I was two seconds away from punching Lorelei right in the kisser, no pun intended. But then Calvin began to respond, and my swell of territorial fury abruptly died. His hands twitched, and Lorelei felt it. Her fingers weren't shy at all – they reached right up and went into his hair.

I was sure that Calvin was about to wrap his arms around her at any second, and my humiliation would be complete. But he didn't. He seemed to be trying to resist – after the hand twitching, he had balled his hands into fists. I fantasized it was because he wanted to punch Lorelei too. I wanted to tell him that I could do the punching – all he had to do was stop the dang kissing! Before either of us could take action, Lorelei abruptly pulled back. Like me, she stopped and looked into his eyes. But there was no intimacy in her gaze, only puzzlement, like she couldn't understand why he did not react as she expected. She stood up and went back to her seat. "I'm bored. Let's do something else."

I knew that tone – that was Lorelei's pissed off tone. Well, she wasn't the only one who was pissed. I wanted to ask her where she got off, right then and there. I might have done it, too, if Mabel and Lorelei hadn't started talking about Jezzie and ghosts as they kicked dirt over the dying fire. Instead, I looked over at Calvin. He had not moved, but was still sitting with a stunned expression on his face. In a hot wave, my anger shifted towards him. He hadn't given in exactly, but he hadn't pushed Lorelei away either.

Once the fire was extinguished, Mabel and Lorelei decided it was time to conduct a séance up in the hayloft. I didn't even care about that anymore. All I could think was how awful I felt, like I'd been betrayed, and I how I did not want to spend another minute with my sister. But I couldn't say so, not without showing how hurt I was.

Angela Hoke
A Whisper of Smoke

When the slumber party moved toward the barn, I followed because I couldn't reason a better alternative. Glancing back at where Calvin was pulling the hay bales to one side, safely away from any remaining embers, I wanted to say something, but I didn't know what. Should we discuss what just happened? Did we need to establish new boundaries for our friendship? Should I tell him that the kiss meant something to me, and point out that it I was sure it hadn't meant a thing to Lorelei? But I didn't say anything. Instead, I climbed the ladder to the loft, lost in thoughts that made no sense.

He startled me when he called out a good-night. But that wasn't the worst of it.

He sounded infuriatingly normal, like nothing had changed at all.

Chapter 3: Shelly and the Jerk

For the rest of the summer, I went on native hunting expeditions in the woods, fished for bull sharks in the mystical creeks, and rode horses to escape from wild Indians. In other words, I used fantasy as a way to avoid reality, whatever that was. When I wasn't occupying my mind with adventures, I alternated between feeling extremely irritated that my world had been so rudely upended by the events of that night at the campfire, and dipped in melancholy thick as molasses to think Calvin might prefer Lorelei to me, or worse, that he was completely unmoved by me at all.

Immediately following the camp-out, I'd taken my cues from Calvin, who behaved as though the kissing never happened. It wasn't quite as easy for me, but I was more than agreeable as we immersed ourselves in activities that didn't require much talking or close physical interaction. Careful avoidance was the objective, in the hopes that memories would dull. And as we rode horses in single file along narrow trails and played stickball with the kids, I almost convinced myself that I must have dreamed the whole thing.

But then the day came when I could no longer fool myself. We were meeting at the big creek for a swim, and though we'd done so a million times before, this time was different. I'd kissed Calvin, and despite my dedication to denial, I no longer looked at him the same way. He had turned adorable, making my insides roll around like socks in the dryer

Angela Hoke   *A Whisper of Smoke*

whenever he flashed his half-smile my way. And without clomping hooves or fly balls to distract us, I worried that all my feelings, which I'd worked so hard to suppress, would overwhelm me in his presence or, worse, become obvious to him.

On top of my anxiety about our pending proximity, I was also dealing with my recent revelation that I was not a kid anymore, and hadn't been for some time. It wasn't that I was ignorant. I'd learned about raging sex hormones and menstruation from the Sisters, and I'd noticed, vaguely, that my body had been changing. Still, I'd vigorously resisted it, to the extent that every four or five weeks when I was reluctantly compelled to strap on my sanitary napkin belt, I'd pretended I was secretly wounded in some imaginary battle across enemy lines, as I nursed myself back to health for the six or seven days it took to "heal". But it didn't end there. Mama had gotten me my first bra, so my headlights wouldn't be on high-beam in t-shirts, as she so delicately put it. But I'd seen old men with bigger boobs than me, and they didn't scoop them up into a harness. So I had been refusing to wear it on principle.

But there was no denying it anymore.

As Hank and I walked through the woods towards the big creek at the rear of the property, I was overcome by an almost clinical self-awareness. And as I began to notice my body in earnest, I realized, with great horror, that I, in all my newly discovered womanly glory, was about to meet up with Calvin wearing a *bathing suit*. Briefly, I fantasized that Calvin would look at me differently, notice that I was becoming a woman. Like I'd so recently done, perhaps he would suddenly awaken to my blooming sexuality and find it irresistible. I even went as far as to imagine a scene where the awestruck hero would swoon at the sight of the princess, so taken by her that he would rush to make half-naked (but heart-felt) declarations of love, like some sort of naughty fairy tale. But when I looked down at my body, how my small breasts were flattened by a one-piece made for little girls and how my knees were scabbed over, scraped up from sliding into third base one too many times, I knew it was no use. I wasn't ever going to compare to Lorelei, with her curves and long silky hair. I'd fought my journey into womanhood for too long, and it was going to take a while to get back on track.

Like most things in life, my imagination held much more drama than the reality of finding Calvin and Mabel fishing from the bank, their appearance there as familiar and comforting as home at the end of a long trip. My obsessive fretting suddenly seemed absurd and, after scolding myself at my foolishness, I was quick to join my two best friends at the water's edge as Hank followed the younger ones into its depths. Determined to regain my sense of footing, I'd been even quicker to demonstrate my vast fishing knowledge as I proudly baited my own hook and cast the line into the blue-green water. But then I caught a turtle which I promptly sent soaring over our heads with my vigorous reeling, and what little remaining pride I had quickly dispersed like the dust cloud I created by diving to the ground. Calvin rescued the little guy, and despite my embarrassment and tinge of envy I felt when I heard the sweet way he spoke to the turtle, I was moved by his kindness.

Fishing was over at that point and we joined the younger ones in the water. When Mabel suggested we play baptism, I went along even though I didn't really get the allure. But she was excited, and as the kids lined up, she drew Elton to stand in front of her. She recited a complicated pledge as she placed her hand on Elton's dripping head. Then she called on the trinity, which was the one part I could understand, as she rather forcefully dunked him backward with both hands. She held

Angela Hoke *A Whisper of Smoke*

him there for long enough that my protective instincts started to kick in, but she hauled him up before it was necessary for me to initiate a rescue. As water flew from his sanctified head, Mabel beamed with satisfaction – Baptists make a big deal about getting dunked. When we were kids, I had tried to explain to Calvin and Mabel about the sacraments and purgatory and all that. They never did get it. When it was Hank's turn, I stepped in. I don't know why, exactly. I guess because I felt like it was my job to look after Hank's soul, and I'd been doing it since he was a baby.

Then someone suggested we play *Tag* and Elton slammed into me, declaring me *'IT'!* But before the game could start in earnest, I noticed that Mabel was distracted, looking towards a spot in the trees at my back. Following her gaze, I found Lorelei standing on the bank, her hands on her hips. She looked torn between making fun of us for acting like babies and joining in. But since she was wearing regular clothes, she settled on scoffing. Maybe she was a little jealous, too. After all, she hadn't been invited.

"Get out," she'd ordered. "It's time to go home and get cleaned up for dinner."

I felt my temper rise at being told what to do, but the others were already climbing up the bank. I wasn't inclined to take her orders on a good day, but things had been strained with Lorelei ever since the camp-out and I was even less enthusiastic about listening to her now. I turned to Calvin and Mabel's reactions, because if they were as annoyed as I was, I was going to give Lorelei a piece of my mind. What I saw instead made my stomach roll – Calvin was staring at Lorelei like he couldn't tear his eyes away. She was wearing a t-shirt that was too small, in my opinion. It was stretched across her bosom like taffy. She had on her white shorts, and the artful, smooth contrast of her brown legs reminded me of sculpted wood.

My stomach lurched, launching acid into my throat, as I considered my own appearance. I glanced down at my chest, at the baby breasts I was just getting used to – Lorelei liked to call them mosquito bites, and I could see why when I compared them to hers. I looked at her pretty long hair and I felt my own matted wet pony tail, tangled with a couple of sticks and some leaves. I didn't think it was possible to feel more of a complete contrast from Lorelei.

She's not as sexy as you think, Mister, I'd thought crossly, looking again at Calvin's dumbstruck expression. I pictured how awful Lorelei looked without her makeup, or how frizzy her hair still got on rainy days, and how ridiculous she looked with her head covered in juice cans. I told myself that if Calvin could see Lorelei the way she really was, he wouldn't be drooling over her. But then a worse thought occurred to me, crooked in a sneaking finger of insecurity – maybe Lorelei's kiss had meant more to him than the one he shared with me.

As this horrible idea took root, the air whooshed from my lungs like I'd been punched and tears sprang to my eyes. I looked up at the trees until I could bite them back. When the stinging subsided, it was replaced by the burn of jealousy as ugly words itched at my tongue, rolling against my teeth. I glanced at Lorelei, who was standing a little awkwardly against a tree, alone. I wanted to hate her, and a little part of me did. But I couldn't bring myself to blame it all on her. Calvin was the one staring at her, like an idiot. The more I considered it, the more I couldn't believe that he was so openly gawking, especially with me right beside him. If he weren't my best friend, I would have smacked him upside the head until he got his senses back.

Angela Hoke   *A Whisper of Smoke*

If I hadn't been such a chicken, I might have tried to convince him to look at *me* that way, instead.

Things were not the same after that day. By summer's end, I was chagrined to find that I had wasted more than a few perfectly lovely summer afternoons listening to love songs on my transistor radio and writing poetry that no one will ever read in this lifetime. Adding to my consternation was the sad fact that my interactions with Calvin had become painfully awkward – so much so that we weren't really hanging out anymore. And while Mabel was still one of my best friends, I was growing weary of the energy it took to deflect her unending questions about why I was perpetually spaced out.

By the time school started in the fall, I knew I had to do something to get my mind off Calvin and I decided new friends and cute boys were just the answer. I considered it destiny that I met Shelly in lunchroom purgatory on the first day of eighth grade. It's the place you pass through just after you've picked up your tray but before you find someone you know, the one lonely buoy in a sea of white Peter Pan collars and plaid. We'd locked eyes over lima beans and country fried steak.

Shelly couldn't be more different from the Conners – she smoked Virginia Slims in a brass cigarette holder behind the dumpster out back of the parish rectory, and wore white lipstick and Jean Nate splash between her breasts. She carried her contraband smokes, personal products and even snacks in the waistband of her highly elasticized white cotton panties. I learned this one day when I made the mistake of asking for a piece of gum – I've never thought of Juicy Fruit in quite the same way again.

As far as boys were concerned, she considered herself a broker of sorts. She convinced me that the Catholic boys' schools were full of guys looking for someone exactly like me, and that dances were the perfect place for a little transacting. I'd already made up my mind to try to forget about Calvin – at least in the romantic sense. So by the first dance of the season, I was up for a little commerce.

"Who do you think will be there?" We were in my room getting ready together so that Shelly could monitor my wardrobe choices. I speculated about a roomful of cute boys which all began to look like Calvin in my imagination. Shaking my head to clear it, I focused on trying to tame my cowlick into a side part with VO5 while Shelly ironed her own hair.

"All the cute guys from St. John's. I told you about Kenny, that boy that goes to my parish. He's very cute, and so are his friends. Me and Lydia used to walk by the basketball court when they were playing with our bras padded out to here," she said, gesturing out from her chest. Shelly was referring to her former best friend, who had transferred to the public school to be a cheerleader.

"Did they notice you?"

"Of course. Oh, they acted like they didn't, but once this dark-haired boy with the tightest butt ran right into another boy because he was so distracted by us."

She told me other stories while we got ready, making me laugh at her audacity. When we were finally done, Shelly's hair was three inches tall at the crown, and she wore false eyelashes. My hair was formidable too, but I refused the lashes – I knew Mama would notice Twiggy eyes in a heartbeat, and I wasn't about to give her an excuse to detain us. I did let Shelly put a little mascara and blush on me – the effect was suitably subtle, and I figured it would pass muster. But I declined the lipstick, at least while we were still at home. So Shelly tucked the Yardley Slicker tube in her bra so we could apply it in the car.

Lorelei drove us to the dance, which I suppose was nice of her. But I wasn't of a mind to act appreciative. I was still pissed about what she'd done at the camp-out, though I'd refused to give her the satisfaction of voicing just how much she'd hurt me. Turned out, I didn't have to say it. It was obvious she knew she'd acted despicably, given her uncharacteristic solicitousness in recent weeks. This was a familiar pattern with my older sister – she'd do something mean and spiteful, sometimes I think without even knowing why, and spend weeks surreptitiously trying to make amends. Driving me around and spontaneously lending me her prize Schwinn Starlet was her messed up way of apologizing, and I knew it well.

After she dropped us off, we paused in the parking lot to check our outfits, but we didn't linger. The gymnasium beckoned to us with thumping percussion that rattled loose window panes and the murmur of excited voices, floating on the air like ghost whispers, and we hurried after them. Inside, the dance floor was defined by awkwardly draped streamers, but the effort was wasted. The dancers seemed to be unconsciously sticking to the boundaries formed by the basketball court markings. The band consisted of five high school boys dressed in black turtlenecks and sporting shag haircuts. Their band name, *The Breckenridge Sound*, was inscribed in psychedelic script on the face of the base drum, and the decent rendition of *I Want to Hold Your Hand,* confirmed their obvious musical inspiration. There were a few couples grooving on the dance floor, but otherwise the gymnasium was as divided as the Red Sea just before Moses' passage, with a tide of shy and giggling girls on one side, and a wave of deliberately disinterested boys on the other.

As we stood on the fringe, Shelly scanned the crowd for familiar faces, and finding some, grabbed my arm and dragged me towards the sea of females. Amongst the larger group of girls from school was a cluster of girls in serious discussion off to one side. Zeroing in on them, Shelly deposited me next to the wall. "Stay here," she said. "I'm going to find out what's the scoop." She slid off and I watched as she deftly melded into the group. After a few minutes, she slipped away.

When she got back to me, she was smiling. "Oh, this is great."

"What?"

"Kathy and Chip broke up." She almost squealed, she was so downright gleeful about it. "He's so cute. If I didn't like Kenny, I would definitely have a thing for Chip." I asked which one he was, and she discretely pointed out a boy with curly black hair, wearing a blue shirt. He was leaning casually against the wall, laughing at something one of the other guys was saying. His feet were crossed and his hands were in his pockets, and he looked like he was not the least bit interested in any of the girls in the room.

I had to admit, on the cuteness scale, he was off the charts. I thought immediately he was out of my league. Add to that the fact that I had no experience attracting boys. Needless to say, I was a little nervous about what Shelly had in mind, but I tried to play it cool. "I see him – he's not bad. But you don't think I'm going to go after Kathy's ex-boyfriend with her standing right over there?"

"Who gives a flip what Kathy thinks? And you are not going to go after him, we're going to get him to come after you." Before I could respond, Shelly pulled me out of the gymnasium and into the hallway where the bathrooms were. Shelly reached her hands around my waist and grabbed my skirt.

"What are you doing?"

"I'm setting the bait," she answered as she methodically rolled the waist band on my skirt until it was a good three inches shorter. "I hope you shaved."

"Of course I did," I lied, not wanting to admit that she didn't really have to shave my legs that often. We went back in and moseyed over to the refreshments.

"Just look at me, not at them," Shelly instructed. "Laugh like I said something funny. Oh look, what a lovely shade of chartreuse this tablecloth is. It reminds me of puke. Doesn't it you?" She kept on until I was laughing in spite of my jangled nerves. A crash behind us made us both start. When we turned, one of the boys was being hauled off the floor – it was Kenny.

"Kenny, is that you? I didn't realize you would be here."

"How's it going, Shelly?" He was leaning up against the painted block walls again, cool as a cucumber.

They made small talk for a few minutes, and she introduced me. When Kenny didn't make introductions, Shelly prompted him. "Who're your friends?"

Kenny looked startled. Emily Post he was not. "This is Keith and this is Chip," he finally said.

A Whisper of Smoke   *Angela Hoke*

"Hey," they both replied in unison, before turning their attention back to the dance floor and to the four or five brave couples that were getting down to the music. We stood there for a few awkward minutes, giving them ample opportunity to ask us to dance. When the song changed and the band starting playing *I Can't Get No Satisfaction*, by the Rolling Stones, Shelly took my cup and handed both our drinks to Kenny.

"Hold these for a sec, will you? We're going to dance."

"Uh, sure."

Shelly pulled me onto the dance floor.

"Time to get their attention," Shelly said as she began to move to the beat of the song.

"I think that's impossible." I tried to copy Shelly's swivels and side-steps, not quite successfully.

Shelly twirled around so that the hem of her skirt sailed to a most revealing height. "Let's do the *Jerk*," she said, and began performing an emphatic version of the dance we'd seen on *Bandstand*. I tried to join in, but could not muster quite the same enthusiasm.

"Come on, Susanna. Put some *oomph* into it."

"I can't do it like you can, Shelly. Some talents are just beyond me."

"Of course you can. Boobs are power, and you need to learn to use them to your advantage." Shelly said, as she stuck hers out as far as they would go. Truthfully, it wasn't that far. But she made me laugh and even forget about the boys we were trying to impress.

When the song ended, we hung on each other, out of breath. I barely noticed as Kenny and Chip walked up.

"You girls sure like to dance, huh?" Kenny asked with his stunning vernacular. Our drinks were gone, I noticed. Behind him, the

Angela Hoke   *A Whisper of Smoke*

band played the opening chords of *Unchained Melody*. "Wanna dance?" he asked, and I began to wonder whether Chip could speak.

"Why not?" Shelly answered for both of us. Grabbing Kenny, she pulled him into the middle of the dance floor.

"Hi there," Chip said, coming up to me. He reached out his hand and I took it. My stomach flipped as he led me onto the dance floor. I'd never danced with any males other than Daddy and Uncle George, but I quickly saw that teenage dancing was different. I draped my arms around his neck and tried not to stare at his chin.

"You go to St. Catherine's?" Chip asked near my ear. His breath tickled.

"Yes. I'm in eighth grade."

"Me too," he said.

We were quiet for a moment as I hunted for something to say. "Do you like school?" I finally asked, inwardly groaning at the inane question.

"I love it. If I didn't have to leave for summer break, I'd stay there all year long."

"Oh, okay," I said, not sure what else to say.

"I'm joking, silly. School's okay. I mean, I want to be a doctor or lawyer or something. So education's pretty important."

It took me a minute to catch back up – I'd not been expecting a sarcastic response. *So that's how you're going to play*, I thought. I had plenty of experience with sarcasm, living with Mama.

"Not as important as your soul," I said. "I'm planning to be a nun. I'm just waiting until I'm sixteen to enter the convent."

"Wha??" I really got him with that one. He actually came to a standstill.

"Kidding," I laughed. And after a beat, he chuckled in my ear. We started dancing again, without speaking. I'd thought myself momentarily clever, but now I was searching for something else to talk about.

"You and Kenny been friends for a long time?" is what I came up with – brilliant, I know. But I *was* curious how he could be friends with someone so obviously not an intellectual.

"Yeah. We've known each other since we were kids," he said. "His mom died a few years ago, so he's had it pretty rough."

For a second I wasn't sure whether to believe him. I smirked, searching for a sarcastic response. But then I glanced at his face and saw that he was serious. I immediately assumed a sympathetic expression. "That's awful," I said, meaning it.

"It was a real bummer," he agreed, and I couldn't tell from his tone whether he'd noticed my very inappropriate, if brief, lack of compassion.

The song was ending, and I thought I'd blown it. I was sure he would say a polite good-bye and I'd be off to sit by myself on the bleachers while Shelly made out with Kenny behind a balloon column. But he didn't ditch me. Instead he asked me if I wanted to get some chips.

"Sure," I replied, biting my lip so I wouldn't giggle at his unintended pun. We got some refreshments while most everyone else danced to *Twist and Shout.* There was a glass window next to us and I caught my reflection – I was biting my bottom lip and moving my body in ways that could not be called dancing. I looked ridiculous and I hoped he hadn't noticed. I guess he didn't, because next he suggested that we go outside to get some air. I mumbled something like assent in reply, and we walked outside into the autumn night. The sky was bright from the

Angela Hoke   *A Whisper of Smoke*

harvest moon and dry leaves skipped on the pavement, doing their own dance in the moonlight.

"Tell me about yourself. Do you have brothers and sisters?" Chip asked as we sat carefully on the curb. I tucked my skirt under my thighs.

Was he looking for a witty reply? I settled for a straight answer. "Yes -- two sisters and a brother. What about you?" The wind lifted my heavily sprayed hair in one piece, pulling at my scalp. A horrid image flashed through my mind, of me taking flight by the hair, soaring around over the parking lot. I slipped my hand up to my head and tugged my hair back into place.

"I have four older sisters and a younger brother."

"Big family."

"Yep."

We stared out into the dark street, sitting just a few inches apart. When I shivered, he offered me his jacket. He draped it around my shoulders, settling his arm across my back.

"I noticed you come in with your friend," he confessed. He was close enough that his breath brushed my cheek, and his eyes were dark under the shadow of his lashes.

If this were a movie, I would have said something really cheeky right about then, which he would find charming and irresistible. But my mind blanked, and all that remained was the obvious question.

"Really?" *Why?* Even without voicing the second part of my surprise, I sounded incredulous, which I was. His chin was nearly resting on my shoulder, and it was making me a little uncomfortable. I could smell corn chips on his breath, and I wondered what he smelled on mine.

"Yeah. We thought you were pretty." I knew I should have higher self-esteem, but all I could think was he must need glasses.

A Whisper of Smoke   *Angela Hoke*

"Don't tell me that you don't know how pretty you are," Chip said, bending to look into my face. I blushed – I couldn't tell whether he was being sincere or just trying to "take advantage." I said something silly, like that I wasn't as pretty as Kathy (his ex-girlfriend). He put his finger under my chin and forced me to look at him. Don't get me wrong – he was nice to look at. I just wasn't sure I wanted him to be able to study my face that closely.

"You're kind of a dunce, aren't you? What you need is to be educated," he said to me, with a slight grin. Before I could decide how to react, he leaned in and kissed me.

I waited for the belly flips and chills, like I'd felt with Calvin. They didn't come. He kind of assaulted me with his tongue, and I wasn't sure if I liked it or not. In any case, it didn't last long, so I would have to ponder it later, match it up against kissing Calvin. Maybe I could write a paper on it in English – Sister Margaret loved a good compare and contrast essay.

While I thought about essays and comparisons, Chip stood up and offered me his hand.

"You ready to go back inside?" he asked. I nodded. I grabbed hold of my hair and followed him.

As we walked back into the gym, we were just in time to see Sister Mary Agnes (or as Lorelei always called her, Sister Mary Anus) prying Kenny's and Shelly's faces apart with her ruler. As we made our way towards them, I could feel the dirty looks from Chip's ex-girlfriend Kathy boring into my back. I tried to ignore it, focusing on Shelly, who had a smug expression on her flushed face as she calmly smoothed her mussed hair, and Kenny, grinning like a fox beside her. By the time we reached them, I could feel Shelly's excitement that we'd both scored boyfriends – it hummed around her like an electromagnetic field. It was contagious, and I buzzed with excitement too.

At that moment, for the first time in weeks, I wasn't thinking about Calvin at all.

Chapter 4: Climbing Everest

There should be some natural law in the universe that keeps you from getting sick too early in a relationship. Six weeks was just too soon to think that Chip wouldn't be tempted by some other girl, and there were plenty of them around – trampish carhops in knee-high socks and roller-skates, shamelessly flirting for extra tips, and high school girls in convertibles, trolling for boys with the highly effective lures of tight twinsets and padded bras. It wasn't fair at all, I decided. Now, not only was I laid up at home, sick, but I had the added worry of whether I would still have a boyfriend by the time the weekend was over.

Maybe I wouldn't have been so insecure if we were going steady. But he still hadn't asked me. I couldn't help thinking it was because he wanted to keep his options open. At least Shelly would be with him tonight – Chip was going to tag along on Kenny and Shelly's date. That made me feel some better, but I knew how distracted Shelly could get with Kenny and a big back seat. So I tried to take her assurances to keep an eye on Chip, well intentioned as they were, with a grain of salt.

My head was hurting. I tried to clear my mind of all non-productive thinking and just rest, and it was working too. But just as I had gotten to a nice calm state of relaxation, I heard the back door slam. The booming outside voices of Hank and Annabelle filled the kitchen where I knew Mama was busy cooking large quantities of Cincinnati chili for the

Angela Hoke   *A Whisper of Smoke*

party tonight. It was going to be Mama's first dance party, and she planned to showcase some of her dance students (fellow parishioners to whom she'd taught the Fox Trot and the Rumba) and their newly acquired skills. And of course Mama wouldn't be opposed to providing demonstrations for any novices in attendance.

In any case, there's no way Mama would put up with them in the kitchen when she was prepping for a party. Sure enough, I heard Mama shooing the kids out of the kitchen, and directly thereafter, the sound of pounding feet on stairs. Hank and Annabelle burst into my bedroom and Annabelle bounded onto the bed.

I groaned. "Belle, I'm sick! Settle down and no jumping."

"Oh, sorry," said Annabelle, jumping off the bed with a loud thump that made me wince.

"Sorry to bother you, Susanna," Hank said solemnly. "Mama wants us out of the way for her party."

"I know, Hank. It's okay. Just try to talk in quiet voices," I replied, as I nervously kept an eye on Annabelle. She was exploring my room and knocking things over right and left.

Hank gave me an appraising look, apparently not liking what he saw. "Have you had anything to eat today?"

"I'm not really hungry."

"You need to keep your strength up, you know. You look pretty awful." *Thanks, kid.* "If you want, I could warm you up some soup."

I smiled at him. "Aww, thanks, Hankie."

He didn't acknowledge my use of his pet baby name, which I took as a sign that I must look like death. "You took care of me enough growing up. I want to be able to take care of you sometimes," he said, and blushed deeply. I swelled with pride at his considerate nature – after all, I practically raised him.

"You're not grown up. You're only seven," Annabelle pointed out.

"Seven-and-a-half," he mumbled.

As he turned to leave the room, I stopped him. "Can you please take Belle with you?" I pleaded.

"Sure." He rolled his eyes and shook his head at me in mutual exasperation. Little cutie pie. Ignoring her protests, he grabbed Annabelle's hand and dragged her out the door.

Within a few minutes, Hank and Annabelle returned with Mama, who rushed over to me.

"My poor darling," she cooed, adjusting my covers and fluffing my pillow. Turning to Hank, she said, "Pull the covers off of Lorelei's bed and get the chairs from my bedroom."

"What's going on?" I wanted to know.

"We're making a big tent," said Annabelle. "And you are going to be in it."

"We're pretending that we are climbing Mt. Everest," Hank explained, as he came in carrying two chairs he got from Mama's room. "This is base camp, and you have altitude sickness."

"Oh, I see," I said, blowing my nose. Daddy and Hank had been reading about mountain climbing and Edmund Hillary's expedition to summit the tallest mountain on earth. Mama, Hank and Annabelle set about constructing the tent with blankets and clothespins and chairs. Hank retrieved his plastic walkie-talkies and the transistor radio, and Annabelle went in search of flashlights.

When they were done, Mama said. "I'll go down to the village and round up your provisions." When she'd gone, we started playing.

Angela Hoke   *A Whisper of Smoke*

Hank checked my pupils and my pulse. "Do you remember what happened?"

"Not really. It's all a little hazy."

"We were up at Camp Four and you fainted."

"It was scary," Annabelle added. "You about fell off the mountain."

"Oh, yeah. I remember a little now. I was climbing and everything got fuzzy and I started seeing spots."

"Classic signs," Hank confirmed, nodding gravely. "It was a good thing we got you down when we did."

"What about me, Hank?" Annabelle asked.

"You carried Susanna's pack back down, Belle. Without you, we woulda run out of food and water and she'd probably be dead by now."

"You're lucky I was there," Annabelle said.

Hank checked in on the rest of the climbing party with his walkie talkies while, in the background, we heard the sounds of adult voices filling the rooms downstairs. Music was playing now and there was laughter, and I hoped that Mama remembered to bring us up some supper. A little while later, there was a knock at the door. Hank made the decision to brave the blinding snow to answer it. Holding on to an imaginary length of rope, he made his way to the door. It was Mama, wearing a red dress despite the blizzard and holding a tray of thermoses, crackers and utensils.

"Sorry it took me so long to get these to you. The weather was just awful. I had to hire three Sherpas and two yaks to bring everything I needed."

"It's okay," Hank said. "You got here just in time."

A Whisper of Smoke   *Angela Hoke*

She handed us the thermoses then ducked back out. After a few more minutes, Mama came in out of the blustering wind carrying three bottles of Coke, an effective bribe designed to curb unwanted interruptions at her party. Blowing kisses, Mama left us to our climbing exploits and returned to the adult festivities.

When we finished eating, I suggested we write letters to our loved ones in case we did not survive the harsh mountain conditions. Hank retrieved a notebook from my book bag, and we all took turns dictating letters as I wrote them out. I started, to get them in the spirit. My letter was to my husband Chip and our three adorable children, Marcus, Elizabeth and Peyton, and told of a monumental love and life together. Annabelle wanted to go next, and she had me write two letters: one to Mama and Daddy and one to her stuffed animals. Her letter to Mama and Daddy consisted mostly of instruction on how to distribute her belongings, the most controversial items being her bubble-hair Barbie and Raggedy Ann and Andy. Her letter to her animals included a specific schedule detailing on which days each one was allowed to sleep on Annabelle's bed in her absence. By the time it was Hank's turn, I was getting tired. I was about to suggest we take a break when the doorknob rattled.

Assuming it was Mama, I improvised. "Oh, good," I said. "More medical supplies."

The knob rattled again and the door flung open, banging against the doorstop. Hank lifted aside the tent flap just enough for us to peer out, but it wasn't Mama.

Framed in the doorway was a large man, a beer bottle in his hand.

"Who's in here?" His voice was loud and commanding, like Sergeant Carter on *Gomer Pyle*.

Hank and Annabelle were quiet, but I shushed them anyway.

"What's this, a tent?" he said, lumbering into the room. Hank let the flap drop closed and Annabelle turned off her flashlight. The drunken stranger shuffled closer, his shadow an ominous silhouette on our tent wall. Hank reached for my hand in the dark and gripped it. From somewhere downstairs, I could hear Mother's tinkling laugh, and I wondered where Daddy was.

"Come out, come out, wherever you are," the man said. The words weren't themselves scary, but there was something slightly menacing about the way he said them. We watched as his shadow moved closer, and the shape of a hand materialized out of the larger form. He paused, and the sheet fluttered from his breath.

I knew I should do something, but I was paralyzed. *If he pulls open that flap, I'll let him have it,* I assured myself, and hoped it was true.

Then he did. His face was overlarge, like a cartoon caricature. His pores were craterish pits, and his bulbous nose had broken veins mapping tributaries across it.

"Well, isn't this cute?" he said, then laughed from his gut, spewing spittle in our faces.

"You're not supposed to be in here," I croaked, sounding significantly less authoritative than I'd hoped.

"Aww, now. Don't be like that," he said, settling into his squat.

I sneezed, not trying to cover my mouth. He recoiled from it, and I felt my control surge. It didn't last long.

He took a handkerchief from his pocket and blew his nose noisily. Then he stuffed it back into his pocket and reached that same

A Whisper of Smoke   *Angela Hoke*

hand towards us. We all leaned back, but it was Annabelle he was reaching for.

"Now would you get a look at those curls?" he said, pulling one and releasing it like a spring or a Slinky. "A regular Shirley Temple." That chuckle again.

I cast a glance at Annabelle – she was scowling, as I knew she would be. She hated being compared to Shirley Temple. Her hair really was much longer, and though her face was round and babyish, she had no dimple. And her eyes often blazed (she was fiery little one), but never twinkled.

"Wanna play, little princess?" he asked, then made a tickling gesture against her stomach. She squealed, but not with delight.

It snapped me out of my fog.

"Stop that!" I snapped, slapping his hand.

He jerked his hand back, and smiled at me. "This one's got spunk."

He reached for me, and Hank said a soft "no" at my shoulder.

I felt conspicuously naked under my flannel nightgown, my new breasts pushing against the fabric.

"Sam, what the hell are you doing?" It was a familiar voice, coming from outside our door.

"I don't know," the man said, moving away from us. "I was trying to find the bathroom."

I heard Uncle George come in. "Well you are on the wrong side of the hall." Hank pulled the flap back again, and we peered out to see Uncle George shepherding the strange man across the room. "You big jackass. You see a john in here? You think these dolls are fancy toilet paper covers?" Uncle George laughed loudly as he clapped the guy on the shoulder and shoved him into the hall. The guy stumbled, but didn't seem angry at being man-handled.

"You never know. My ma, she's good at that crocheting," the man said stupidly.

Uncle George glanced back at us, flashing a grin. "Is that where you learned it from?" he joked. "Come on now. Let's get this Yeti out of here." Uncle George was always good about getting into the spirit of whatever we were pretending, but I was impressed that he'd picked up on it so quickly. Probably Mama told him.

The man looked perplexed. "Huh?" Not real quick, that one.

"Nothing. Bathroom's that way." After another directional adjustment from Uncle George, the man staggered into the bathroom. Uncle George watched him until the door closed, then turned to us. Only then did I let out a breath I didn't realize I'd been holding.

"You okay?" he said, his face becoming momentarily serious.

"Yeah, thanks," I croaked. Whether my voice was faint from fear or illness, I worked to clear my throat and tried again. "Thanks, Uncle George."

"Might want to keep this locked," he said, then smiled, his expression returning to the jovial one we knew and loved. "Those abominable snow-types are sneaky bastards." He winked as he turned the lock behind him and pulled the door closed.

I appreciated Uncle George's attempt to make light of what had just happened, or almost happened, because it seemed to calm Hank and Annabelle. But the intrusion was sobering, and all at once our game of pretending to be on Mt. Everest was over. Without discussion, Hank and Annabelle set about dismantling the tent, while I lay in my bed unable to do much to help. When they'd finished, Annabelle asked me if she could sleep with me. Despite concerns that they would get sick, I suggested that both Annabelle and Hank get their blankets and pillows so we could all sleep in the same room together. It just didn't feel right for us to be separated tonight.

Just as they got their pallets made up and settled in, we were startled once again by the sound of a rattling doorknob. My chest seized up with an irrational fear, and I was ashamed of myself.

"Susanna?" Annabelle whimpered.

The rattling turned to pounding. "Open the damn door!" It was Lorelei.

"Go ahead and open it, Hank," I said, sighing with relief as Hank rushed to the door. Lorelei slipped in, smelling of smoke and beer.

"Move out of the way, please," she said, pushing her way inside. "And lock that door back!"

Hank did, and Lorelei collapsed on her bed. "Thank God I made it in here. Mother is in rare form down there."

"Why? What's going on?" I asked.

"She and Daddy are into it. She's going off about some idiot at the party."

"Oh, no," I groaned. "Did she see you come in?"

"I don't think so." We both hoped not. When Mother was drunk and in one of her moods, Lorelei became public enemy number one.

Downstairs, the music stopped abruptly leaving a void that was instantly filled by the shouts of our parents. Outside, car doors slammed as the guests made a quick exit. Lorelei crept to the door and opened it silently.

"What are you doing?" Hank asked. He sounded scared.

Angela Hoke   *A Whisper of Smoke*

"Shhh, I want to hear." Once Lorelei suggested it, we quickly joined her.

"Damn it, Elise! Do you have to say everything that pops into your head?"

"If you hadn't brought that ignorant bigot into our house, I wouldn't have had to put him in his place." In the background, car engines started in quick succession.

"I work with those people. Unless they are wearing sheets or swastikas, I'd like to think we could at least wait until they leave before we judge them."

"If you think I'm going to sit by in my own home and let your jackass co-workers spout off like the idiots they are, you have lost your mind," said Mama.

This wasn't the first time Mama had stood up to bigots. Mama didn't tolerate prejudice against Negroes or anybody else, for that matter, and wasn't afraid to say so, even when Daddy was too polite to make a fuss. I had no doubt that Mama probably had made an ass of herself, but still I couldn't help but feel a little proud.

"Who the hell do you think you're married to?" Mama was saying. "Some delicate little wallflower like that MaryAnn?"

"At least she knows how to show a little respect to her husband," Daddy retorted, and Lorelei and I both sucked in our breath.

There was silence for a moment. "Get the hell out of my house!"

"This is *my* house." Daddy said after a beat, his voice eerily calm. But something in it sounded like even he realized he might have gone too far.

Mama lost it. "Get out, you son of a bitch!" she screamed, followed by the crash of breaking glass.

A Whisper of Smoke   *Angela Hoke*

We heard the front door open. "Right now I'd do anything to get away from you!" Daddy shouted, and then the door slammed shut.

"Oh, shit," Lorelei whispered.

Turning around, I ordered Hank and Annabelle to get in bed. For once, not even Annabelle argued – they immediately scrambled to their spots and squeezed their eyes shut. It was just in time too, because we could hear Mama stumbling up the stairs, muttering curses.

"Lorelei, you little slut, are you home? Goddamn it, you'd better be!"

"Shit," Lorelei said again, and we both rushed to our beds, just as Mama opened the door with a bang.

"Lorelei? There you are. You'd better be glad your ass is home in bed. You're sorry-ass father is sleeping on the lawn tonight, and don't you dare let him in."

She walked over to Lorelei's bed.

"Do you hear me?" she hissed.

"Yeah," Lorelei mumbled into her pillow.

"What?" Mama shrieked, turning Lorelei over.

"Yes, Mother," Lorelei said, unable to hide the disgust in her voice.

"You'd better listen to me, you ungrateful shits," she said to all of us. Annabelle started whimpering, and I reached over and patted her, quietly shushing her.

Whatever sense of pride I had for Mama had disintegrated into a pile of ground glass tinged with bourbon.

Mama stumbled back out the door, clumsily slamming it behind her. We all listened without breathing until we heard the door to Mama and Daddy's bedroom shut. Then Annabelle burst into sobs. "Why did Mommy say those things?" she cried.

"Mommy's drunk, Annabelle. She didn't mean what she said," I told her, rubbing her little back.

Lorelei harrumphed in her bed.

"I hate it when Mama drinks that liquor," Hank said quietly.

"Me too," I said. "But everything's going to be okay."

"What about Dad?" Hank asked. "He'll freeze out there."

"Don't worry about Dad," said Lorelei. "When Mother passes out, we'll go and get him."

We all lay in silence in the dark, waiting and waiting, listening for any sign of life from Mother. After twenty minutes or so of perfect quiet, Lorelei and I crept out of our beds. We opened the door and tip-toed down the hall to Mother's door. Leaning close, we listened for the sawing sounds of her deep alcohol snores. Once we were confident she was passed out, we rushed down the stairs on quiet feet.

The front door was indeed locked, Daddy presumably on the other side sulking. Grabbing our coats, we opened the front door. I was alarmed when we didn't immediately see him, but then Lorelei nudged me in the ribs.

"Hell, he's passed out too."

I looked where Lorelei indicated, seeing that Daddy was indeed passed out on the porch. First we tried to rouse him. When that failed, we each hitched our grips under his arms and pulled. He didn't budge. We tugged and pulled and lightly slapped his face, all to no avail. Finally, we looked at each other.

"Let's go get him some blankets," Lorelei suggested with a sigh.

Together we rounded up all the blankets we could find and a pillow too, and we wrapped our sleeping father up with care. We both kissed him lightly on the forehead, and then headed back to bed. Sometime later, after hours spent chasing sleep that was elusive as a flickering phantom, I heard Daddy stumbling his way up the stairs, shushing himself. It was only then that the binding on my chest fell away and I could breathe properly. At last, I drifted to sleep, thoughts about boyfriends and childish games far from my mind.

Chapter 5: Attack of the Snow Queen

February 1966

I loved the way snow made the world look brand new again, virginal almost. I loved how it piled heavy in the trees and blurred the boundaries between properties, even disguising the changes in terrain. I loved everything about it except how it compacted into frigid concrete walls that could block your escape, creating an igloo-like prison where you were trapped to weather the cold with all the members of your family, both those you adored and those you abhorred.

On this day, I could have used a little alone time, even if just to ponder recent events in my life, both positive and negative. Good things about the last few months included: Chip finally asked me to go steady; I made good marks for the semester; my boobs grew another size. Not so good things about the past few months included: Calvin still acted weird around me, I had two pimples that would just not go away, and Mama and Lorelei had been fighting constantly.

"*Annabelle!*" Lorelei screeched, and it was like the scream of a banshee, or an air raid siren – a shriek that climbed inside your skull, made worse by the sensation that you were trapped with whatever monster could sound like that.

Annabelle was sitting on the floor in front of me, playing tea party with her dolls. I didn't know what she'd done, but a look of guilty terror flashed across her round face as she scrambled to hide behind me on the couch. Hank looked up from where he was reconfiguring his train tracks on the coffee table just as Lorelei stormed into the living room.

I jumped back in my seat when I saw her. Lorelei's eyes were icy and striking even without their furious gleam, with pale blue irises ringed in dark brown. But now they were hideously uneven – one was made up with liner and mascara giving it a three-dimensional quality, like an oracle, and the other was bare, naked by comparison. And she'd only filled in one eyebrow with her brown pencil, but it was over the eye that was not made up. She looked like a psychotic clown. To top it off, Lorelei's head was covered in a puffy flowered cap, its elastic trim framing her furious face. Sprouting out from the cap, a hose dangled like a giant tentacle. It expanded and contracted from her head, like an accordion or the head of a jack-in-the-box, mocking the angry heaves of her chest.

My mouth twitched as I suppressed a laugh.

"What… did you do… to my hose," Lorelei said slowly, each word low and menacing.

"I only used it for a minute," Annabelle cried, huddling against my side for protection. "It was a tunnel for my Barbies. They were trying to escape the jungle prison." Annabelle buried her head under my arm and whimpered. Her brown curls curved over my bicep like creeping vines.

"You know you are not allowed to touch my stuff! What the hell am I supposed to do now?"

Hank crept up beside her.

"Let me take a look, Lei," he said, and his soft high voice drew her attention long enough for him to reach up on tip-toes and remove the elasticized cap from her head. In doing so, he unmasked Medusa, and once again I had the urge to laugh. Lorelei's head was covered in orange juice cans, her wet hair wound around each one like oily, coiled snakes.

Lorelei looked back to Annabelle. "Answer me," she snapped, and Annabelle began to cry.

From where he stood behind Lorelei, holding the hair dryer cap and hose, Hank looked at Annabelle and frowned. He couldn't stand to see her cry. In a flash of inspiration, he put the hose up to his nose, and silently trumpeted it like an elephant. Belle still shivered in fear. When that didn't work, he held the cap over his bottom and, rotating his hips like a miniature Elvis, swung the dangling hose like a tail, grinning ridiculously. All the while, Lorelei continued to glare at Annabelle, and Annabelle shrank. Determined, Hank snapped the hose towards Lorelei like a whip, and Annabelle at last began to calm. She hiccoughed what I knew to be a tiny laugh, though it sounded enough like a sob that Lorelei didn't notice.

Encouraged, Hank's face assumed a mischievous expression, and I was suddenly certain that he was two seconds away from holding the hose over his crotch and pretending to pee on the back of Lorelei's leg, or worse. But before he could do anything else, Mama walked in, carrying a basket of laundry on her hip.

"What's going on in here?" It was a logical question, and shouldn't have been scary. Hank immediately stopped fooling around and receded into the shadow of the dining room.

"I'll tell you what's going on," Lorelei snapped. "Belle broke my blow dryer and I can't finish fixing my hair."

"Are you planning to go somewhere?" Mama asked. Her voice was perfectly neutral, lilting even.

"I have a date."

"Oh, I don't think so," said Mama, and her eyes shone with a dare.

Lorelei stood there fuming, her face and neck blotchy with angry red spots. Mama was still, the fire in her eyes at odds with the unnerving smile on her lips.

I saw Hank slip out of the room from the corner of my eye. *I don't blame him,* I thought. Annabelle only burrowed deeper.

"Belle," Mama snapped, and Annabelle withdrew from her hole and looked at Mama, her lip quivering.

"You didn't mean to, did you sweetie?" Mama said then, her voice sugary.

"No, Mommy. I didn't mean to."

"Well, then," said Mama, looking back at Lorelei. "It was just an accident. It doesn't matter, really, because the snow is much too deep to be going out."

Lorelei's glare could have melted steel. I could almost hear her thoughts – how she was dying to tell Mama off, to say how Mama had no right to keep Lorelei from going out, that she was old enough to decide for herself.   And that Mama always took Annabelle's side. All true, probably. But, based on her silence, Lorelei also must have realized that there was no winning against Mama in a fight – that it was better to keep silent and wait for the right moment to try a different approach.

Hank came back in then, quiet as a whisper, carrying the blow dryer case and a roll of duct tape. Lorelei never took her eyes off Mama, and Hank had no trouble withdrawing to the wingback with the hose, the case and the tape. I watched as he went to work on it, methodically inspecting the contraption and the broken seals. After a few moments, he pulled Daddy's pocket knife out of his jeans and cut small strips from the big gray roll. Like a surgeon, he applied the strips here and there, attached the hose to the case, then affixed another piece. He tugged on the hose and blew into it to check his seal. Apparently he was satisfied with it because he carefully closed the case and latched it.

Meanwhile, the Mama-Lorelei stand-off was ongoing. While I'd been distracted watching Hank, Annabelle had made her way to Mama's side, where she stood at her leg with one finger through Mama's belt loop. Belle's expression alternated between smug and terrified, and I sent mental messages to Annabelle not to look too triumphant. Lorelei was fast, and Belle was within slapping distance. But then Hank was there, having approached Lorelei as silently as he'd made his repairs. He placed the handle into Lorelei's clenching and unclenching fist, and she looked down in surprise.

"I fixed it, Lei," he said, flashing his dimples. She wordlessly took it, leaving him to retreat to the coffee table and resume his intricate plan to traverse the magazine stacks with well laid tracks.

Now that there was no longer a reason to rant, Lorelei calmed herself. We both knew that Lorelei's only chance of getting out of the house tonight was if she let it all go. Glancing out at the drifts of snow, I had to admit that perhaps Mama had a point. Not that I was that concerned with whether Lorelei got to go on her date tonight or not. Annabelle had recovered and become fascinated with her own feet – she practiced first and second ballet positions while Mama raked her fingers through Annabelle's curls.

Lorelei murmured a thank you to Hank, then without another word, slid past Mama and ran back up the stairs.

Mama stood there a moment longer, looking at me as though waiting to see whether I cared to defy her – I didn't. Instead, I looked back down at the cross-stitching in my hand, and purposely pierced the fabric with the needle, pulling the fine pink thread through until it was taut. After a moment, I looked up and saw that Mama was gone, and that she had taken Annabelle with her. Annabelle's tea party remnants were left behind like ruins of a lost civilization, her dolls sprawled, dejected and abandoned.

Sometime later, I finished the last stitch in my hoop. As I put my materials away, I wondered what I could do the rest of the afternoon to avoid attention. Hank was busy with Daddy — they were tinkering with the washing machine. Lorelei was reading a book while her hair set, obviously still determined to find a way to go out on her date. And Annabelle had disappeared with Mama, pursuing some magical adventure. With no one to care for, I was left feeling superfluous and restless.

The sharp knock at the door startled me. Opening it, I found Mabel standing there, bundled in snow pants and a hooded coat, lime green mittens on her hands.

"Can you sneak away?" she asked, her eyes sparkling.

I looked over my shoulder. No one was around, though I could hear voices from throughout the house. I looked to the coat rack by the door and the basket of hats and gloves on the floor beside it. They beckoned to me.

"I think so," I finally said, and Mabel clapped her hands. As quickly as possible, I threw on my outerwear, and with a parting yell to Mama, I was out the door before anyone could stop me.

Outside, Mabel grabbed my hand and together we trudged through shin-high snow. The sky was so light it almost blended into the white ground. There was the faintest yellowish cast to the clouds, but no blue poked through and the air was still.

"Where are we going?" I asked.

"You'll see."

And then I did. On the far side of the barn was Calvin, sitting on Gertrude, the lovely, spirited palomino – the horse of my dreams. Beside him was Franny, the gentle old nag, and he was holding the reins of both. He grinned at me.

"Want to go for a ride?"

"Oh, yes!"

I clumsily ran toward the horses, Mabel at my heels. When we reached the horses, Mabel mounted Franny and settled her seat in the well-worn saddle. I was confused. Usually I rode Franny, and Calvin rode Gertrude or Sampson. And if Mabel came with us in the past, she rode with Calvin.

"Did...did you want me to come?"

"Yeah, of course." Mabel replied. Then she looked at Calvin and seemed to understand my confusion. "Mom said I was finally big enough to ride Franny all by myself." She grinned. "You haven't had enough practice to ride Gertrude alone, so I made Calvin come."

"You'll have to ride with me," Calvin explained, unnecessarily, bowing his head in embarrassment. "Unless you'd rather not."

I stood there for a moment and felt my cheeks flush. *No big deal,* I told myself. I was Chip's steady girl now, ever since Christmas, and going riding with Calvin didn't mean a thing.

"Uh, sure," I mumbled, and my stomach jumped.

He took his foot out of the stirrup and scooted back on Gertrude's rump, giving me room to pull up. Once I was settled in the saddle, the saddle horn pressed against my pelvis, he gently lowered himself into the swell of the seat behind me. He reached around both sides of my waist and took hold of the reins, his head looking over my right shoulder, almost resting on it.

Omigosh, omigosh, omigosh, my rattled brain repeated. My heart was galloping faster than I'd ever experienced on a horse, and I hoped he couldn't feel it. I prayed I didn't spontaneously combust at his closeness – the closest we'd been since the campfire – even as I tried to tell myself I didn't feel anything at all. Mabel giggled at the sight of us, and I could feel the intensity of Calvin's scowl, which was severe enough to wipe the grin off her face.

I could feel his breath on my cheek – it was minty, like he'd just brushed his teeth. His coat smelled of wet hay and motor oil, but I didn't mind. It was comforting, like the way Daddy smelled after working all day. I tried to focus on that, and ignore the impulse to melt back against him. I was pretty certain he'd be off that horse and away from me before I could say, "Getty up."

As we started off, and settled into the calming rhythm of the ride, I could feel the heat radiating from him. It stirred some deep muscle memory in me and I twitched involuntarily. Trying not to think about the night of the campfire, I turned my thoughts instead to the first time I'd taken advantage of his heat in the snow, back when we were kids – I had frightened him with my imagination that day, but he'd come to understand me just a little, too.

It was March of my sixth year, and winter had made a surprise return to teach the daffodils and red buds a lesson in humility. After a noisy night of pelting ice and cracking branches, we awoke to an amazing landscape. Ice covered every surface and dripped from the trees, and it looked like the land of the Snow Queen, one of those stories that Lorelei used to read to me at bedtime.

I'd spent the morning staring wistfully through frosty windows at the expanse of snow and all that it promised, waiting for Lorelei to take me outside to play. But by ten o'clock, she still wasn't ready and I was running out of patience. When I couldn't stand it one second longer, I put on my winter gear all by myself and slipped out the door.

It was very cold outside, and the snow was much deeper than I'd expected. Working slowly, I kicked my way through drifts up to my knees. It took a long time, but eventually I crossed the yard over to Calvin's farm, past the barn and the pasture, all the way to the frozen pond. By the time I reached it, I felt like I'd been on an arctic expedition that had lasted months. I gazed at the landscape before me, feeling warm and cozy in my multiple layers of clothes (that I'd remembered to put on, without anybody reminding me). I was proud to think I didn't need Lorelei after all.

"Goin' ice fishing?" someone asked and I jumped. I was relieved to see it was just Calvin.

"You trying to give me a heart attack?"

"Naw." He said, straight-faced – he never really was one for sarcasm. "Just saw you standin' out here and thought I'd see what you were up to."

"Well," I began, but then I had to stop and think. "I'm not really sure. I just needed to be out here, because we must have crossed into the Snow Queen's kingdom while we were sleeping." I didn't even know I was going to say that until it came out, but that was how I knew I was about to start an Adventure. Just like Mama taught me.

Calvin looked at me like I had lost my marbles. Besides not understanding sarcasm, he also didn't appreciate the gift of Imagination. Mama always said Imagination was God's favorite talent of all, because it was what convinced people to believe magic could be real, even when life tried to tell you something different.

"Did you have a better idea?"

"Well," he said, his words sliding out slow as a snail. "I was thinking about skatin' on the pond."

"Oooh!" I exclaimed, clapping my hands in a muffled cheer. "That sounds like loads of fun." I jumped up and down a couple times, until Calvin's eyes widened with something close to fear, like he wanted to run far, far away from me.

I stopped jumping.

"Oh, no. I don't have skates," I suddenly remembered.

"Don't worry. We have three or four pairs. I could go get them."

"Yes, please."

"Kay," he replied, and started walking in slow motion to the barn, as I stomped my feet to warm them. There was no telling how long Calvin would be, so I decided I had better prepare to protect myself from the Snow Queen's evil foot soldiers, so they wouldn't kidnap me and make me a servant princess. I bent over at the waist, but the snow was high and I reached it easily enough. I made one snowball, then another, and another, and despite how the wet snow clung to my mittens, I soon had an impressive stack. As I assessed my armory with satisfaction, I wished for a moment that I could rely on Calvin to be my Knight and protect me, but I didn't think he would cooperate about that. And even if

Angela Hoke   A Whisper of Smoke

he did, he was so slow I figured he'd get stabbed by a thousand icicle swords in the first two minutes.

I sat down on the bench and waited, plotting how I might persuade Calvin to participate in my adventure. I realized that the Snow Queen might be too much for him, for his first time. So I came up with an alternative plan, one that didn't involve quite so much fantasy.

When he'd finally gotten back with the skates, I grabbed his coat.

"We have to hurry and deliver this very important equipment to the science station. There's a blizzard coming," I said. He looked startled.

"Huh?"

"The scientists at the North Pole said they need some special equipment so they can investigate the polar bears," I patiently explained.

When he still looked blank, I expanded my explanation.

"The polar bears accidentally found Santa's workshop and then they tried to eat some of those poor elves." I knew about the dangers of polar bears because of the scary sign at the zoo that said 'Beware of the Polar Bears' which went along with some pretty frightening stories Mama told about polar bears eating children that accidentally fell over the wall.

"What in the world are you talking about," Calvin said, but he didn't actually look like he wanted to know. I decided to ignore the way he was looking at me like I was crazy and dangerous at the same time.

"Of course Santa Claus doesn't approve of polar bears eating elves. So he shot them with tranquilizer darts full of fairy dust. That's how come the polar bears were in a trance and went back the way they came."

"Fairy dust?" Calvin said, sounding skeptical. "Aren't you getting your stories all confused? Fairy dust is from fairies," he said. I found his tone very annoying, because of course I knew all about fairy dust.

"I know that. But fairies are related to elves, and that's how come Santa has a secret supply of fairy dust for if some Reds attack or something. And that's also why they let the fairies hide in Santa's bomb shelter at the North Pole."

He shook his head at me. "Where do you come up with this stuff?"

"Can't you just play and stop all your complaining?" I snapped.

He looked at me for a second, like he was trying to decide something.

"Well," he said kind of slowly. "That blizzard is coming any second. We better hurry and deliver this stuff to the scientists. They need it to… to put in some booby traps to catch the polar bears if they try to go after Santa's elves again."

My jaw dropped and I nodded dumbly, all the while beaming at him. Calvin got a peculiar look in his eyes just then, and I thought he was finally getting the big secret – which was if he would just cooperate with my adventures, everything would be so much easier.

As we began discussing our options, he set the skates on the end of the bench and sat beside me. The bench was small, and our arms couldn't keep from touching. I leaned against him just a little because he was warm as a kerosene heater.

"Well," he said, once we'd decided what supplies would make the best polar bear booby traps. I shifted away from him before he could tell me to.

Angela Hoke   A Whisper of Smoke

"We better start crossing that glacier before it melts," he pointed out. "The science station is on the other side." It didn't occur to either of us that melting glaciers and blizzards implied different weather conditions.

Instead, all I could think was how much I really liked that boy. I spontaneously threw my arms around him in a great big bear hug, and we fell right off that bench in a big heap, the snow crunched flat underneath us.

My chin landed on his chest and all I could see was his red scarf and the underside of his jaw as he looked straight up at the sky. I watched his breath, puffing like Old Faithful into the air, and I thought that those could be mad puffs. Then Calvin's shoulders began to vibrate, like an earthquake tremor, and I just knew he was about to explode with a bad temper. Not that I had ever seen Calvin lose his temper, but I knew what the Exploding Temper looked like and was familiar with the Warning Signs. I'd learned it from Mama. I wished my legs were working so I could get away while the getting was good.

As I braced myself for it, he tried to sit up. He raised his head to look down at me, and I winced in anticipation. I was shocked at what I saw.

He was laughing! Calvin's whole face turned beautiful when he laughed like that. I started laughing too, giggling until my stomach stitched up.

"Susanna!" someone yelled, and I knew right away it was Lorelei because of her bossy tone.

Calvin jumped right up, and I was impressed with his agility, dressed as he was in some serious snow gear. I was sure his nice gestures had come to an end, but he surprised me again – he stuck his hand out to help me up. I thought that was very Christian of him, even if he wasn't Catholic.

As we brushed snow off ourselves, we saw Lorelei coming towards us, her skates draped over her shoulder by the laces. Her pigtails peeked out from under her knitted cap like extraneous puff-balls.

Behind her, Mama and Daddy followed. Daddy was wearing his funny Russian snow cap and his black skates were hanging from his neck. Mama was wearing her white wool coat with the whipped cream trim of fur, and she had bright white skates dangling from her wrist. She took Daddy's arm, and as they made their way through the snow, she flashed in the diluted sunlight, throwing sunbeams like lightning bolts. As they drew closer, I could see it was the sharp shine of the skate blades and the glitter on the laces that were catching the light and sparkling like jewels. Mama was royalty that day, and as she approached, we knew to make way for her so that when she reached the bench, it was ready and warmed for her to sit.

Daddy helped her with her skates before putting on his own, but Mama didn't wait for him. As soon as she was outfitted, she made her way onto the ice, gliding before the other skate ever touched down. She made a few graceful turns around the pond, and then skated to the middle where she stopped. Slowly and deliberately, she pointed one toe into the glassy surface and spread her arms wide. We were all transfixed, as we awaited whatever was coming. I was imagining something mystical – her drawing the winter elements into a swirling frenzy, anxious to do her bidding. Or even better, some sort of holy ascension, like Jesus at Pentecost or like the Blessed Mother, after she appeared for those lucky, lucky girls in Fatima.

Angela Hoke   A Whisper of Smoke

Instead, she started to spin. Round and round she turned, precise as a drill bit, and I worried for a moment that she would drill her way through the ice to the frigid waters below. Then it was over, and Mama's face was raised towards heaven, triumphant. Were it not for the self-satisfied smile (and if I hadn't known her better), I might have described it as angelic. Still, it was awe-inspiring, the way only Mama could be.

I wasn't sure who started it, but suddenly everyone was cheering, even Mabel, who'd just walked up. I was proud, to have a mother like that.

But it was Calvin who really figured it out. He leaned towards me so he could whisper in my ear.

"The Snow Queen?" he asked, so only I could hear.

"Exactly," I'd whispered back, smiling at his exceptional progress.

Calvin coughed, startling me back into the present. I was surprised to find that I was no longer nervous, being so close to him. Somehow, while I'd reminisced, he'd transformed from the cute guy with whom I shared my first kiss back into the little boy from my childhood.

The horses walked slowly through the snow, and were almost to the woods at the edge of the pasture. No cars passed by on the road behind us, and the other animals were hiding under blankets, huddled in stalls, perched side by side in dusty rafters. When we finally reached the edge of the trees, I held my breath until we crossed over. It was like entering Narnia, or some other winter wonderland.

The horses huffed puffs of smoke, equine fog machines. There was no sound except the crunch of horse hooves on the crystalline snow and the snorts and breaths of the horses. We didn't even talk to each other, because it would have been improper – disrespectful, somehow. By the time we reached the clearing, it seemed as though we'd left the whole world behind us. It was hard to imagine that other human beings inhabited this perfect world. It was the most beautiful thing I had ever seen.

Calvin reined in then, surprising me. He dismounted and, taking the reins, walked to a nearby tree and tied Gertrude to it. He pulled out some oats from his pocket, and she munched them happily from his palm. After a moment, Mabel had tied Franny up too, and was giving her a carrot.

I felt a little ridiculous, seated on the horse while my two friends were at my feet, so I climbed down as well. My boots sank in the snow.

"Come on," Calvin said, grabbing my hand. Again, I was startled by the sudden intimacy and my heart skipped – I was glad I couldn't feel the calloused flesh of his hand on mine. When he grabbed Mabel's hand too, I calmed myself. He pulled us both along, until we'd navigated a huge drift where the creek would normally be, and he led us along an invisible path, back into the woods.

After a few moments, we reached a miniature clearing among the trees. This one was dotted with spruces and cedars, though, and each one was dripping in white like a picture of Victorian Christmas. At the sight, I had to retract my earlier assessment – *this* was the most beautiful place I'd ever seen.

When we were standing in the middle, Calvin dropped my hand. I'd almost forgotten he'd been holding it, but now his hand was conspicuously absent and I missed it. I was overcome with the irrational fear that I would sink without it. But the beauty pushed its way in and with it the fear vanished and was replaced with awe.

We each took a few moments just to take it all in – the way each branch was coated by the thinnest layer of ice, transforming the trees into ice sculptures. And how even broken trees and heaps of undergrowth and pine cones looked like works of art the way the brown and dark greens poked through the bright white.

We might as well have been in another world.

"What do you think?" Calvin asked, and even his soft words were jarring.

"I love it," Mabel replied.

"Beautiful," was all I could manage.

"Do you hear it, though?" Calvin asked.

Mabel looked at him. "What?"

Calvin just closed his eyes, and an impish smile turned up one corner of his mouth. "The most perfect silence."

I closed my eyes then too, and I could hear what he meant. There were no animal noises, no rustling of leaves, no chirping insects – none of the sounds that I had always associated with these very same woods. There was nothing to disturb the senses, as if we'd entered a void – some rip in space and time where the senses became useless. You could get lost here, and no one would find you unless you wanted to be found. It was seductive, this nothingness. And that's what made it lonely.

Perhaps it was the feeling of loneliness, but I suddenly wanted the sounds and the smells and the presence of others. So I took a step, as if to symbolically reenter the world, and the silence retreated. I heard cracking branches in its place, and one lone bird in the distance – a quail, or a dove maybe – and I knew I had returned home.

Only then did I begin to hear something else in the distance, and I knew it probably wasn't real, but I felt the thrill as if it could be and gasped.

"What?" Calvin asked, turning towards me, his eyes flashing with instinctive alarm.

"Do you hear them?" I whispered.

"Hear what?" Calvin was growing a little agitated, maybe wondering if I had heard a wolf, or whether a rogue bear had made its way here from the Appalachians. Mabel turned too, her expression wary.

"The foot soldiers of the Snow Queen," I replied.

Calvin was lightning quick, the way he grabbed a handful of snow and formed it into a perfect sphere within milliseconds. I couldn't help but be impressed, even as the snowball smacked my face and crumpled into a wet landslide. My eyes were blurry, but I could hear Calvin laughing. Then someone, presumably Mabel, placed a snowball in my right hand and, with a well placed throw, the battle had begun.

Angela Hoke   *A Whisper of Smoke*

Chapter 6: Beware the Wolf

June 1966

"Good grief, Susanna," Shelly sighed, holding up a depressingly boring brown tweed skirt. "Everything in here is outdated. Not a mini-skirt to be found."

"I like the repressed matron look. I think it works for me," I joked, but secretly I was glad she was helping me.

It was the Friday before Lorelei's graduation, and Shelly had come over after school to help me pick out the perfect outfit for Lorelei's graduation party, scheduled for the next afternoon. I needed the help. I was a fashion flop under the best circumstances, and I was so nervous about Chip coming to the party and meeting my family for the first time, I'd probably end up wearing some old lady shirt with yellow sweat stains and shorts too small to contain my droopy granny panties, if she weren't there to set me straight.

Shelly looked at me seriously. "I might get why you'd wear something like this if you didn't wear anything under it. Chip would dig that." After regarding me for a moment, she shook her head and resumed rifling through my drawers. Apparently I didn't look as though I was ready to jump from granny panties to no panties. Finally, she settled on some turquoise shorts and a cute white top with turquoise butterflies. She did have good taste. And without me suggesting it, she picked out my most feminine (and young) bra and panties too, laying them atop my outfit.

"Are you going out with Chip tonight?" she asked now that she was done. She flopped on my bed so and turned to face me. I was reclined on Lorelei's bed.

"No, he's doing something with his friends, since he's coming over here tomorrow for the party. You're still coming, aren't you?"

"Of course, I wouldn't miss it. I'm looking forward to meeting your farm-boy, Calvin. He sounds intriguing," Shelly said, raising her eyebrow suggestively. Shelly and Kenny had broken up a few months before, and since then she'd been on the prowl for a new man.

I felt a surge of jealousy, even though I knew I had no claim on Calvin. Plus, I was over him. I really was. Not that there'd been anything to get over.

"I've got Chip," I said.

"You don't have to rub it in."

I blushed. I hadn't realized that I had spoken out loud.

"So am I spending the night tonight, or not?" Shelly prodded.

"Sorry, Shel. Mother says we have to spend the night cleaning and getting ready for tomorrow. She said no guests."

"I could help," Shelly offered, and I wondered why she'd rather stay at our house than go home to her own.

"I wish you could, but the Queen has spoken."

Shelly sighed, and pried herself from the bed.

"Well, then I'd better get going. I have to walk home before it starts getting dark."

"Do you want my Dad to take you home?"

"Nah, I'm used to it. That's how I keep my girlish figure."

"I never knew walking made your boobs big," I joked.

"Why, yes it does. So you'd better get out there and start making tracks," Shelly said, darting out of the room just as the pillow I threw hit the wall where she'd been standing.

I lay back on Lorelei's bed and listened to Shelly calling a good-bye to Mama, Hank and Annabelle on her way out. Anxiety turned my stomach as I worried about Chip coming over for the first time. I couldn't imagine what he would think of our house, now that I'd seen his. And what would he think about my family? About Mama? Would she be nice to him, or would she see him as weak and eat him up? Or worst of all, would she flirt with him? Just the thought of that made me shiver.

Uncle George came over for dinner under the guise of pitching in with party preparations. But after we'd finished our pork chops and white rice, his biggest contribution was the entertainment value he always brought. He found some Mo-town on the radio, and he turned it up as loud as it would go. The sound was distorted, but we didn't mind. And when he started swing dancing with Mama in the living room, we all stopped to watch. Even Daddy came in, taking a break from patting ground beef and bread crumbs into hamburger patties.

Uncle George twirled Mama around and around in intricate loops and vines. Her face was lit up with a huge smile and she barely registered surprise when he flipped her around his back and through his legs.

"You scoundrel," she cried. But she kept up with him.

My foot tapped as I watched, and I wished that Chip would learn to dance like that. It looked like so much fun. When they finished, Mama collapsed on the couch, panting, and George reached a hand out to me.

I looked at Mama questioningly, not sure if I was asking for permission or courage. She smiled and nodded at me, and then I was twirling around and around, dizzy and happy.

He didn't do any flips with me, and I doubt I looked very graceful. But by the end, I thought I was beginning to get the hang of it. When we finished, he kissed the top of my head before announcing that he needed another beer.

Mama followed him into the kitchen and I heard the screech of kitchen chairs being pulled out and the creak of their sitting. Daddy had gone back to his task, and they settled into amiable chatter. Meanwhile, in the living room, we'd all caught the spirit. I took turns dancing with Hank and Annabelle, spinning them around and around until they toppled over onto the floor.

Not much cleaning was happening, but we were having the best time. We barely noticed that Lorelei was late. When I realized it was nearly nine o'clock, I froze, sure that at any moment Mama would notice it too. She would be livid, I knew. As if I was clairvoyant, I heard Mama say, "Well, hell. Do you see what time is it? Wonder where my darling daughter could be?"

We all heard the warning in her tone, and the frivolity abruptly ceased. Hank and Annabelle dove back into their dusting, swiping feverishly, heads down. I renewed my silver polishing with vigor, wishing Lorelei would hurry up and get home. It was a little insensitive for her to be out with her friends while the rest of her family sacrificed their Friday night preparing for her party. She could have at least called. But, then again, I knew why she didn't. Mama would have given her an earful and demanded that she come home.

Angela Hoke   *A Whisper of Smoke*

"Give her a break, Elise. It was her last day of high school today. I don't blame her for wanting to be with her friends," said Daddy.

"That's what tomorrow is for," Mama said acidly. "Do you think I'm throwing this party for me?"

Daddy harrumphed. "Give it a rest."

"I don't blame her one damn bit," Uncle George said. "Go crazy while you can, I always say. She won't be young forever."

"Bring me the bourbon, Hank," Mama called, and Hank at once retrieved it from the liquor cabinet in the dining room.

"Thank you dear," Mama said, and Hank darted out of the kitchen, back to his dusting post. I don't think that coffee table had every gleamed so brightly.

Everyone was quiet for a few minutes. Then someone pushed back from the kitchen table, by the sound of the chair moving across the floor.

"I better head on." It was Uncle George.

"Do you have to?" Mama sounded like a little girl.

"What can I say – places to go, people to see."

"I'll walk you out," Mama said, and we scattered. I withdrew to the wingback chair by the window to continue my polishing, and Hank and Annabelle hurried to dust the end tables on the back wall. Our locations were strategically selected because they were outside Mama's direct path.

Mama held Uncle George's arm as he went to the door.

"See you, kids," he said to us. "Don't get too wild now. Save it for tomorrow."

I smiled at him. "See ya, Uncle George." Hank and Annabelle mumbled their good-byes.

A Whisper of Smoke   *Angela Hoke*

At the door, Mama and Uncle George paused. She put her hands on his cheeks, and he immediately reached up to pull them off. His instant rebuff was so automatic as to be practiced. I could imagine that they'd shared this exchange a million times, since they were kids.

Now he held both her hands in his, hanging loosely in front of them. "Remember what we talked about," he said quietly. And there was no flippancy in his tone.

"You are a sweet man," she said to him, and hugged him. As she squeezed his neck, he looked a bit uncomfortable, but content too.

"Aww shucks, Ma'am," he said. Then he pulled away, kissed her forehead and slipped out the door. She stood there for a beat, and I could feel how much she loved him. When she turned to us, I could see the conflicting emotions on her face, like she couldn't decide whether to convey her affection upon us, or whether she wanted to go back to being pissed that Lorelei still wasn't home.

But Daddy came in then, drying his hands on a towel. As he passed the radio, he turned it to a forties' station. Glen Miller filled the room, and Mama's shoulders at once relaxed. He swept her into his arms, and they did a few turns around the living room. By the time they'd completed the circuit, Mama was smiling again, and Lorelei was coming through the door. We held our breath to see what Mama would do, but she just grabbed Lorelei's hand and twirled her around, calling her the "sexy scholar." Even Lorelei, who'd obviously come in prepared for a fight, couldn't help smiling. The pressure in the room ratcheted down a few notches, and I think we could all sense that the danger had passed. We danced and cleaned until the house sparkled.

By the time we'd finished cleaning, and with the baking finished earlier in the day, all that was left was to make the potato salad, and I had been elected to do that since mine was the best. Lorelei took the kids to bed while I got started in the kitchen.

"Do you need some help?" Daddy called as I began accumulating all of the ingredients.

"No, that's okay Dad. You just relax. You've had a long day."

"Thanks, Susie. Let us know if you change your mind."

"Okay," I replied. But I was content to enjoy the solitude of the kitchen while Mama and Daddy relaxed in the next room.

"Rub my feet, sweetie," I heard Mama say. She moaned and I hoped the foot massage hadn't graduated to higher anatomy.

After a moment, Daddy said, "Now, can we please talk about this college deal?"

Mama sighed. "I don't see why we need to discuss it again."

"Because it's not settled. Like I said before, I don't feel comfortable borrowing money from your brother."

"Henry, you know good and well that Lorelei's scholarships won't pay for all of her expenses. This is her dream. Our baby girl is going to college. We can't take that from her."

"I know!" Daddy said, and I could hear the frustration in his voice. "I want that for her, too. She's worked so hard for it. Damn it." He was quiet for a beat, then he sighed. "If I was a better provider, this wouldn't even be an issue."

"You listen to me," Mama said, and I knew that tone. I hoped Daddy was paying attention, even as I prayed Mama was kind. But she surprised me with what she said next. "I don't want to ever hear you talk like that again. You're a damn good provider, and a wonderful father. And you are obviously brilliant, since you did choose *me* for a wife."

I cringed at the sound of kissing, but it made my heart glow a little too.

When the noises didn't stop, I started to worry I'd be trapped in the kitchen for a while. But then the smacking subsided, and Mama spoke. "Look, George doesn't have any kids, and if he marries Cheryl, he never will."

Well, now that was interesting. Was Uncle George, the eternal bachelor, in love?

"Why is that?" Daddy asked, voicing the very next question that had come to my mind.

"She can't have kids, apparently. Anyway, you know George thinks of our kids like they were his own, without the responsibility of course," she joked.

Apparently, Daddy was still feeling uncomfortable, because Mama lowered her voice and spoke gently.

"Remember when he loaned us money for Christmas, what was it, five or six years ago? The year that the car broke down and we had to repair it with our Christmas fund."

"How could I forget."

"He was perfectly gracious about that, you have to admit. He never once brought it up. And we were able to pay him off in no time, because you *are* a great provider."

"This is a little bit more than money for Christmas," Dad said with quiet resignation.

"I know, great love of my life," Mama said tenderly. From someone else, the sentiment might have seemed a bit overdramatic, or even cliché. But from Mama, it somehow rang true.

Angela Hoke   *A Whisper of Smoke*

"Henry," said Mama, and for some reason I held my breath. "It's the right thing."

The house was still, too much so, and I realized that I had not moved a muscle for the last five minutes. I purposefully clanged a pot to remind them of my presence.

"How's it going in there, Susie?" Mama called.

"Almost done," I called back, feeling almost content. I figured that as long as Lorelei never found out where the funding came from, all would be fine.

I'd just put the potato salad in the refrigerator when I heard a creak on the stairs. I wondered if maybe Mama or Dad had forgotten something, and I waited for someone to come into the kitchen. When they didn't, my heartbeat jumped, but I stayed calm. I put the dish towel on the counter and began tiptoeing towards the doorway to the living room, telling myself it was probably nothing. The floor squeaked as I walked, and I froze every time it made a sound.

At first I heard nothing else, and I was beginning to think I'd imagined the noise. But then I heard another creak, and it didn't come from me. The hair on the back of my neck stood straight up. Reaching over beside me, I slowly withdrew a knife out of the butcher block and took one more step towards the door. I swiveled around on my sock feet and placed my back against the wall, as I silently counted one... two....

At three, I jumped into the doorway with the knife raised, ready to face my attacker. When I saw the dark figure at the front door, my heart nearly stopped.

The person spun around and cursed.

A Whisper of Smoke   *Angela Hoke*

"Damn, Susanna. You scared the shit out of me."

"Likewise, Lei," I said, lowering the knife as I tried to calm my pounding heart. "What are you doing?"

"Shhh, don't wake them up." Lorelei's eyes shone bright, even from across the room. I walked over to her so we could talk in whispers.

When I'd gotten close enough to her, I asked again. "What the hell are you doing?"

As if in answer, I heard tires crunching on gravel and pulled back the curtain to see. A car was creeping up the driveway, headlights extinguished. Pushing me aside, Lorelei flashed me a devilish grin and darted out the front door. I toyed briefly with the idea of locking her out, but I didn't. I figured it was better to have her owe me one.

I considered going on up to bed, but I thought I should keep an eye on that shadow car and make sure it didn't go anywhere. I decided to work on my poetry while I waited for her to get finished with… whatever. As quiet as I could, I ran up the stairs, stopping by Annabelle's and Hank's room to check on them. I lifted up on the door to keep it from making noise and smiled at the sight of Annabelle, who was already turned sideways in her bed, her small feet dangling off one side. Hank was burrowed into his mattress and blankets like a little hedgehog, dead to the world. I crossed over to my bedroom and pulled my poetry notebook from its secret place, then quickly tiptoed back downstairs.

Back in the living room, I settled on the wingback chair, draping my legs over one arm. As I thought about what I wanted to write, I wished again that I could just come out and express what I was thinking and feeling, like in a diary. But it was Lorelei's diary (which Mama read) that really started the wars between them, and I knew that a diary would never be safe. Still, if I could write in a diary, I would write about how

Angela Hoke   *A Whisper of Smoke*

Chip was pressuring me to go all the way. Not so much in words, but with his body. We'd been going together for almost nine months, and we spent nearly every weekend together. In the beginning, our dates were nice, safe – sharing burgers and fries at the soda shop, going to movies, meeting friends at parties and dances. But lately, we spent most of our time "taking walks" on his property, which really meant making out on a blanket on the grass, where the houselights couldn't reach.

It started out as kissing, which was fine by me – I loved kissing Chip (either he'd improved since that first time, or I had). But things quickly escalated. One night a few weeks ago, after we'd kissed for what seemed like hours, I suddenly found myself sans pants, his fingers inside my panties. As soon as I noticed it, but before I could protest, he put on a full court press – his kisses deepened and moved to new places, on my neck, on my nipples. He played me like a Les Paul guitar, and my body sang.

Since then, it was like my body had been awakened. And as much as I was ashamed to admit it, I ached for him to make me feel like that again. So when he led me away from his house, telling his mother we were going to take a walk and look at the moon, I went right along with it, anxious for the moment when he would consume me.

But two weeks ago things changed again. We were making out on the blanket, and he was kissing me and touching me and sometimes even sucking on me, and I was feeling like there wasn't anything I would deny him. I knew he wanted more from me, needed more. I understood that he got some pleasure from our encounters, but I sensed that he was becoming more and more dissatisfied. So when he took my hand and placed it on the outside of his pants, and I felt his erection big and hard underneath the zipper, I thought I owed him a little rubbing.

A Whisper of Smoke   *Angela Hoke*

After that night, I felt educated – womanly. I thought I knew what he expected, and I was prepared to do a little voluntary stroking through his pants. As I got ready for last week's date, I even felt a little powerful, knowing that I was going to take charge and show him I was as passionate as he was. But when the time came, and I inched my hand down his belly and reached, with confidence, for where I expected to feel his tight, hard body straining against his trousers, I found flesh instead. He had released himself from the restraints of his pants, and suddenly I was touching it.

His penis was hot, like a fire poker, and it pulsed in my hand. It was surprisingly big and solid. As I searched my mind for some comparison, I thought of roasted Kielbasa, or boiled brats, and I fought the urge to take a bite out of it. Instead, I just held it – too unsure to proceed, and too committed to withdraw.

Thoughts of food quickly faded as he went nuts at my touch. His tongue invaded me – my mouth, my ear, my neck, and then he kissed his way down my chest and sucked on my nipples. I gasped and my body responded. I stroked him, once, tentatively, and he groaned and starting thrusting into my hand. That scared me a little, and I let go. But he was in another place by then, and he wasn't deterred by my retreat.

Instead, he seemed to take it as some kind of invitation.

He leaned over me, his penis making sticky tracks on my leg as he rubbed up and down against me. He sucked at me then bit my nipple as first one finger, and then two (*oh God*) slid inside me. Distantly, I registered that I was naked, but I was gone at that point, lost on the road to a new frontier called Orgasm-land. When his knee slid between my thighs, slowly pushing them apart, I barely noticed. I just happened to open my eyes and caught the look on his face, his longing so clear it

Angela Hoke   *A Whisper of Smoke*

seemed a transformation – the conversion of boy to wolf in the full moonlight.

Somehow, miraculously, I withdrew myself from the haze of desire, and I knew at that instant that he was about to be inside me, but not with his hand.

Something gave me the strength to stop – the niggling fear of pregnancy, the knowledge that this was a sin, the thought of disappointing my parents. And I had the feeling that, if I gave in, it would be like stepping over the edge of the precipice. There would be no going back with Chip. I thought it might become the price for his love.

Instead, I stroked him in apology until he climaxed.

Now, sitting in the chair waiting while Lorelei made out, or more, with some guy, I shook my head to clear the images. I picked up my journal, clicked my pen, and let the emotions flow out, writing:

> *Rocks of fire, beds of grass*
> *Burning blankets, lapping waves*
> *Repeating tides from an enveloping sea,*
> *Liquid of salt and moonlit darkness.*
>
> *To the brink, fear and delight*
> *Weighted neck, dragging down*
> *Starving lungs, thirst for relief,*
> *Swimming strong strokes, seeking the surface.*
>
> *Erupt into darkness, erupt from the dark*

Moonlight highlights, illuminating the highs
Breath of life, a thousand deaths,
Alive in a million pieces, numb to the core.

When I finished, I quickly closed it away, anxious to shut down the simultaneous feelings of arousal and guilt my composition evoked in me. I looked at the mantel clock and saw that almost forty-five minutes had passed since Lorelei went outside. It always amazed me how time could fly by when I was writing. But now it was getting late, and Mama had not drunk enough to ensure that she would not wake back up. To speed Lorelei along. I flipped the porch light on and off a few times, which was our signal to each other that there was a danger of getting caught and to wrap it up. Through the window, I watched for Lorelei to emerge from the car. The car windows were steamy and stayed that way – they didn't seem to be in a hurry to stop whatever they were doing.

Just thinking about what was happening in the car made me flash back, briefly, to Chip and the way he touched me. At that moment, my resolve to be good didn't seem quite so strong. I thought that, if he were there with me at that moment, I would not be able to resist taking all of him inside me.

I shook my head hard to clear the sinful thoughts, and shot up a quick prayer for forgiveness, while also making a mental note to confess my shameful lust.

Finally, Lorelei opened the big car door, and she stumbled out giggling. She came tip-toeing up the walk, exaggerating her steps and almost losing her balance. I quietly opened the door on the dark porch, and Lorelei slipped inside, smelling of boy scent and beer.

"Thanks, Sus," she whispered.

Angela Hoke   *A Whisper of Smoke*

"Yeah. You owe me."

"Right," she said, as she continued her stealthy progress towards the stairs. I followed her up the steps, hoping that Lorelei could make it to the bedroom without making too much noise.

Chapter 7: White Elephants and Graduation Caps

The graduation had been hot and long. By the time we got home and piled out of the steamy station wagon, I reeked from my own perspiration and also Hank's little boy sweat, as he'd been smushed against me in the backseat. We all were in need of freshening up before the party, but there just wasn't going to be time for us all to do it properly. It was going to be a case of survival of the fittest, in terms of who would get access to the bathroom and who wouldn't. And while I appreciated that this was Lorelei's party, and that Mama was hostess, I couldn't afford to be swayed by courtesy – Chip was coming to the party and would be meeting my family *for the very first time*. And I needed to be firing on all cylinders, good hygiene among the most basic of requirements.

I raced to the bathroom as soon as I got inside the house, but Mama still beat me to it. She grinned and disappeared behind the door, so I sat down on the floor in the hall and staked my claim to be next. My anxiety ticked upward with each passing minute and was at full capacity by the time Mama emerged twenty minutes later, looking pretty. Before anyone could muscle their way in front of me, I quickly slipped inside and locked the door behind me.

I stripped in record time and climbed into the shower, careful to preserve the hot water which I knew would be in short supply. As I stood under the water, I tried to calm my nerves, telling myself everything would be fine. And when that didn't work, whispering Hail Marys to the showerhead. When I finished, I darted to my room to get dressed, glad that I didn't have to worry about finding something to wear. I put on the outfit Shelly picked out for me, and wound my wet hair around orange juice cans. I put the hair dryer cap over my head and started working on my make-up. Just as I was taking the cap off, Shelly burst in.

"Good grief," I said. "You scared the crap out of me."

"Well, don't you look like a freak at Mrs. Frankenstein's beauty salon." Shelly climbed up behind me and started pulling the cans from my hair. "Oow, ooh, ouch," she complained, as she flung the hot cans and pins to the floor. "Let me help you with your hair. Do you know what time it is? People are going to be here soon."

"I know!" I cried. Already, I could smell the scent of the charcoal grill being fired up through the open window. "Don't make me nervous when I have a wand of stinging mascara pointed at my eye – I'm uncoordinated enough as it is."

"Sorry," Shelly said, as she began brushing my hair. "So when's Calvin coming over?"

"Don't know, and you leave him alone. He's too sweet for you." Well, now. I wasn't sure where *that* came from.

"Uhh! I object to that! I'm very sweet – he can taste me to find out!" I threw a pillow over my shoulder, and missed entirely. "Want to know what I think? I think you are secretly in love with Calvin. I think when you're kissing Chip and you close your eyes, it's Calvin's mouth that you are imagining."

A Whisper of Smoke   *Angela Hoke*

I froze mid-application, a tube of pink lipstick paused against my lower lip.

"That's ridiculous," I said, but even to my own ears, I didn't sound convincing.

But Shelly didn't seem to notice. "Well, I should hope so!" she said. "Chip is gor-gee-ous. He sure would keep *my* attention." I realized she'd been teasing me and inwardly sighed with relief.

"Are you going to finish putting that lipstick on? Or are you trying to look like a geisha?" Shelly asked. I glanced in the mirror and it did look funny. I folded my hands together and bowed to her.

"Oooh, stay like that," Shelly said. She grabbed a comb and starting teasing the crown of my hair. When I flipped back over, my hair was a huge mane, and we both collapsed into laughter.

Finally we were ready, and we walked outside just in time to meet Mabel, Elton, Cora and Kathleen as they arrived. The younger ones quickly found Hank and Annabelle and together they all went off to play stick-ball. Mr. and Mrs. Conner were close behind, carrying casserole dishes with potholders. Mr. Conner looked awkward holding the casserole, so I offered to take it from him. Mr. Conner seemed relieved to no longer be carrying a dish, and went to stand by Dad at the grill. Dad offered him a drink, and Mr. Conner accepted a cold bottle of RC from the ice chest.

With my hands full, I suggested that Shelly pour herself a glass of lemonade and make herself comfortable while I helped Mrs. Conner. I rolled my eyes when Shelly took a seat in a lawn chair behind my dad and Mr. Conner and immediately started flirting with them. She just grinned at me, completely incorrigible.

Mrs. Conner and I took the food into the kitchen and placed it into the crowded oven to keep warm until it was time to serve. Mama was even gracious about it – apparently (thankfully) she and Mrs. Conner had spoken beforehand and had agreed on what dishes the Conners should bring. Since I wasn't needed, I left Mrs. Conner chatting with Mama, and followed Lorelei back outside. Lorelei was carrying the transistor radio and she set it on the patio and tuned it to some rock and roll, which livened up the atmosphere.

The party preparations had gone well, and so there wasn't really much to do until it was time to eat. So I stood on the patio, surveying the landscape. It took less than a minute to realize I was looking, not for Chip, but for Calvin. Where was he? I had expected him to come over with the rest of his family, but I didn't see him anywhere.

Apparently Shelly thought that Dad's and Mr. Conner's conversation had grown boring, and she moved her chair over by where Lorelei sat and now Mrs. Conner was also sitting. Mrs. Conner remained perched on the edge of her seat, clearly uncomfortable to be sitting still and not preparing or serving. But she was smart enough not to intrude on another woman's party, particularly when that woman was as capricious as Mama. I joined them just in time to hear Lorelei speak excitedly to the others about attending Northern Kentucky University in the fall. She was going to be a nurse, like she'd always planned. I was excited for her, and proud of her.

When there was a break in the conversation, I attempted to ask casually about Calvin's whereabouts. I saw Shelly's ears perk up as Mrs. Conner responded, "He'll be here soon..." (and then followed that hopeful statement with the fateful and devastating words...) "He's just gone to pick up his girlfriend."

GIRLFRIEND, Girlfriend, girlfriend... The word echoed horrifically in my head. I sensed Shelly's scrutiny, and sure enough, she was watching me curiously. I flashed a smile and excused myself to go help Mother.

Susanna, get a grip, I scolded myself. I had a boyfriend, for goodness sake! And why was I so surprised anyway? Calvin was sixteen, sweet and cute in a wholesome kind of way. Of course he would have a girlfriend. Suddenly, I found myself hoping that Chip would arrive before Calvin and his (gag) girlfriend.

Cars were pulling up and parking in the designated portion of the adjacent field, and I was relieved to see Chip's mother's car pull up and let him out. My stomach did a little flip at the sight of him, as it always did. And I ran over to greet him, throwing my arms around him in a spontaneous hug. He grinned at me in response and gave me a quick kiss. Feeling reassured at his presence, I grabbed his hand and led him towards where my family was gathered, feeling a confidence that I hoped would hold.

I took him over to where Lorelei, Shelly and Mrs. Conner were sitting and introduced him.

"How do you do," he said, shaking first Mrs. Conner's hand and then, to my surprise, Lorelei's. "Hi," he said to Shelly with a nod.

"Hey there," Shelly answered back.

Just then, Dad came out the back door carrying a platter of raw hamburger patties.

"Dad, this is Chip," I said.

"Hi, Sir. Can I give you a hand?" Chip asked, solicitously.

"You sure can. There is another plate of hotdogs inside. If you could bring them out to me, that would be great."

"No problem, Sir," he said. I led Chip into the kitchen where Mama was mixing a pitcher of mint juleps.

"Mom, this is Chip," I said. And held my breath.

She turned to look at him, appraising him with a long glance. Then she held out her hand for him to shake.

"Hello, Chip. It's nice to finally meet you," she said.

"Hi, Mrs. Braden. It's great to finally meet you too. I told Susanna she's kept me away for too long," he added brazenly, and I looked at him. He was smiling in his charming way, and I glanced at Mama to see if his charm was working on her.

"Well, next time, don't wait for an invitation," Mama replied, batting her eyes once, twice. *Oh, good grief.*

I cleared my throat. "Daddy wants us to bring out the hot dogs," I said, and Mama pointed us to the covered plate on the counter.

"There they are. Chip, I hope we have more time to visit later."

"You can count on it," Chip replied. And I led him back outside with the platter of weenies before he and Mama exchanged numbers.

"I hope you brought your dancing shoes," Mama called after us.

When we got outside, I was alarmed to see that Calvin had arrived and his apparent girlfriend was with him. She was pretty and demure, with wide blue eyes and very smooth, dark hair. She was wearing an exceedingly chaste blue gingham sundress, and suddenly I felt audacious in my cropped shirt.

They were standing between the grill and the cluster of lawn chairs talking with Daddy and Mr. Conner. Calvin was gesturing about something, and the girl was standing close beside him, her face bowed

A Whisper of Smoke   *Angela Hoke*

in shyness. When I first saw her, the girl had been holding Calvin's hand in both of hers (an awkward grasp given that she was standing just behind him to one side), but Calvin had needed his hand to describe whatever it was he was talking about. When he let her hand go, it was clearly unconscious, but it left her looking lost. Like a pathetic little puppet, her head imperceptibly bobbed as she seemed transfixed on the position of his hands. And her hand twitched as though it wanted to snatch his flying one out of the air and calm it back down into submission.

"Are you coming?" Chip asked curiously, and I realized that I had stopped in my tracks while Chip had continued walking with the tray of hotdogs directly *(gulp)* towards the grill and Calvin.

"Oh... yeah," I said and trotted to catch up, catching Shelly's bemused look from her casual observation post on the green plastic-straw lawn chair. Shelly caught my eye and smiled wide, apparently enjoying the anticipation of whatever it was she expected to happen. I rolled my eyes and then rubbed my nose with my middle finger, clandestinely flipping her the bird. Shelly burst out laughing, and I couldn't help but smile, just as I saw Mrs. Conner and some of the other neighbors look over at Shelly strangely.

Then Calvin and his girl were directly in front of us, and I watched in slow motion as Dad took the tray from Chip and Chip turned to introduce himself to Calvin. They were shaking hands like men and words were being exchanged, but I didn't hear them. I only saw Calvin as the butterflies in my stomach launched disobediently into a frenzy.

I was angry at myself for reacting this way. I'd been over Calvin for months. Just because he had a girlfriend now didn't change a thing.

Angela Hoke   *A Whisper of Smoke*

Calvin was talking at me, saying something about his little puppet girl…

"…is Christine," I finally realized he was saying, by way of introduction.

'Hi," I said, trying to neutralize the rogue muscles of my face into a benign expression.

"Hi," Christine said back, still looking at the ground, which was just as well, because I had no great desire to get lost in her baby blues.

Chip and Calvin talked about school and sports for a minute, then the conversation seemed to dry up in the heat.

"Well," I said, interrupting the awkwardness before it became too pronounced. "I should introduce Chip to some other family members. This is the first time he's met my family," I explained to Calvin and Christine, and Calvin was nodding, too long.

"Okay, then, I guess we'll see you later?" he said, and Chip said 'sure.' Calvin led his puppet girl over to his mom, and Chip looked over at me with a smile.

"So who's next?" he asked, good-naturedly.

"Um, Uncle George," I offered, and we went to find him.

By the end of the night, Calvin and Christine had said their good-byes, as had the rest of Calvin's family. It was no coincidence that their departure happened just after Lorelei's "friend who was a boy but not a *boyfriend"* Martin knocked over a table of cups when he drunkenly crashed into it. The party had become "after hours," and the light-weights were bailing out.

A Whisper of Smoke   *Angela Hoke*

Shelly had left too, reluctantly adhering to her twelve o'clock curfew.

Chip was feeling pretty good at this point, as he was on at least his sixth cup of beer. I had drunk a few cups, but when the ground started bucking and no one else was ducking for cover from the earthquake, I figured I'd better stop drinking.

Looking around at the inebriated group, there was obviously no one there that would be sober enough to drive Chip home. Thank goodness he had already called his parents and asked for their permission to stay the night in Hank's room. They said yes, obviously having no idea how loose the supervision could be at the Braden house.

By 1:30 am, I could barely keep my eyes open and the jokes and stories that were being passed around lost much of their hilarity. They had disintegrated in complexity to the stupid elephant jokes that guys seemed to find so funny.

Even Daddy was laughing. I looked at him in surprise, watching his stomach jiggle with his laughter as he doubled over on the lawn chair. Mama was spread languidly beside him on the chaise lounge, her ankles crossed and her top sliding down revealing the white caps of her breasts. I shook my head at them, and Mama smiled in response. We shared a momentary kinship, until Mama laughed at something Uncle George said. I closed my eyes.

"How do you shoot a blue elephant?" Uncle George was asking now.

"I don't know, darling brother. How?" Mama replied, setting up the punch-line.

"With a blue elephant gun!" he revealed, and the guys cracked up.

Angela Hoke   *A Whisper of Smoke*

"How do you shoot a yellow elephant?" he went on.

"How?" prompted Lorelei, before losing her balance (ironically, from a sitting position) and falling with a thud to the ground. There was a delay in George's response as everyone tried to get their crying laughter under control.

Finally, he said, "Have you ever seen a yellow elephant?" to which everyone erupted again.

Is that it? I thought, totally not getting it. Maybe you had to be drunk.

"How do you shoot a red elephant?" he continued, unbelievably.

Oh, good lord, I thought, rolling my eyes.

"Hold his trunk shut until he turns blue, and then shoot him with the blue elephant gun!" he roared. Everyone was rolling, gasping for breath as they laughed themselves silly. I gave a half-hearted laugh, just to fit in, but what I really wanted was to go to bed.

"Hey, I've got one," Chip piped up when the laughing had largely subsided. I turned to look at him in surprise. I was sitting between his legs, my back resting comfortably against his chest.

"Let's hear it," Uncle George said, leaning forward in (*good grief*) anticipation.

"Okay," he said. "What's harder than getting a pregnant elephant into a Volkswagen?"

"What?" came several voices.

"Getting an elephant pregnant in a Volkswagen!" he cried, and people started toppling over everywhere with uncontrollable laughter. It was really too much.

"I'm going to bed," I announced.

"Awww, no, Sus!" Chip protested, grabbing my hand as I tried to stand. I stumbled, and he caught me in a tight embrace around his lap. I could feel his erection under me, and I instantly blushed with embarrassment, thankful for the cover of darkness.

Uncle George was already telling another stupid joke, attention diverted. I removed Chip's hands deliberately, one at a time, and stood up quickly to escape his clutches. My head swam, and I swayed on my feet.

Chip jumped up and steadied me. "I'll take you," he said.

"I'm taking sleepy-head to bed," he announced, leading me away. I waited for a biting comment from Mama, but she just smiled and waved at Chip with her fingers.

I rolled my eyes again, and we headed inside. We went upstairs slowly, as Chip tried to keep both of us in balance. He giggled when he slipped down one stair.

"Shhhh!" I admonished. "Hank and Annabelle are asleep."

"Okay," he whispered loudly back. Then he continued his ascent with exaggerated tip-toed steps. At the threshold of my bedroom door, I turned to tell him good-night and was assaulted by his tongue. He fell against me, pushing me into the door with a thump, as he kissed me deeply.

Part of my mind worried that he might have awakened Annabelle, and the other part responded disloyally with a flood of desire. He sensed it, and put his knee between my legs, applying pressure to my crotch while he spread them ever so slightly.

The sounds of drunken laughter erupted outside, breaking the spell that had come over me. With both hands, I pushed Chip back. "No!" I whispered harshly. "Are you crazy?"

Angela Hoke   *A Whisper of Smoke*

"No, just in loooove," he said seductively.

"Oh, go to bed," I said firmly, but I was slightly amused. I gave him a quick kiss on the lips, then slipped inside my room, closing the door swiftly behind me.

I stood there with my back against the door and my hand on the doorknob, prepared to force him back if he tried to come in. He didn't, though. After a moment, I heard him stumble his way to Hank's room and open the door with a squeak. I winced at the sound, and then relaxed my shoulders when I heard Hank's door click shut.

Chapter 8: Valley of the Dolls

After Mass on Sunday, everyone was still in a good mood from the party, and even managed the effects of various stages of hangovers with relatively good humor. Chip's parents had picked him up early so that he could go to Mass with them, and I smiled as I remembered his face as he tried to hide his pounding headache from his mother. Annabelle was the only one that was cranky, but then she had stayed up much too late the night before. So right after lunch, I offered to take Annabelle up to her room for her nap.

"I'm too old for naps," Annabelle complained, as she pulled against my grip the entire journey up the stairs.

"If you keep doing that and if I accidentally lose my grip on you, you are going to go flying."

Annabelle sighed dramatically, but she stopped pulling.

"You stayed up really late last night at the party," I explained as we reached the top of the stairs and entered the bedroom. "Today you need a nap, no arguments." With my hand, I nudged her into the bed, stroking her long soft curls as she lay down. Her hair was soft as silks from unshucked corn.

I was just about to leave when Annabelle said, "Uncle George liked my dolls."

I paused at the foot of her bed. "Oh yeah? When did you show Uncle George your dolls?"

"Last night at the party. He kissed them good-night." She giggled, then turned serious. "He slobbered on them though. I could have done without that."

"Bet that was gross," I smiled and sat next to her. "Why was Uncle George in your room anyway?"

"Because Mama told me to get my PJs on, and Uncle George came up to help me," she replied, yawning.

George was our favorite uncle, but something about the thought of him helping Annabelle with her PJs didn't sit right with me. Still, even as I asked the next question, I told myself the knot of worry in my chest was unwarranted. "Did he help you change clothes?"

"Uh huh," she answered, nodding. "We played tickle."

I felt a little light-headed. "Where did he tickle you?"

"You know, on my neck, under my arms, stuff like that," Annabelle said. I relaxed my shoulders, until Annabelle added, giggling nervously, "He wanted to play tickling the privacies."

My stomach turned over and I tasted bile. I swallowed. "Are you sure?"

"I'm not dumb, I know what the privacies are," Annabelle said, pointing down.

My mind started spinning, but I forced myself to think. I thought I should ask more probing questions, but I was suddenly afraid of the answers.

Lorelei, I thought. Lorelei would know what to do.

Annabelle was looking at me intently, as though gauging my reaction. I shook myself and pasted on a smile. "Time to go to sleep now," I said and kissed her head. Then I hurried out of the room, before my façade cracked. In the hall, I paused to steady myself, then raced downstairs to find my other sister.

Lorelei was outside in the hammock, reading *Valley of the Dolls* with her shades on. I walked through the short grass and stubbornly resilient dandelions to where Lorelei swayed in the breeze, suspended between two green apple trees. My stomach rolled with anxiety. I could have been going to meet my executioner.

"Hey," Lorelei said, not looking up.

I took a deep breath. "I need to talk to you about something," I said. Lorelei peered over the tops of her sunglasses at me, and something about my expression made her pause. She folded over the page in her book and swung her bare legs over the edge of the hammock.

"Come sit," she invited, patting the netting beside her. "Tell me what's going on."

I sat beside her, and we both lay back across the width of the hammock, our feet grazing the grass. Without conscious thought, we began to push against the ground, gently rocking the hammock.

"Is it Chip?" Lorelei asked, sounding genuinely concerned. Hearing the sincerity in her voice made my pulse slow as she I gathered up the courage to tell Lorelei about what Annabelle had said.

"No," I began slowly. "It's Annabelle."

She sat up quickly. "What's wrong, is she alright?"

"She's okay. She's sleeping," I quickly assured her, and Lorelei lay back down. "It's about something she told me a few minutes ago."

"Okay. What is it?"

Angela Hoke   *A Whisper of Smoke*

"It's about Uncle George," I began. The sick feeling returned to the pit of my stomach, and suddenly the rocking motion was making me nauseous.

"Go on," Lorelei said with a dull voice, but she had stilled her feet. Now we both lay still on the netting of a stationary hammock, our legs dangling and our eyes glued to the flashing leaves and clusters of growing apples hanging heavy and precarious above our heads.

I took a deep breath and told her about my conversation with Annabelle. As I spoke, I couldn't see Lorelei's reaction behind her dark glasses. When I'd finished speaking, I waited patiently for whatever wisdom she might impart. The seconds ticked by, and then Lorelei gave a big sigh. She looked defeated, and I realized that Lorelei wasn't going to take charge and spare me the burden of deciding what to do.

Lorelei *loved* bossing, and I was unsettled by her reaction.

"I'm sure it was nothing, but I still think we have to tell Daddy," I ventured, half hoping Lorelei would disagree.

"Don't you think she's telling the truth?"

I wanted to doubt her, but something about Annabelle's recounting had the ring of truth.

"I can't think why she'd make that up."

"Of course she didn't," Lorelei replied, her voice hard. I looked at my sister, hoping that her dislike of Uncle George wasn't making her biased. Because while I didn't think Annabelle was making it up, none of it reconciled with the uncle I knew.

"I can't imagine telling Daddy. What do you think he'll say?" My stomach flipped over. "What if I can't say the words?"

A Whisper of Smoke   *Angela Hoke*

"You'll say it because you have to. Hell, we'll tell him together," Lorelei pronounced, mustering some of her old authority. It felt good for Lorelei to be bossy – it was a comfort.

"Might as well get it over with," Lorelei sighed, then hoisted herself up, dragging me with her.

We made our way slowly towards the house, hoping that Mama was asleep so we could talk to Daddy alone. When we walked inside, Daddy was sitting at the kitchen table reading the Sunday Courier Journal and drinking coffee. He looked up at us and put a finger to his lips, pointing upstairs to indicate that Mama was indeed napping (translation, sleeping off her hangover).

"Daddy," Lorelei said quietly. "We need to talk to you." I stood in the background wringing my hands, useless.

Daddy smiled and motioned for us to sit.

"So what's going on, girls?"

We looked at each other, then Lorelei took a deep breath and told him what Annabelle had said. Daddy was eerily silent during the short account, but his face reddened and his expression darkened.

Finally, he asked, "Did she tell you anything else?"

I spoke up, "No, I didn't ask her anything else. I didn't know what else to say."

"It's okay," Daddy said distractedly, patting my hand. "You girls did the right thing telling me. I'll talk to her when she wakes up, and I'll deal with this."

His grip on the coffee mug was so tight that his knuckles were white. I worried that he would break the cup and hurt himself, but then he set it down and said he wanted some time alone.

Drained, we shuffled outside, heading mutely back to the hammock. I was too nervous to sit, though, so instead I grabbed hold of a sturdy limb and swung my leg up and over. I started climbing the tree until I reached a crook that submerged me into the protective cover of criss-crossing branches and blanketing leaves. Lorelei lay back down on the hammock, but did not reopen her book. She rocked silently as I hid among the pregnant branches.

Finally, Lorelei spoke. "Did you ever wonder what made Mama get married at fifteen?"

I thought about that. The truth was, I had not really.

"I did," Lorelei said, answering her own question.

"Wait a minute," I said, a thought dawning. "Was she pregnant when she and Dad got married?"

"Nope, at least not with me. I was born almost two years later," Lorelei replied. I was relieved, but remained puzzled.

"What I mean is, did you ever think that there were reasons that Mother didn't want to be at home anymore?" As I pondered that, Lorelei continued. "Uncle George has given me the creeps since I was a kid." I looked at her, and there was none of the usual smirking disgust in her expression. There was something else, something way too vulnerable to sit comfortably on her face.

I wanted to say something to comfort her, and I opened my mouth, unsure of the words. "Me too, sometimes," I managed, not realizing it was true until the words left my lips.

Lorelei took her sunglasses off and looked at me for a long moment, then put them back on and resumed swinging.

"There's always been something weird about Mama's relationship with him. Don't you think?"

A Whisper of Smoke   *Angela Hoke*

I shrugged. "If he did something to Mama wouldn't she have told us?"

She looked at me over her shades. "Are you kidding? We're talking about Mama here."

This felt wrong. "Maybe nothing ever happened to her," I said, but even to my own ears my words lacked much conviction.

"Of course it did. She's a nut-case. Always has been. Hell he probably diddled her all the time."

"But he's younger than her," I said.

She paused at that. "Well, even if it wasn't Funny Uncle George, *something* happened to make her crazy. And they've always been in it together. Shit – maybe something happened to both of them."

"Oh, come on!" I exclaimed.

"Are you that naive?" She looked at me with disdain. "It would explain how Uncle George became a diddler." I winced. "And you have to admit it would explain a hell of a lot about Mother."

My mind was whirling with too much new information. I felt sick.

"She could have warned us," Lorelei barked, and I was so startled I jerked in my seat, shaking apples loose so they rained like bomb shells.

Lorelei didn't seem to notice, as her anger grew. "How could she have ever let us be alone with him, if she knew he was a big pervert? Annabelle didn't deserve this. She's just a little girl!"

Shit. She's right. Anger welled up within me, and I rode its rising tide, my vessel built from indignation that a grown man, a trusted relative, may have robbed my baby sister of her innocence. *How could he be so vile?* I wondered, though I would not have accepted a response. There was nothing that could serve as justification for this.

Angela Hoke   *A Whisper of Smoke*

A more troubling question poked at me. *Did Mama really know what he was capable of?* There also was no good answer to that question. So I pushed it aside.

After some time had passed, there was the sound of a door slamming in the house, and then raised voices. I was emotionally exhausted, as though I'd been crying for hours, but somehow I roused myself. In unspoken accord, Lorelei and I made our way to the house to investigate, readying ourselves to come to Annabelle's defense, if needed. I latched back onto my receding anger and stored it, ready to loose its accusations like a flood.

When we entered the house, we saw Mama holding onto Daddy's arm, apparently trying to keep him from going to confront Uncle George.

"Henry, this is ridiculous!" she exclaimed, sounding a bit frantic. "She doesn't know what she's saying! I'm sure it was innocent."

Daddy gritted his teeth. "I will not stay here and argue with you, Elise. I talked with Annabelle, and she told me what happened."

"Then she made it up!" Mama spat.

Daddy raised his arm, and I sucked in my breath, suddenly afraid that he was going to strike her, though such an act would be completely uncharacteristic. But he didn't, of course. He remained true to our perceptions of his nature, the one constant in this whole mess, and I was utterly grateful for that.

Instead, he grabbed Mama's hand and pried it forcibly from his arm, then slung her onto the couch. Mama looked like she could spit venom, she was so furious. And Daddy, for once, seemed as though he would welcome her strike and an excuse to shake some sense into her. For some time they stared at each other, she sprawled on the sofa, chest heaving, he standing by the door with his arms hanging stiffly away from his body.

"It wasn't that bad," Mama whispered at last.

Daddy looked at her. A look of sadness flickered across his face, then his expression hardened. "It was bad enough," he finally said. And though his voice was quiet, it was steely and cold. Without another word, he stormed out of the house, and Mama sat stunned on the couch, her eyes full of wet fury.

She then appeared to sense our presence, and she whipped her head around.

"What are you two looking at!" she screamed.

I shrank under Mama's maniacal glare, and neither I nor Lorelei said anything, but instead scrambled upstairs where we found Annabelle crying on her bed, and Hank with his arm protectively around her. He was patting her back comfortingly, and whispering that it would be okay. If Annabelle hadn't known that there was anything improper about what happened, what Uncle George had done or almost done, before, she certainly knew it now.

Lorelei walked over and picked Annabelle up. She rocked the little girl in her arms, shushing against her soft head. Hank was left sitting on the bed, shock written all over his face. I went to sit beside him and covered his hand with mine. He was shaking. I wanted to ask them what had happened before we came in, but I didn't want to add to their trauma, so Lorelei and I just looked at each other.

Downstairs, we could hear Mama rampaging through the house, her anger punctuated with crashes and breaking glass. When it finally grew quiet, I figured Mama had gone to her most reliable source of solace – the liquor cabinet. I imagined that she had opened the bourbon and was slowly drowning any annoying residual feelings of guilt or shame with each burning swallow.

Turned out, I was not wrong.

We were quiet during dinner, and the kids went to bed without a fuss. Mama was passed out in her bedroom and, with luck, would be until morning. By ten o'clock, Daddy still wasn't home, and Lorelei and I kept exchanging looks of concern. With an unspoken agreement, we took up positions in the living room, she watching the *Tonight Show* while I attempted to read, and we both waited for the sound of our father's station wagon in the drive.

Without realizing it, I fell asleep, and awoke to the soft sound of a car door closing. I looked around a little disoriented and saw Lorelei asleep on the wingback chair and the television showing static where the station had gone off air for the night.

"Lorelei," I whispered, and Lorelei jumped.

"What?" she growled.

"I think he's home," I replied in a quiet voice. Lorelei came fully awake then, and both of us listened intently. We heard the sound of uneven footsteps, crunching up the gravel path.

"You sure that's Dad" Lorelei asked, at which point we heard a loud thump and the unmistakable voice of our father voicing an expletive.

"Yep, that's him," I said with a grim smile.

We heard the key fumble in the lock and we looked at each other. Suddenly, I was filled with anxiety and craved the ignorance that was the *before* to this unfortunate *after*. The keys dropped on the concrete, and Daddy cursed. Lorelei and I seemed to transmit the plan for retreat through telepathy because, all at once, we bolted on feather-light feet to the stairs. We were both tucked safely in our beds by the time Dad finally connected his motor skills with his brain's instructions and came into the house.

Anxious for oblivion, I dove into sleep with panicked strokes and finally sank down, leaving the residual flotsam of this horrid day floating just below the surface.

Chapter 9: Invitations

Lorelei moved away and started her new life, leaving me behind. In mid-August, Mama drove her to northern Kentucky and helped her get settled into the dorm. When she returned home, she reported that Lorelei's roommate was a skinny little girl named Wanda with stringy hair and enormous eyes. She was an art major and her clothes were black fabric and paint-spattered. Mama chuckled at the thought of the pair, and I wondered what she found so amusing about it. Maybe she thought Wanda was the type of girl that would appreciate the genius of teaching someone lessons in caretaking by pretending to be an escaped mental patient, like Mama had done for Lorelei not long before she graduated.

Lorelei got a job right away waiting tables at a college hangout called Hannigan's to help pay her tuition, since her secret supplemental tuition source had mysteriously disappeared. She used a fake ID to get the job, so everybody there thought she was twenty-one. She had always looked older than her real age.

At first Lorelei was resentful about having to work, venting to me and taking every opportunity to lament about her hardships. After all, she had not been expecting to have to work her freshman year other than her student worker job in the library. She thought that Mom and Dad had it covered, and was oblivious to Uncle George's planned involvement. But now she acted as though it were her idea all along, and seemed to take on more and more hours at the pub in some kind of defiance.

She called once a week and usually talked to me for ten minutes or so – long enough to say that she was making good money in tips and that the college guys were cute. Her descriptions of the pub were charming and evoked a vivid (though unlikely) image – red-faced smiling bartenders with chipper Irish brogues and a décor of giant shamrocks in Kelly green, rows of cracked bar stools and thick wooden tables and chairs solid enough to support the rambunctious antics of all the short-haired boys with giant chests and shoulders, and swaying friends locked arm in arm united by Greek letters emblazoned across their stylish sweaters. It sounded so free and bohemian, in a swash-buckling blue collar kind of way.

Lorelei rarely mentioned her classes, so I assumed they were going well.

"How are Mother and Dad?" Lorelei began asking, once she finally accepted the state of her financial condition and became resigned to her life as a waitress/college student, which really meant, "Are things back to normal?"

I always replied that things were fine, meaning that they were speaking to each other, but that the white elephant had taken up residence in our lives and was not going away any time soon. By December, Uncle George had been completely absent from our home since the party, which was over six months earlier. I missed his boisterousness and larger than life way, a fact that I was shamefully determined not to admit.

In any event, things might have been fine, but they weren't normal. Mother and Daddy were deliberately civil to each other, but with an aloof restraint that was completely unlike them, and it left the entire household feeling unnerved.

Thanksgiving had been strange – Lorelei had stayed conveniently away, claiming work and studies as her excuse. Mother flared up for a moment about that, and then seemed to lose her steam, so Lorelei got by with it. That left the rest of the family to make the annual lunchtime pilgrimage to Grandmother's and excluded Lorelei from the awkwardness of pretending to believe that Mother was feeling too ill that evening to go to Uncle George's and Cheryl's first Thanksgiving dinner.

An invitation had arrived in the mail two weeks before Thanksgiving inviting the Braden family to '*Please join George and Cheryl in giving thanks for another year of good health and prosperity.*' The invitation was embossed on thick card stock and had a colorful cornucopia at the top. The address was Uncle George's house, but the wording made it seem like it was *their* house. Mother's expression as she read it was a strange mixture of her characteristic snickering at the pretentiousness and intermittent, brief eruptions of naked longing.

Once it arrived, Mother was visibly anxious (which was unusual in and of itself), and I risked being sucked into the quicksand and hung around the periphery out of morbid curiosity, wondering just how she would ask Daddy about it. Mother's manipulations were masterful, and this one would have to be one of her very best efforts. But I never heard it spoken of. Mother's tactics were atypically subtle, as the invitation sat conspicuously by the coffee pot for a few days, a place where Daddy was sure to see it.

But then it was gone, and I didn't know whether it was because Mother had given up and stashed it away or whether Daddy had finally had enough and tossed it out.

So Mother self-medicated her mysterious ailment that Thanksgiving night with whiskey and Coke, and Daddy was Mr. Thanksgiving himself. When bedtime finally came, we scattered to the sanctuary of our bedrooms, anxious to leave the odd holiday behind.

When another invitation arrived in the mail just a week after Thanksgiving, familiar calligraphy transforming their ordinary address into an elegant destination, I slapped it on the credenza with the rest of the mail, assuming it was an invitation to *'Join George and Cheryl for a very merry and snooty Christmas celebration to sing carols in operatic voices and pat each other on the back in self-congratulations.'* But Mama's gasp as she read it indicated something altogether different.

"Holy hell," she said, destroying the illusion of elegance that the invitation implied. "They're getting married."

I stopped doing my homework at the kitchen table and stared at Mother. She was suspended in a posture of shocked paralysis, one hand gripping the invitation and the other gripping the credenza for support. Then, she seemed to recover herself and she calmly laid the invitation back on the credenza, carefully smoothing out the wrinkled cardstock with her hands. She took a deep breath, and then went to the liquor cabinet and poured herself a glass of clear liquid, drinking it like it was the life-giving water whose appearance it mimicked.

Mother was obviously shaken and I wondered what was going through her complicated mind. Unbidden, I cruelly wondered if Mama was planning to call George and offer to let Annabelle be their flower girl. I shook my head to clear the disturbing thought.

Angela Hoke   *A Whisper of Smoke*

When Daddy got home from work, Mother was clearly nervous. She flitted around the kitchen and living room and dining room, attempting to serve dinner but somehow falling short of the mark. Daddy knew something was up, I could tell, but he had no desire to inquire about it. He was, after all, a smart man and pragmatic – he knew that the storm would find him and that he need not go looking for it.

All evening long, I was torn by the self-preservationist instincts that told me to hide, but an inconvenient fascination overrode my better judgment and, again, I found myself hovering – a pathetic and obvious voyeur.

Dinner, though, was inexplicably boring, and neither Hank nor Annabelle seemed to notice the haze of discomfiture that had settled over the table. At least not until Mother abruptly dismissed us all.

"Kids, go on up to bed now," Mama said, as she shuttled dirty dishes back and forth, nervously, between the dining room and the kitchen.

"Mom, it's not even 8:30," Hank replied, confused. He had been trying to help clear the table, only to be oddly relieved, repeatedly, of the dishes he was carrying before he could even make it to the threshold of the kitchen. The effect was a peculiar assembly line.

"Just do it!" she yelped. "Please," she added, and Hank looked at me with wide eyes, wondering at the use of the word.

I sensed that The Conversation was about to ensue, so I got up and ushered my bewildered brother and irritable sister towards the stairs.

"I'm supposed to get a story," Annabelle snapped. "You better not forget," she said as she languished on the stairs.

"Don't sass," I scolded, patting her bottom. "You'll get your story, just get on up there and brush your teeth."

A Whisper of Smoke   *Angela Hoke*

Once I finished reading to Annabelle and got her tucked in and settled down, I crept back out of the bedroom I now shared with her and into the hall. Finally, it seemed as though some discussion was occurring downstairs. I could hear voices – steady but not shouting, and seeming to come from the kitchen. I crept down the stairs, careful to place my feet on the spots that wouldn't squeak, and making agonizingly slow progress. Finally I was at the foot, and I sat down just in the shadows.

"Why should I have anything to do with him? Why should any of us?" I heard Dad say in whispered anger.

"Henry," Mother said with amazing calm, pleading. "Please."

"But tell me why? How can I ever trust him? How can I forgive him for what he did?"

"He has called me a hundred times, apologizing more times and more ways..."

Dad harrumphed with skepticism and derision.

"Henry, please," Mother said again, followed by a congested, wet sniffle. *Could Mother be crying?!*

I didn't think I had ever seen my mother cry.

"Elise," I heard Dad say, his voice like a tender sigh, almost a surrender. There was more movement, and I imagined him wrapping her up in a hug.

"Will you at least please talk to him?" Mother pleaded, and she hiccoughed and sniffled, seeming to cling to her composure. "You know what kind of home we lived in growing up..." she added in a thick, ashamed voice.

I held my breath, waiting.

Angela Hoke   *A Whisper of Smoke*

"I know it was awful," Daddy said after a long silence. "But, damn it..." It was the beginning to a thought, the prelude to a noble protestation.

"I'm not excusing anything," Mother hurriedly added. "But... he's still George. He is the only family, apart from you all, that I have left," she spilled out, and her voice caught in a sucking sob. Even that comment was a little confusing – apparently Gran and Pappy didn't count for much. I wondered what that meant.

There was no mistaking, I now clearly heard the sound of weeping, and it was unbelievably coming from Mother. I couldn't help but imagine how humiliated Mother must be feeling, showing weakness like this, and I marveled at it.

And then I got it.

Lord help her, she adores him, I thought. *Even after what he's done. But how can Dad possibly forgive him? How can Mother expect him, or us, to forgive him? We're her family too!*

I was sure Daddy would say no, preferably even "hell no." I still loved Uncle George too, but this was black and white. What he did was beyond wrong, and to forgive him would be sacrilege to the sanctity of our family. It would be appalling, a deliberate choice to choose someone else over their own child.

But then I heard him, astonishingly, say, "Alright." And Mother erupted in the first and only real sobs I ever heard her emit.

I expected to feel empathy, or something, for my mother. But I felt nothing but disgust for them both – that, and extreme disappointment that my father, my sweet daddy, would go along with it.

I thought I had been angry before, but it was nothing compared to the toxic outrage that swelled in me now, burning its way through me body, heaving through my stomach, scorching a path through the ventricles of my heart. It forced its way over my carefully constructed dam of self-containment in a river of caustic tears. With blurry eyes and roaring ears, I turned and somehow dragged myself up the stairs, opened the door, and entered the false sanctuary of my bedroom. There, I gazed on my sacrificial, angelic baby sister, asleep in her bed.

I swayed at the foot of Annabelle's bed for a few moments as the little girl swam in and out of focus. With movements that seemed to be guided from beyond, I found myself floating to the little shrine by the window box, the one where I used to kneel and say the Rosary when I was a little girl. I wrapped my warm hand (which was surprisingly steady and solid-looking) around the cool ceramic of the little Virgin Mary statuette. I gripped it firmly but carefully, carried it to the bed where Annabelle slept, then placed it on the shelf over her headboard as some kind of protectorate talisman. Would it matter at all? I wasn't sure anymore. After all, the Virgin had been watching over the girls in this room for as long as I could remember, and it had not kept the demons away.

How ironic, I thought bitterly, that the Virgin could not protect, in our family at least, the one virtue that most symbolized her divinity.

Part II

Chapter 10: In Search of Magic

Summer 1967

It was the worst possible convergence of unfortunate circumstance culminating in a Friday night with no plans. Chip was out of town for the weekend with his parents, visiting his grandparents in Cincinnati. Shelly was going to see *To Sir With Love* with her new boyfriend. Calvin was probably lining the bed of his rusty old truck with quilts so that Christine would be comfortable when they got down to necking. Even Mabel couldn't be relied upon to save me this time. She was on a camp-out with the Girl Scouts.

The result was that I was stranded at home, with my parents, whom I'd barely spoken to over the last six months, ever since they inexplicably forgave George and thereby thoroughly betrayed their own children. Even my daddy, who I had always trusted more than anyone, had permitted himself to be persuaded to participate in the unthinkable, all because he couldn't stand to disappoint Mama. That's what hurt the most, because Daddy had always been the one that stilled the earth when Mama got it to spinning.

What they did, forgiving George like that, was inexcusable, and in the months since, I had been constant in my resolve to castigate. Still, I wasn't blatant about it. I never had liked confrontation, but rather preferred protestation through silence, which I'd found could sometimes speak volumes louder than snide comments and insults. So I shouted at them with my withdrawal, screaming my frustration through my obvious absence, both physical and emotional, and I hoped they spent nights steeped in their feelings of guilt while I secretly ached at the betrayal. I wrapped myself up in my anger so I wouldn't feel the hurt.

I perfected my embargo through relentless occupation and, as a result, I'd never been so socially active. I obsessively dated Chip, to the point of excess. I did needle-point with Mabel and her sisters on their front porch until I'd rubbed calluses into my fingertips. I threw the baseball with Hank in the backyard, and turned into twilight zombie monster to make the kids scream. I walked in the woods, fished with a stick and some line in the creek on repeated occasions, though the most I ever caught was one tiny little bluegill, and I climbed trees so that I could feel closer to God. I even volunteered to babysit the Taylor twins on a cyclical basis, defined by the natural progression of my memory and just how long it took me to become convinced that they couldn't have been as terrible as I remembered. And when all else failed, I crawled into the hayloft next door with my box of poems and I wrote until my hand cramped up.

But not this time. The day was waning, guests would be arriving soon for Mother's party, and none of my stand-bys were panning out for me.

Mother had been spastically prepping for the last two hours and I had done my best to stay out of the way. To discourage her from talking to me, I decided to give my hair a mayonnaise treatment, and I wrapped my head so thoroughly in tinfoil I honestly nearly didn't hear her when she called to me from my bedroom doorway and told me to get my ass out of bed. But I had my back to her, and I buried my nose in *The*

Outsiders, until she eventually gave up, evidently deciding that eliciting my help wasn't worth the journey across my messy floor. I'd just rinsed my hair and finished brushing it out when I heard the first car pull up. Mother screamed at me to get downstairs to help, and I knew this time there was no escape. So I pulled my damp hair into a ponytail and exchanged my grungy shorts for some clean capris. I looked in the mirror, but I had no time for make-up so I just inspected my sunburned nose and cheeks to be sure there weren't any scaly pockets threatening to flake off. Stepping back, I looked at my wet hair and my scrubbed face and I realized I looked like a little girl. No one would guess that I was nearly sixteen, practically grown.

Downstairs, Mother put me to work painting pigs in a blanket with a spicy glaze. Hank was standing on tip-toes in front of the freezer chipping at ice with a pick. Annabelle was carefully stacking napkins in a criss-crossing pattern. Mother, meanwhile, rushed to the record player. She set the needle on the record with one hand while she used the other to blindly apply lipstick. When she'd finished, she smacked her lips and stuck the tube between her breasts. A scratchy hiss, then the music started – Dean Martin. Mother put both hands on the console, bent at the waist and legs straight, and swayed with the music. She did sexy like some moms did Donna Reed. Daddy came in then, his dark hair slicked back and his black suit starched to a sheen. He put his arms around Mother and his face in her neck, and I turned away. I could smell his cologne, a combination of English Leather and a musky scent he only got when he was close to her. I blushed at what it might imply and busied myself with the cheese tray.

A Whisper of Smoke   *Angela Hoke*

Within half an hour, there were thirty people or more in our house. Voices and laughter weaved through the music, carried on warm breezes from the open windows. These were mostly my Dad's folks, from GE, which I found amazing. I mean, you'd think they would have shied away from our house after some of the spectacles at previous parties. But perhaps that was part of the allure – at our house, you never knew what to expect.

The evening got off to an inauspicious start. There were a handful of tee-totalers in the group, and Mother thought of them as completely foreign and slightly deranged. She'd made it her personal mission to convert them, and she was constantly pouring liquor in their glasses of punch when they weren't looking. I had to trail after her like some sort of counter-intelligence unit, removing the glasses as soon as she'd moved on before she could cause some poor alcoholic to fall off the wagon or push an unsuspecting diabetic into a coma. It was tedious work that required a level of hyper-awareness that made my eyes hurt, but at least it kept me busy.

Once Mother believed her job was done, she moved on to other things. Relieved, I resumed my assigned duties. People had spilled out onto the back patio and were sitting on our lawn chairs and stone planters. I was in charge of refilling drinks, so I walked around with a bottle and a pitcher and topped off glasses and cups. The light was beginning to fade, trailing purple across the blue. The clouds in the distance would light up before long, and I kept an eye on them so I wouldn't miss it as I went back into the kitchen to uncork another bottle and refill my pitcher.

120

I almost didn't notice Hank and Annabelle sitting on the floor in the corner. They were playing Jacks, and I wondered how she'd convinced Hank to do that.

I squatted down beside them. "Whatcha doin'?"

Annabelle looked at me like I was dim. "Playing Jacks."

I pushed down my irritation. "I meant, why are you guys sitting in here in the corner?"

"Oh, we was gettin' underfoot," Hank said without looking at me. Those were Mama's words, I knew.

"Why don't you go upstairs and play, then?"

"It's hot up there," Annabelle complained.

"Plus, Mama said she could hear us pounding the floor from clear down here."

Well, hell, I thought. They were just kids. Was she going to make them stay in this little corner all night?

I straightened. "I'm going to talk to her."

Hank looked up in alarm. "No, Sus. Please don't. It's okay. I mean, we can't really play this game on the carpet anyway."

I looked at him hard, but he cast his eyes down.

"I got fours!" Annabelle cried.

"Good job, Belle," he said kindly.

I watched them for a few more minutes, warring within myself. *Dang Mama!* She was so thoughtless sometimes.

"You lost!" Belle said gleefully. Hank glanced at me and shrugged his shoulders.

"You're just too good," he said.

"Let's go again!"

"I don't mind playing it, Belle. But you did promise we could play something I wanted to play."

"Just one more game," she pleaded.

Don't you give in, I thought.

But he sighed. "Alright."

"Hank…"

He looked up at me and smiled. "It's okay." And then they were doing onesies, Annabelle shrieking when, strangely, Hank wasn't coordinated enough to hang on to one measly jack. After another minute of watching Annabelle squeal with delight and Hank smile at her pleasure, I sighed and drifted away, wondering if he'd ever get her to play the game he wanted.

In the living room, I checked on the cheese tray and rearranged the crackers into a smaller ellipse. Scanning the room, I took in the clusters of people chatting and laughing. Everyone seemed to be having a good time. Andy Williams was on now, and I'd always liked him even if he wasn't considered cool by most kids my age. I hummed to myself and, using a napkin, rubbed the side table to remove a water ring before it became permanent. Behind me, I heard Mother complaining.

"No one is dancing, Henry. This is not exactly what I had in mind." I could just imagine the pout that was probably on her face.

"But everyone seems to be having a good time, Elise," Daddy said, mirroring my own observation.

Mother harrumphed. "They don't know what a good time is," she muttered. I pocketed the damp napkin and listened to hear whether Mother would launch into a tantrum.

When she spoke, I realized it was going to be worse than a tantrum. "I think we need to shake things up," she said.

Angela Hoke   *A Whisper of Smoke*

Uh oh, I thought. But Daddy just said, "Whatever you want, dear. Just tell me what to do." Geesh, had he always been so nauseatingly accommodating of her?

"I'll be back," said Mother, and there was something in her voice that made me look back at her. Her eyes were gleaming from alcohol and mischief as she disappeared upstairs, and I thought to myself that these poor party-goers were in for it. I didn't know exactly what was coming, but I knew Mother well enough to know that it would very likely be something shocking. That could mean anything from a conga line to a drinking game to some kind of dramatic performance. I was annoyed that Mother couldn't just be normal, but I was curious too. So I found myself an empty seat in the corner and I waited.

After five or ten minutes, Mother sauntered down the steps wearing her fur trimmed coat and carrying a record. A few guests noticed her and openly gawked – it was eighty-five degrees and she was dressed for a stroll in the snow. But she just flashed them all a bright smile and made her way over to the console stereo. Unceremoniously, she interrupted Andy crooning *Moon River,* and replaced it with the record she carried. With her back to us, she carefully set the needle down. The music started – it was Vaudevillian, or Burlesque, and it reminded me of… of a strip-tease.

With her back to us, she began to shift her hips from side to side. When the first big chord boomed from the speakers, she turned her head over her shoulder to look at us and dropped her coat to the floor. Underneath, she wore one of her many red dresses with black satin gloves then extended past her elbows. She whipped around, and the skirt flared. Facing us now, she began pulling her gloves off, one tug with each beat of the music.

A Whisper of Smoke   *Angela Hoke*

Oh… my… God. By this time, I realized that she fully intended to strip her clothes off. I glanced around – all the guests stared at her in astonishment. I looked for Daddy and even he was speechless, his glass of brown liquor suspended just below his chin. I told myself I should do something, but I couldn't move. Like everyone else, I was paralyzed with shock.

Her gloves removed, Mother reached under her skirt and worked off her stockings, one at a time. She mostly pulled them off under her skirt, but she did give one little Betty Boopish reveal, then coquettishly covered her mouth with her hand as though it had been an accident. Next she moved to her dress. The dress she wore had buttons all down the front, but she was efficient, flicking them open one at a time with the beat of the music. When she finished with the buttons, she used one hand to keep her dress closed until just the right moment. We could sense the coming climax in the song, and we all held our breath. No one said a word. There was not a catcall or whistle, which I'm sure Mother had been expecting. We were all waiting to see where this was going, unable to turn away.

And then it came – the big moment. With a dramatic flourish, she threw open her dress and I instinctively shut my eyes. I couldn't bear to see Mother standing their naked like a fool. I waited for the gasps, or the prayers for her soul. But instead, I heard someone laugh. Then someone else joined in. Before long, several people were laughing and even starting to clap.

What in the world?? With a deep breath, I opened my eyes. Mother was standing there wearing a red bathing suit and a sash across her torso that said *Give Me Liberty, Or Get Out.* From somewhere she'd

Angela Hoke   *A Whisper of Smoke*

produced a tiara which she'd perched on her head, and she posed blowing kisses like the beauty queen she believed herself to be.

Daddy set his drink down and staggered over to her. I hadn't realized how much he'd had to drink until that moment. When he reached her, she gave him a huge smile. He grabbed her and dipped her, kissing her deeply while the drunker guests began to cheer. Only the tee-totalers inched their way towards the front door.

I had to get out. The whole display sickened me, especially when I thought how Hank and Annabelle had been banished to a corner while Mother held court. As the crowd moved toward Mother, I squeezed through and darted to the kitchen.

At the back door, I paused and looked at the kids.

"Everything okay?" asked Hank. "What's going on in there?"

"Nothing," I lied. "It's fine. I'm going out for a while."

He looked at me like he wanted to say something. Maybe it was *"stay,"* or maybe it was *"let me come too,"* but whatever it was, he kept it to himself. He nodded at me once and went back to playing with Annabelle – Old Maid, by the look of it. Then I was outside.

The sun had just set, and the sky was lit up with God's colors. It looked like He'd painted the sky with cotton candy – pink, orange, blue, like they had at the State Fair. I darted past the few guests that lingered on the patio and by the time I got halfway across the yard I was running. I didn't stop until I got to Merlin, where I collapsed against his enormous trunk. Taking deep breaths, I tried to reason out why I was so upset. And I tried to remember back to when I'd loved Mama's unpredictability, when I thought it was part of her magic.

From the time I was a little girl, I understood that Mama wasn't like other mothers. It wasn't just that she knew how to get her way, which she did, it was how she saw opportunities that other mothers didn't. She saw magic in shiny surfaces and wizened oaks, heard songs in rushing waters and television static. She chased wishes around like floating dandelion seeds even though it left her exhausted, with no time for sewing and fancy cooking, or being Troop Leader for the Girl Scouts. She was a surprise every day, and not always a good one. But she birthed adventures like golden eggs, and that was the secret treasure of my childhood.

So on the night that Mama called the angels, back before Hank was born, I knew they would come. She knew when angels were around, and how you could tell them apart from ghosts or just plain noisy wind. She knew things like that, though she never explained how. Maybe Mama had noticed that it was too hot for crunchy brown leaves, or how the bony trees were bent over like Satan's claws, great big angel traps waiting to spring. Maybe she recognized the too-warm winds as his angry snorts of frustration. But the point is, I believed her in these matters, so when Mama came flying through the house, trailing sheets and shouting instructions, I abandoned my dolls to their tea party and took up my sheets, without hesitation.

By the time I got to the back door, Mama was in a tizzy and Lorelei was waiting for us, looking superior with her feet planted wide and fists punched into her hips, her frizzy hair wiry as Mama's old brillo pads. We'd already fought that day, about rights to Corrina, the doll that cried until you picked her up – a doll she had given to me as soon as she graduated to Barbies. Lorelei had taken her back, like the bullying Indian Giver she was, on account of Corrina was now supposedly a "collector's

Angela Hoke   *A Whisper of Smoke*

item." And nothing Lorelei said made me feel one ounce better – especially not her empty promises that she'd let me borrow it once I was old enough to "handle the responsibility."

Hmmph.

Now, looking at her, I felt mad all over again, and I gave her a little kick before I could talk myself out of it. Right away I knew I shouldn't have done it, and I winced, waiting for the smack. But Mama distracted us, swooshing us through the backdoor in a cloud of cotton, and then we were outside linking hands. I forgot all about Lorelei and Corrina as we snaked through the backyard. Instead, I focused on trying not to stumble in the matted grass or from the way the sheet wrapped my ankles in loose bandages, snagging on the buckles of my Buster Browns.

When we'd gotten about halfway across the yard, Mama paused. "It's perfect," she said, and glanced back with a secret smile.

Lorelei acted bored, but she asked, "For what?"

"For the Ceremony, Lei-Lei."

I frowned, remembering that Daddy was working the Double Shift at GE, and I thought maybe we should wait for him. But when I suggested it, Lorelei looked at me like I was dumber than a box of rocks.

"It's only for girls," she said, like she knew everything.

Mama stopped and turned, raising one hand to the side of her mouth.

"It's just for special girls with the Magic Gift," she corrected, and her breath puffed the secret, mixing with the itchy smell of dry grass. It was nice how Mama made you believe it could be true.

I didn't know much about Ceremonies except First Communion, which was when you got to wear that beautiful dress and pretend to marry Jesus. Lorelei had already married him, which made me wonder what made her think she could possibly marry Elvis too. This may not have been First Communion, but Mama's tip-toes through the grass and tinkly laugh promised something special. So I mustered my courage and scooted past Satan's demon trees, and before I knew it, we'd reached Merlin, the grizzled old oak at the edge of the yard. Merlin's knobby black branches felt protective, not dangerous. He was a loyal tree – he changed his clothes of leaves but not who he was.

Once I saw this was our final destination, I tried to let go of Lorelei's hand but her face flashed, as though someone pulled a shade of mad down over it. Her mouth turned up at the corner and she squeezed. "Oww," I groaned, but not loud enough to interrupt Mama's concentration. Instead, I worked at prying Lorelei's hooked fingers off in stubborn segments like the shell of a hickory nut.

Finally I got free, my fingers tingling as I shook out the cramps. But I quickly forgot about them. With a giant gasp that lifted my hair, Merlin gestured grandly towards the sunset, and I could see why – it was rich as sherbet and there were clouds skipping across in the bubbly ripples of geese landing on a pond.

"It is gorgeous," said Mama, and I jumped at her sudden closeness.

"We don't have much time," Mama said then, her voice suddenly urgent. I felt the urgency twist in my stomach as she wrapped me in my sheet, tying the ends in a knot. She did the same for Lorelei and herself, and suddenly we were all ancient princesses, our sheets glowing ghost blue in the twinkle-light.

Around us, the moon bled black, a giant bullet hole in space but in reverse, like negatives from the Instamatic. Before it could soak the edges of far off hills, Mama formed us in a wide ring and started to walk

Angela Hoke   *A Whisper of Smoke*

in a circle, swishing and curving. We copied it, creating a swirl in the grass – a Christmas wreath of matted blades. Round and round we went, our arms floating away from our bodies in arcs and waves. After a moment, Mama began to sing. The words fell fat as raindrops, bursting on sharp brown grass into grown-up pleas, meant for God. The meaning floated away from me, leaving behind the notes, eerie how they changed directions unexpectedly, but convincing somehow – like how chants at Mass led you towards heaven without telling the directions.

By the time Mama had finished, the bright colors were gone, and the sky was dark blue and black as new bruises. Warm night air lifted the edges of our sheet gowns with the whoosh of a furnace grate. When a cool wind snuck in, it was a cold finger poking, and it raised the hairs on my neck and arms.

"The angels are here," Mama whispered, and I didn't doubt her for an instant. The trees cheered for the arriving angels, rustling their black leaves against the navy sky. Stars blinked on, counting off the spirits as they joined us in the mysterious place that used to be the backyard.

"Close your eyes, girls," Mama ordered, pulling us into a tight circle. "Close them and say your prayers, quick, before they fly away."

I didn't have to be told twice. I shut my eyes tight as I could, and gripped fingers so the angels couldn't take me away to heaven, like that creepy bed-time prayer Gran always made us say. The wind whipped up, blowing my hair into my mouth and tugging at my sheets.

"That's right, bless my baby," Mama said, and I opened one eye. Mama had let go of one of Lorelei's hands and was holding her stomach where the baby was growing.

A Whisper of Smoke   *Angela Hoke*

I hadn't realized the ceremony was for the baby, but it made perfect sense to me. I warmed, thinking of this baby who would be specially blessed, and I loved it already. I'd been practicing for ages with the babies at Mabel and Calvin's house, just waiting for my chance to be a big sister. They were loads better than some silly old doll.

Just then a whisper sounded next to my ear, and it told me a secret – one I wouldn't share, not even with Calvin and Mabel. That baby was a boy, and he was going to be mine. I smiled, imagining him already – how he would sit on the crook of my arm, like a sack of sugar, and settle into the nook at my neck; or how when he was all clean and fresh from the bath, he would smell better than warm bread straight from the oven. I would carry him around on my hip, and clean his spit-up with a cloth diaper, and I would even smear sticky Desitin on his butt if he got a rash. I would play pea-pie to make him laugh and watch him blow spit bubbles till they popped, dripping slobber down his chin.

But even as I imagined all the good things, a sliver of insecurity wormed its way in. Of course I was glad God would pay special attention to this new baby boy, when he came. But, seeing how Mama was going to so much trouble, I couldn't help wondering – had Mama ever had a ceremony for me? If she did, I was pretty sure it hadn't worked. Maybe Satan had captured my guardian angels with those claws of his, and that's why I hadn't turned out at all the way Mama'd intended.

"Maybe the third time's a charm," I muttered, remembering a phrase Gran sometimes said, and thinking how Lorelei wasn't all that spectacular either.

A cluster of leaves rose from the ground nearby and swirled like a devil. It frightened me, and I clamped my eyes shut. I began whispering words that probably weren't too fitting since they weren't from the Rosary

Angela Hoke   A Whisper of Smoke

or the Lord's Prayer. "Please God, keep us safe," is what I said, over and over.

I knew God could be kind of particular about those things, but it seemed to have worked because the winds calmed and the rustling quieted. The angels were leaving, I could feel it, and with them, and whatever chased them, most of my fear drained away.

Mama squeezed my fingers and tried to let go. "Susanna," she said, and there was no magic in it.

I peeked, and gripped her hand to steady myself – looking up at Mama was disorienting, like bending over to see into the Conners' old well. And the way our sheet gowns hovered, glowing and ghostly, chased a chill into my hair. Only the lightning bugs – winking, secret pals – seemed familiar.

"Are you hungry?" Mama asked, but I didn't answer. I felt like my voice wanted to escape on the winds, maybe chasing after those angels. I worried it would drag my soul right along with it.

"I'm starving," Lorelei said, because apparently her voice didn't enjoy travel. And despite my uneasiness, just hearing her say it made my stomach growl.

Mama started to pull off her sheet gown. "Let's go inside then," she said.

My sheet pooled around my feet. I picked it up and shook it out as best I could to get rid of the grass clippings and any lazy grasshoppers that may have been looking to hitch a ride. But by then, Mama and Lorelei were already walking toward the house. Daddy swore monsters weren't real, but I wasn't convinced and I definitely didn't want to be caught outside alone in the dark with lurking bogeymen or Satan's *claws. So before I was left to fend for myself, I ran to catch up, my sheets trailing behind like angel's wings.*

A loud crash from inside the house brought me back to the present, and I was surprised to see that night had fallen. Lightning bugs hovered nearby, as if to check that I was okay. A tree frog croaked from somewhere above me. More sounds from the house drifted over, and I winced. Remembering the way Mama used to be, and the way I used to feel about her, only drew tonight's events into sharper contrast. Suddenly, Merlin's boughs were not far enough away. I jumped up and ran towards one of my few sources of refuge – the woods on Calvin's farm.

I broke into the trees, but I didn't slow. I liked listening to my breath and the blood pounding in my ears as I ran. It helped to distill everything else. Before long, I was deep into the woods, and nearing the creek bed. We'd seen a fair amount of rain that summer, and there was a trickle of water running through it. I paused beside it and bent to dip my hand into the current. The cold sent a shock up my arm, and I hastily withdrew. I stood, wiping my hand on my pants, and took in my surroundings.

The woods were quiet except for the wind rustling through the high branches. I didn't hear the party at all anymore, and I was glad of that. The path continued on the other side of the creek, and I looked down it, but I couldn't see far. Just ten yards or so from the creek was the dense section that always elicited both fear and a thrill in me. It was the part where I'd thought I'd spied Jezzie, and where Calvin had touched my face. It was a place that still held magic, and suddenly I was moving towards it. I needed magic tonight, needed to know that I could still believe.

I hadn't ventured through this part of the woods at night in some time, but this section of the woods was just as dark as I'd remembered. Like before, I hesitated before stepping across its threshold, because it really did feel like crossing into another world. But I was determined, so I took one step, then another, and then I was making my way down the path. I walked more carefully here because I could barely see. I tripped a few times on tree roots and rocks, but otherwise my progress was unimpeded. I rounded a bend, deep into the thicket, and darkness closed in around me. Fear crept across my scalp and I paused. My heart was beating a track up my chest and I concentrated on slowing it as I also focused my other senses. I'd been here before, many times during the day, and there was nothing to fear.

It worked. My fear drained away, and I was left feeling disappointed. It was the sense of the unknown, of this place's magic, that had originally frightened me, two years before. That was what I had come here in search of, and I was rationalizing it away. All at once, I was profoundly disappointed that it could in fact *be* rationalized away.

I had nearly convinced myself this was a fool's errand and was about to turn back when I saw it – the white flashing through the trees, off in the distance, elusive as smoke. Adrenaline gushed inside me and my nerve endings came alive. *This* was why I was here – this was exactly what I needed in order to remember the magic that surrounded us.

Without hesitation, I took off after it. Immediately, I was off the trail and into brambles and ivy that snagged at my feet and legs. I felt them clawing at me, and I knew I'd leave this little adventure covered in scratches. But I didn't mind. I felt alive, chasing this phantom, and when I glimpsed it again, I took off faster. I pursued it with purpose for some time when I came to a small clearing. The moonlight poured into it and pooled to its edges. I bathed in it for a moment as I gathered my bearings. It was impossible to see the flash of white with all this moonlight, so after a minute or two of appreciating the beauty of this little spot, I headed back into the trees. I could only hope I was moving in the right direction. I didn't even think about how I would find my way out.

I'd barely crossed back into the dense trees when I saw the flash of white again, and I was thrilled, and frightened, to see that it was closer. Determined to reach it before it could disappear, I moved as quickly as I could towards it. As I moved, it flashed in and out of view as my excitement grew. I found myself whispering, "Come on Jezzie, stay with me. I'm coming."

When I found the phantom, I didn't at first realize it. It was not immediately visible, though I'd just glimpsed it a few seconds before. So I stood still and waited for it. From some distance away, the wind gathered in the treetops and pushed its way through. They bent and swayed, whether in protest or submission, I wasn't sure. But it built in energy until I could feel its approach. When it arrived, it blew through me and I stepped back. And there it was. The white, that I'd chased all night, and for many nights in my dreams, was right in front of me, revealed as the wind caught the leaves of a silver poplar just right, so that it flashed the white underbellies of its leaves in a rippling illusion.

I was crushed. My phantom, my personal ghost, my magic was nothing but a trick of the wind in the trees. And as the wind blew past me and rippled through the white-backed leaves again, mocking me, I felt all the wind leave my spirit. I collapsed on the ground and put my head in

Angela Hoke   *A Whisper of Smoke*

my hands. Before I knew it, I was crying. And though I wasn't sure exactly why, I knew it wasn't just because Jezzie turned out to be a tree.

I don't know how long I sat there, sobbing into the night, wailing my part in a symphony of crickets and frogs. But at some point I realized I wasn't alone. The hair stood up on the back of my neck and arms, and I wiped the tears from my eyes so I could see. A deer stood in the grass just a few feet from me. A doe, with big glassy eyes that reflected the moon. It watched me and I watched it, and neither of us moved. She was beautiful, strong and delicate at the same time, and she had wisdom in her eyes. Sensing I was no threat, she bent to eat from the grass. My nose was running and I itched to wipe it, but I was afraid I'd startle her. Finally I sniffed, just barely, but she raised her head sharply. She looked at me again, but she didn't dart away. She snorted, as though in sympathy, and walked slowly towards the trees. She stopped by the silver poplar and looked at it, then back at me. And in a flash, she took off, her white tail disappearing into the foliage before I could register that she'd gone.

After a bit, when she did not return, I got up to go. It took me a few minutes to get my bearings, to work out which way was east and therefore must be the way home. Reluctantly, I began walking that direction.

I'd not found my magic in the woods, at least not the magic I had expected. But I had found something a bit magical, and maybe a little more real. Still, as I made my way back to the trail and then along its bumpy path towards the farm and my home beyond, I couldn't help feeling that I'd left my childhood behind.

Chapter 11: Shades of Red

I was supposed to be out on a date with Chip. And why wasn't I? I was not entirely sure. He had called just thirty minutes before he was supposed to pick me up and said that a family emergency had come up, and that he'd tell me more about it later.

Later. When exactly was 'later?' Later tonight? Later this week? I knew I shouldn't feel uneasy. After all, I had no reason not to trust Chip. But him having a family emergency, and not including me, felt like some kind of rejection – maybe because I had been trying to dial back the fooling around, despite Chip's repeated non-verbal attempts at persuasion.

Anyway, because my plans changed so late, it was too late to make alternate arrangements. But thankfully, this time, no one else was home. Mother and Daddy had gone to some friend's home for dinner and drinking and had dragged Annabelle along with them to play with the other couple's children. And Hank was spending the night with his new buddy Roger, which I thought was great.

It had been a long time since I'd been in the house alone on a Saturday night. Days and weeks and months had ticked by, and I'd continued to avoid my parents as much as possible. Nothing had changed, as far as I was concerned. They were seeing Uncle George like things were the way they'd always been, when in actuality our family would never be the same again. And Mother would never apologize.

Even if she believed she was wrong, which I was sure she did not. Instead, Mother's way of talking things through was trying to force a confrontation. She pushed my buttons, gave me a hard time about stupid stuff, but I didn't engage. Unlike Lorelei, I did not enjoy warring with Mother. It never did any good anyway – Mama always won. But I couldn't act like everything was okay, either. So our estrangement persisted, and I wasn't sure anyone besides me even noticed. Or cared.

But I didn't have to think about any of that tonight. And I didn't have to spend half the night anticipating the moment when I would have to refuse Chip intimacies that I considered to be sacred but that he thought he was entitled to.

As I focused on these positive points, I began to relax. And I decided that this was an opportunity. I tapped my chin. What should I do? I needed to take advantage of this rare respite.

Yes. I knew just the thing.

With purpose, I hurried to Mother's room and took a seat at her vanity. It felt deliciously wrong to be sitting there, and even more illicit when I took Mother's favorite red lipstick and applied it to my lips. I smacked them together and used my finger to clear the smudges away at the corners. Then I got a flash of inspiration, and I went to the closet and retrieved Mother's most luxurious red negligee, complete with feathered fringe at the collar and hem, and slipped it over my head. I fished out Mother's highest heeled pumps and put them on, practicing my walk in front of the full-length mirror.

I admired the transparency of the gown's material and thought how my jeans and top looked a bit ridiculous underneath. So, feeling especially wicked, I reached underneath the gown and removed first my pants, then my top. Then I thought, what the heck, and took off my bra and panties.

Naked under the caressing fabric, I stood in front of the mirror and looked at myself with fresh eyes. I looked like a young woman, standing there – a little sexy, even.

Feeling very grown up, I made my way on wobbly feet down the stairs and into the dining room. I pulled out a bottle of red wine and looked at it for a moment, considering. I didn't drink very often, but I felt so cosmopolitan and adult in my attire, that a glass of wine seemed appropriate. Decided, I found a dusty bottle in the back of the cabinet which I hoped would not be missed. I took the cork screw and opened the bottle, pouring myself three fingers in a crystal glass.

Tasting it with a careful dip of my tongue, I winced at the bitter taste, then tentatively took another sip. I felt the red liquid warm its way down my esophagus and settle in the bottom of my stomach. Glass in hand, I swished my way to the console turntable and put on a Sinatra record. Then I twirled around the living room like a spinning diva, quickly setting my glass down and abandoning the shoes so I could maintain my balance. I grew dizzy with spins and wine, and laughed with the simple joy of it.

It was several minutes before I collapsed on the couch, head spinning and exhausted. With a flash of inspiration, I jumped up and hurried to the stairs where I started to climb them at the same hurried pace. Unfortunately, my feet caught the hem of the negligee and I plowed face first into the shag carpeted step. Even that was hilarious, and I lay there for a few moments with tears streaming from pain and laughter.

Angela Hoke   *A Whisper of Smoke*

If Chip saw me now, he would think I was completely nuts, I thought. And then, as I caught my breath, I realized that was the first time I'd thought of Chip since I first came downstairs over an hour before. I felt a little liberated by that realization, and my sense of empowerment buoyed my collapsed form up off the floor.

At the top of the stairs, I hurried to the bathroom and looked in the mirror. My face was flushed and my hair was all mussed. But my eyes were bright and glassy with mysterious depths. I rooted through the drawers for some bobby pins and, finding them, I went to work pinning my hair into a messy up-do. I wished I had a fall to attach – something along the lines of Barbara Eden. Even without synthetic help, sections hung down around my face and over my eye in movie star fashion and I felt a thrill at my sudden sex appeal.

Back downstairs, I got out another record and put it on, then realized I was hungry. Retrieving my wine, I sashayed to the kitchen and started making sauce for spaghetti. As I cooked, I danced around sipping on my wine. It felt really good to have this time alone – no shrieking Annabelle, no arguments between Mother and Dad, no one to tell me what to do or to invade my privacy. *This is what's it like to be grown up,* I thought.

When the food was done, I lit candles on the dining room table and set myself a place. I sat down to eat and exhaled a long breath, relaxing my shoulders. I watched the candlelight skate across the surface of my wine, and I started thinking about Chip. What was going on with his family, I wondered? Had there been an accident? Was someone sick? Had, God forbid, someone died? I certainly hoped it was nothing too serious. Though, if it were serious, that would excuse the way he disappeared. But if it weren't life and death, why had he rushed off without even explaining?

I thought about him and how we had been arguing about stupid things over the past several weeks. Lately, he'd starting getting really defensive whenever I asked, innocently, what he had been doing – after school, after practice, it didn't matter. I knew he had a lot more freedom now that he had his own car. I also knew that he was very cute, and that he was a big flirt. But that didn't mean I distrusted him.

Chip had always had a healthy ego, but it had reached huge proportions now that he had his 'Righteous Ride' (Kenny, the idiot, came up with that one). His dad had bought him a new Mustang for his sixteenth birthday, and he was in love with that thing. It was black with chrome bumpers and shiny black vinyl seats that froze in the winter and would probably be hot as the dickens in the summer. He washed and waxed it every Saturday morning religiously, and he wouldn't let anyone eat or drink in it. It made it a little awkward for carhops, because, just as they were bringing the food out to the car, Chip would make everyone get out and eat at one of the lonely picnic tables.

And it had been a new experience going out on car dates – it was fun and a little scary at the same time. Now we could go parking with no risk of parents interrupting, like we needed even more opportunity than we already had. Some girls might see it as a positive, but for me it just made it harder and harder to come up with excuses for why we shouldn't take things further.

Maybe it was all that unfettered access and its implications that were contributing to my feeling of relief that he'd canceled our date for tonight. Because I really wasn't all that upset – in a way, I felt like I was getting a little break. We had been going out for two years, and I loved him. Of course I did. But besides the constant pressure to take our fooling around to the next level, he could be moody and distant. And lately our conversations had been rather empty and hence shortened. I already knew so much about him. I knew that he had played baseball from the time he was five and that he still hated being picked on by his sisters. His favorite foods were roast and potatoes and cherry pie and he hated Brussels sprouts and yellow squash. He loved basketball but had a deep aversion to running track because his coaches had always made his teammates run laps as punishment. He had never had to wear hand-me-downs and every year his Christmas got bigger and bigger. And his family took vacations every summer, without fail, but his dad worked all the time and was often away on business trips.

Chip believed in lower taxes and less government and hated the Vietnam War because his friends did. His secret ambition was to be a senator or even the president, but believed that he probably wasn't smart enough to get into an Ivy League school, which he believed was a pre-requisite. He figured he would have to settle for being a doctor or lawyer instead. He was aware of the civil rights movement but had no real opinion of it since it didn't really impact him. He was a Catholic and a former altar boy, but he sometimes secretly wondered if God was real.

And, of course, he was very cute, though increasingly roguish. And he was a great kisser with an arsenal of ways to push me to the edge of abandon, and almost beyond.

He knew all about me too. He knew that I loved my younger siblings, but particularly adored Hank, and he always paid Hank special attention as homage to my feelings. He knew that I rode horses with the farm kids next door but never thought to ask whether Calvin was one of my riding companions. He knew that I wrote poetry, though he had never asked to read any. He knew that my mother was free-spirited and sharp-tongued and that she could be played with flattery and flirtation, but that my father could see through sycophancy. He knew that my family didn't have much and though I sometimes worried that he thought I was second class, he never acted like he did. He knew that I was tough and not girly about stuff like getting dirty or bugs, and that I fought mean when I had to.

So what else was there to learn about each other? I hadn't experienced much of life outside of school and family, and he was experiencing similar things – he too was a high school sophomore with a big Catholic family. Truth be told, we spent most of our time together making out or trying to find a place to make out, or reminiscing about when we made out last (Chip could make some dirty talk).

I sighed, and carried the dishes to the kitchen. I was a little melancholy, and wasn't sure if it was because I was feeling some dissatisfaction with my relationship with Chip or if it was just the wine. I knew I was very lucky. Most girls my age would kill for a good-looking, rich, jock boyfriend like mine.

And I wasn't really interested in any other guys, though that could be because there *were* no guys at St. Catherine's (though that technicality would be rectified if I could just convince my parents to let me go to John Adams High next year, which was the public school that Shelly had started attending at the beginning of this school year because her parents couldn't afford parochial school tuition after the divorce). So I struggled to understand why I was suddenly feeling unsure about things. For a brief second, Calvin flashed across my mind. The way he had of looking over his shoulder and giving me that half-grin. My stomach flipped, and I admonished myself verbally.

Angela Hoke   *A Whisper of Smoke*

"Stop it, Susanna."

It didn't work. Calvin was taking off his shirt in the hot sun, wiping his arm across his sweaty brow and then resuming pitching hay. Calvin was riding Sampson ahead of me, his cute little butt firmly nestled in the saddle. Calvin was giving me that look with his big brown eyes, a cross between annoyance and affection, or at least amusement. I flopped on the couch and closed my eyes, wanting to let go of the fantasy that was desperate to play out in my mind.

No, stop it, I told myself again, this time silently, squeezing my eyes tight and trying to force out this disloyal train of thought. "I love Chip," I said aloud. "I love Chip, I love Chip, I love Chip," I repeated like a mantra.

I forced myself to picture Chip, and the first thing to come to mind was the image that seemed to define us -- him kissing me and touching me, and my body gushed with instantaneous desire. *See?* I said to myself, as if that proved it.

Suddenly I felt silly lying there on the couch looking like some cartoonish version of a sex kitten. My eyes were feeling heavy, and I became concerned that I might fall asleep on the couch. The last thing I needed was for Mother to come home and find me drooling on her best chiffon.

I hauled myself up, blew out the candles and stowed the wine and other evidence of my evening, then took off the shoes and carried them up the stairs in my hand, the other hand firmly on the banister. My head was swimming just a bit as I went to my room to change into some pajamas.

Through the window, the eerie glow of the full moon caught my attention. I went over to the window and stood at it, looking out at the shadows that I knew were trees and bushes, despite their ethereal appearance. I suddenly flashed back to the slumber party night, when we'd all sat around the campfire and ... *Calvin and I kissed!* my mind shouted, disobediently. *No! Don't even think about it,* I scolded my subconscious. *Anyway,* I continued silently, as my thoughts settled back into line – it was at the campfire when Calvin mentioned how clearly he could see into our bedroom window at night. I wondered if anyone was out there right now, looking at my ghostly silhouette and thinking that I was a beautiful apparition.

I sat down in the window seat and gazed out, and then opened the window so the cool, early autumn breeze could sweep across me. It brought with it the sounds of the night, the rustling of the trees, the bullfrogs croaking from the catfish pond, the crickets chirping their constant rhythm. The wind blew in through the window and went through my gown as if it weren't there. My nipples stiffened in the cool air, and shivers traveled my body. *Too bad Chip isn't here,* I thought naughtily.

Good thing Chip isn't here, I amended in my mind, trying to squash the instantaneous guilt that seized my conscience.

In the cool night breeze, I felt awake again, so I thought I'd write a little poetry. The lonesome moonscape was a good inspiration. So I turned on my lamp and got out my poetry journal from my new secret hiding place (one had to keep changing it up to avoid security breaches – Mother was clever). To get the right mood, I put my red scarf over the lampshade like I often did when I was searching for a muse, and propped myself back in the window seat.

My mind was swirling with the effects of the alcohol and inspiration, and I wrote for quite a while before I noticed the car driving slowly by outside, ominously creeping with its headlights extinguished.

Angela Hoke   *A Whisper of Smoke*

The car snaked down one street and turned the corner to the next. *Maybe it's leaving,* I thought, hopeful. But then, to my horror, the car made its way back by and came to a menacing idle below my window. My blood turned icy cold, and traveled like a freight-train through my veins, weaving a trail of shivers in its rumbling wake.

I ducked down and crawled over to the electrical outlet. I unplugged the lamp, extinguishing the scarlet light with a flash that left a momentary residual on my retinas, giving the darkened room an exposed relief, like a photographic negative. For a moment, I sat on the floor beneath the window with my chest heaving, trying to slow the pounding of my heart, coaxing it to stay put and abandon its efforts to escape forcibly from my chest.

In the dark, the quality of my hearing seemed to intensify, and I could hear the soft chugging sound of the idling car engine. I focused all the power of my senses into my auditory nerves, pushing the limits of my hearing through the open window, along a winding path through the cross-currents of the nighttime winds, and trained my ears like sonar on the sounds of the car, listening for the opening and closing of a door.

After a few seconds of constancy, I risked peeking out the window. I raised up slowly, wondering if the highlights of my hair would glow in the moonlight, despite the extinguishment of the artificial light. Nevertheless, I risked the exposure so that I could better assess the danger.

My head moved up like a jack-in-the-box in slow motion, but stopped when my line of vision cleared the window sill. There the car sat in the dark, the moonlight giving it a pewter glow but not betraying its true color. I could tell that it was a sedan, and I discerned the shadows of two men in the front seat. Though it was impossible to really tell, I imagined that both men were turned towards my house, looking up at my just darkened window.

As I knelt there, spying my voyeurs, my breathing began to slow and I regained some clarity of thought. Now, all of my sensory ability was focused on my sight, as I watched for any betraying movement, for a sign of decision to turn the moment from voyeurism to intrusion. I mentally went through each room of the house, thinking about whether I had locked the doors and windows, and mentally berating myself when I was uncertain. I searched my mind for weapons, coming up with only Hank's baseball bat or the large, marginally sharp butcher knives in the kitchen. Daddy didn't believe in guns.

I thought about my absent family, and fantasized that they would come pulling up the drive with bright headlights and radio blasting, and that they would scare the two men into hasty retreat. Then my mind made a dark turn as I imagined that, instead of retreat, the two men took them all hostage.

Oh no you don't, you sons of bitches, I thought, feeling anger rising inside along with a fierce instinct to protect my family and my home.

I had never been drawn to violence, but right then I wished I had one of Calvin's shotguns. I imagined loading the shells then pumping a round into the chamber so that the loud and ominously unmistakable *cla-click* sound would travel like a warning through the air.

Then I nearly hit my forehead at my obtuseness. *Calvin!* I thought. *Maybe Calvin's home,* I dared to hope, knowing that he would be at my side in two minutes, well equipped to be my protector.

I've got to get to the stupid phone, I thought in frustration, not wanting to leave my observation post. *Why couldn't Mother have put a phone extension in here like Lorelei and I begged and begged!* I silently cursed, in vain.

I decided that the best option was probably a mad dash to the hall, where I could grab the phone and bring it back into the bedroom. The cord was not long enough to reach all the way back to my post at the window, but I hoped I would be able to stand a little further back, masked in shadows, and still be able to watch the car outside.

Steeling myself with some deep breaths, I bolted through the room in a crouched run, holding the layers of gown up around my waist in a ridiculous vision, an odd ostrich with red feathers flying.

In seconds, I had grabbed the phone and pulled it to the wall of my room where I had an adequate vantage point to what was happening outside. I stood there shaking, gripping the phone to my belly as I lifted the receiver. I started to dial with trembling but deliberate fingers, but then became frantic when I saw the strike of a match in the car and a tiny orange light that glowed bright and then faded into an arcing pin-prick of light. The smoke from the cigarette circled out of the open car window and swirled up like a phosphorescent fog.

Please, please, I silently begged, as the phone call connected and began to ring on the other end. Two rings, three rings, four... *Shit! He's not home. Please, anyone! Pick up!*

"Hello?" answered a soft male voice, tinged with a touch of annoyance.

Oh, dear God, thank you! I heralded, a praise of gratitude to hear Calvin's voice on the line.

"Hello?" came the voice again, his irritation growing, and no doubt about to culminate in a disconnection.

A Whisper of Smoke   *Angela Hoke*

"Calvin!" I whispered with as much force as my tightened chest could manage.

"Yes?" he answered, questioning.

"Calvin," I whispered again, but with a catch in my throat.

"Susanna? Is that you?"

Relief flooded over me, giving my vocal chords a small boost of efficiency.

"Yes! It's me," I said, and the words indicated a working larynx at last.

"What is it? Why are you calling so late?" he asked, not sure whether to be alarmed, but clearly recognizing this whispered call as an unusual occurrence.

"Where are you? Has Chip done something? Are you alone somewhere?" he asked, his own voice rising as he jumped to conclusions.

"No!" I snapped in a hushed voice, wanting him to stop jabbering and listen.

"I'm by myself at my house, and there's a car with strange men outside," I gushed. "I'm scared!"

"I'll be right there," he said with an intensity that implied competent action. "Where are you? What room are you in?"

"In my bedroom."

"Lock the door and the window, and watch for me," he ordered, then abruptly hung up.

Normally, I would have been pissed that he'd hung up without saying good-bye, but I only felt relief that he was coming and a building tension that he might be putting himself in danger.

Angela Hoke   *A Whisper of Smoke*

Obediently, I locked myself in my room, then, standing to one side, slowly closed the window and locked it, hypnotized all the while by the lazy arcs of the man's cigarette.

Across the road and over the field, I was heartened to see the back light come on and Calvin's lanky figure stride with purpose to his faithful Ford pick-up. He jumped into it, maybe carrying a gun, it was hard to tell, cranked it and turned on the bright headlights. Though I couldn't hear it through the closed window, I knew he had peeled out of their gravel drive because of his quickening speed and the cloud of glowing dust that rose in his wake.

I watched without breathing as he sped towards the hovering shadow car, and wondered what they might be thinking. They weren't fleeing, which was a bit curious, and I observed the man closest to me take one more long drag on his cigarette, the end glowing bright for a moment, before it flew in its final arc out the window to the ground below. It extinguished itself immediately in the dewy grass.

Then Calvin's truck was alongside them, looking large and brutish beside the dwarfed sedan. He got out of the truck and walked up the driver's side window, no gun in his hand (but perhaps waiting in the seat directly behind him?).

They talked for a few minutes, as my breath ran out and I sucked in another one. Calvin wasn't making any mad lunges for hidden weaponry, and the men weren't fleeing in fear.

What in the hell is going on down there? I wondered.

Then the discussion seemed to come to a close, and Calvin gave a slap to the top of the car before it leisurely pulled away, the sound of its chugging engine fading with the sound of expanding distance. Just as I stood up and let out a sigh of relief, Calvin collapsed on the ground.

A Whisper of Smoke   *Angela Hoke*

"Oh, please God, no!" I cried, and went flying out of my room and down the stairs, towards my fallen hero. I threw open the front door and ran in bare feet through the cool damp night to where Calvin was lying in a heap.

"Calvin! Please God, please be okay! Calvin!" I exclaimed as acidic fear spread through my stomach. In a flash, I reached him, alighting next to him like a red angel.

He was retching on the ground, his head on his knees, his shoulders heaving.

"Oh, Calvin!" I cried, pulling him into my arms. "What happened? What did they do to you?"

He started to speak, but couldn't get the words out past his overwhelming emotion, so I crushed his head harder against my chest and kissed the top of his head, stroking his hair and face.

"Susanna!" he finally mustered, taking my hands and pushing himself free. Then he took one look at me, and he doubled over again.

That's when I realized it – he was *laughing*! I jerked away like I'd been stung. "What are you laughing at? Are you crazy?"

He just continued to guffaw, his laughs catching in his chest as tears streamed down his cheeks.

"If you're not hurt, you're about to be!" I snapped, dumbfounded at his behavior, and with half a mind to storm back inside the house. But my curiosity kept me still, as I waited to hear what had transpired with the strange men in the dark car.

When it was obvious that he was indeed unhurt, I leaned back on my knees and crossed my arms with what I hoped was a terrifying scowl.

Angela Hoke   *A Whisper of Smoke*

His laughter finally started to abate, and he gulped air as he wiped at his eyes. Before he finally regained his composure, he erupted into a few more fits of sputtering, snorting giggling – the kind that would cause milk to spurt out your nose, if you were drinking any. I waited patiently for him to get a grip, seething at his completely inappropriate response to my obvious peril.

Finally he took some big hiccoughing sighs, and sat back on the weight of his arms, his hands planted on either side of him in the wet grass. He just looked at me with mirth and shook his head, his eyes sparkling. He looked so smug, I almost wished I didn't have to probe him for an explanation.

"Are you going to explain or not?" I asked, my voice tight.

"This is classic," he said, his deep laugh rumbling like an aftershock.

He seemed to be mocking me, and I bristled with annoyance. I refused to give him the satisfaction of having me draw answers out of him. I closed my face and stubbornly waited.

"They thought you were a… a…," he couldn't even finish it.

"Spit it out already."

"Do you have a red lamp in your room?" he finally asked.

"I put a red scarf over it to make the light look red," I said slowly, wondering what that had to do with anything.

"That explains it, I guess. They thought you were a housewife hooker," he said and, snorting, burst into laughter again. He had tears streaming down his cheeks.

I was stunned. "They thought I was a *what??*"

"Did you know that a red light in the window was the sign for 'we're open for business?'"

A Whisper of Smoke   *Angela Hoke*

Of course I had not known such a thing!

"N-no!" I sputtered, and Calvin laughed yet again at my expense.

"Apparently some of our neighbors have a little side business going on," he paused, and I wondered if were both thinking of Mrs. Kingsberry down the street. The way she flirted with the paper boys and yard boys, with her low-cut blouses, she seemed a likely suspect. But then again, to an outsider, so would Mother. "A red light in an upstairs window is the signal that it's all clear. I'll have to pay more attention to our neighbors' windows," he said to himself, trailing off. "Anyway, they said this wasn't the first time they'd seen a red light in your room, but every time they had come close, it had gone off, like you were... hmm, mmm, busy."

There it was again – that infuriating snickering. But even as I fumed, I thought about the cars I'd seen driving slowly down the road with extinguished headlights. I had speculated that they were mafia or government agents or something, and my imagination had gone wild. But it turned out they were something I could never have imagined – pathetic johns looking for a little suburban hanky-panky. I waited for him to continue.

"Anyway, tonight they were checking out their options, and they were quite excited when, not only was your light on, but you were actually sitting in the windowsill in a... in *that*..." He looked down at me and burst into laughter again.

I was appalled and completely, utterly mortified. Groaning, I buried my head in my hands.

"This is *awful*."

"Hey," Calvin said, a little sympathy interrupting his amusement.

Angela Hoke   *A Whisper of Smoke*

I heard him rustle around and move beside me. He put a hand lightly on my back, and patted me awkwardly.

The more I thought about what he'd told me, the more humiliated I felt. "Oh...my...*gosh*."

"It's okay," he said, and gave my back a friendly little rub.

He noticed me shiver, and bumped my arm with his in a brotherly gesture to get my attention.

"What?" I snapped, looking over at him.

He smiled a slow smile, and then looked me up and down with that same mocking expression.

I looked down at myself, shrouded in stupid chiffon, absurdly naked underneath, and suddenly laughter was bubbling from my own belly. It burst out like an explosion, and then I couldn't stop. My laughter shook my gut so hard, I lost the ability to draw air and my chortles turned into silent, agonizing hacking. This set Calvin off again, and we both laughed until our sides were splitting, and tears covered the sore muscles of our stretched grins.

"Here, take my jacket," he finally said, removing his warm flannel coat and placing it on my shoulders. I was at once warmed, and not just where the jacket lay, as I inhaled his comforting smell.

"Let's get you inside, Miss Madam," he joked. "Before any other clients arrive."

He helped me up and walked me to the front porch. When we got to the door, I reached inside and turned on a light. Suddenly, my ridiculous attire was highlighted, as were its sheer qualities. Calvin blushed, and told me to keep the jacket for tonight. With a quick, friendly squeeze of my hand, he turned and walked down the sidewalk, shaking his head the whole time. I watched him for a second, until I saw headlights turning towards us from the end of the street, a few blocks away. Hoping to avoid either another hopeful, prospective client or (*eeek!*) my parents, I dashed inside and transformed back into fifteen-year-old Susanna with a change of clothes.

Climbing in my bed, safe in my locked house and with my guardian living next door, I reached over and decisively jerked the red scarf from the top of my lamp, like an angry magician, then turned it off.

Chapter 12: Gertrude in Goldenrod

Spring 1968

I walked into an empty house at two minutes until 11:00. As I let myself in to the creaky quiet, I rubbed my lips where Chip's kisses had chafed them sore and tried to remember more of the movies that had been showing at the drive-in. The first feature was *The Jungle Book*, which I'd already seen and thus had a description at the ready if I fell under Mother's scrutiny. But the main feature was *The Planet of the Apes* (which I had not previously seen) and I ran through fuzzy snippets in my mind, hoping I could piece enough together to fake a synopsis. I had actually wanted to see *The Planet of the Apes,* because (a) it was an interesting premise and (b) Charlton Heston was always good to watch. But Chip had made a consistent viewing impossible by his repeated and persistent mauling. Every time I tried to sit up and pay attention, he was all over me, kissing my neck and running his hand up my leg and under my skirt. Then, inexplicably, I would find myself lying across the back seat of Chip's Mustang shrouded in the cocoon formed by his long lean body.

But now I was back home exactly on time, not even a minute late. I had become militant about meeting my curfew of 11:00, without any prompting from my parents. I had not even asked for a later curfew when I turned sixteen in November. I told Chip that it was because my parents were too overbearing to ever permit me to miss my curfew much less entertain the suggestion of a later curfew. But while my mother could be overbearing and spiteful, my parents usually weren't even home by 11:00 on nights when they went out.

Could I have requested and received permission to stay out later? Probably I could have. But I had a secret reason for my obsessive compliance with my 11:00 curfew.

As I put my purse down and kicked off my shoes, the phone rang. *Speak of the devil, here's the reason now.*

"Hello?" I answered.

"Hi, Sus," came a boy's voice, sweet and soft.

"Hi, Calvin," I said with a quiet sigh of satisfaction. I pulled the phone as far as the cord would allow and draped myself across the puffy wingback chair. Ever since the 'Brothel Debacle,' (as we'd come to call it, and never without laughing), Calvin had called me every Friday and Saturday night at a few minutes after 11:00 as soon as he'd returned home from dropping off Christine.

He said that it made him feel better to know that I was safe.

It made me feel better, too. It was great to know that I had such a good friend, someone to look out for me.

"How was your night?" he asked, making small grunts as he settled into a comfortable position, preparing for a long conversation. I pictured him sprawled on a messy bed in his darkened room, his white t-shirt glowing in the dark, talking ridiculously on the white princess phone that he pulled in from the hall extension.

"It was fine. We went to the drive-in," I said without thinking, then winced as I waited for his sarcastic reply.

"Ooohh, the *drive-in,*" he said, and I could almost hear his eyebrows wiggling up and down.

Angela Hoke   *A Whisper of Smoke*

"We watched two very good movies, I'll have you know," I bluffed.

"Oh, yeah? What were they?"

"*The Jungle Book* and *The Planet of the Apes*," I said, then sucked in my breath, hoping he wouldn't ask too many questions.

To my surprise, he got all excited. "Oooh, me and Christine went to see *The Planet of the Apes* last month at the cinema. What did you think about the ending? Wasn't that unexpected?"

"Uhhh, yeah. It was definitely unexpected," I said, as I racked my brain. Unfortunately, the ending happened to be one of the parts that was a little fuzzy.

"Hmmm, how much did you actually watch of the movies?" Calvin asked.

"I watched it!" I insisted, indignant.

"So what was the big surprise at the end?" Calvin pushed.

"It was a statement about society and our prejudices," I said, bluffing as best I could.

"You are such a little tramp!" Calvin said with affection, laughing.

"Am not! Thanks a lot."

"Oh, quit your pouting. You know I'm just kidding with you."

"Yeah, sure," I said, not ready to concede. I was quiet for a minute, then I couldn't resist asking, sheepishly, "So what did happen at the end?"

Calvin burst into laughter. "I don't think I should tell you."

"Why the hell not?" I demanded.

"You haven't earned the right to know. I think you are going to have to go see it again," he said.

Well now, he was being completely unfair.

A Whisper of Smoke   *Angela Hoke*

"Come on, tell me," I pleaded. "Now you've got me curious."

"No way, little girl. If you can ever get through the movie without making out the whole time, call me and we can discuss it. In fact, I'll make you a deal. If you can call me and tell me what happens at the end of the movie (and I mean, from actually having seen it yourself), I'll..." he paused as he tried to think of a good reward.

"Take me to a movie of my choosing," I finished without thinking.

Calvin was quiet for a moment.

"Okay, I'll take you to the matinee of your choice. It's a deal."

"Deal," I confirmed, noticing how smoothly he had turned the prospect into an afternoon event. "Can we talk about something else now?"

"Sure. What do you want to talk about?"

"How was your night with Christine?" I asked out of politeness.

"It was fine. We went to the malt shop for dinner and then we were supposed to go to some friends' house to listen to music." I picked up on the use of the phrase 'supposed to' versus that they actually did, but I let it slide for the moment.

"What did you talk about?" I asked, not being able to help myself.

"That's such a girl question," Calvin said, but then he considered it. "We talked about her mom and dad – they are having problems and have been fighting a lot. She said that half the time they don't even sleep together. She's worried they are going to get a divorce."

"That's not good," I sympathized.

"No, it's not. She's been pretty emotional about it. She cries real easy at things that don't seem to have anything to do with it. Like tonight. When we got her hamburger, it had mustard all over it even though we had specifically said no mustard. She is allergic to mustard, so she really can't eat it. It's not like she was just being picky," he explained, seeming to feel the need to justify her behavior.

"Right," I said without judgment.

"So anyway," he continued, "usually we would just take it back to the counter and get them to make a new one. But this time she just started crying. People looked at us weird, and then some of the girls started giving me dirty looks like I had done something to her."

"That must have been awkward.".

"Completely. I tried to comfort her. I even went around to her side of the booth and put my arm around her, even though I usually hate public displays of affection." I smiled to myself and rolled my eyes.

"That was sweet. What did she do when you did that?"

"She started crying even harder. She was really embarrassed, you could tell. She kept looking out the window as she tried to compose herself and she kept using the napkins from the little metal dispenser on the table to wipe her nose. She was making this big pile of crumpled napkins, and we hadn't even eaten yet. Finally, it was obvious she was getting more and more upset, you know, starting to do that sucking, hiccoughing sound. So we just had to get up and leave. Neither one of us got to eat, but it cost me half of my week's pay. Not that I'm complaining about that part," he added.

"So where did you guys go when you left?"

"We went up to, um, Cherokee Park," he said reluctantly. "We didn't go there to park," he swiftly added. "We just went there to have some time alone so she could get calmed down."

"Uh huh," I said, and resisted the urge to rib Calvin. "Did you get her calmed down?"

"Not until she bawled all over me for over an hour. I had absolutely no idea what to say to get her to stop crying."

"Calvin, my dear boy. You weren't supposed to get her to stop crying. You were supposed to be a safe place for her to cry and let it all out."

"Really?" he asked, perplexed.

"Yes. Believe it or not, we are not always looking for our boyfriends to fix our problems or make things better. Sometimes we just want to be held when we are sad."

Calvin pondered this for a few minutes. "Really," he said again, but this time more as a statement. "So you're saying that I wasn't supposed to do anything?" he asked skeptically.

"Well, not exactly. You weren't supposed to fix it, because some problems, like the ones with her parents, can't be fixed. At least not by you. But you were supposed to be there for her, listen to her and comfort her."

"I did that. I mean, I tried to suggest some ways she could handle it better. You know, like maybe help clean up a little more at home so that her dad wouldn't get so mad about it. Or talking to her mom about not putting so much pressure on her dad about the hours he works."

I put my head in my hands in frustration at his lack of good sense.

"Calvin, Calvin, Calvin."

"What?" he asked, a little sharply.

"Honey, no offense, but you are such a guy," I said. Then I heard him huff, and I knew he was getting irritated and defensive. "Sweetie, telling her how to handle it better is exactly the wrong thing to do."

Angela Hoke   *A Whisper of Smoke*

"Why?" he demanded.

"Because, first of all, how do you really know what she should do with her parents' situation? You don't live there. You're not really experiencing it. Plus, you are really lucky with your parents. You probably have never even seen them fight."

"Sure I have," he insisted. "They got in a fight just last month about my dad's mom. She wanted to make Easter dinner even though it was going to be at our house, and my mom said that it wasn't her place to do that. She said Grandma could bring a few dishes, but that was all. Then Dad told her that Grandma's potato salad was better than Mom's so she should be allowed to bring that. I thought my Mom was going to spit when he insulted her cooking *and* took my Grandma's side. She was mad at him for two or three days, and he was too stubborn to apologize. She didn't let him off the hook until Grandma called and asked what specifically Mom would like her to bring. Apparently, Dad had talked to Grandma about it and taken up for Mom."

I thought about how to respond. I knew I'd have to be delicate, or else Calvin would shut down and the conversation would be over. I'd have to somehow suppress the urge to shout, *"Are you kidding me? That's not a fight, that's a tiny little spat."*

"I'm guessing that her parents' fights are a little more serious than that," I said carefully. "The kind of fight your parents had was a normal marriage kind of fight – I mean, you never wondered whether they'd stay together, right?"

"No," he admitted.

"See, in my house, my mom and dad get in some massive fights sometimes – especially when they've been drinking a lot. They say nasty things to each other, and I mean nasty – cussing each other and stuff. At least my parents still have sex, but if my parents were fighting like that *and* not sleeping together, I'd be pretty worried about them splitting up too."

"Yeah, I guess so," he acknowledged.

"Also," I began, choosing my words, "when you give Christine advice like that, about how she could have handled things better, it kind of implies that maybe she's partly to blame for her parents not getting along. And I'm guessing that she already worries that she's partly to blame."

"I'm completely confused. Of course it's not her fault," Calvin said, exasperation clear in his voice.

"I know you don't think so, but do you see why it might make her feel that way?" I said, thinking of how I would feel, how I often *did* feel.

"I guess," he said slowly. "Then what was I supposed to do?"

"Again, you weren't supposed to do anything other than listen and comfort her. Let me give you a little tip – if she wants your advice, she will ask for it."

I could tell that Calvin was struggling with the female psyche and the whole concept of being told a problem but not being expected to fix it. But I also had faith that he would think it through and try to do better.

Finally, he sighed. "Okay," he said. I knew the topic was closed for the night.

"What are you doing tomorrow?" I asked, changing the subject. "Do you have to work?"

"Yep, in the morning. I've got to milk the cows and feed the animals. But we've already planted, so there's no crop work at the moment. It's supposed to be pretty out tomorrow – do you want to go riding with me after lunch?"

Angela Hoke   *A Whisper of Smoke*

"I'd love to!" I exclaimed.

"Okay," said Calvin. "I'll let you know when I'm done working, and we'll head out. It'll probably be around 2:00 or so."

"That sounds great," I replied.

"Okay, good."

My ears perked up to the sound of crunching gravel. My parents were home, and I wanted to be in bed before they came in.

"Calvin, I gotta go. They're home."

"Okay, sure thing. I'll see you tomorrow." He paused then added, "Susanna, thanks for listening to me and giving me advice – even though I didn't really ask for it." I could tell he was needling me at the end.

"Of course, my darling. Any time," I responded, not taking the bait.

"Sleep tight, Susie," he said sweetly.

"You too, Calvin," I answered back.

The next day was indeed beautiful. Before taking the horses out, Calvin insisted that we brush them down and that I saddle my own horse. Putting a saddle and bridle on a horse always made me nervous, particularly because I had never before been expected to do it by myself, but it was worth it on this day because Calvin was letting me ride Gertrude, the glorious palomino of my childhood dreams, for the first time on my own. So I was overwhelmed with elation as we trotted out of the corral, through the first pasture, and entered the woods, not even minding the sore bottom I was sure to have.

Conversation was light as Calvin and I did the first part of our ride. I was not surprised that Calvin didn't bring up Christine or the conversation we'd had the night before. Our nighttime conversations were always more intimate and deep than the daytime ones. During the day, it was almost like we had not shared secrets in the night. Except that, even during the day, the closeness was there, percolating just under the surface. As we rode companionably along, moving single file when the trail got too narrow, Calvin talked about the new spring calves and what it was like sowing soy beans with his dad's new tractor. I laughed at two squirrels that seemed to be having a quarrel over an old acorn, and watched the blue birds with their red breasts flit colorfully through the trees. The ride drained the tension as we got further and further away from home. We were heading to the back side of the farm, and no other person was anywhere around.

As we rode, the sun played hide-and-seek behind the branches of the trees, firing beams of sunlight in surprising bursts when you least expected it. In the shade, it was still a bit cool, so the windbreaker was a good idea. But when the sun found us, the warmth came over us like contentment. The day was perfect, and I rode with a stupid grin on my face. So I was glad that Calvin had let me ride lead so he couldn't make fun.

After we'd ridden for a while, I gripped Gertrude's flanks tightly with my thighs and peered over my shoulder at Calvin. He was moseying along on Sampson, their youngest horse, keeping a pace that was contrary to Sampson's rambunctious nature. I was itching to go fast, but was cautious because Gertrude was pretty tall, and the hard, rocky ground seemed a long way away. But today in the bright spring sunshine, with all the trees budding with tiny green clusters of life and the cherry trees raining white and pink blossoms, it seemed as though the pretty blond horse and I would be able to fly.

Angela Hoke   *A Whisper of Smoke*

When I saw that the trail was about to open up ahead into the pasture land, the urge to gallop overcame me and I knew I wouldn't be able to resist. I felt my eyes grow bright with mischief, and I dared not look around to Calvin, who was whistling through his teeth behind me, oblivious. Our pace quickened as Gertrude steadily closed the distance to where we would emerge from the woods, and I rose up a little from my seat in anticipation. Behind me, I heard Calvin mutter a mild curse at Sampson who had apparently stopped again to try to steal a bite of the new grass. I knew that Calvin would be jerking on the reins, showing the young Sampson who was boss, and that I might have a couple of seconds to get to the clearing and break away before he noticed.

Not that I was trying to get away from him. I loved being with him, and only felt safe enough to run Gertrude because I knew he was riding protectively just a few feet behind me. It was just that I was on the precipice of living out one of my oldest fantasies— a dream of flying on this beautiful mare, our blond hair intermingling in the wind. It was a vision I'd had for as long as I could remember.

Finally, Gertrude broke free into the clearing. My inner voice told me it was now or never, so I gave the reins a firm shake and kicked my heels into the horse's hindquarters. Gertrude reacted immediately and, it seemed, with delighted surprise. She broke into a joyful gallop, like she was young again, and I laughed out loud as I clung on, ignoring Calvin's shout of alarm receding in the distance.

We ran and ran across the flat field, whizzing by old cows who looked at us with the mildest of interest before turning back to grazing. The goldenrod was swaying around us like a seabed of yellow anemone, and the puffy cumulus clouds followed us in cheerful encouragement. Gertrude's hooves pounded on the grass in a muffled thunder that formed the baseline for my booming heart. Blood rushed in my ears further muffling the sounds, adding to the surrealism.

When I noticed that a pure yellow butterfly had landed on the saddle and was joining in the ride, I thought, *This IS a dream,* and I closed my eyes and gave in to an intense joy that approached rapture. Head back and eyes closed, I wanted to let go of the reins and spread my arms wide, but prudence prevailed and instead I opened my eyes and lowered my head. My horse and I thundered on, heading to a cluster of centennial oaks, but I could feel that the great animal was tiring and that her enthusiasm was beginning to wane.

As we approached the large trees, Gertrude slowed even more, and I pulled gently on the reins, giving the sweet horse the permission to rest. *Okay, if you insist,* Gertrude seemed to say, clinging to the vanity that was her due. We came to a stop and I loosed the reins so Gertrude could graze, and only then did I hear the thundering gallop of Sampson coming up fast.

I sat lightly on the saddle of the glorious palomino, holding the reins loosely and stroking the horse's neck with affection, as I watched Calvin coming towards me like an angry locomotive. His face wore either an intense look of concentration or a deep scowl, though I couldn't read his eyes behind the reflective flashing of his glasses. But his body language shouted that he was annoyed.

He's coming in awfully fast, I thought, but my euphoria blanketed any anxiety I might have otherwise felt with a shroud of dampening calm. Calvin rode that horse hard until he was almost up on us, then he reined in abruptly, coming to a halt just beside me. Gertrude barely looked up from her voracious grazing.

Angela Hoke   *A Whisper of Smoke*

Before Sampson had even come to a complete stop, Calvin was off and striding towards me. I watched him with a kind of curious detachment, until he unceremoniously grabbed my hand and jerked me off the saddle.

I tumbled down into his arms, and he held me fast so I wouldn't fall.

My mind swirled in confusion, desperately trying to process the anger that was emanating from him and reconcile it to the dream that he had so rudely interrupted. But then I realized that he was holding me against him, his arms locked in a death grip under my arms and around my waist, my face in his neck where I could smell his sweat. My breasts were mashed against his chest, he was holding me so tightly, and I could feel his heart pounding against me.

"Are you alright?" he asked tightly.

"Yeah, yeah," I said breathily. "You're killing me, though."

"Sorry," he mumbled, letting me go.

Then, he took my shoulders and stared at me. His brows were furrowed, and he searched my face for injuries, or explanation. I had the absurd impulse to cross my eyes at him, stick out my tongue or something.

"Are you okay?" he asked again, this time looking directly into my eyes with his intense brown ones.

"Yes, I'm fine," I said, then couldn't help but laugh with residual happiness.

This seemed to anger him, and he let me go abruptly. "Then what the hell were you thinking, Susanna?" he snapped. "I mean, damn it!" He ran a hand roughly through his hair and kicked at the ground.

My laughter died in my throat. I looked at him curiously, cocking my head to one side. My long blondish hair whipped in the wind and wound around my face. I spit it out and used my fingers to pry it back.

Calvin had turned his back on me and was kicking at some rocks in the grass, muttering. The back of his neck was red with emotion, but despite his obvious discomfiture, a smile erupted back on my face. I tried to wipe it off, because it was in opposition to the flip of my stomach, but my emotions were mixed up.

"Calvin," I said carefully when my voice seemed safe.

"What," he muttered.

I risked going up to him. When he didn't move, I laid my hand lightly on his forearm.

"Calvin," I said again, softly.

He turned to me. Anger, fear, something else flashed across his features.

"I'm sorry," I said, but wasn't exactly sure what for.

"Susanna, you could have been killed," he said. "You're not an experienced rider. And you don't know this terrain."

"I'm sorry," I said again, and left my hand on his arm. He looked down at it, then slowly lifted his other hand up and put it over mine. It was shaking and sweaty. He gripped my fingers, gently picking them up and lacing his fingers with mine, pulling me close.

"I thought the horse had gotten away from you, and all I could think was that you'd be thrown. I kept thinking you'd break your neck," he said, his warm fingers interlaced with mine, our palms touching. His thumb stroked mine with reassuring repetition.

I looked up into Calvin's eyes, and for once he didn't break away. We just stood there, two breaths apart, hands palm to palm, transmitting bolts of electric chills, up and down. He brought my hand up to his chest and pressed it flat, bringing me yet another step closer.

My mind struggled to make sense of what was happening and I was suddenly shy. I looked down, and then back up at him through my lashes.

He was looking at me intently, standing close enough that I could breathe in his sweet exhalations. Around us, the birds were singing and the big old trees were rustling as they slowly arched to one side and then the other in a slow dance with the wind. Calvin's brown eyes were so earnest and beautiful – big brown circles surrounded by blue white, lids fringed with thick dark lashes, magnified through the lenses of his glasses. His nose was very straight and narrow. His clear skin was browned from the sun.

I was breathless, and I guiltily willed him to kiss me. My mouth watered with the thought of it. Then I cursed myself, worried that I'd jinxed it.

Sure enough, I saw the change in his look, and I knew at once that the moment was retreating. Then my hope surged as he leaned towards me, but he closed the door with a firm, affectionate kiss to my forehead. With a quick squeeze of my hand, which was still glued to his chest, he stepped back, breaking the seal.

"You know, if you wanted to learn to run her," he said, nodding towards the horses, "all you had to do was say so. I would have ridden alongside of you."

"Right," I said, nodding stupidly, still clinging to the memory of his closeness.

He squinted, surveying the pasture with his gaze. Then he turned to me. "What do you say we get these horses back to the barn?"

A Whisper of Smoke   *Angela Hoke*

Without waiting for an answer, he went to Sampson and mounted. Sampson skittered sideways with youthful exuberance.

I just stood there, not sure what had happened, or almost happened. I felt exposed and frustrated.

"Are you coming, or what?" Calvin asked, cantering around me.

"Of course," I said, snapping out of my pointless reverie. I went to Gertrude and patted her neck as I grabbed the reins. Gertrude gave me a sideways look like she wasn't ready to leave this moment.

"Tell me about it," I mumbled, and then mounted the big blond horse.

Calvin and I rode side-by-side at a modest gallop back towards the wooded trails and the barn beyond, abandoning my waking dream in a field of goldenrod.

Chapter 13: Chips Go Stale

I was dreading my date with Chip. Lately, we argued virtually every time we talked, and things had never been tenser between us. Things had deteriorated so much that, up until a couple of hours ago, I didn't even know if we still *had* a date tonight. Not after Wednesday night's call.

Chip had been very terse when he'd called me before bed. I tried to ask him questions about his day, and he answered in one-syllable words.

"What's the matter?" I'd asked.

"Nothing, Susanna! Why does something always have to be wrong, just because I'm not in the mood to talk about stupid stuff?" he snapped.

I cringed on my end of the phone. I was silent, frightened to speak for fear of saying the wrong thing. I bore the silence in agony, until finally he cleared his throat.

"How's your algebra class going?"

I hesitated, sensing a trap of some sort. He knew that algebra was hard for me and that I had really been struggling with it.

"It's going okay. I've been trying to study at least an hour a night just on algebra. I really want to get a C at least."

"Are you sure that's enough?" he said, and I heard the antagonism in his voice that I despised. "If it's that hard for you, maybe you're just not smart enough to take it."

"That was a hateful thing to say!" I said, stung that he would needle me about something that I was already sensitive about.

"God, Susanna!" he scolded, condescension dripping from his voice. "Can't you take a joke? You are so damn sensitive!"

I knew what this was – it was one of *those* conversations. I had been strolling along a beautiful path, and had suddenly found myself in the middle of a minefield. I'd been here before. And even though I could see the blackened holes where some of the mines had exploded, I knew there were so many more out there, hiding in the innocent grass.

If there was one thing I'd learned from Chip and Mother, when you are standing in the middle of a minefield, the best thing to do is not to move at all.

After interminable seconds of silence, he sighed loudly. "So what, are you not talking to me now? That's really mature, Susanna."

"I think I need to go now," I said tightly.

"Why?" he said, his voice belligerent. "You got someone else to call?" I could hear the sneer in his voice, the challenge.

"I'm just... really tired," I said, finally. "I need to go to bed."

"Yeah, if you say so," he said. Then, there was silence again, and I knew we were entering into no-man's land, a stalemate to see who would cave and say "I love you," first.

I knew I should just suck it up and say it first, but I was feeling a surge of resentment that made me feel stubborn and rebellious. But the longer the silence persisted, the more I sensed the lurking danger. So I gave in.

Angela Hoke   *A Whisper of Smoke*

"I love you, Chip," I said softly.

"Hmmph. I love you, too," he said, with what sounded like a trace of reluctance.

"Okay, goodnight," I said, before anything else could be said.

"Yeah, goodnight," I heard him say from the receding handset as I hung up.

I'd stared at the phone and tears threatened again, tasting bitter on my tongue. The acid rolled in my stomach making me slightly nauseous and anxious to fall into the oblivion of sleep – anything so I didn't have to remember the conversation, or dwell on the sad fact that every conversation had been like that, or near to it, of late.

He hadn't even called on Thursday. I had spent the whole night filled with anxiety, worried that he wouldn't call, and then worried that he would.

But when he didn't call at all, I wondered what that meant. And I felt a niggling fear mixed with my relief that I didn't have to worry about protecting myself against his subversive verbal attacks.

So Friday afternoon, when he called to confirm our date acting as though everything was fine, I was surprised, but yet I couldn't bring myself to call him out on the abrupt shift in behavior. Now I was getting ready, brushing my hair and pinning it behind my ear with a side part, carefully brushing mascara on my lashes. I wondered what the night would hold, and then the doorbell rang, and I realized I was about to find out.

When I got to the front door, I stopped and took a deep breath. I could see Chip's silhouette through the window sheers.

"Susanna, are you leaving?" Mother called from the basement.

"Yeah, Mother. I'm going! See you later," I called, and quickly made the decision to open the door to Chip.

He smiled when he saw me. It was a charming smile, but it didn't quite reach his eyes.

"You ready?" he asked, pleasantly enough, then stepped aside for me as I walked down the path to the shining red car.

In the car, he turned up the radio, excusing either of us from making conversation, and I was relieved. I looked out the window, my mind drifting. I was sitting on the border of the passenger seat and the middle of the bench seat, riding the fence between taking my normal place in the middle right next to him, and hugging the sanctuary of the passenger seat. I felt conspicuously indecisive, my awkward seat placement a metaphor for my inner turmoil. But Chip didn't comment on it.

After a few minutes, Chip turned down the radio to speak.

"So I thought we would go grab a burger and then go to Patty Wilson's party. You remember her from that night at Kenny's, right?"

"Yeah, I remember," I said, trying to keep my voice neutral. Patty had gotten drunk on Kool-Aid hooch at Kenny's out-of-control party, and had been falling all over Chip. I suddenly wondered how Chip got invited to this party. He obviously didn't know Patty from his *all-boy school.*

"I take it Kenny will be there?" I asked carefully.

"Um, I'm not sure," he said vaguely, and my inner alarms started ringing.

"I love this song," he said, turning up the radio, abruptly ending the conversation.

I stewed on what this might mean, if anything. At dinner, I was on edge, waiting for Chip to say something biting, to pick a fight. But he

Angela Hoke   *A Whisper of Smoke*

didn't. Instead, he kept up a running monologue about school and practice, an overly cheerful account that required very little interaction from me. My suspicion grew, and with it my throat thickened making it impossible to swallow the soggy French fries and giant cheeseburger. Chip didn't seem to notice, and didn't even make a snide remark about how I was wasting his money by not finishing it.

With dinner behind us, we got back into the dark car and Chip put it into gear, peeling out of the parking lot. I gripped the dashboard and door, trying to keep from sliding across the seat. I could sense Chip's pent-up energy from across the seat, like he was feeding off the rumble of his V-8 engine.

Before long, we pulled up to an orange brick ranch home in Middletown. It was lit up all across the front, and cars were parked to overflowing in the driveway and all over the yard. We went inside, where music was blaring from the stereo and kids were drinking beer and talking everywhere. I surveyed the room, searching for people I knew. There weren't many. Then I saw a thin blond girl with a very short skirt and sleeveless top, talking animatedly to a group of people, and I recognized her vaguely as Patty.

I shifted my gaze away, looking around the room once more and wondering why we were there. When I turned my attention back to Chip, I realized that Patty was heading towards us, an odd smile on her round face.

Patty finally arrived, bringing a cloud of *Chanel No. 5* with her.

"Hi!" she said in a breathy voice, her round cheeks flushing an apple red, making her blue eyes pop. From close up, her bright pink top and coordinating plaid skirt looked expensive, making me feel a little self-conscious in my own, home-made clothes, worrying it would be evident that they were a cheap imitation.

"Hi," I heard Chip respond. "Thanks for inviting us," he added with a smile.

"Of course! I'm so glad you could come," she gushed, her attention focused on Chip.

"Hi," I said, inserting myself into the conversation.

"Oh, yeah," Chip said, seeming to remember her. "You remember Susanna?"

"Sure!" Patty replied, too brightly. "It's good to see you. Glad you could come, too!"

"Uh, thank you."

My gaze flicked between Chip and Patty – they were both smiling wide smiles, looking at each other. Then from the other room, the sound of breaking glass interrupted whatever spell seemed to be holding them captive. Patty turned her head to the sound, just as someone called her name. Her pretty face turned serious, as she muttered about people disrespecting her family's things.

I thought that if she wanted people to respect her family's possessions, perhaps having an unsupervised party with beer and teenagers was not the brightest idea.

"Let's get some beverage," Chip said, grabbing my hand and dragging it towards the keg in the corner. We stood in line for a moment, and then were both handed cups of frothing, overflowing beer from some preppy boy in charge of the tap.

I didn't really care for beer, but I sipped it so as to not draw attention to myself.

"C'mon," Chip instructed over his shoulder, with barely a backwards glance. I had no choice but to follow him like some stupid puppy. We walked through the room to a group of kids sitting on two identical, facing sofas. I didn't know them, but apparently Chip did.

"Hey man, what it is?" some guy with big arms said, getting up from his seat.

"Hey man, give me some skin," Chip replied, and they exchanged some secret handshake.

The guy looked at me, subtly eyeing me up and down.

"Are you going to introduce me to your lady?" he said, assuming a refined voice, but not able to disguise the lurking leer in is bloodshot eyes.

"This is Susanna," Chip said, gesturing to me where I continued to be relegated by space limitations to a spot just behind him and to the right.

"So nice to meet you Susanna," the guy said, taking my hand in his and giving it an inappropriate caress on my palm. "I'm Quentin."

"Hey Chip," some of the others called.

"Hey guys," he responded, not offering any further introductions. I assumed that all these kids went to Fern Creek, because I recollected that's where Patty attended. But I still didn't understand why Chip and I were there.

Someone made space for Chip, and he sat, leaving me standing awkwardly by myself.

"Here, you can sit by me," Quentin said from behind me, using his beefy body to scoot the others over to make a space wide enough for maybe one of my hips to wedge between him and the arm of the couch.

I surveyed my options, thinking that if I didn't take the spot by Quentin, I would be completely left out. I elected to accept the semi-seat, to Quentin's delight. His face lit up as I wedged myself in, trying to angle my body away from him, but realizing too late that this caused my bottom to be firmly pressed against his thigh.

I figured it was better than having my breasts smushed against his arm, but not by much.

After a few minutes sitting in this awkward position, anger flooded my chest that Chip was oblivious to my discomfort, and in fact was basically disregarding me. Quentin, on the other hand, was quite focused on me, leaning over my shoulder and breathing his beer breath into the side of my face as he tried to make uncomfortable conversation.

As he leaned over me, he rested his hand on my exposed outer thigh, feigning inadvertence. I squirmed to pull down the hem of my short skirt, and Quentin sighed in unexpected pleasure. My skin crawled with revulsion, and my anger towards Chip flared, especially when I saw that he was laughing with people I didn't know, as if I wasn't even there.

I decided my best bet was to block it all out. I ignored Quentin's advances, figuring he would eventually give up. He did finally quit asking questions and trying to engage me in conversation, but his hand didn't leave its resting spot against my leg, much to my annoyance.

After some time had passed, I snapped out of my self-imposed oblivion as Patty entered the cozy seating area.

"Hey, Patty," everyone greeted her enthusiastically, shifting around as they tried to make a spot for her.

She was carrying a beer and staggering around a bit. As she made her way in between the sea of legs, she tripped, sloshing beer everywhere and stumbling, somehow landing in Chip's lap. She giggled

Angela Hoke   *A Whisper of Smoke*

stupidly, her legs splayed in a very unladylike manner. He was laughing too, his eyes bright as he held her around her waist.

"Oops!" she exclaimed, apparently realizing that her skirt was virtually pooled around her hips. She straightened up to pull it down, sitting upright in Chip's lap as she squirmed around to fix it. He was laughing, obviously enjoying every sickening moment.

Patty finally got herself rearranged, but she showed no sign of vacating her spot in Chip's lap. My eyes narrowed in disgust, even if Chip's hands were now resting at his sides.

"Do you want us to make you a spot?" some perky girl asked.

"I'm pretty comfy where I am!" Patty replied, giggling absurdly. Chip laughed too loud, going along with the joke.

I glared at Chip, incredulous. He didn't even glance in my direction, the bastard. My anger was coursing through my body now. How could he humiliate me like this?

When it was clear that neither Chip nor Patty showed any signs of altering their seating arrangement, I found that I could take it no longer.

"Quentin," I said over my shoulder.

"Yes!" he replied, instantly at attention.

"Could you help me up, please?".

"Sure, of course!" he replied, apparently deciding to restrain himself from taking advantage as he lifted me up without touching me inappropriately. Maybe he wasn't a total slime after all.

I looked at him gratefully as we stood, and he smiled in response. It dawned on me that he may not know that Chip and I were dating. Chip certainly had not introduced me as his girlfriend, and now he was sitting, quite relaxed, with that slut Patty sprawled across his lap.

Now that I was disentangled, I stood next to the couch looking at Chip, waiting for him to acknowledge me. Quentin was standing beside me, saying something into my ear.

"What, huh?" I said, turning to him.

"Do you want to go outside and get some fresh air?" he asked, and I was reminded of the first time I met Chip, when he asked me basically the same question before taking me outside and kissing me on the curb. I felt the anger swell up and I wanted to scream at him.

"No, thanks," I said tightly, turning to Quentin with a rueful smile. "I appreciate it, but I think it's time for Chip to take me home," I explained further.

"Oh," he said. "Oh!" He finally got it, and his gaze flickered to Chip with obvious confusion.

I'm right there with you, I thought bitterly.

As I stood there like a fool, watching Chip laughing with some slut in his lap, totally ignoring me, I was reaching my limit. I was two seconds away from asking Quentin to take me home, but I didn't know him and some remaining sense of self-preservation restrained me.

So I stood there like an idiot, my face flushed with humiliation, waiting for Chip to notice me. To make it easier, I walked right up next to him and looked down on him. In my shadow, he couldn't help but look up. Patty somehow managed to pretend like she didn't notice my looming figure.

His eyes were all bright as his gaze met mine, but they turned cold when he saw my expression.

"I guess you're ready to go," he said, dripping sarcasm and acting like I was somehow putting *him* out. Anger raced through me anew, as I thought, *Oh, he's good.* I wondered with chagrin whether he had been taking secret lessons from Mother.

"I guess I have to go," he told the group apologetically, rolling his eyes towards me. "Up you go," he told Patty as he lifted her waist and set her on the lap of the guy next to him. *Why couldn't he have done that to begin with?* I wondered.

When he finally rose from his seat, he bid everyone good-bye then pushed past me without looking at me. Again, the humiliation was intense as I realized I was supposed to follow him. I was seething, thinking about how he had subjected me to one indignity after another tonight.

I followed him outside, shooting daggers into his back with my eyes.

Outside, he marched to his car, not bothering to open the door for me. He had it cranked and in gear before I could even get the door shut behind me. Then he peeled out of Patty's yard, digging up the grass as the car caught and jerked out into the road. We drove in deafening silence for a while, but I could tell that Chip was angry. That vein in his temple was throbbing and his face was screwed up tight. I was irate, and the dominant thought playing through my mind was, *Bring it on.*

We came to an abrupt halt in front of my house, and my body pitched forward. My hands shot up just in time to brace myself and prevent a face-first collision with the glove compartment. I froze with my hands on the dash and my hair flipped over my face, taking deep breaths. Then I slowly turned my face towards Chip, my eyes blazing.

"Well?" he asked, before I could begin my tirade. "What do you have to say for yourself?"

I was stunned! Oh, he was a master indeed.

A Whisper of Smoke   *Angela Hoke*

"What in the hell are you talking about?" I hissed, as mad as I'd ever been at him. Maybe as mad as I'd ever been in my life.

"How could you embarrass me like that?" he spat.

"Embarrass YOU?" I replied, my voice rising.

"You just sat there like a lump on a log all night. Couldn't you have socialized a little? Oh, wait. I *forgot.* You DID socialize – you were all over Quentin."

"You son of a bitch," I said, my words dripping venom as a fury like I'd never known overwhelmed me. "How DARE you try to put this on me! You ignored me all night, then sat there with that slut Patty practically screwing you on the couch!"

"Oh, Susanna, my God! You are utterly ridiculous. I am so *sick* of your jealousy," he said, and I just stared at him. Again, he was diverting this back on me! I was not normally a jealous person, at least I didn't think so. But I had a right to be jealous tonight, didn't I? Aaaghh! How did he do this? How did he turn situations where he was completely at fault into some attack on me? He was infuriating!

Still, I thought carefully about my words. I was not going to fall into his trap.

"I will not let you turn this around on me," I said slowly, deliberately trying to keep my voice neutral. "You know *exactly* what you did tonight. Your behavior was… unbelievable. You didn't treat me like a girlfriend. Hell, you treated me like you didn't even know me. I deserve better than that."

Chip looked at me for a long time, calculating.

"Listen, Susanna," he said, his voice dangerously soft. The change in his tone made tears spring to my eyes, which I willed back.

"If you can't understand why I would want to make new friends, maybe you need to re-evaluate things. And if you can no longer appreciate what we have, maybe you need to be with someone else."

I listened to the words, trying to see around the corner and anticipate where this was all headed. But the paths all led to places I never thought we'd go.

Was he *trying* to get me to break up with him? Was that what this was about? I was so furious, that right now I wanted nothing but to get away from him. It seemed easy to give up, when there was no apparent way to win. I knew I'd probably regret it tomorrow, but right now I wanted to make him pay for this night and all the manipulative crap that had led up to it.

"Fine," I finally whispered. "I guess that's it then."

"So you are breaking up with me," Chip clarified, and it wasn't a question.

"We are breaking up," I confirmed, without accepting sole responsibility.

Chip looked at me intently for a few minutes, and I looked away when I felt the tears threatening again.

He sighed and turned away. "I guess you should probably go in, then," he said to the window.

Now the tears spilled out, and I was grateful that he was not looking at me. "Right," I managed in a ragged whisper, and I opened the door and stumbled out before he could hear the sob that was rushing up my throat.

I closed the car door hard behind me and staggered to the lawn. Then he was peeling away, catching second gear with another screech of tires, lending a sound to the ripping of my heart.

A Whisper of Smoke   *Angela Hoke*

When he was out of sight, I collapsed on the curb as the sobs racked through me. Behind me, the front door opened and Hank called out to me.

"Susanna? Are you okay?"

I sucked in my breath and tried to hide the sorrow in my voice.

"Yes, Hank," I said. "I'm fine. I'll be in later."

He was quiet for a moment, no doubt hearing the emotion in my voice despite my attempts to conceal it.

"Okay," he finally said, and I could hear the compassion in his voice, as well as his conscious decision to honor my unspoken request to be left alone. The light from the door shrank and was extinguished with the click of the latch.

I knew I should not stay on the road. I wouldn't want a repeat of the brothel misunderstanding. So I drew myself up off the pavement and staggered around to the hammock in the back. I collapsed on it, and looked at the black leaves in the trees above me with blurred vision.

When my sobs subsided a bit, leaving my ribs sore, I noticed the tell-tale beam of headlights swinging around in the distance. *Calvin*, I thought. And without consciously deciding to do so, I was wandering towards his idling truck, reaching it just as he turned the motor off and cut out the lights.

He opened the door, and shut it behind him, looking handsome and sweet in the half-moon light.

"Hi," I croaked, and he jumped.

"Holy cow, Susanna!" he cried, his hand on his chest. "You scared the shit out of me."

"Sorry," I mumbled, and, annoyingly, my voice cracked again.

"Hey, what's wrong," he said with concern, as he rushed to my side.

"Chip and I broke up," I managed before bursting into fresh tears. He drew me to his chest and surrounded me with his strong arms.

"Shhh, it's okay," he whispered, smoothing my hair as he held me.

After a few moments, he suggested that we walk around to the pond behind the barn. I couldn't speak without erupting again, so I just nodded. He slowly led me around back, his arm around me, supporting my every step.

When we got to the pond, he spread his jacket out on the ground and helped me sit beside him. There, he took me into his reassuring embrace again. He was being so sweet – it made me realize the sharp contrast between him and Chip, and the tears flooded out yet again. I vaguely wondered just how many tears one girl could produce.

My nose was running pitifully and every ounce of make-up that I'd started the evening with had been washed away and replaced by a swollen red mess. I tried to inhale but my nose and throat made a clogged sucking sound.

"Here," Calvin said, and without another word, he took off his button-down and removed his t-shirt (*Oh my lord*) before putting his button-down shirt back on, leaving it unbuttoned. He handed the t-shirt to me.

"Blow your nose on this," he offered.

"I can't," I protested, distracted by his glowing chest, which peeked out from his unbuttoned shirt.

A Whisper of Smoke   *Angela Hoke*

"Sure you can," he encouraged. "My mom always told me that I should carry handkerchiefs with me – it's my own fault that I was too stubborn to listen."

I gave him a pathetic smile, and then blew my nose repeatedly on his shirt until my nasal passages were once again clear. That's when I realized that his t-shirt was full of his scent, so I feigned another blow just so I could clandestinely inhale his woodsy smell.

"Do you want to tell me what happened?" he asked gently.

"Noooo," I wailed.

"Sorry, sorry," he mumbled, drawing me close again. This time my face was pressed against the bare flesh of his chest, and I closed my eyes to better absorb him.

Then I realized that I was making him all wet, and I sat back, trying to pull myself together. I hiccoughed for a while as I tried to reign in my gulping sobs, thinking that I should be embarrassed but realizing that I wasn't. He was quiet during all this, just sitting beside me and gently rubbing my back in small circles.

Calvin did not like Chip, I knew. Even without telling him about the way he had treated me tonight, I knew that he was probably glad that we were no longer together, though, unfortunately, not for the reason I'd like. But to his great credit, he didn't make any derogatory comments about Chip. He didn't even act superior or say *I told you so.* He usually wasn't shy about telling me when he thought I was being stupid or making stupid decisions, but he gave me a pass tonight. His judgment was suspended, or at least the expression of it. For that, among other things, I was grateful.

When I had finally gotten all the tears out, we sat in the silence for a while making sure that I was really done. But when no new bouts erupted, I suddenly became aware that Calvin was sitting against me with an open shirt, and that he was still rubbing my back in a constant caress. My breath caught, as I felt his hand burning through my shirt. He seemed to sense it at the same time, and his rubbing stopped. He gave me a friendly double-pat, then his warm hand was gone. And with his retreat, the sadness rushed back in.

"You know, you used to scare me when we were little," he said out of nowhere, interrupting my self-pity. I knew he was trying to distract me, but I couldn't help but be curious about that statement.

"Why?" I finally asked, when I felt that my voice was under some kind of control.

"Because you had so much energy, it always seemed like you were going to combust or start spinning in a tornado or something, and I was afraid to get caught up in it."

I looked at him with what I imagined to be an inscrutable expression, which made him laugh softly.

"I guess it was because you were so free and unpredictable. You never followed a plan, never acted like your whole life was mapped out for you. I didn't know how to relate to that. I didn't want to acknowledge that such freedom could exist, when I'd never known it myself. It made me feel odd inside my own skin."

I looked at my friend, and I knew that he was revealing something new to me. That in these sweet words, offered as a way to distract me from my pain, he was opening up to me at a deeper level, and at the same time risking a vulnerability that would be uncomfortable for him. It made my heart swell with affection for him, and I squeezed his hand, before speaking again.

"That is so … surprising," I said, my voice embarrassingly thick and hoarse. I cleared it and tried again. "That you thought *I* was free, I mean. Because I always felt like my home was totally controlled by my mother. Even our moods and thoughts were dictated by her and her mood of the day. Maybe that's why I let loose when I was with you, when I was away from her – because I was finally *feeling* some freedom."

He pondered this, as he absently shredded a rogue wheat stalk. When he didn't say anything else after a few moments, I opened up a bit more to him.

"Actually, I was always jealous of you," I said.

"Me, why?" he asked, appearing genuinely perplexed.

"Because your family seemed so normal to me. Like Father Knows Best or something, except on a farm. Yeah, you had lots of rules and responsibilities, but at least you knew what they were. You have no idea how difficult it is not knowing the rules. Or thinking you do, and then having them change on you in an instant. It makes you walk on eggshells all the time, always feeling things out to figure out how to act, or what to think." I picked up an exceptionally large acorn and hurled it at the pond, gratified by the satisfying plunk it made in the water and the way it made the bullfrogs stop and take notice.

"You've got the Cleavers for your parents and I've got Endora for a mother – how in the world did that happen? In what universe is that fair?" I joked, trying to lighten the mood.

He smiled at my characterization, but I could tell he was still considering my words.

"I guess I see what you are saying. It would be hard to live like that. But the grass isn't always greener, Sus. My home probably was all those things you described, but it also lacked the imagination your family

Angela Hoke   *A Whisper of Smoke*

possesses in spades. And it takes imagination to be able to see anything outside of your own experiences -- to be able to have an open mind, and accept that your kids might turn out differently than you, or (God forbid) might want different things." The passion in his voice drew my gaze, and I yearned to see the expression in his dark eyes, which were trained straight ahead and shrouded in the darkness of night.

"Your family might be unpredictable, and I'm sure they can be difficult to live with, in ways that I couldn't even begin to understand or appreciate. But yours seems to be a family that believes in following your dreams. My dad doesn't even understand that concept. He's a pragmatist to the core. And he has always treated me more like his apprentice than his son," said Calvin, his voice quiet now. Something in the way he said these last words made me stop feeling sad for myself and begin to feel sad for Calvin, and I reached over and took his hand. For a moment, he let me take it, even let me intertwine my fingers with his.

Then he shook his head, clearing it, and let go of me yet again.

"Well, sorry to be so melancholy. You must be exhausted. Do you think you are okay to go home?" he asked then, and I knew the moment was over.

I sighed – with contentment, with frustration, with disappointment that this sweetness was ending.

"Sure," I answered back, and my voice sounded close to normal.

"Okay, sweet Susanna," he said, addressing me with an uncharacteristically affectionate endearment. He rose gracefully and offered me a hand. He hauled me up, retrieved his jacket, and we both started back towards home.

As we walked in silence, my nerves were frayed and my emotions sliced raw. I buried the anxiety about the pain I'd inevitably feel tomorrow, and the next day, and for many days after that. But I also had a sense of peace – a feeling that I would survive it, and a belief in something better.

I granted myself a small smile, which widened as I glanced over at Calvin who was surreptitiously buttoning his shirt as we walked.

"You better not let your mother see your buttons all undone – she'll think you were taking advantage of me out here in the dark," I teased.

"As if *I* could ever take advantage of *you*," he said back, grinning. "She knows what a good boy I am. If anything, she'd think *you* would be the one taking advantage of me."

You don't know how close to the mark that may be, I thought ruefully.

When we got to his house, the intimacy of the comfort he'd provided had passed, and he stood with me by his darkened truck looking sweet and awkward. My heart flooded with affection for my dear friend, and I threw my arms around his neck in a tight hug.

"Thanks, Calvin," I said into his neck.

"You're welcome," he mumbled, embarrassed. And I was already stepping back.

"See you tomorrow?" I asked tentatively.

"You know it," he said, then smiled his half-smile.

We parted, and as I walked the dark lonely path from his house to mine, I knew he was watching over me, making sure I stayed safe. As I opened my back door, I heard his back door closing, and I knew I would sleep well tonight, after all.

Angela Hoke   *A Whisper of Smoke*

Chapter 14: Armed Services Harbingers of Death

I waited under the big silver oak, spinning in leisurely circles in the tire swing. Calvin sounded tense last night on the phone, and I wondered what was bothering him. I hoped that he would tell me about it on our ride today, but I never could predict when Calvin was going to be in a sharing mood.

As I grew dizzy by the spinning tree limbs, I thought of how I couldn't have gotten through the past few weeks without Calvin. Breaking up with Chip after we had been together for two and a half years had been very difficult, probably the most difficult thing I'd ever done. He was my first boyfriend, and after Calvin, only the second boy I'd ever kissed. And I had given myself to him in ways that still made me blush. We had shared intimacies that inspired in me overwhelming passion and crippling guilt, simultaneously and with equal force.

For the first week or two, I had not been able to eat, and had craved sleep like a drug. I sought oblivion to flee the pain, only barely resisting the urge to use bourbon or vodka to aid in my escape. Calvin had spent at least an hour with me every night that first week, apparently worried that I would do something stupid. He had all kinds of pretenses for coming over, but the one that seemed to have the most practical use was his claim that he wanted to tutor me in algebra.

A Whisper of Smoke   *Angela Hoke*

At first, the tutoring was not very effective because I couldn't concentrate. To his credit, he was really trying to teach me. So he grew frustrated when I couldn't get the simplest concepts right. He was patient, though, and by the second week, I was beginning to come out of my fog when I was with him. And I was grateful that he was so annoyingly persistent.

For the hour that we were together, my mood would lift as Chip receded from my thoughts. But when Calvin left, all of the memories would come flooding back in, and I would sink back into my pit of sadness. That's when Hank would come sit with me.

In the beginning, I was annoyed that Hank would not leave me alone, but I couldn't bring myself to hurt his feelings by kicking him out. So I had pursed my lips and forced myself to push back the pain so that it didn't always cover my face like a scary mask.

Sometimes Hank would just sit next to me and quietly do his homework. Other times, he would sit close to me on the couch as we watched TV, content to be near me. But my favorite times, in retrospect, were the times that I was most blue and couldn't seem to make myself get out of bed. He would climb up next to me, pick up whatever book I'd been reading and start reading to me where I'd left off. He never said a word about why he was doing it or why I was too sad to join the rest of the family for dinner, he just sat snuggled up to me on my twin bed and read to me. Even when I couldn't bring myself to concentrate on the words, I found his young voice soothing, and the halted cadence of his inexperienced pronunciations a calming rhythm. It was a sweet reversal of a familiar scene in years past, where I would read to a compact Hank before he was old enough to read for himself.

Angela Hoke   *A Whisper of Smoke*

Between Calvin and Hank, I didn't have the opportunity to sink too far into the abyss, and after a while I found that I was no longer sinking.

Now the pain was no longer sharp, except when someone mentioned Chip's name or I happened to see him. After I made it through the first few weeks, I only suffered the stabbing pain the one time that I actually ran into Chip and Patty out on a date. Thankfully, Shelly had been there to remove me quickly from the premises and help re-assemble my shattered pieces with cheerful (on Shelly's part) Chip-bashing and milkshakes.

As it turned out, those milkshakes were one of the few things that didn't make me feel nauseous and helped keep me from wasting away during my first weeks of mourning. Nonetheless, I lost over ten pounds, and all of my clothes hung off me. It was a good distraction when I had to alter all my clothes so that they fit my new gaunt frame.

Now, as I spun around on the tire swing, I looked at my thighs, finally thin, and thought about the price I'd paid for them. I sighed, not willing to go to the sad place.

"Hey, girlie," said Calvin, and I looked up as his face came into view, upside down.

"Hey," I replied, hauling myself up.

"Ready to walk with me?" he asked, offering me his hand.

"Sure. We're not riding today?"

"No, I thought we'd go for a walk around the pond, if that's okay," he said, looking at me tentatively. "I thought it might make it easier for us to talk," he added, then promptly turned his back on me as he led the way down the path to the pond.

I registered surprise, but quickly trotted to catch up.

We walked in silence for a while, as I waited for him to speak. I knew better than to try to engage him in idle chit-chat. He would clam right up if I chattered pointlessly, and I didn't want to do anything that might discourage him. But I was impatient with a burning curiosity.

When we got to the pond, the dragonflies were buzzing the water and the cat-tails were swishing the air clean. Calvin picked some rocks out of the dirt, and threw them over the water, watching them skip across.

I waited, my hair blowing around my face.

"I've decided to join the army," he said, so quietly that I thought I'd misheard him.

"I'm sorry, what did you say?"

"I've decided to join the army," he said again, and it made no more sense the second time I heard it.

I was momentarily speechless. "Wh-why?" I stuttered, too shocked for a more articulate response.

Calvin sighed, then flopped on the ground. He leaned over his knees, and pulled the fibers of a dandelion stem apart. I sat next to him, close.

"But why?" I asked again, once I'd regained control of my voice.

"You know I've always wanted to go to college, right?" he asked. I nodded, though he didn't seem to be waiting for a response. "I've been talking to my dad about it for the last couple of years, and he promised he would think about it. But now he says that we can't afford it and that he needs me on the farm."

I was silent, waiting for him to continue.

"When I tried to argue, he got real angry and silent. See, he never even finished high school. He thinks that I think I'm better than

Angela Hoke *A Whisper of Smoke*

him," he said, frustration in his voice as he ripped the poor weed to shreds.

"I'm sure he doesn't think that," I said gently. "He knows you better than that."

"I don't think so," he said bitterly. "I talked to my mom about it, hoping she would talk to him for me. She just said that he worked his whole life to build that farm so that he could pass it on to his children. Talk about a guilt trip. And that's so unlike her!"

"Hmmm," I said, listening and thinking.

"What *is* your dream?" I asked after a moment.

"To work with animals. Maybe be a veterinarian," he responded. Of course, I knew that. I'd always known that. How could his parents not realize it? Besides, Calvin was so smart, he was meant to go to college. He had scored very well on his SATs, and colleges were begging for him. But none of them could offer full scholarships, and even the reduced portion ascribed to him was too much.

"I want it so bad, Susanna. Not just that. I *don't* want to be a farmer," he said with force. "Don't get me wrong, I love the farm. But what I love are the animals. I don't enjoy the planting, or the harvesting, or any of the administration."

He put his head in his hands. "Am I being selfish? I don't want to let my parents down."

"You've never let anyone down in your whole life," I proclaimed without hesitation. *Think, Susanna,* I told myself, anxious to help him think this through.

At a loss, I went back to my original question. "So, what does all this have to do with the army?" I asked, half afraid to hear the answer.

He sighed again, and his eyes looked troubled. "If I join the army, I'll have to leave the farm. Dad won't be able to do anything about it. And I'll be serving my country, like he did when he was my age. Then, when I get done with my service, I can go to college on the GI bill," he explained.

I chewed on that. It seemed to make sense, but I was still uneasy. Then, with a rush, I realized why.

"You'll go to Vietnam," I whispered in shocked realization.

"Probably," he acknowledged. "Even if I stayed home, I'd probably get drafted anyway. I mean, it's not like I'd have a deferment for college." His voice was bitter and sad.

My mind raced as I absorbed all this. It was hard to sort out my thoughts, when they were clouded by acidic fear of Calvin going to war.

"What if... what if something happened to you?" I asked, my voice sounding far away.

"Sus, nothing's going to happen to me," he said with his half-smile, pushing me on the shoulder.

I must have looked doubtful, because he turned serious again. "Hey, really. I know how to use a gun like a pro. Nothing will happen to me."

"Are you sure you want to do this?" I asked, turning to look into his eyes. He held my gaze, and his eyes softened.

"Yes," he said, then hesitated. "I don't see any other way. The thought of being trapped here on the farm, giving up any chance for a different future... Well, it's unbearable."

"Then I support you," I said, reaching out and squeezing his hand.

"Thanks." He flashed a weak smile.

Then his expression faltered.

"How will Dad get the work done, though, if I'm not here?" he asked, as though talking to himself. He put his head on his arms. He looked suddenly deflated.

I snorted. "Well, Elton sure could pitch in a lot more. He's just a big old lump, always letting you do all the work."

Calvin laughed. "He's an athlete."

"Athlete, shmathlete. When you were his age, you worked five times as much as he does. Let *him* help your dad out. It will do him good."

He smiled at my fierce expression, then turned serious again. "I know you're probably right," he said. "So does that mean you think I'm doing the right thing?" he asked hopefully.

I looked at him for a long moment. Could I truthfully tell him what he wanted to hear? Again, my mind was flooded with nightmarish thoughts of Calvin in danger.

His eyes were so earnest, I couldn't bear to be the one that upset him.

"I think that you should do whatever you believe is right for you," I said, hedging.

His shoulders visibly relaxed. "Thanks, Susanna." He reached out and squeezed my hand, a return gesture for the squeeze I gave him before. "It means a lot to me that you support me. Christine didn't react quite so well."

Hmm, Christine! Well, she wouldn't, now would she? Because SHE'S NOT RIGHT FOR YOU! my mind screamed.

He shook his head. "Man, I can't believe I'm going to be graduating in two weeks."

A Whisper of Smoke   *Angela Hoke*

I can't believe you're turning eighteen in a couple of weeks, and that you'll most likely be going to war shortly thereafter, I thought grimly. But I didn't vocalize it. I figured that those thoughts were better left unspoken, lest I risk losing Calvin's trust. And I cherished being his confidante, especially knowing that Christine was being unsupportive. I liked the thought of him contrasting us this way.

But I wasn't supporting him just so I could look good compared to Christine. I would never do that, not when his life was potentially at risk. I was supporting him because... well, because I *believed* in Calvin, more than I'd ever believed in anything or anyone (except God, of course).

I believed in him with my whole heart, and I trusted implicitly that he would do what was right, and what was best. With the tiniest part of my brain that harbored the smallest sliver of doubt, I prayed that my trust wasn't misplaced in this case.

"Are you going to tell your parents?" I asked, and he knew at once that I was not talking about graduation.

"No, I can't," he said. "If I tell them, it will just upset them, and it won't change anything. I'm just going to wait until my birthday and when I go register for the draft, I'm going to swing by the army recruitment office."

He said this so nonchalantly that I just stared at him.

"What?" he demanded.

"You're just going to 'swing by the army recruitment office'?" I mimicked. "You make it sound so... insignificant."

"What would you rather I say? That I'm going to sign my life away with the armed services harbingers of death?" he said with a smirk, but clearly trying to tease me.

I glared at him. "This is *not* funny," I insisted. "Listen, I respect your choice. And I know why you think you have to make it. And again, I totally support you if you are *sure* that this is the right thing for you. I mean, answer to prayer, destiny, fate, meant to be, and all that."

He looked at me. "Okay...," he said warily, waiting for me to continue.

"But you listen here, mister. You can't make a decision like this and ignore the fact that you will be putting your life at risk. You have to accept that you could DIE, and decide whether you are still driven to make this decision. But if you are doing it out of rebellion, or avoidance, or whatever, you better think again. Because so help me, I'll come to boot camp, or Saigon, or wherever and kick your ass right back home again!"

My chest was heaving with emotion as I finished, and I glared at Calvin, daring his smirk to reappear. His mouth twitched and he burst into laughter. Then he uncharacteristically grabbed me in a big bear hug.

"I love you to death, you know that?" he said into my hair, chuckling.

Oh, how I wish you'd left out the 'to death' part of that sentence, I thought. *I know the translation for that is 'I love you like a sweet, sometimes cute, but never sexy little sister.' Damn it all!*

"Yeah, yeah," I said with a muffled voice, pressed, as I was, against Calvin's substantial side. I pushed myself away, not able to withstand the closeness without severe repercussions.

"So Christine didn't take it well?" I said, trying to divert the discussion.

"Uh, no. That's an understatement. Every time I talk to her, she berates me and cries. I finally had to tell her I changed my mind, because I was afraid she'd rat me out."

"You *lied*?" I was astonished.

"I know, I know," he said, putting his head in his hands again. "I'm a terrible person."

"No, you're not," I told him, instantly softening, eager to console him.

"I just can't stand to see her hurt," he added, and I harrumphed with barely concealed disgust. I crossed my arms, and tried not to look annoyed.

"Do you really think she'd tell on you?"

"Yes, in a heartbeat, if she thinks it would keep me here. But what she doesn't realize is that it would destroy me to stay. The closer I get to graduation and the knowledge that my life is pretty much set after that, the more panicky I feel. It makes me feel like I have no future. At least now I feel like I've got a chance – that my life doesn't have to end at eighteen."

At that, I was sick in the pit of my stomach and a dark chill raced up and down my spine. I hoped it wasn't some kind of bad premonition. I shook my head to clear it.

We were quiet for a while, sitting side by side in one of the most peaceful places imaginable.

"What can I do?" I asked. "How can I help you?"

Calvin turned to me and smiled that adorable, heart-melting half-smile. There was some version of love in his eyes, though I was sure it was that sisterly kind, as he said, "You can support me when no one else does. And you can keep my secret, for now."

Angela Hoke   *A Whisper of Smoke*

"You got it," I replied, meaning it. After all, I would do anything for Calvin – even if it took him away from me. I just prayed that this was the right thing.

Chapter 15: It's My Party and You'll Cry If I Want You To

Calvin went off to Basic Training right after graduation. He wrote and called occasionally, but he seemed distracted and weary so I kept the conversations light. After eight weeks, he moved on to AIT, his advanced training, and I was beginning to ache from his absence. Summer was a dry husk of nothing without him.

Then, as his formal training was coming to a close, he officially received his orders – infantry, in Vietnam, of course. I was devastated but Calvin seemed resigned. After a few private cries in the boughs of the old oak tree, I worked to pull myself together. Somehow I reined in my boiling emotions and kept them locked away so that when he came home for his final leave before going over, he didn't seem to notice that my heart was in tatters. And, together, we spent the last month riding and swimming and laughing with all the kids, and acting as though we would be young forever.

Now it was time to really say good-bye, and I wasn't sure if I could. I felt unstable, as though those emotions I'd so carefully locked up were on the verge of a revolt.

"Are you sure that I'm allowed to go to this party?" Shelly asked, snapping me back to the present. Shelly was peering at her profile in the mirror, sticking out her chest in different postures.

"Yeah, of course. Calvin said he'd love for you to come," I said, as I pulled on my pants and shook my head to dislodge the lurking despair. My hands shook as I tried to fasten the button at the waist. My fingers kept slipping off, and finally I just sighed and flopped backward on the bed.

Shelly came over and flopped down beside me.

"What's wrong," she asked, as we lay side by side looking at the popcorn ceiling.

"I just can't believe he's going," I said quietly, my voice thickening.

"Why don't you tell him how you feel?" Shelly asked.

"What are you talking about?" I replied, wiping a tear away.

This time Shelly sighed, as she propped herself up on her side, her hand under her head.

"I'm talking about the fact that you're in love with him," she said with no trace of flippancy.

I looked over at her, poised to deny it. But when I looked into my friend's eyes, my face crumpled. I covered it with my hands and wept.

"Aw, Sus," Shelly said, as she rubbed my arm. "Let me get you some tissues."

She retrieved a box of tissues from the dresser and handed them to me.

"I am so scared, Shelly," I whispered through my tears. "I'm terrified that something will happen to him."

"Have you told him that?" she asked gently.

"No, I can't!" I wailed. "I promised him I would support him, especially since his family is having such a hard time with it. I can't add to his pain." I paused to blow my nose. "Plus, I don't want to make him doubt his decision. It's not like he can change it now anyway. And he needs all his confidence to survive." When I finished, I burst into tears again.

"You really do love him, don't you?" Shelly said. "I've known it for a long time, but it has been even more obvious since you and Chip broke up. You should hear the way you talk about him – your voice gets all dreamy, and you smile like a big goof. But I don't think I ever realized before just how *much* you love him." She was looking at me with an expression that was a cross between aching sympathy and amazement. "You never loved Chip like this, did you," she said as an afterthought, not really a question.

I didn't respond. I closed my eyes and took deep breaths.

"You should tell him how you feel," Shelly said again, this time as a suggestion.

"How can I?" I whispered, not denying my feelings. I realized it felt good for Shelly to know.

"How can you *not*?" Shelly asked. "He's going to *war*. You may never get this chance again."

She stopped when she saw my face.

"I'm not saying that something is going to happen to him," Shelly added quickly. "But something could," she added, her voice kind. "Give him something real to come home to."

"He's with Christine. He *loves* her," I protested.

"He loves you, too," Shelly countered. "You know he does. He may not even realize how much."

"I know he loves me, but he loves me like a sister, or at most, like a best friend."

Angela Hoke   *A Whisper of Smoke*

"Please," Shelly said, rolling her eyes. "You guys are starting to piss me off!"

"Sorry," I said, my voice wavering.

"Oh, good grief," Shelly said, rubbing my arm again. "I didn't mean it… Or, I did, but I didn't mean to make you cry."

"I know," I sobbed, covering my face.

"You have to tell him tonight, Susanna. You will never forgive yourself if you don't. You don't really want to look back, years from now, and wonder what might have been if you'd only had the courage to tell him you love him."

I didn't answer right away. I was trying to get my emotions under control, and using the time to think about what Shelly said.

"What if he rejects me? What if he tells me that he doesn't feel that way about me?" I whispered.

"Well, then at least you'll know," Shelly said, compassion in her voice. "And you can send him off with all the best wishes and prayers that he needs from his very best friend."

My eyes filled with tears again, and they spilled over, running down my temples and into my hair.

"Okay, enough of that. Let's get your face washed. You've got to fix your make-up, or you're going to scare small children," Shelly joked, trying to lighten the mood.

"Right," I said, letting my very good friend hoist me off the bed.

By the time we walked across the road heading to the campfire in the heart of Calvin's going-away party, my face looked almost normal. It would probably pass as such in the darkness. My eyes scanned the large group of people standing around, clusters of dark silhouettes flickering in the firelight. As we got close, I could see Mrs. Conner standing stiffly next to a table of food and drinks, looking like she was barely holding herself together. As I watched, Mr. Conner walked up and squeezed Mrs. Conner's hand, making her jump but then smile a rueful smile when she realized it was him. It was very sweet, and also very uncharacteristic – I knew that Mr. Conner was not an outwardly affectionate man.

"Susanna!" a voice called, and Hank came running towards me, followed closely by Elton. I smiled at the open expression on my brother's face, but then noticed that when he called my name, many people turned to look at us.

That's when I saw Calvin. And my stomach fluttered uneasily.

Christine was right beside him, of course, and she glanced at me for a moment, then quickly turned away, focusing her attention back to the people around her. Calvin's gaze lingered though, his face looking anxious to my practiced perspective. He gave me a small wave and that half-smile that melted my heart.

"Susanna, are you listening to me?" Hank asked, shaking my arm.

"Oh, sorry," I said, shifting my focus back to my excited brother.

"Calvin's giving me his comic book collection! Can you believe it?" Hank asked, his excitement bubbling over as he nearly jumped up and down.

I glanced at Elton. "Elton, didn't you want them?"

"Naaa," Elton replied. "I'm not really into comic books. He gave me his Colt 45."

Angela Hoke   *A Whisper of Smoke*

My eyes grew large. "I don't want to hear that you boys are playing with a gun, *ever*," I said firmly.

Elton rolled his eyes. "Don't worry. My dad won't let me use it until I'm fifteen. It's locked in his gun case. But *then* it will be mine!"

"Well, that's a relief," I said, meaning it. Then I wondered with mild alarm, *why is Calvin giving away his things?*

"C'mon, Sus," Shelly was saying, tugging on my arm.

"Well, well, well," Elton said, noticing Shelly for the first time. "What have we here? *Two* gorgeous girls!"

I tried to suppress a giggle. Elton was becoming such a flirt!

"Well, aren't you a cute thing?" Shelly said, eating it up. "How old are you, anyway?"

I could have sworn I saw his blush, even in the darkness.

"I'm twelve," he said standing up to his full height, proud of his almost teenage status.

"Well, I tell you what – in about ten years, you give me a call." She ruffled his hair, and walked away. Hank snickered at Elton's love-struck expression, as I followed my friend towards the rest of the guests.

I saw my mom and dad sitting together on a bale of hay, drinking beers and looking out of place but not uncomfortable. They were both smiling – even Mother, and with no trace of condescension. I felt a surge of affection for them, slightly softening my resolve to be angry for what happened with Annabelle and how easily they forgave Uncle George... Well, I didn't want to think about that right now.

Everyone in my family was there, even Lorelei with her new boyfriend Mark. Lorelei's friend Martin was also there, looking jealous as he glared at Mark with his arms crossed. *How can she be so oblivious?* I thought, shaking my head.

Calvin's whole family was there, too, of course, as were all the kids from the neighborhood and several of his friends. There were also two uptight people standing next to Christine looking awkward and anti-social, and I guessed that they must be her parents.

Shelly was chomping at the bit to dive into the throng of people and start socializing. I wished her good luck, but couldn't make myself fake social niceties just yet. Instead, I headed to the keg and, when no one appeared to be looking, furtively poured myself a large tumbler of beer. Even though I didn't really like it, and I was technically too young to drink, I craved the numbness that it could provide.

It was unusual for me to drink, so no one really paid much attention when I casually refilled my cup, time after time. By the time the party was in full swing, my perception had grown fuzzy. I *did* feel calmer, and for that I was grateful. I sat alone on a hay bale, watching everyone else, and I gradually noticed that the older folks had started to thin out, so that it was mostly teenagers that remained. I sought out Calvin, and found him in a group of his friends, Christine holding his hand in both of hers, standing in his shadow.

Now that I was a little more in control of my emotions, I wanted to spend some time with him. But I couldn't bring myself to go over with Christine glued to his side.

Shelly came over and plopped down beside me. "So, how are you doing?"

"I'm fine," I said, turning to my friend, just a moment later than my brain intended. It was like there was a slight time delay between my brain's instructions and my actions.

"Are you *drunk*?" Shelly asked incredulously. She peered into my eyes, looking for signs. "Oh, my gosh. You ARE!" she cried, then started laughing. "I've never seen drunk Susanna before. This should be entertaining."

"No, no. I don't think I could ever compare to you when you're inebriated. By the way, aren't you drinking tonight?" I asked, surprised.

"No, damn it. I haven't been able to get past the keg Nazis over there," she replied, gesturing to the post that Mabel and her friend Walter had taken up in front of the table. "They are only letting people that are eighteen or older get a drink."

Then she turned to me. "How did *you* get booze?"

"No one paid any attention to me," I said, shrugging. "I guess I'm just not as noticeable as you."

"Yeah, right," Shelly said acerbically. "They are just used to you being a goody two-shoes, you mean."

"No, I'm definitely not that. I'm not as good as people may think," I said, feeling dangerously close to some kind of confession, but Shelly blew it off.

"So, have you talked to Calvin yet?" she prodded.

"No. How can I, with that waif stuck to his side like a barnacle?"

"Good point," Shelly acknowledged. Then she peered over at Calvin and Christine with calculation in her eyes.

"I wonder if I could get her away from him somehow..." she mused, tapping her bottom lip with one finger.

"No, Shelly. Don't bother. Besides, I don't think it's possible. Unless, that is, you brought an anti-fungal with you."

Shelly burst into laughter. "I *like* drunk Susanna!" she declared, then excused herself to go back to the guys she'd been talking to before.

I waved her away, content to sit by myself in the glow from the fire. I was in a bit of a daze, and so didn't notice Calvin standing there at first.

"Hey, Susanna," he said, taking the seat vacated by Shelly.

"Hi!" I breathed. *Don't be desperate,* I scolded myself.

"Were you ever going to come talk to me?" he asked, looking a little hurt. "It *is* my party, after all."

"I'm sorry," I said, meaning it. "I just didn't want to intrude on you and that Christine," inadvertently using the 'that' qualifier that I usually reserved for my private thoughts. He didn't seem to notice. "Where is she, by the way?" I asked quickly, trying to cover.

"She's getting her things together. I have to take her home. Her parents left earlier."

"Oh," I said.

"I was wondering – will you be here when I get back? It won't take me long, and I really want us to get to talk."

"Sure. I'll be right here."

"Great," he smiled and patted my hand. "Be back in a jiffy." And he was off.

As soon as he left, Shelly zoomed back over for the scoop.

"So, what did he say?" she asked urgently.

"He said he was taking that Christine home, and that he wanted me to wait for him. He wants to talk when he gets back."

Shelly fixed me with a hard stare.

"What?" I asked, not liking the intense scrutiny.

"You know this is going to be your chance, right?" she asked pointedly.

I closed my eyes. "Not this again," I muttered, noticing that I seemed to be swaying slightly.

"Yes, this," Shelly said firmly, taking me by the face and forcing me to pay attention.

"Don't chicken out on this, Susanna. I know you will regret it."

"We'll see," was all I could say. The truth was, part of me really wanted to tell Calvin ... well, *everything*. But the other part of me was scared to death of damaging our friendship.

I must have dozed off, because the next thing I knew, Shelly was making out with some boy on a hay bale across the way, the crowd had thinned out even more but those that were left were rowdier, and Calvin was striding across the grass towards me.

My stomach lurched as I wondered if Shelly was right – if this was my one chance. When he got to me, his eyes were flashing with intensity, and he grabbed my hand and pulled me away from the crowd.

"Where are we going?" I asked, stumbling beside him.

"To the barn. I want to say good-bye to my horses, and I want you to be with me," he replied, and I could swear that I heard him get a little choked up.

When we got into the barn, he left the lights off, so it took us a few minutes for our eyes to get accustomed to the even darker interior. I followed him around, wordlessly, as he went from stall to stall. In each one, he stood next to the horse's head and stroked it as he murmured into its ear.

Do I really need to be here for this? I wondered idly. But then he spoke, and I realized he was talking to me.

"So I guess I'm really going," he said in a defeated tone.

A Whisper of Smoke   *Angela Hoke*

"Yeah," I croaked, then cleared my throat to try again. "Yes, I guess you are," I said, and this time my voice sounded strong, rational.

"My dad is finally talking to me again," he offered.

"Calvin, I'm so glad. It was really sweet of them to throw this party for you."

"You have no idea. This has been ripping my mother apart. I think Dad was as mad about that as anything."

We were quiet for a moment.

Then, Calvin turned to me. "I'm scared, Susanna."

"Oh, Calvin," I said, rushing to him without a thought. I wrapped my arms around his middle and laid my head on his chest. He started, at first, with surprise, but then embraced me warmly, squeezing me tightly. He buried his face in my hair. His breath was hot, as was the rest of him. He radiated heat, like he did safety and security.

"I'm scared," he whispered, repeating it. "I can't tell anyone else that but you – not my parents, not Mabel and certainly not Christine. For them, I have to act like I know exactly what I'm doing, and that I'm sure it's the right thing."

I squeezed him tighter.

"But I'm not sure," he admitted in a soft voice. "I'm not sure at all, and now I'm scared to death that I've made a huge mistake."

My eyes welled up, but I held my tongue until I could be sure that my emotions were in check.

"Calvin," I said, drawing back gently so I could look up at him. Our faces were only a couple of inches apart, and, realizing the danger of such proximity, he let me go, and stepped back. He sat on a bale of hay and I sat on one across from him. We could hear the sounds of the party from outside, and the startling flutter of a barn owl in the rafters.

Angela Hoke   *A Whisper of Smoke*

"Anyone would be scared – you'd be crazy not to be. What you're feeling is totally normal, and it doesn't mean that you made the wrong decision," I said, with more conviction than I felt.

"Do you really think so?" he asked, his voice lilting with a vulnerability that was unnerving.

"Yes, I do," I said firmly, careful not to waiver in his presence. "Tell me this – before tonight, when you've been by yourself, alone in your thoughts and not influenced by crying moms or girlfriends, did you feel, in your gut, like it was the right decision?"

He hesitated. "Yes, I think I did," he said, then qualified it. "Well, I knew that it felt totally wrong to stay here and do nothing."

I was quiet as I thought about this. Frankly, I was disconcerted that he was not more sure that his decision had been the right one. But it was way too late to second guess. And he was probably right when he said he would likely be drafted anyway. In this moment, though, it was vitally important that I not reveal any doubts. He needed me to be strong for him.

"You are doing the right thing," I told him. "God would have convicted you strongly if it weren't. You would've felt it in your gut."

He looked at me, and I could see the little bit of filtered moonlight reflecting off his eyes. *No glasses!* Maybe he was hoping to view the night through a filter, too.

"I'm really going to miss you," he said softly, his eyes locked on mine.

My disobedient tear ducts sprung leaks again (*damn it!*).

"Come here," he said, patting the seat beside him. I went over to him, crying freely but silently.

A Whisper of Smoke   *Angela Hoke*

He looked into my face and wiped away my tears. His gaze held mine for a long while, then he smiled at me. It was the sweetest, most tender smile I'd ever seen.

"Calvin," I whispered. *Lord, be with me – here I go.*

"Hmmm?"

"I have something to tell you," I began.

"Okay," he said, reticence entering his eyes.

Be brave, and just do it!

"I'm…. I'm in love with you," I said, then ducked my head down.

There was silence. *Oh, no! What have I done?* I anxiously waited for him to say something. When seconds ticked by and he didn't, though, I began to get a little angry. I raised my head and met his gaze with indignation. Then my face fell at the sight of his obvious agony.

"Susanna…" he began in a tortured voice.

"Shhh," I said, then leaned forward and kissed him. His lips were just as soft and moist as I remembered, and I was filled with a surge of desire and love, fueling me to press hard against him. My hands found his shirt and gripped it in fistfuls. My tongue searched, and when it found his, it sent electric shocks down my body, through my middle. He felt it too, because all at once he grabbed me up and pushed me against the wall, as his hands ran all over me.

Oh lord, I was in ecstasy. It was surreal, like I had crossed over into my dream world without noticing the threshold. He was everywhere – his tongue probed me, and then he was kissing my neck and my ears. His hands moved down my back and brushed the hot skin of my waist where my shirt had ridden up. They settled there, burning me as he pulled me tight against his chest. Desire ripped through me and I wanted him with a ferocity that I had never experienced before.

Angela Hoke   *A Whisper of Smoke*

Then suddenly he pulled back, and stared at me with horror.

"Oh, no," he said, "Oh, God, no." He jumped up and away from me like I was on fire. Almost frantically, he paced across the short distance to the opposite stall and back again, three times in quick succession.

"What am I doing?" he asked himself, sounding wretched. "What have I done?"

"Calvin," I pleaded.

"No, Susanna, stop," he said, stopping to look at me. He looked down at where I sat in a puddle of exposed nerve-endings on the hay bale at his feet.

"This was so wrong," he said. "I am with Christine. I *love* Christine."

My eyes filled, as the delicate threads that held my heart together, already strained after my heartbreak with Chip, tore open and my heart fell apart into a million, unmendable pieces.

Though I couldn't see clearly through the tears that were streaming down my face now, I thought I saw his eyes soften a bit. But then they hardened again, not with anger but with determination.

"Susanna," he said, his voice gentler now. "I don't do this. I don't cheat on my girlfriend, not ever. I love Christine, and we are together."

"But Calvin, *I* love you," I said, now sobbing. All hope for dignity had been abandoned, as I literally and figuratively threw myself at his feet.

"*I* love you," I repeated again, grabbing his hand. He shook his head at me, trying to negate my proclamation, or trying to clear his own defiant thoughts, I wasn't sure.

"Susanna, no," he said, prying my fingers off. "I can't and won't do this. You know I'll always care deeply for you as my best friend, but... I love Christine. Please don't make me keep saying it. I don't want to hurt you."

"But you kissed me!" I blubbered piteously.

He hung his head in shame. "I know, and that was so, so wrong of me. It was ... a moment of weakness, and I sincerely apologize. You are very..." he paused, searching for the right words perhaps. "You are very attractive, and it would be hard for anyone to resist you when you ..."

"Throw myself at them, you mean," I said bitterly.

"No," he said, his voice kind. He sat down beside me again, but was careful to not touch me. "No, what I mean is, no man could resist kissing you if you got too close."

"Is that supposed to make me feel better?" I cried, tears and clear mucus spilling from my eyes and nose.

"Am I going to have to give you my t-shirt again?" he joked, trying to lighten the mood. I just bent over and put my head in my hands.

"Let me walk you home," he said. I was in no shape to argue, as I had become a blubbering mess.

He put his arm lightly around me, his body transmitting a clear message of, *Don't touch me inappropriately, and don't read too much into this,* as loudly as if he were saying it. I felt dejected, ripped in half, and all I could think now was that I wanted to get away from him, away from everyone, so that I could cry until my tears dried up, and try to somehow piece together my pulverized heart.

When we got outside, I saw Shelly looking around for us and finding us. Shelly's eyes grew wide, and she started toward us. Calvin made some gesture, and she stopped. She held up her open hand, showing *five,* as in she was giving us *five minutes* to get out whatever was left to be said, and then she was coming to comfort me.

Calvin nodded, and we kept walking towards my darkened house. It must be very late, I realized, and I was glad that no one was awake to see me like this.

When we got to the door, Calvin turned me towards him. I could not meet his eyes.

"Susanna, I'm very, very sorry I let this happen. I hope you understand when I tell you that I..." he sighed a huge sigh, like he carried the weight of the world on his shoulders. "That I don't think I can be around you anymore. I shouldn't have betrayed Christine like that, and I won't betray her anymore by continuing ... this."

I started to collapse, and he caught me. *This cannot be happening! Why, oh why did I tell him? WHY?*

Shelly ran up just then and swooped in to take me away from Calvin. Though she hadn't heard the conversations, she read the meaning in our body language and the atmosphere around us.

"You can go now," she said to Calvin, her voice cold.

He nodded once, and was gone.

Shelly half carried, half dragged me into the house, up the stairs and into the bedroom. She lay down on the twin bed with me, and held me until I fell asleep. My last thoughts as I drifted off were of Calvin, and how I hoped this nightmare would be over when I woke up tomorrow.

Calvin left three days later, without saying good-bye. My nightmare had just begun.

A Whisper of Smoke   *Angela Hoke*

Chapter 16: Sexy Girl Next-Door

October 10, 1968

Dear Calvin,

I have waited as long as I could, trying to hold out, but I can't take it any longer. I've tried to respect your wishes. I realize that I shouldn't have said the things I said to you at your going away party. You are with someone, and you clearly love each other. She even seems like a nice girl, if you go for the big eyes, gorgeous hair and adorable smile look (I guess everyone has a weakness...). Anyway, kidding aside, I know that it is inappropriate for me to try to interfere with that. But please try to understand that I was afraid I might never ... well, that I might not see you for a very long time. I just wanted you to know how I feel, even if you didn't feel the same way. Okay, that's not really true. I fantasized that you would suddenly realize you felt the same way about me. Don't worry, though – that delusion has been thoroughly squashed. Your virtue is intact, even if my heart is in pieces. (Sigh)

I've re-read my first paragraph, and I am an idiot. But since I have already made a fool of myself, I might as well continue. After all, without you as my best friend, I have absolutely nothing left to lose. Calvin, you are and have always been precious to me. It breaks my heart to think I can no longer have you in my life, just because I was stupid enough to express my feelings for you. So this is where I find myself in a little bit of a conundrum. I could lie and say that I was drunk and that I

Angela Hoke   A Whisper of Smoke

didn't mean it, that I didn't mean all the embarrassing things I said, but I don't think I can do that. As tempting as it is to pretend like it never happened (even if it would help me regain a little of my dignity), what I feel for you is too special for me to dishonor it that way. And even though my memory of that night is a little fuzzy, I did mean it – every word.

No, I can't and won't take it back, but that doesn't keep me from wishing that I had not made my ill-fated confession to you that terrible night. I do desperately wish that I had continued to keep it to myself, as painful as it might be for me – even though there was a satisfying release in finally telling you how I feel, like the words finally loosed the knot that had been in my stomach since our magical (at least for me) first kiss, and even though it was like I had unlocked a secret place in my heart, filling me up with all the rushing, overpowering emotions I had suppressed for so long. Still, I would undo it all if it meant that I would not lose you. You know I hate crying, but I have shed a river of tears since you left. Even now, the place between my eyes is burning, threatening to unleash the pain again. If you see a drop or two on this letter, please ignore – I guess I have a girly side after all.

This is about the tenth version of this letter I've written – I kept starting it, thinking that I could be detached and just your friend, hoping that I could reverse time. But they all seemed so false. With you leaving, and with everything else that has happened, I've come to feel that life is too short to hold back and not share my feelings for you. Besides, I want, no, I need to be authentic with you, especially. I've always felt my most authentic with you anyway, and I refuse to become disingenuous now.

So instead of trying to pretend that our fateful conversation (i.e., pathetic admission on my part) never happened, I'm going to embrace that it did. I'm going to find joy knowing that you know how much I care for you, and that I'm praying every morning and every night that you will be safe, even if it is so you can come back home to Christine and enjoy homemade muffins and drink tea from little breakable cups while her mother and father talk about golf handicaps and which undesirable has just been allowed to join the country club (gasp!). I'm sure that will all be very... comforting. Actually, I'm being snide. I'm sure she will wrap you up in love like a tight little tamale, or like a tightly swaddled baby that she can cuddle and bottle-feed. (Sorry! I can't help myself).

No, I can't pretend that I don't feel the way I feel or that I didn't say the things I said. But I do promise to try very hard not to make you feel uncomfortable with me, and not to pressure you for anything more than your wonderful friendship – if only, if only you will just give me another chance to be your friend.

I know you, you stubborn, good man – I know that you will likely not wish to correspond with me anyway, either to avoid the appearance of impropriety or (in my fantasy!) because you don't want to be tempted by me. If that is your decision, I will (try to) respect it. And, I will say this only once – if you ever decide to dump sweet adorable Christine, I love you, and I want you, and I am here.

Since I'm writing this in a letter and don't have to see the rejection on your face, and since I doubt you'll write me back anyway (though if you do, I promise to limit the proclamations from now on), I would like to have this one last chance to tell you what's in my heart (since I was so rudely interrupted before). Anyway, here goes – I love you! I love you. And, seriously, I love you. You are an amazing person, to whom I could attribute a thousand incredible adjectives – however, I'm trying not to go overboard (if you ever change your mind about me, I'll list

Angela Hoke   *A Whisper of Smoke*

them out, a kiss at a time). Speaking of kisses, I have relived our campfire kiss a million times. It, by far, was the most amazing kiss I've ever had. (In fact, I'm tingling even as I write this ... okay, I know you'll say that's crossing the line. Sorry – I won't bring it up again.)

In all seriousness, I miss you so very much – I will always, always cherish the friendship we shared, even if you choose never to be my friend again. Regardless of whether you decide to let me back into your life or not, the fact remains that I really do love you, as much as we both might wish it weren't so. And if the love of a silly girl from your hometown, a girl that has known you since you were a goofy little boy, can make prayers more powerful, then you will be mightily protected over there. And that is what I want more than anything else in the world.

All my love (heartbreaking but true),
always,
Susanna

* * *

October 1968

Dear Susanna,

I should not be writing you back, and you should not be writing me at all. It was painful enough saying what had to be said the first time. You know that I care very much for you and I would never want to hurt you. But it's not just that. It also feels disrespectful to my relationship with Christine. It's even hard to write those words, because then I have to admit I know it's disrespectful yet here I am doing it anyway. But really, you should have listened to me. This is a bad idea.

I know all of those things, but my heart doesn't care.

The fact of the matter is, I have an overwhelming compulsion to write back to you. You've been my best friend since we were kids. I always felt a strong connection to you, but even more so this past year. You make me feel safe. You make me feel that no matter how much I might change, you will always see the real me. You'll know I'm still in there somewhere, even if I am no longer sure. That's an incredibly wonderful quality in a friendship, especially when you are over here.

Geesh, I'm not making any sense. I'm not very good at expressing my feelings and it's probably dangerous to try too hard. Besides, it makes me feel exposed. I'm guessing you're thinking I'm being vague. I'm hoping you won't be too frustrated with me, and then I feel guilty for worrying about what you think of me.

I'm praying for forgiveness for many things these days. And even though I know it's wrong, writing to you is not even close to the worst of them. Maybe you can tell me how this sin ranks in the severity of sins ... you Catholics are expert at that (and no, I'm not making fun of you, at least not much – but if this is a mortal sin, I need to know it right away!! I can't afford many of those where I am.)

Anyway, here's the point. Even though I know it's wrong, and you really should stay away from me, I would really like it if you would consider being my best friend again while I'm here. I can't promise you anything, Susanna, when I get back. I'm so sorry. I have to be honest with you on that point, while I'm hoping that you will be gracious and wonderful enough to be there for me anyway. I hate to ask you for anything, because I don't deserve it. But Susanna, I need you. I'm finding that I need you more than I could have imagined. Is it bravery or cowardice that I can only admit that to you on paper, and from 8,000 miles away?

Angela Hoke   *A Whisper of Smoke*

You probably think I'm selfish for saying in one breath that we can't be together, and in the next breath begging you to be the wonderful best friend you've always been. I have no explanation for how I can be so selfish. It's just that everyone over here has people that love them but who can never know the truth of this place. And then there are those special few who can know it all and, somehow, love us anyway. I know I have no right to ask, but I am asking whether that person, for me, can be you.

I have no right to expect anything from you, and I have no idea how you'll respond to this letter. You might tell me to go to hell, but frankly, I'm already there. I hope that you won't. I'll be anxiously awaiting a response. I hope that I haven't overstepped too far.

> Your very true friend –
> always and forever,
> Calvin

P.S. I promise that, if you'll agree to keep writing to me, I will not be so self-absorbed next time. I very, very much want to know how you are. I confess that I've read and re-read your letter about a hundred times, and you still make me laugh – even from across the world.

* * *

October 22, 1968

Dear Calvin,

You crazy thing! What part of me adoring you and being here for *you do you not understand? I thought I made that clear in my last letter, but maybe I didn't. Granted, you did crush my dreams of us being together into dust beneath your olive drab army boot. I won't lie – that did hurt. But after I wallowed for three or four days, I decided that I would be here for you no matter what. (Am I successfully hiding my devastation beneath false bravado? I hope so. It would be awfully embarrassing to continue to be so transparent, even after your repeated rejection.)*

Seriously, I understand what you are saying, and I am working hard to accept it. The truth is, I couldn't refuse you no matter what. I miss you like crazy, and I'm willing to take any part of you I can get. And as for you writing to me despite your guilty conscience, that is a minor sin – say two 'Hail Marys' and call it a day. (Do you even know the words to 'Hail Mary'? I'm betting not, you poor Protestant fool).

How has it been over there? I heard that you've learned some demolitions. Hank and Elton think it's the cat's meow to be able to blow stuff up. Personally, I can't imagine you doing that. I can, however, picture you with your rifle slung over your broad shoulder, sweat streaming down your forehead as you traipse through the jungle, your muscles rippling under your t-shirt... Okay, this line of thought is not doing me any good.

So what has it been like? I think it is still the rainy season over there – is that right? I'm so curious as to what the landscape is like. I'm picturing Tarzan vines and swinging monkeys. Is it like that? I know that you hate snakes – have you seen many? It seems like you might be more prepared than some of the guys, since at least you've been camping many times and have been shooting for years. Is that a completely naive comment? Over the course of our correspondence, I may ask many foolish questions. I'm not going to be obsessing over that though. I'm afraid it might inhibit my letters, and I know that you seek total honesty.

I can't imagine what it must be like to be fighting an enemy in the jungle. Do you know where the enemy is, or are you literally wondering if they are hiding behind every tree? Maybe you can't answer that. I'm not asking where you are or where the enemy is, I'm just wondering whether, generally speaking, you have, I guess, a front-line. It seems so different from the way it must have been to fight the Germans. Every night, I try to picture where you might be, what you might be experiencing (ignoring the fact that when it's night here, it's the next morning over there). Can you see the sky, or is the jungle too dense? Can you sleep at all, or is it too scary and dangerous to even close your eyes? I hope that you at least find enough rest so that you are sharp and alert when you need to be. I'm sending a thousand prayers to that effect, and for protection for you and your friends.

I feel like I'm hounding you with questions. I'll give you a chance to respond to these before I ask any more. In the meantime, I'll tell you what's been going on around here. So Chip (asshole) is going steady with a girl named Holly White. She's as pure as her name implies, and while I hate her with a cursory enmity, I also feel a little sorry for her. I'm not sure what kind of bull Chip has fed her, but I have no doubt that he's messing around with other girls while he's dating her because I'm sure that she's not given it up to him yet. She's a good girl – just the kind of challenge he loves. (Is it weird to you that I'm talking about my ex-boyfriend? If we were dating, I wouldn't mention Chip at all. But since you've made it painfully clear that we are not together, I figured what the hell – all's fair in love and, ironically, war.)

So not sure if I've mentioned that I have since found out that he had been cheating on me (I know, you're probably thinking big shocker). But it was, actually – a big shock, that is. And when I found out through the grapevine a few weeks ago, even though I don't love him anymore (at least, not like I did), it was like I had been punched in the stomach. But oddly, at the same time, it felt like it was proof of what I'd suspected all along. I don't mean that I knew he was a lying, cheating bastard, I didn't. I just couldn't believe that he really loved me – not deep down. I always felt a seed of doubt. I chalked it up to a self-esteem issue on my part. But now I think it was my women's intuition screaming out to me, but I didn't know how to interpret it. Damn it. I did love him (but not like ... never mind). I did.

Here's what I've learned after two months of solitude and self-reflection -- sometimes love just isn't enough. I used to think that you would only fall in love if it was destiny – God's will. Now I believe that there are many people that you can fall in love with, some that are good for you and some that are bad. But I still believe that there is one person you are meant to be with. I can't help it – I'm still a hopeless romantic. Maybe it's the poet in me.

We're going to have our first school dance week after next. A month ago, when I didn't have Chip or you anymore, I would have told you there was no way I would want to go. I was pretty depressed. But now I have my best friend back, my memories of Chip and what happened are still painful but they are dulling, and I'm looking as good as ever (Ha! Joking on that one). I'm feeling quite a bit better, and I think I'm going to let Shelly drag me along. It will probably be fun.

I guess that's it for now. I could probably write a book to you, but then you would have to wait forever to get my letter. And I have to save

Angela Hoke   A Whisper of Smoke

something for next time, right? I'm sending you two Hardy Boys paperbacks from Hank and a Perry Mason paperback from Dad. If there is anything else you need or would like, will you please tell me? You can ask for anything at all. I'm here for you, now and for always.

Love your incredibly sexy
girl next-door,
Susanna

* * *

October 1968

Dear Sexy Girl Next-door,

It was so good to get your letter! You are the greatest to agree to still be my friend even after all that happened between us. Thank you, Sus. You'll never know how much that means to me. And before I get too distracted with my own meager problems, I want to say that Chip is a fool and a royal jackass to cheat on you and to let you go. You deserve a hundred, no a thousand times better than him. Trust your intuition next time. I've always found that you have excellent instincts. Please don't settle for less than you deserve, and you deserve the very best.

I'm going to try to answer some of your questions. You asked so many, it may take me several letters to get to them all. But don't stop asking questions – I love your inquisitive nature as much as ever.

You are right – I can't tell you where I am or what I know about the enemy. I will tell you that I have never been so wet in my entire life. It is the rainy season, as you thought, and I never knew that it could rain so much. It rains all day, straight down in buckets. Non-stop rain. Nowhere to get dry. My biggest fantasy right now is sitting in a big armchair in a cozy den, my feet warmed by a roaring fire, and drinking a beer. When I think I'm about to go nuts, I try to go there in my mind. It doesn't really work, but I continue to try anyway.

You'll probably notice that these pages have been wet. I keep them in a plastic bag, but as I'm sitting here writing to you, it is impossible to keep them completely dry. It's first light, and I'm sitting in my hooch on the edge of my air mattress holding my poncho over my head with one hand so I can attempt to write to you on my lap with the other. Sometimes I make it through with the letter intact, but other times a gust of wind blows rain in and your letter melts away. Let's hope this one survives.

There is a period some nights, from about 2:00 am to around 6:00 am, when the rain stops for some reason. It happened last night, and we were rewarded not just with a reprieve from the rain but also with an explosion of stars, glimpsed through windows in the canopy. Me and Max agreed to pull the hooch flaps back so we could lie on our backs looking up at them. The Milky Way was clearer than I've ever seen, even from the darkest corners of our farm. I marveled at it, just as I tried to ignore my mind's subconscious association of lights in the night sky to the Mad Minutes that are as terrifying as they can be reassuring.

For those brief moments, it seems unbelievable that the rain will start up again in just a few hours. And looking up at the stars through the trees, as I listened to Max muffling his belches and smelled his dirty sweat beside me, I could pretend, for just a moment, that I was camping out with a friend in the woods behind my house.

The rain is not pounding yet, but it's steaming. I'm hoping the socks I'm wearing inside my shirt can dry a bit more before I have to put them on. I've got two pairs of socks, one that I keep in a plastic bag during the day and the other that I wear. They never get totally dry, but every night I put on a dry t-shirt and

Angela Hoke   A Whisper of Smoke

put my socks against my bare chest, hoping they'll be mostly dry before I have to put them back on. Does it sound like I'm obsessed with my wet feet? I am. We can get jungle rot if we can't get them dry enough, and that is disgusting and painful.

In the dry season, apparently, you are dying for water. That seems impossible to imagine right now.

I will admit that I was scared shitless the first month of my tour. I was so scared that I might be killed, I don't think I slept a wink. And I didn't fire a single round until I had been here for three weeks. I was worthless.

The difference now is that I've come to accept that I am going to die here.

I'm thinking that might shock you. Please don't freak out. I need you to be strong and not overreact to what I tell you. I need to be able to tell someone.

Anyway, I know I'm going to die here. We all do. Knowing that is the only thing that makes it bearable. It takes the fear away. There is a feeling of invincibility to know that your destiny is to die fighting – I think it provides some clarity. It's very important to have clarity in a fight. It helps tremendously when you have to make life and death decisions by instinct and in a matter of seconds.

We only have a couple of cherries on our squad at the moment. Their inexperience is dangerous. And their naked longing for home is hard to take, since we've all worked so hard to suppress such thoughts. Hopefully, they'll pull themselves together and live long enough to know what they're doing. Does that sound callous? I hope not. Please don't think me uncaring. I love these guys already – they are like brothers, but more. It's just our coping mechanism. We can't feel it too much, or we'll become paralyzed by fear. My fear now is that I'll suffer another kind of paralysis – a numbness of spirit from not feeling for too long.

A Whisper of Smoke   *Angela Hoke*

I had a good buddy, Sanchez, that got killed a few days ago. We called him Sanchez because he had Indian blood in him – Pueblo, from Arizona. His real name was William. He was our squad leader, and he was killed in an ambush that killed him and two of the other guys that were walking point. He was in his second tour, poor bastard. Anyway, four of them got into the kill zone before the first guy, we called him Tank, hit the trip wire. Then all hell broke loose. At least they didn't know what hit them.

Sanchez was a good guy – couldn't hold his liquor worth a lick, but great in a fight. He had a girl back home. They were supposed to get married when he got back. Now we have a Shake'n'Bake lieutenant, green as baby shit. I can't tell yet if he's going to be a good leader or not. If he doesn't get killed, maybe he'll be alright.

I've got to go now. We're packing up to head out. Please tell Hank and your dad that I said thank you for those books. My entire squad thanks them. We are passing them all around to keep the boredom away – it's a much less hazardous distraction than our other main pastime, combat. We love to get care packages – cigarettes, cookies, books, magazines are all great. But don't feel pressured to send anything but your lovely letters. They are what I find myself looking forward to most.

Your strapping soldier-boy,
Calvin

P.S. Will you send me a picture of you? I've been sharing a bit of your letters with the guys. They think you are funny and sound sexy as hell. They are dying to see what you actually look like (they won't be disappointed).

Chapter 17: My Dear Strapping Soldier-Boy

November 3, 1968

Dear Strapping Soldier-boy,

I love that salutation! It fits into my fantasy of you quite well. Again, I'm picturing you (especially now, after your description of the constant rain) soaking wet, your clothes melded to your body, outlining your firm chest, your... I have to stop this! Are you trying to encourage me? Don't answer that. I don't want you to feel guilty and I don't want you to stop being, well, harmlessly flirty. I won't expect anything as a result. And if I'm making you uncomfortable with my retorts, tell me and I'll stop (as long as you stop egging it on!). But if you are okay with it, if it brings a smile to your face (or a chill down your middle – a girl can dream!), then don't stop. You deserve this minor diversion. Say another four 'Hail Marys' and you're slate will be wiped clean – you can flirt and fantasize about me all you want! (And I've included a prayer book, for your reference, you sweet little Protestant ignoramus.)

I can't tell you how weird it is to read the cynicism in your letter. I can tell that you have changed – hardened, I guess. It's okay though. I can also still see the real you between the lines – you are not lost. I can still see you and reach you. I'll always be here to pull you back, if you'll let me.

A Whisper of Smoke   *Angela Hoke*

I'll admit that it was disturbing to read about your philosophy over there – I mean, that you're sure that you're... not going to make it. But I think I understand what you are saying. I cannot, on the other hand, allow myself to think that. For me, it makes this – you being away at war – completely unbearable. But I will respect whatever you say, even when it scares the hell out of me – because I definitely do want you to continue to confide in me. Plus, I'm guessing that this is one of those things that you can't share with your mom (bless her) and darling little delicate Christine? (Please ignore any sarcasm you might have detected in those words). I can understand that. You don't want to cause them more pain or worry than they are already enduring.

I'm reading between the lines here, because I know you so well, and guessing that Sanchez's death hit you pretty hard. I know you can't let yourself feel it, but when you get back here, you can talk about Sanchez and Tank and any other of the boys that you loved and lost to me. You can cry on my shoulder until I'm as wet as a Vietnamese monsoon, and I will never judge you. Will you give me that gift, in return for being your brutal confidante while you are there? Will you let me hold you (with no inappropriate touching, I promise) and absorb your pain? You'll probably say no, that Christine gets to do that. But I can't help but ask (and hope) anyway.

I've been thinking a lot about your description of the unending rain. It must be enough to drive you crazy, after a while. It was raining here the other day, and I went outside in Bobbie Brooks pants and a t-shirt, boots and a poncho. I sat under the big solitary oak tree in the back (no, it wasn't a thunderstorm) for an hour, trying to understand how it might feel. By the end of the hour, my feet and hands were numb, and I was shivering uncontrollably. I was so wet, that the fabric was chafing my (tender white) thighs. I couldn't stand it any longer – I came inside, changed into warm dry clothes, pulled right out of the dryer, and drank a steaming cup of hot chocolate. (Is it cruel to describe such things to you? I don't mean it to be.) My point is, I couldn't even stand it for an hour. I don't know how you can stand it for months on end, except that you have no choice. It's funny what you can live with when there is no other choice.

While I was sitting there, Mother came in and looked at me oddly, but didn't say a word. Honestly, I think she knew exactly what I had been doing and why. She may or may not read my letters from you (I know she knows we are corresponding), but Mother is very intuitive about these types of things. Sitting out in the rain to try to understand the experiences of the man you… a man you really care about, serving our country in war, is exactly something she would do. Does that make me like her? A scary thought. Maybe that's just an indication that I may have inherited the best parts about her – the part that could understand why such an experiment was important. See? I'm optimistic enough for both of us. My optimism is like the sun, overcoming and drying out your damp cynicism. I'm good for you.

How do you like your new squad leader, the 'Shake'n'Bake', as you referred to him? (By the way, could you tell me what that means? I'm picturing a chicken leg, covered in golden breading…). Is he a good leader? How has it been since you wrote to me last? I pray that this letter finds you unharmed, if not dry and, by our limited civilian definition, "safe."

I guess I'll go now. Oh, I almost forgot. I went to that dance. It was fun – there was a very cute organ player in the band, but he has a *girlfriend (damn!). I danced the night away, and it was a nice distraction from my thoughts of you. Other than the cute keyboard player, no other promising prospects presented themselves.*

> *Until next time,*
> *Love Sexy Girl Next-door*
> *(and your friend forever),*
> *Susanna*

P.S. I've inserted (I hope) a flattering picture of myself into the prayer book – that way, after you guys have finished lusting after me (Don't I wish! By the way, do you have any single, worthy soldier boys over there that would be looking for a cute and spunky Catholic girl? But I digress…), you can immediately do your penance. Thoughtfully convenient, don't you think? Just make sure they know that if any viewing of my picture takes place out of sight from others (ahem, insert innuendo), the penance is twice as much (devilish grin!).

* * *

November 1968

Dear Sexy Girl (we might as well get straight to the point),

Your letters have become the bright spot in my miserable existence. Please don't stop sending them. And I wouldn't be offended if you wrote more often (but I don't mean to ask too much).

Sorry it's taken me so long to write you back. I've had malaria, and have been quite sick. As you can imagine, there are mosquitoes everywhere. We are supposed to take a quinine tablet every day to keep the malaria away. I'm pretty sure I only missed mine once or twice. Anyway, we were walking through the jungle and I was sweating (as I always do), but I realized I was feeling clammy. McMillan was walking in front of me, carrying our radio, and he turned around at one point and saw my face – it was apparently white as a sheet. I still didn't really know I was sick – you get accustomed to feeling uncomfortable, hot, sweaty, tired, and sometimes even lightheaded and dizzy. You just push through it. I mean, what other choice do we have?

But then, just when we were about to camp down for the night, apparently I passed out. Just dropped like a sack of potatoes. Willis, our medic, said I was burning up. So much so that they called in a medivac helicopter to the closest LZ, and carried me in a litter to the helicopter. I felt like an idiot, having to get medivac-ed out for malaria, when there are guys getting shot and blown up all around us. But, I guess it was a good thing they got me out. My temperature got up to 105 degrees, and they put me in a tub of ice to get it down. I don't remember any of it.

Then, I was so weak for the next four or five days, I was laid up in the infirmary in the rear. By the end, I was itching to get back to my unit. I felt worthless, and that my squad was out there risking their lives while I was sipping Pepsi and looking at pretty nurses.

Anyway, I've been back in the jungle for a week now, and I finally feel the energy to write you a letter. Please forgive me for not writing you sooner.

While I was in the rear, at the base, a USO troop came through. It was very weird to be sitting there watching people perform songs when just a few days before I had been at the edge of the earth, in a wet hell. It was almost out-of-body. I imagine that it's a little bit like how it feels to be back home.

Not long before I got sick, we pulled palace guard. There were

A Whisper of Smoke   *Angela Hoke*

prostitutes everywhere on base – little bitty things with too-wide smiles and funny English. They would ride in and out of base on scooters, wearing the same bright outfits two or three days in a row. Before you ask, no I didn't use their services. But I would be lying if I didn't admit that some of the guys did. It may be hard to imagine, but most of the working girls don't seem to mind being with the guys.

All except for one. There was one girl that seemed out of place. She was terribly shy and she wore the most subdued clothes – modest, almost. Her name was Mai, I learned. And we called her that, when we called many of the others Girl-san. It was a sub-conscious sign of respect, I think. Unlike the others, Mai looked troubled when she wasn't smiling coyly at some GI. And there was something about her, an innocence and something else – despair, maybe, lurking beneath the surface. And though I knew it was completely foolish, I began to think of my own sisters. I started thinking about if circumstances ever pushed them into prostitution. Man! I wouldn't be able to stand it. It makes me sick just to think of it. So it was with these errant thoughts that I took it upon myself to be her protector – uninvited. She was polite enough to me, but she didn't exactly act appreciative. Mostly she ignored me. And any fantasy I had of her opening up to me about her life, well that didn't happen. Instead, I sat like a grumpy troll outside the tent they used and hoped that with my new musculature and a fierce expression, the guys might shy away.

I congratulated myself that it was working until I noticed that two and three guys were "visiting" her whenever I vacated my post. That ticked me off, and I was about to break some skulls, when I got a visit from Mama-san (the "madam", if you will). She laid into me about messing with things that weren't my business and that I knew nothing about, and she told me I was being watched and would, well, really regret it if I didn't learn my place and back off. (Her actual threats were quite colorful but not suitable for this letter.)

Even after that memorable warning, I still felt a compulsion to help Mai,

Angela Hoke   *A Whisper of Smoke*

to somehow save her from her situation. But I had no idea how, so I backed off. Also, and I'm not proud for being swayed by this, but the guys would have killed me if I caused a big falling out with the girls. And I'm not even sure I don't mean literally. There are times, after a fight, when our adrenaline is pumping so much and we feel an overwhelming need to feel alive. Sex accomplishes that for lots of guys. I can see why it would be a release, but not so much that I would consider using Mai or the other girls that way. Plus, I would never want to betray Christine.

I hesitated whether to even tell you about the prostitutes because I know, to you, it must seem very disturbing. Back home, my civilized side would probably have been appalled, while my soldier side is no longer shocked by anything. And in the grand scheme of the things we have seen, and done, having a good time with a girl-san does not really seem all that remarkable.

Do you think we're awful for doing these things? You would not be totally wrong. Men turn into animals when there aren't societal pressures and consequences to keep them in check. It's a sad realization, but it's true. You can lose your soul here, in more ways than one. I can't change the fact that I have, and will continue to, kill people here – it's the only way I can stay alive. I hate every second of it, but I accept it. But I can control other parts of myself. I don't have to give in to those primitive instincts. I may want to sometimes, but I can still control whether or not I do. God help me the day that I ever give in and lose myself completely. Pray for me that I'm strong enough never to do that.

Okay, so enough of that. How about you? How have you been, and what have you been doing? I love that you sat out in the rain to try to feel my pain. You are a big sissy, to only last an hour, but it was a very sweet gesture all the same (joking!). The guys think you are great, when I tell them about some of your antics. And your letters get us all a little hot under the collars (though, admittedly, we are easily excited). Are you trying to tempt me? It's okay if you are, as you say, engaging in or encouraging harmless flirtation. If I were back home, I'm sure I'd have to get on my high horse and lecture you, or worse, stop talking to you all together. But you are making me laugh, while I'm here, and that's a gift. And if I get hot and bothered at the same time, well that's just the price I have to pay, I guess.

And sometimes you say something in one of your letters that, unexpectedly, makes tears spring to my eyes. How do you do that? I'm a tough soldier -- I'm not supposed to cry. How is it that you can get right to the heart of what I'm going through with just a few words? How do you know what I'm thinking and feeling, when I know I'm not putting it into my letters? It's like you can read my thoughts. I love that about you. There's a part of me that would really like to use your shoulder to cry on when I get back. But you are right, I don't think Christine would appreciate that (regardless of your commitment to no inappropriate touching! Besides, I'm not sure I could promise that ...)

Alright, I guess I'd better go now. I can't wait to see what you will write to me next. I hope you won't find it too much of a burden to keep those letters coming. I'll use my prayer book to pray for your fortitude. That's assuming it's still usable – I think a couple of guys used it for penance after being behind a tree with your picture... (Just kidding!)

Your (slightly more jaded but as always,
true to you) Strapping Soldier-boy,
Calvin

P.S. The 'Shake'n'Bake' Lieutenant (ha! A chicken leg... you make me laugh), a guy named Wilson, is doing okay. He's a good kid (listen to me – you'd think I had aged 10 years and was 28 instead of 18. I guess that's how I sometimes

Angela Hoke   A Whisper of Smoke

feel.). Plus, I'm pretty sure he's older than me by at least a couple of years. And Shake'n'Bake means he was a cherry officer – straight out of OCS. But he's got good instincts and he cares about his men, so he'll be alright. If he lives.

* * *

November 16, 1968

Dear (in hot water, mister!) Strapping Soldier-boy,

I was so relieved to hear from you! I was starting to get really frightened that something terrible had happened to you. My heart was in my throat for three weeks, waiting for your letter. Don't ever scare me like that again! I don't care if you send me a letter with one sentence saying "I am alive – I'll tell you more later." Anything would have been better than not hearing anything. I wanted so badly to go ask your mom if she'd heard from you but (a) I wasn't sure if she knew we were writing to each other, and (b) I was afraid of upsetting her if she had not heard from you either.

So I just suffered alone, and prayed my heart out. I'm so glad you are okay. And I'm going to punish you when I see you! Just so you're prepared, I'll be the one in the Catholic school-girl uniform (with the skirt rolled up at least three times), 3-inch heels, and a nasty-looking ruler in my hand, looking stern and sexy…

I'm trying to joke a little so that I don't get too scared for you. I know that's not what you need from me. I do want to say this to you, though – you should NOT feel guilty about getting sent to the rear and taking the time to get better. Think of it this way—if you had been in the jungle with your unit, the guys around you counting on you to help keep

A Whisper of Smoke   *Angela Hoke*

them alive, and you had passed out from malaria (or worse), you could have put their lives at even greater risk. You could have been a deadly distraction. Plus, I've read that some people have feverish hallucinations with malaria – just think how terrible it would have been if you had stayed in the jungle too long and accidentally hurt one of your own guys because you imagined them to be the enemy? So I don't want to hear one more word about this guilt for being sick and having to get better. It is a selfish notion, to think that you would rather have stayed with your unit and put them at risk. This was about them, not you. (Okay, partially about you. And I am still thanking God that you are okay. By the way, have you taken your quinine pill today?)

I've been thinking a lot about Mai and the other girls. I guess I always suspected that there were prostitutes over there. I worried that you might be tempted by one, but I was too afraid of the answer to ask you about it. Plus, I didn't know how to ask without seeming judgmental. So I'm relieved that you are abstaining, but I can tell that it's a complicated business – more so than we, as Americans, could possibly understand. But one thing I do know – you are still the most moral person I know, and I love that about you.

Also, it's interesting to realize, as I read these words, that what you are describing would, normally, make me cringe or rush to judgment. But because they are written by you, and because of the great respect I have for you and the person I know you to be, I am reading each word of your letters with an open mind. I try to put myself in your shoes, particularly in the context of what I know about your character. It is a very interesting insight onto the effects of serving in war. I wonder if, ten years from now (when we are sitting by a fire, you drinking your beer and me

Angela Hoke   *A Whisper of Smoke*

sipping a glass of wine, and you are slowly rubbing my feet, and Christine is only a distant memory...), we'll share these stories again? Will we have an even greater perspective then? Or will our perspective forever be limited by what we know and feel right now? In any case, I'm trying to be more adult about this than I've ever been about anything in my life. I owe that to you, because you are having to be as adult as a person can be asked to be. You are teaching me to be a better person, I think.

Did I tell you I switched schools this year? You know I had been thinking about it. I have always wondered what it would be like to go to public school, especially after Shelly made it sound so wonderful – full of cute boys, and all that. So Mom finally agreed, and now I'm at John Adams High, your old alma mater, reunited with my great compadre Shelly. Anyway, I think that finally giving in to letting me change to public school had more to do with not being able to afford my tuition than anything else. But I'll take what I can get.

Since Shelly's been here with me, the adjustment hasn't been too bad. I saved up babysitting money all summer to buy some regular clothes, since I no longer need my uniforms. I've been babysitting for your mom a little, and also babysitting the Simmons' kids and the Taylor twins. It was fun getting a new wardrobe. Plus, Shelly and I bought some fabric at the Woolco and I've been making some ultra-short minis (eat your heart out!). I've got one dress that's so short that when I drop something on the floor, I have to squat down very carefully so not to show my goodies to the world. Okay, it was kind of an accident to make it so short (I must not have made adequate allowance for my ass – I'm always underestimating it!). But I can't let it go to waste. And it has (ahem) gotten me a little bit of attention at a few school functions. I can't wear it to school during the day because, unbelievably, it does not meet the school dress code. I guess I thought that public school was like the proverbial den of iniquity (not, of course, that such a notion was my reason for wanting to go there). Turns out, in some ways it is almost as square as St. Catherine's. Oh well. It's probably a good thing that I can't wear my shortest minis to school – can you imagine the leg cramps I would get constantly maneuvering to pick up the pencils and books that boys just "accidentally" knock off my desk? (Hoping to make you just a teensy bit jealous – did it work?)

So we just had the Sadie Hawkins dance at school. Did you ever go to it? If not, that's where the girl asks the guy. I thought long and hard about asking somebody, but I just couldn't get excited about it. Plus, I've been feeling a little bit shy in these new surroundings (shocking, I know). So Shelly and I just went stag. It was a blast. We danced with abandon – there's no greater freedom than two Catholic girls at a dance with no nuns! And that same band was playing – you know, the one with the cute organ player? I'll refer to him as "Cute Rocker" from here on, so we are both clear as to whom I'm referring. They all had on black turtlenecks and they played Beatles and Credence and other cool songs. Apparently, Cute Rocker's girlfriend is named Lindy, and she goes to my school. She went up to him on his breaks and mooned over him. Then she looked at him with basset hound eyes while he played. It was a little much.

Okay, so enough about me. It has been so interesting reading your letters. I mean, not just because of what you are sharing about your experiences, but because I feel like I'm reading your soul. Your letters

Angela Hoke   *A Whisper of Smoke*

paint pictures for me. You are so smart – which I always knew, but you are deep too. Your letters make me feel more... I don't know, grown up I guess. That's not a very eloquent way to say what I mean. Let me think of a better way to express it...

Okay, I'll give it a try. You are teaching me a transcendent way of relating to another human being. You inspire me. I'm feeling compelled to write you a poem, but I'm shy about it. As odd as it may seem, for me, writing a poem creates a path, the only path, to my truest self. It is intensely intimate to me. The moment that I share that with you, you'll know that I've handed you a key to my soul.

Well darlin', I've got to go now. It's very late, and I have to get up early in the morning. I hope this letter finds you well. I pray for you every day.

Love your Sexy Girl,
Susanna

P.S. (Something told me not to send this letter yet.) Here's a brief peek into my poetic compulsion – a few words that will no doubt inadequately convey my feelings about your letters, and what they mean to me:

A letter from you is a surprise of stars in a velvet pouch;
Softness – enclosing, scorching.
It is worthy – its contents radiate, promising brilliance;
Exquisite purity.

The feel of it weighs on me, in my hand, like a stone on my chest.

Yet its density is restless, animate.

I pull it close, to protect, but its core spills through my fingers;
Fleeing, denying, floating just out of reach in the night sky of
dreams.

Your words find their way to me,
Beams of light traveling millions of miles through space;
Reaching their destination light years after their transmission.
In this same way, your words connect me to you –
A thousand suns warming my soul.

Well, I've handed you my key. You can unlock me – but then,
you always could.

* * *

November 1968

Dear Sweet and Sexy Girl,

What a beautiful poem. I have read it over and over, and it makes me
feel like I've climbed into your soul, and I feel safe and warm. Thank you so very
much for sharing it with me. I know what your poetry means to you, and I am
honored and humbled that you would not only share a poem with me, but that I
could possibly have inspired it.

Rainy season is finally ending here, thank God. The land is in a weird
state of transition, and recently we were in bogs for two days straight. The

Angela Hoke   *A Whisper of Smoke*

receding, brackish water invaded our boots and soaked through our pants and made our fatigues smell of sour animal dung. Our arms ached from constantly lifting our gear up out of the swamps. Whenever we came to a spot of dry land, it still wasn't dry the way you would think. It would still be spongy, though curiously not muddy, but at least up and out of the water. Then we would pull the leaches off.

But, at last, the ground is drying up. After walking in swamps for so long, my legs feel light and springy – as if they have been unburdened by pounds of weights that had been dragging them down. I think I could run a marathon on this drying earth.

We lost three guys from our squad in a big fight this month. Jackson was not by me and then he was, his intestines spilling out through this gaping hole in his abdomen. He was still talking to me the whole time, telling me that he couldn't find his grenade, that he was afraid he'd accidentally pulled the pin and he couldn't find it. Jackson was a friend of mine, and he always carried four grenades in his pistol belt. They were all still there. It was not his grenade that had blown his guts out. I tried to tell him that as I stuffed his guts back inside. They kept squishing back out, like they were never meant to be in there in the first place. Then the wound was closing back up around his intestines, but with feet and feet still hanging outside of him. It was like one of those little rubber change holders, you know, the kind where you squeeze the sides and the middle opens up so you can put the coins in? Then, as soon as you quit squeezing, it closes back up and anything on the inside stays in and anything on the outside stays out. I tried to push the other part back in, but every time I pried the wound open to push it in, more came out. And he wouldn't stop yelling about the damn grenades. He was hysterical with fear, until finally I grabbed one out of his pouch, pulled the pin and threw it somewhere in the direction of the NVA.

A Whisper of Smoke   *Angela Hoke*

"That was it, Jackson," I said. "That was your grenade – you threw it at the enemy – did you hear it? Did you hear it?" I was yelling and gripping his blood-soaked jacket. He finally focused on me, and he let out a sigh like he was glad that I had found that troublesome grenade. And then his life left him. It was only then that I realized I was sobbing, and that Max was at my back, covering me. The sounds of the firefight came rushing back in, and I fell over Jackson, trying to control my damn emotions. But then Max was in trouble, the NVA was advancing, and I came back to my senses. I retrieved one of Jackson's remaining grenades as I lay over him, pulled its pin, and counted off 1-2 before throwing it at the enemy that was almost on top of us. Max and I instinctively hit the dirt, and then when the blasts went off, we crawled out of there, leaving poor Jackson until the fight was over and we could safely retrieve him. I didn't know that the fight would go on for another 18 hours.

Jackson was 20 years old, but already had a wife and a little baby in Michigan. He tried not to let anyone see it (I guess he thought the guys would razz him), but he carried around one of those little New Testament bibles that they give you when you are a kid. It was baby blue. He read it every night under his poncho, and no one said a word to him about it, even though I'm sure I'm not the only one who saw it. He had enlisted too, dumb bastard. He would have had a deferment, because of his little girl.

Red was a funny looking kid with bright red hair (inventive nickname, I know). He was barely eighteen and had only been in country for 24 days. He got drafted almost as soon as he registered on his eighteenth birthday. The guys were always giving him a hard time for being a virgin (not that he's necessarily the only one, but he was an obvious one). His face could turn as red as his hair when he had a full blush on. He seemed like a baby, not much older than Elton or Hank. I realize, before you say it, that we were almost the same age.

Willis was a staff sergeant who had taken ROTC in high school, to be *like his dead daddy (who had died in Korea). He was our medic, and he helped get me out of the jungle when I had malaria – I may have mentioned him. He was sending his pay to his mama and his four younger sisters. He had a huge crush on you, and was always threatening to get out before me and go to Kentucky to sweep you off your feet. He knew how much that aggravated me, because he was a good-looking guy. You would have liked him, I'm sure. You would have liked them all.*

I hate this fucking place and this fucking war. Not a one of them deserved to die. They had their whole lives ahead of them. And for what? For what did they die? To satisfy the commanders that we were carrying out the orders to search and destroy? There were no lands gained, no people liberated. We have no front-line, no clear lines of battle, no logical military objective. It is illogical and unending. And I came here voluntarily. Most of these guys were drafted – they are not a volunteer army. Many of them had never before held a gun, never hunted, never slept a night out in the woods. Most had never even been in a fist fight.

I remember when my dad talked of his older brothers going to fight in WWII. They both fought in Europe, and they rushed to the call. Millions of young men enlisted to help fight tyranny and evil. They were still soldiers, still human, and no doubt some of them committed inhuman acts while they were there. But their cause was noble. They were giving their lives for a reason – to secure the continued freedom of their families, of the free world at large.

I would gladly give my life to save my brothers here. I'd die for Max in less than a heartbeat, and he would do the same for me. But why are any of us here? How do our deaths make you safer, or make any other country safer, for that matter, other than potentially South Vietnam? And that is very debatable, given that the battlefields take place in their villages, in their rice fields, in their homes.

A Whisper of Smoke   *Angela Hoke*

I am sorry to be so cynical and melancholy. I will put this letter down and pick it back up when I have something better to say.

It's been four days since my lamentation. Sorry about that. It don't mean nothin'.

Let's talk about lighter things. I keep picturing you in your ultra-short mini-skirts. The guys want you to send a picture of you wearing one. That's as much as I'll ask. I won't tell you what position they wanted you to be in for the picture. Or what kind of undergarments (or lack thereof) that they wanted you to wear under your skirt. Their minds are in the gutter, that's all I've got to say.

I'll admit that I do feel a pang of jealousy to think of guys looking at you bending down in your short little skirts. If only I... could be there to defend your honor! If Cute Rocker is the type of guy that would stare lasciviously at you, tossing pencils on the floor to watch you bend down, you stay away from him! That sounds like Chip behavior to me.

Okay, sweet Susanna. I'm going to close now. Thanks for sending those Louis L'amour books. The guys liked them. Any books you can send would be great. I can't wait to get your next letter. It's almost Thanksgiving, and I'm missing you all so very much. Rake up a big pile of leaves and let all the kids jump in it, in my honor.

Yours always,
Calvin

P.S. Happy birthday, my little Susie! Seventeen – I can't believe it. I still see that skinny little girl with long braids, balancing Hank on one hip. Man, how time flies!

Angela Hoke   *A Whisper of Smoke*

Chapter 18: How a Real Man Loves a Real Woman

November 29, 1968

Dear Calvin,

I am really missing you. We just had Thanksgiving, and it was so awful not having you around. The leaves are all off the trees and the sky is gray – it's just the right kind of riding weather. I keep thinking back to just a year ago, when you and I set out on Franny and Sampson on the Friday after Thanksgiving. Do you remember? It was cool outside and rather bleak, but we were dressed warm and the world seemed silent except for the sound of our horses breathing hard and clomping through the dry leaves. It was like we had the woods to ourselves.

We rode for over an hour without saying a word – do you remember? When we finally stopped to water the horses at that pretty creek in the woods, you sat close to me on the rock to help me stay warm. You patiently listened to me obsess about Chip, and why he was so moody, and we ate pimento cheese sandwiches. We took drinks of water by scooping our hands into the frigid creek. Then, when my hands were like ice, you took them between yours and blew on them with your warm breath before we got back onto the horses to ride back home. Did you know that I loved you then? Could you see it in my eyes when I looked at you? Could you feel it radiating from my skin?

A Whisper of Smoke   *Angela Hoke*

I confess that I fantasized that you secretly loved me too. There were a few times that you looked at me, and I thought I saw something in your eyes... I read something in them that was not really there, but it warmed me inside to believe it, even if I knew deep down that I was fooling myself. When we were sitting on that rock, your hands surrounding mine and your lips almost on my fingertips, I thought that you might kiss them. I thought, for a stupid moment, that you might kiss me.

I went to your house Thursday for Thanksgiving lunch, but you weren't there. We all said prayers for you and thanked God for you. Mabel had her boyfriend there. Did you know she had one? His name is Jacob, and he was bashful but cute. He had that flushed cheek look and blond eyelashes, and he sat close to Mabel all afternoon. She was animated and blunt as ever, telling stories and keeping us cheered up. Hank was there too, and I think he was a little bit jealous that Mabel had a boyfriend. She's cute as can be, and all spunk.

Your mama seemed a little sad in the eyes, but she smiled a lot and made us all feel special as she expertly put us to work helping her get the meal ready. Your dad was outside until the moment we sat down to eat – he led the prayer but otherwise was silent, not that his silence is all that unusual.

And Christine was there – did I mention that? I tried to be friendly towards her, for your sake. She was a little aloof to me though. Does she know what I said to you at your party? Or does she just sense that I adore you? She teared up four or five times during dinner, as your brother and sisters told funny stories about you. It was (sickeningly) sweet. She was your mother's right-hand woman, which I found a little annoying. She acted as though she were a daughter-in-law already. Is there something I should know? Please don't spring that one on me without some warning – have a heart for a pathetic love-sick girl who clings to denial.

After your family's Thanksgiving lunch, your dad and your brother went into the living room to watch football while your Mom, your sisters (with Mabel grumbling the whole time about how her lazy brother ought to get his butt into the kitchen and help), and, of course, sweet Christine, cleaned up the mess. Hank and I helped for a while, and then we had to hurry back home to get ready for Thanksgiving at Grandmother's. He was the only boy that helped – even little Jacob seemed to think his place was yelling at the crazy football players on the television (he was starting to come out of his shell). Hank is a sweetheart, as always, but I have to wonder if he didn't help in the kitchen at least partly to impress Mabel. An older woman! Well, he always did have mature tastes. Why he doesn't go for Kathleen or Cora, I don't know. On the other hand, Mabel is pretty special – she knows herself already, and she's strong.

So I was just re-reading what I wrote to you so far, and I feel incredibly insensitive. Here I am, sitting in my safe bedroom in my safe country, whining about having a wonderful Thanksgiving dinner with delicious food and in a warm cozy house, surrounded by loved ones, and complaining about missing you. I am so selfish. I am sorry. I was writing that purely from an emotional place, and I was not thinking. Please forgive me if I made you feel bad. Sometimes I don't know what to share and what not to. I want to transport you and give you that mental vacation that you no doubt need, but I would never want to make you feel worse. Please instruct me here – I need your direction.

Calvin, I have no words to express the sorrow I feel for you over the loss of your friends. It must have been so terrible. And you were trying so hard to help Jackson. I do think you helped him – you took away his anxiety, so that he could let go in peace. He must have been worried that he was going to hurt one of you with the grenade he thought he had lost. He was hanging on desperately to try to keep you safe (or so I imagine), and you gave him peace of mind. Even in the midst of great danger, you helped him. And your friend Max, tell him I would give him a big kiss, if I could, for keeping you safe when you were trying to help Jackson.

From what you described, the fighting sounds almost hand-to-hand. That's not how I pictured it at all – I guess I was picturing fighting scenes in the woods in WWII movies (only much greener and with some monkeys thrown in here and there), but where there is still some distance between the two sides. Now, instead, I'm picturing you slashing your way through dense green vines and bamboo with machetes, constantly in danger of hidden ambush, the threat of North Vietnamese soldiers hiding behind the vegetation at every turn. I'm very scared for you right now. Please, please be safe. I'm sure there are military tactics for maneuvering in that type of environment, and I'm also sure you can't describe them to me. I just pray that you all use them expertly and that they are exceptionally effective.

Again, I apologize. I don't want to cause you more stress. And I certainly don't want you to worry that you are scaring me. I'm strong, I can take it. Please keep writing to me whatever your heart needs to tell.

52

I'm going to close now, my sweet Soldier-Boy. I look forward to reading your next letter. Please write to me soon.

Love,
Susanna

* * *

December 1968

Dear Susanna,

Thanks for your letter. Again, you know my heart. Your words bring comfort to me – I'm trying to convince myself that you are somehow right about Jackson, and that I at least helped ease his dying moments. But I miss him and the others.

I have been drowning in despair lately. The death of brothers can do that to a person. But I don't want to be bitter – it makes me afraid that I am changing into someone I don't recognize. And I'm afraid that you won't recognize me either. Help me come back from this dark place, will you? Write to me in your witty way, with your outrageous flirting. Bring me back from the brink of my despair. I hope that is not asking too much.

And before you start to apologize again about the solemnity of your last letter, please know that your last letter was what I needed. Yes, your letter was a bit darker than usual, and I was momentarily sour that you all had such a normal Thanksgiving while we are all stuck here, but you forced me to feel the emotions that I've been trying to suppress, and to let them out. If I'd known what you would write, I might have been hesitant to read it, afraid of crumbling. But in retrospect, I know that it is what I needed. It is poison to a soul to repress grief for too long – grief over the loss of my friends, grief over what my friends have lost,

A Whisper of Smoke   *Angela Hoke*

grief over what I have lost.

I don't feel that I am explaining this very well, and I worry that I'm going to make you feel bad, which is the last thing that I want. What I am trying to say is that your last letter was raw, and went to the heart of things – important things that should not be ignored. I felt sorry for myself for a while, then I was angry, then I was incredibly sad and I constantly hid my tears from the guys. But now I feel some semblance of peace – not acceptance, but a peace, like I have been cleansed, or purged, and that my inner self has been fortified.

So thank you. Thank you for missing me in the undisguised way that you have, because it reminds me that you care for me unconditionally.

You are never going to believe this, but guess what? I get to go to Hawaii in a few weeks for R&R. Can you believe that? Me, who had never even been on a plane before joining the army. I'm going to paradise. I am picturing brown-skinned hula girls with grass skirts and coconut bras. I am picturing tiki bars where it's perfectly acceptable for soldiers to order fruity drinks with pineapple wedges and little umbrellas. I am picturing palm trees and sunsets and turquoise ocean lapping across lava rock and sand.

Can you tell that I am really looking forward to it? I'm not sure if it's because I've imagined it to be such a paradise and a retreat, or if it's because I'll get to be away from here, or both. But even as I write this, my brain is screaming that I'm jinxing myself by acknowledging my anticipation – that something will probably spoil it, or that I might even be dead before then. See the danger of having something to live for, of hoping that you'll make it? My invincibility armor that was constructed out of the knowledge that I'll die here now has a big crack in it – plenty big enough for a round or two to enter.

I know I shouldn't admit this, but there's a part of me that wishes that you could meet me there. I fantasize that I'll come off the C-130 and into the

Angela Hoke   *A Whisper of Smoke*

airport, and there you'll be at the gate, smiling with your whole face and waiting to put a lei around my neck. You'll throw your arms around me and I'll hug you like I'm trying to absorb you. Then we'll run out together, laughing, and somehow we'll be running right towards the beach. We'll pull outer clothing off until we are wearing our underwear, then we'll jump into the surf.

We'll swim and swim, and then we'll let the tide push us onto the beach, where we'll lie covered in sand and baking in the sun. We'll lean up on our elbows and watch the sunset, and I'll feel safe and present again.

Christmas will be here soon, and I won't be with you, but I'll be thinking about you all (and probably getting drunk here). But enjoy it – life is too short not to treasure those moments together.

I can't believe that Mabel has a boyfriend! She has mentioned him in her letters, but she made it sound like they were just buddies. And Hank is jealous, huh? Does Mabel notice it?

Okay, sweet Susanna, I'm going to go now. Please take care and know that I am with you – Sanchez used to say if we smoked the peace pipe, our astral beings could travel out of our bodies and anywhere we wanted. (It makes me wonder what they smoke in those things). But it is a nice thought – I like to think that I can travel to you, and can look over you to see that you are all safe, and that the world outside of our small one still goes on. So next time you feel that breeze across your shoulder as you are drifting to sleep, imagine that it's me, visiting you on an astral plane, tucking you in.

Yours always,

Calvin

P.S. When I let Max read your last letter and he saw where you said you'd like to give him a big kiss, he said he'd like to give you more than that, that he wants to show you how (and I quote) "a real man loves a real woman." (He's looking over my shoulder right now to be sure that I am telling you this – I guess he means it as some kind of offer. You can do better – Ouch! I mean, no girl could ever do better!)

* * *

When I finished reading Calvin's letter, I sat back on my bed and my eyes widened. Was he inviting me to come? Or was I reading too much into it? Oh, how I would love to go to Hawaii to be with him and somehow convince him that we were meant to be together. Surely, after the hints he's made that he might be attracted to me (at least a little), he wouldn't be able to resist me, were I there in the living, breathing (heaving) flesh?

I got goosebumps up and down my arms as I imagined our passionate reunion, and in one of the most romantic spots on earth. At the thought, I bolted up from my bed and to my jewelry chest. I unlocked it and took out the false bottom to reveal my hiding place for money. Even though it was more than I'd ever saved, it did not seem like enough. How was I going to make this happen? *Should I even try?*

Realizing I needed an objective opinion, I put the money away and locked it back up, then tore out of my bedroom and down the stairs. I grabbed the hall phone extension, pulled it into the broom closet for some privacy, and dialed Shelly's number, hoping she was home.

Shelly answered on the first ring.

"Shelly! It's Susanna. No time for chit-chat. Can I read you a letter from Calvin? I need your advice."

"Nice to talk to you, too," she replied drolly.

At my great sigh of impatience, Shelly relented. "Sure, of course.

Go right ahead."

Shelly was quiet as I began reading, and I could hear the hope in my own voice. When I finished, I held my breath, waiting for Shelly's reaction.

"Why you two just don't get a room and get the dirty deed over with, I'll never know."

"So I'm not imagining it? It does sound like he's interested in me?" I asked, barely daring to hope.

"Oh, he's interested. I've told you all along. I don't care what he says, he's attracted to you. It's everywhere between the lines – too bad it can't be between the sheets!" She laughed at her own joke. "Besides, you know he cares about you."

"I know," I said. "I know he cares about me, I've never doubted that. But is he feeling something more? I just can't tell! I'm afraid I'm reading more into it than I should. And I don't just want him to be attracted to me – he'd probably be attracted to a knotty pine at this point. I have no interest in seducing him, even if it did not take much effort. Not unless I can seduce his whole heart, too."

"Why the hell not? If you get him to want you, then maybe he'll *want* you," Shelly reasoned.

I sighed. "That's not Calvin. Even if I could melt his resolve and he wanted me, it's much more likely that he would feel so much guilt that he would cut off all contact with me. That's how I almost lost him to begin with – I pushed it too much and he felt morally convicted to sever all ties with me."

"Yeah, until he didn't anymore," Shelly said.

"What do you mean?"

"What I mean is, he couldn't stay severed from you, could he?

He reached out to you, and now you two are all intimate, sharing stuff that I can't even comprehend. How can he not have deeper feelings for you?"

"Because he's a rock," I protested. "He has the moral strength of a priest. Even if he had feelings for me, he would not admit it to himself, not as long as Christine was around."

"Then we must take her out," Shelly suggested darkly.

"I'll get the gun," I replied without hesitation, and Shelly laughed.

"So seriously, tell me what you are thinking. What does your gut tell you?"

"It tells me to gather as much money as I can and fly to Hawaii to meet him so I can try to fulfill his fantasy and more. It tells me that this may be my last chance to win him, because when he comes back home, Christine will be here waiting." Even as the words came out of my mouth, I was surprised at my admission.

"Then that's what you should do. But... would your mom let you go?"

"I don't know..." I tapped my chin in the dark. "If I could somehow convince her it was her idea, that she was helping me play out some romantic plot, she probably would put me on the plane herself. But do you think I should go for it? I mean, really go for it?"

"Isn't that what I've been saying? Anyway, if you don't go, I may have to fly to Hawaii myself. Strapping Soldier-Boy makes me weak in the knees, and maybe he won't notice it's not you."

"Witch!" I laughed.

In the end, I decided to do the very thing that my instinct warned me against – leave my letter out so that my mother would just "happen" upon it, and hope that Mother wouldn't become suspicious. To heighten the drama, I decided to draft a desperate response to Calvin, declaring my love. I sat at the table with my stationary spread out, and Calvin's letter open beside me.

"Dear Calvin," I wrote. "There is something that I have to tell you. I am in love with you." As an added touch, I scribbled the last words out but not so they were illegible. Laying the two letters side by side on the kitchen table, I got up and hurried through the living room and up the stairs, sniffling and wiping my eyes as I flew past Mother. She gave me a strange look, but said nothing.

Hoping that Mother would be intrigued enough to take the bait, I settled on my bed and waited for the wheels of fate to turn

When I later returned to the kitchen to retrieve my things, I noticed that the letter from Calvin was turned over, face down. I was quite sure I had left it face up (could I have been more obvious?). It appeared that Mother had read it. Now I'd just have to hope that Mother would decide that Calvin and I were star-crossed lovers, and that her romantic side would take over. I only hoped it didn't take too long.

Chapter 19: Pappy Has the Right Idea

Christmas 1968

Mother had not said a word about the letter, so I still couldn't be sure that she'd read it. Not willing to give up though, I'd made a point of talking on the phone to Shelly, within Mother's range of hearing, lamenting about my fervent wish to go to Hawaii and try to win Calvin's love. It was more than a little humiliating, but it would be worth it if it worked. Then, for good measure, I'd spent the past few days moping around the house and acting all heartsick about Calvin (not too much of a stretch), just to drive the point home. By Christmas Eve, nothing seemed to be any different, and I was beginning to lose hope.

Then it was time to go to Gran and Pappy's, and Uncle George would be there.

I had barely seen him since everything happened. I had refused to go to his wedding, feigning sickness. Mother had fluctuated between extreme irritation and something else (a guilty conscience maybe? If she even *had* a conscience.) – something else that kept her from going off on me. Thankfully, they'd been gone on their honeymoon that first Christmas *after...* And, as much as I was loathe to admit it, Christmas dinner had been weird without him.

Then, last Christmas, I couldn't avoid seeing him. Enough time had passed that everyone expected things to be back to normal, even if they weren't and would never be again. Chip went with me to Gran and

Pappy's Christmas, and I really appreciated his presence. Uncle George was there, as was Cheryl, whom I had never met before. Cheryl was very thin and tall with short pixy hair – like Mia Farrow or Twiggy. She had stayed by Uncle George like she was his protector -- as if *he* was the one who needed protecting! And Uncle George was strangely subdued, looking at me every now and then with what I interpreted as guilt in his eyes. *Damn right, you should feel guilty!* I'd thought, as I dared him with my eyes to try to deny responsibility. He had not taken the dare. Thankfully, Chip and I had been able to take our leave early, because he had family gatherings that required our presence as well.

Aside from holidays, I hadn't really had to worry about running into him. Unbelievably, Uncle George had not stepped foot inside our house (at least not to my knowledge) since the night of Lorelei's graduation party. Still, if that was his only penance, he was getting off very lightly.

Now I was faced with the prospect of seeing him again, but I still could not bear to be around him. I didn't want to see him acting all gregarious, telling his stupid jokes, drinking too much and getting flirtatious (yuck) in inappropriate ways. I also knew that my anger towards my parents was likely to flare back up when I saw them being friendly towards the traitorous George. I sighed, wishing that Christmas did not have to be sullied with this poison.

I didn't even have asshole Chip to whisk me away when things got too weird! *Now I'm just being pathetic,* I thought, shaking my head clear of the negative thoughts.

By the time Mother called for me to come get in the car, I had spent a couple of hours trying to wrap my head around the coming encounter. Rebellion streaked through me, a residual result of the anger that Mother inspired when it came to Uncle George, and I thought about stalling. But then I remembered that I was hoping for Mother's support to go to Hawaii, and that overrode everything else. I jumped up and hurried down the stairs.

It was really good to see Gran. I hadn't realized how old she was getting, and it made me feel a little sad. Gran seemed so small and breakable, as I bent over to hug her. But she still had that familiar smell, a cross between lemon meringue and old vitamins, and I smiled over her small shoulder.

After Gran had gotten her fill of hugging me, she let me go by and turned her hugs on the rest of the family. I squeezed by her and hurried to the corner of the room, beside the tall white flocked Christmas tree. It was one of the few spaces where a person could stand without bumping into anyone else, and I figured it would give me a good vantage point for evaluating the lay of the land.

So far the coast was clear, so I relaxed against the wall and waited for everyone to arrive. I didn't even notice that Pappy was asleep in the lazy chair until he snorted in his sleep. We both jumped, but he kept on sleeping. He wasn't really walking or talking anymore, since his stroke. I supposed I should be sad about that, but Gran had seemed so much happier since he lost his ability to yell at her, I wondered if maybe it was a blessing in disguise.

I heard a commotion at the front door, and I held my breath. I was relieved when Lorelei walked in with Mark. He was grabbing at her ass, obviously not realizing anyone was in the room. She squealed girlishly as she darted away from him. I was about to clear my throat to identify myself (before I witnessed something I'd rather not), but Pappy snorted and Lorelei and Mark jumped away from each other in surprise. Then Lorelei saw me in the corner, and she looked at me curiously.

I just shrugged a little, and Lorelei seemed to accept that I had my reasons. She sat in the arm chair with Mark, the two of them wedged in tight. Hank came in the room with a jar of marbles and a wad of yarn, with Annabelle following. He was trying to convince her that playing marbles really was fun, but she looked dubious. Nonetheless, a quick scan around the room showed that, until the presents were opened, there was nothing else to play with and way too many things to break. So she plopped down on the floor with a sigh, and Hank delightedly tied a knot in some yarn and spread it into a circle on the floor. He tried to show her shooting techniques, and he was so earnest that he didn't seem to notice how disinterested his little sister seemed.

Then, there was commotion again, and I heard the unmistakable timbre of Uncle George's voice. I clenched my stomach to keep it from roiling over, and I prepared myself to see him.

Cheryl walked in first and her eyes found me at once. She looked at me sternly, as if trying to warn me off. I looked away, ignoring her. Then Uncle George came in, laughing but not in his normal boisterous way. He looked a little smaller, too – as if he was diminished, in more ways than one.

Something about the expression on Cheryl's pinched face must have warned him, because he immediately tensed, then turned slowly and scanned the room. When he saw me cowering by the Christmas tree, he looked at me sadly then quickly averted his gaze.

Mother and Dad came in then and took their places at the extended dining room table, beckoning to the others to join them for cards. Most everyone gladly migrated to the adjoining dining room, but I couldn't bring myself to. Instead I took a seat next to catatonic Pappy, and stared at the television.

I must have dozed off, because I woke up to the smells of Christmas dinner being placed on the table. I had drool all over my chin, and I couldn't help but chuckle at the thought of me and Pappy, drooling side-by-side.

The yummy smells made my stomach growl loudly, so I reluctantly levered myself out of the deep cushions of the loveseat where I'd been sprawled and made my way to the dinner table. More people had come while I'd been passed out, including good old Uncle Mutt and Uncle Magoo. Immediately upon entering the dining room, I noticed that there weren't enough seats for all the adults.

"Someone's going to have to eat at the kid's table..." Gran was saying apologetically.

"I'll do it!" I piped up, eager to volunteer to eat somewhere, anywhere, where Uncle George was *not.*

"Thanks, Jellybean," Dad said sweetly, and my heart melted a little. I gave him a small smile, but it was genuine, and his eyes lit up with that old sparkle.

I pretended to be in a good mood as I ate with Hank and Annabelle. I acted like I'd heard Santa outside, and Annabelle was so excited she couldn't sit still. Hank just smiled, looking happy, neither confirming nor denying his belief in the sneaky, evasive Santa.

When dinner was over, everyone rushed to the living room to open presents. I followed slowly, and nearly ran into Uncle George as he also lagged behind, stalling his entrance into the crowded living room as well. We both halted, but we were already face to face. A range of emotions passed over Uncle George's face – shock, worry, sorrow, guilt, fear.

My face hardened, and I turned and walked away from him, crossing the kitchen quickly and grabbing someone's coat off the pegs by the front door. Then I was outside, pulling on an old man coat, trying not to gag at the weird smell.

I stood on the front lawn, watching my breath erupt in cold white puffs, and trying to slow my speeding heart. Then I heard the creak and thud of the door opening and swinging closed behind me. I didn't turn around, but my stomach flipped with dread. I heard someone's harsh breathing behind me, and then a voice.

"Susanna," Uncle George said softly, his voice cracking like an adolescent.

I didn't turn, couldn't bring myself to face him.

He came towards me – I could hear his boots crunching on the frozen grass, and then he was standing beside me, both of us facing forward, looking at the empty street and the Christmas lights on the houses on the other side.

After what seemed like a long time, Uncle George took a deep breath, and I held mine.

"I know you are very angry with me," he began.

And? I thought sarcastically, angrily. *What the hell do you expect, you bastard?*

"And you have every right to be," he added, echoing my angry thoughts.

"I have done some really terrible things… Things that make me very, very ashamed."

Am I supposed to feel sorry for you?

A Whisper of Smoke   *Angela Hoke*

He seemed to sense my hostility. "I'm not expecting you to be sorry for me." He sighed. "I'm just trying to take responsibility for what I've done."

I was silent.

"And that includes..." he began slowly, "what I may have... what I have done to you." He said the last part very carefully, as if he weren't sure what my perceptions might be.

Neither was I – my mind bubbled with turmoil, as buried memories trying to break free. I was suddenly terrified, and bile rose up, threatening to escape.

I involuntarily bent over, and put my hands on my knees. My hair hung down around my face as I gulped in the cold, stinging air. *Whatever it is you're about to confess, DON'T!* my mind screamed at him. But the words were stuck in my throat.

His breathing seemed to have stilled beside me, as he evaluated my response. Finally, he began speaking again.

Oh, God, Oh, God, Oh, God. I don't WANT to remember!

But it all came rushing back anyway, remnants of a night I'd suppressed for so long.

Mama had gotten off to the hospital when her contractions were still three minutes apart. Daddy drove her, after making sure that Uncle George had agreed to stay with us. None of us knew it yet, but Annabelle was about to make her grand entry into the world.

As soon as Lorelei heard that Uncle George was coming, she had decided she was going to be elsewhere. She was gone to her friend Marcie's before Uncle George even arrived, leaving me alone for a few hours with Hank. It was the first time I'd ever been left alone, and Daddy had been stern with his instructions. But just before he left, he cuffed me on the chin, and told me he knew I'd do fine, and I'd beamed at him, determined not to let him down.

Hank and I spent our few hours alone cleaning the house, pretending to be slaves of a rich and angry ogre. So deep were we in our fantasy that we were in the midst of receiving an imaginary lashing when Uncle George arrived.

"What on earth is going on here?" he exclaimed, opening the door to find us writhing on the floor, our arms and legs restrained by invisible shackles.

I immediately sat up, embarrassed, spontaneously freed from my invisible bonds. Hank, however, continued wincing and crying out from each strike of the nonexistent whip.

I blushed, "We were pretending like we were slaves and that our evil master was making us clean up the house." I turned to Hank, laying a hand on his chest, "Hank, stop now."

Hank ceased his crying out, but continued to lie still, panting.

"That was worser than last time," he whispered dramatically.

I leaned over, whispering back, "Yes, it was."

"Next time, wait for me. I'd like to play too," he said, and we were pleased that our favorite uncle had come to play.

Uncle George, not being a great cook, fixed grilled cheese sandwiches and French fries for dinner, and I helped. While we ate, Uncle George told silly jokes and stories, and had us laughing so hard we could barely eat.

After dinner, we all cleaned up the dishes together and Uncle George put me in charge of baths. Accustomed to this responsibility, I supervised Hank's bath and then took a quick shower. After we put on pajamas, we hurried back downstairs to join Uncle George who was sitting on the couch watching T.V. and drinking a beer.

On the screen, Fred and Wilma were arguing about how cheap Fred was, and Barney was making matters worse by agreeing with her. Hank was giggling, and it made me smile. Soon, Hank was yawning and rubbing his hair. Without saying a word, I drew his soft blond head down onto my lap. Before The Flintstones got past its closing credits, Hank was snoring softly, sound asleep. I stroked his sweet baby face.

Uncle George picked Hank up and together we took him upstairs. Since Lorelei was spending the night elsewhere, I wanted him to sleep with me, that way I could keep watch over her him while Mama and Daddy were at the hospital. We settled him in my bed, and I kissed him on the forehead. He didn't even stir.

Back downstairs, Uncle George headed to the kitchen. "How about I pop us some popcorn and we make some root beer floats?"

"Okay," I replied, jumping up to help. As we worked side by side in the kitchen, I was struck by the sensation that we were playing a realistic version of "house." And when Uncle George teased me, I joked back the way I imagined a grown-up would.

Once the food and drink were prepared, we settled back on the couch. I curled my legs under me and sat close to Uncle George. We watched an episode of 77 Sunset Strip and drained our floats.

As I slurped the last of my drink, Uncle George offered to make me another. He got up, taking both tall glasses to the kitchen with him. As he worked, I called out, "Do you need any help in there?"

"No, darling. I've got it."

Angela Hoke   *A Whisper of Smoke*

I drew the afghan from the back of the couch and covered up in it as Uncle George came back in, two large floats in his hands.

"Here you go," he said, handing me one.

"Thanks," I said, suddenly shy. I took a sip, then said, "Oh. This tastes different."

"I added a little of my secret ingredient," he explained, grinning devilishly. "Now they are root beer coladas instead of root beer floats," he said, and I realized it was alcohol I tasted.

I frowned a little. "What exactly did you put in here?"

"Just a little rum. You don't mind, do you?"

I thought for an instant, knowing that it was a sin. But I quickly concluded it was a minor one, and that it was worth the penance if it made Uncle George happy.

I tentatively took another sip, cringing a little at the foreign taste when I noticed Uncle George watching me. I took my next drink without hesitation, just to show I could. After a few more brave drinks, I realized that it didn't taste so bad anymore.

"Have you been writing your poetry lately?" Uncle George asked, startling me.

"I sometimes still work on it. It's very private, you know." I felt the blush creep up my cheeks. "I usually don't show it to anyone."

"I know. That's why I feel so honored that you once shared some of it with me." I had, once, during one of Mama's parties. Uncle George had acted so interested in me, and I'd been flattered. And when he'd read my Haiku, he'd seemed genuinely impressed.

I felt my blush deepen. I took another long drink of my root beer colada, and to my surprise found that I had finished it.

A Whisper of Smoke   *Angela Hoke*

"How about another?" Uncle George asked, as he removed the empty glass from my fingers.

As he walked toward the kitchen, I watched him go thinking how sweet and funny he was, and how glad I was that he was my uncle. I was still gazing towards the kitchen when he walked back through, refreshed drinks in hand, and I giggled at how time had passed without me noticing.

"What?" he asked, laughing with me.

"I was just thinking how time is going by, and I'm not even noticing it," I said, as I took the drink. "Whoa." My hand tipped and the liquid sloshed precariously.

"Be careful," Uncle George said, chuckling.

"I'm being careful." I took a long drink, tasting little.

"Come over and snuggle with me. We can share the blanket."

I handed him my glass and crawled towards him on the couch, carefully spreading the blanket over the two of us. As our sides touched, I was suddenly overcome with affection for Uncle George, and I hugged his side with my arms, planting a sloppy kiss on his cheek.

"What was that for?" he asked, handing me back my drink.

"Just because," I sighed, thinking that he would make a good dad someday, and simultaneously feeling that he would make a good husband.

He'd changed the channel, and now Rod Serling was introducing the The Twilight Zone. Usually, I wouldn't be allowed to watch this show because it could be a little disturbing, plus it came on past my normal bedtime. My stomach fluttered with the excitement of the forbidden. George gave a running commentary on the various characters, making them seem unreasonably funny.

Angela Hoke   A Whisper of Smoke

"You're very pretty when you laugh," George said softly. And all at once the mood shifted, like when the air gets sucked up into the sky just before a tornado touches down.

"Would you like to sit on my lap?" he asked, and at first I was puzzled.

"I'm too old to sit on someone's lap."

"We can pretend that you're the mom and I'm the dad, and that Hank is our little boy."

Mama sometimes sat on Daddy's lap, I reasoned. After a moment's thought, I nodded, not trusting myself to speak but not quite sure why my voice might have fled.

I felt George's large, warm hands on either side of my waist, and then I was lifted up and onto his lap. As he settled me back against his chest, I relaxed.

"Let me get you situated," he murmured, as he adjusted me into a more comfortable position, and carefully arranged my mid-length nightgown so that it fanned out around me. Then he covered us both with the blanket.

"See, just like a ballerina," he said, almost to himself. "Sit back and relax," he whispered as he put his arms around me, drawing me tight against his big chest.

I closed my eyes and sank into him. He was comfy.

"Just like grown-ups," he whispered, as a lullaby.

"Just like grown-ups," I whispered back, my eyes still closed.

Almost in a trance, I felt his breath on my cheek, and vaguely heard the sounds of voices from the television.

I might have been almost asleep when I first felt the increasing pressure just under my panties. My eyes popped open and I almost asked what it was, but as the bulge swelled, it actually felt good and I bit off the words before they came out. I closed my eyes again, not at all sure what was happening and not trusting my impaired perceptions. I let my mind focus only on the strange pressure against my crotch, and the shivers it was sending through me, straight up through my middle.

As the bulge grew a fraction at a time, sending tingling sensations like electric jolts through my body, I suddenly had the clear realization that it was his penis I was feeling. I pictured Calvin urinating behind the barn and then flashed to changing Hank's diaper when he was a baby and the way it stood up, sometimes, just before he went.

Uncle George must have to use the bathroom, I concluded. "Do you have to pee?" I whispered, eyes still closed.

"No, I'm sorry," he answered. "Are you uncomfortable? Let me help." He lifted me up, and when he set me back down, I could feel that his erection had unfolded inside his pants.

My eyes popped open again and I froze, as thoughts of Mama's scary descriptions of sex filled my mind. Uncle George sighed and squeezed my middle just like a regular old uncle hug. It was affectionate. But the pressure against my crotch seemed more than affectionate.

Suddenly, I had a horrified thought. Does Uncle George want to have sex with me because we are pretending to be married? I had never considered the sexual part of the marital relationship when I'd agreed to play this game. There was no way I wanted to do that, but I had no idea how to tell him.

I never should have told him I'd pretend! I thought, angry with myself. I didn't know all the rules – but if told him that, I'd look like a baby. I shook my head. I probably had this all wrong.

Angela Hoke   *A Whisper of Smoke*

Uncle George did not seem to sense my increasing uneasiness. His arms were relaxed around my sides, and he even chuckled at the television show that was flashing light distractingly across the darkened room. I sat utterly still and, after a few moments, I felt him draw away, and I was briefly reassured that maybe it was all a mistake after all. But then he pushed against me again, almost as if accidentally – just part of a full body stretch as he extended his arms over his head and yawned.

My eyes were now opened as wide as they could go, and my stomach was rolling around like a front-load washer. The TV was absurdly loud, and I realized that there was a new program on. I had the fleeting thought that it seemed more appropriate that we still be watching the Twilight Zone, as I was certain we were now in it.

George had relaxed his body again, but I could still feel him beneath me. He put his hands lightly on my waist again, giving me a gentle squeeze. It was confusing the way this simple gesture was like normal affection and the prelude to something ominous, all at the same time. The confusion caused my stomach to cycle faster, and my head to join in the spinning. The combination was dizzying, and it made my eyes close and my body sag involuntarily. He took this as a sign of comfort, or maybe of submission, and he hugged me close to his chest again. The hug was chaste enough, but my panic was increasing.

Without warning, I vomited.

"Dammit!" he exclaimed with surprise. He jumped up, forearms dripping brown, root beer vomit, and I fell over when he stood up and lay on the couch moaning, my stomach churning.

I heard Uncle George leave the room, and in an instant he had returned with towels. Through slitted eyes, I watched him cleaning up my vomit, leaving only to retrieve fresh towels. Not at all sure what to expect

A Whisper of Smoke   *Angela Hoke*

of Uncle George now, my view of him upended by the last thirty minutes, I was surprised when he knelt down in front of me and cleaned my face and hair with a damp rag.

"Are you okay, sweetie?" he asked, smoothing my hair and comforting me as a parent would do, as an uncle would do. There were no overtones in his soothing words, and I quickly clung to the image of this George, the one I knew and loved.

After cleaning me up as best he could with towels, he scooped me up in his arms and carried me up the stairs. He hesitated at my bedroom door.

"Do you think we'll wake Hank?" asked Uncle George.

"No, he sleeps like the dead," I replied, surprised that my voice sounded so normal.

With that, he awkwardly opened the door and carried me to my bed. A quick glance at the sprawled sleeping boy reassured us that he was out.

After Uncle George sat me on my bed, he went to my drawers. When he found some clean pajamas, he sat down on the edge of the bed and unceremoniously pulled my soiled nightgown up and over my head. I gasped for the few seconds as I sat there nearly naked, shivering in my thin wet panties, feeling utterly exposed. But almost just as quickly, George had my arms up and my nightgown down over them and settled around me.

"Do you feel sick again?" he asked, misreading my gasp.

"The room is spinning every time I close my eyes," I said truthfully.

Angela Hoke   *A Whisper of Smoke*

*He laughed and said, "Honey, you sure can't hold your liquor."
He laid me back on my pillow, gathered my covers up over me, and
tucked me in, just as we had tucked Hank in a few hours earlier.*

*"Try to get some sleep, and tomorrow morning you'll feel better,"
he said reassuringly.*

*I watched him uncertainly as he headed towards the door,
pausing to turn out the light.*

*"Sweet dreams," he said, his voice low and rumbling. "Oh, and
don't tell your mom and dad I let you have booze. They'd never let me
babysit you again." With that, he turned off the light and shut the door
behind him.*

*I lay there feeling disoriented and unsure of my own perceptions
and memories. Did I imagine it all? Could I have?*

*I convinced myself that it must have been a dream. There was
really no other explanation for it. It was a dream, and I would forget it. I
pushed my way into my subconscious to where the hazy remembrances
of the night floated around in a rum mist, and I closed them behind a big,
heavy door. Feeling relieved, I promptly felt my consciousness spiraling
into blackness.*

Maybe George heard my thoughts, or maybe God heard my
prayer and was intervening. But his next words were not a recollection of
that night. Instead, he said, "Susanna, I'm so, so very sorry. You will
never know how sorry I am – for all of it."

He didn't wait for me to respond, knowing I wouldn't.

"I know I can't change it, but I can make sure that I'll never do
anything like that again."

A Whisper of Smoke   *Angela Hoke*

I looked over at him, then, my eyes sharp.

"And how are you going to do that?" I spat, suddenly furious.

His face was full of anguish that looked genuine, but I was not moved.

He looked at me for a moment, as if gauging whether I just wanted to be angry, or whether I really wanted to know what he was doing to change. He sighed, apparently deciding to tell me, even if I had no interest in listening.

"Well," he began slowly. "I told my priest... everything. I made a full confession right after... when things hit bottom. And, to be sure that I have accountability, I still see my priest three times a week."

I looked away as I tried to control my emotions, but I was listening.

He took my silence as a sign to continue. "I told Cheryl, and she broke up with me for a while. When she came back, she said that she would never leave me alone with anyone that I could... hurt, again. Since she can't have kids, she thinks that..."

He paused, apparently trying to maintain his composure. He cleared his throat uncomfortably and took a deep breath.

"She thinks that maybe God brought us together because she's meant to help heal me and make me a better person."

His head was bowed in shame – whether at the thought of the horrible things he'd done or with embarrassment that Cheryl had married him to be his warden, I couldn't be sure.

"I can't ever make it right," he said, his voice wobbling. "But I am going to do everything in my power to... never be that person again."

Then he turned to look at me. He gazed at me until I had to look at him, then his eyes held mine with a pain that was like a tether between us. "Susanna, I would rather die than to ever hurt you or anyone else like that, ever again."

I searched his eyes, since I was unable to look away. The pain seemed real enough. Despite my commitment to anger, I could feel it dulling, as my heart softened just a little.

He seemed to be waiting for something from me.

"I can't forgive you," I started, and his eyes closed. "Yet," I added, reluctantly. "But... I respect that you are trying to change. I'll be watching to see if you can stick to it. Because if you can't..."

"I will!" he said eagerly. "I swear that I will do whatever I have to, Susanna. I don't want to be a bad person," he said, his voice modulating with emotion.

I looked away again, uncomfortable with his show of weakness, his vulnerability. I was not ready to show him sympathy. But I wouldn't hate him anymore, I realized.

"I'm going in," I said, turning from him. I glimpsed his head and shoulders slump in dejection and I paused.

"You coming?" I asked.

His head popped up, and his brief smile looked grateful. He followed me inside, and we joined the family around the tree. Mother and Cheryl both looked up sharply as we entered. Mother's eyes were wary, but then relaxed when she saw that maybe things were a little better. Cheryl's expression was protective, hawk-like as her eyes darted around looking for danger. Something in George's expression must have calmed her, because her eyes smiled, making her face almost pretty.

A Whisper of Smoke   *Angela Hoke*

Chapter 20: Paradise Lost

Lying on top of my covers, I felt a peace that I'd not felt in a very long time. Optimism filled me up like Thanksgiving dinner, and I was filled with the tentative belief that family hurts could heal, that people could change, that Calvin might care for me more than he'd admitted, and that I might get the chance to go to Hawaii and win him, once and for all.

I could even enjoy daydreaming about Cute Rocker – he was a lovely distraction and a reminder that I was still a teenage girl.

Midnight Mass had left me feeling inspired, and my mind whirled with new possibilities. Too wired to sleep, I decided to write Calvin a letter – a real one this time. I retrieved a flashlight from my nightstand drawer, watching Annabelle to see if she stirred, but she was conked, her small hands and feet hanging off the cot at odd angles. Lorelei had reclaimed her bed for the holidays, but it was still empty – she'd spent the majority of her Christmas break with Mark, and I supposed she was with him now.

As I began writing my letter, I alternated between the compulsion to declare my love for him again, and the need to protect myself in case I was misreading the whole situation. I decided not to tip my hand, just in case. Besides, it wouldn't hurt him to get a little jealous (if I could delude myself into thinking that such a thing was possible).

* * *

December 24, 1968

Santa Baby,

    It is Christmas Eve (well, technically it's Christmas Day since it's well after midnight, but it doesn't really count until you've been to sleep and Santa's come), and I am writing this to you with a flashlight under the covers on my bed, as Annabelle snores in the next bed over. I can hear my parents shuttling presents back and forth from their cache to the living room, making Santa's visit a reality. My Christmas wish cannot be wrapped (not unless you care to tie a big red ribbon around yourself, and nothing else!). My wish, my most fervent prayer, is for you, of you, about you – that you are safe, that you are well, that you are happy, that you are thinking about me, that you are fantasizing about my firm young body, that you are planning how you are going to dump your girlfriend for me as you read these words...

    I'm trying to come across as flip and playful, but I fear that my heart betrays me through the words I don't write. I know you want me to be fun and flirtatious, the way that you've come to love and crave, the way I was in the beginning. And I want so very much to give you what you need. But I don't feel lighthearted about my letters to you, and I'm finding it very difficult to pretend that I do.

    Maybe if I tell you about some things that have been going on around here (never dull), that will help to lighten the tone of my rambling thoughts.

    So Cute Rocker broke up with his girlfriend. We had a dance just before we got out for Christmas break, and he was there, playing organ and sometimes bass guitar. As usual, I scoped out the scene for Lindy, and saw her sitting miserably on some bleachers, in the midst of a covey of comforting, sympathetic friends. She looked like she had been crying, and once I pointed it out to Shelly, she was like a bloodhound on the scent of the scoop. Before long, she found out that she was way more serious than he was, and that he broke up with her because he didn't think it was fair to lead her on. Honestly, I thought that sounded a little bit like something you would do, and I was impressed.

Then (and I'm hesitant to admit this to you, except that I suspect you've developed a few vices during your time away), I was outside smoking a cigarette with Shelly and some other kids behind the dumpsters, while Wanda was on the look-out for teachers, when the guys in the band came outside for some fresh air. They walked around to where we were, pushing each other and laughing, as we watched them with eagle eyes. As they walked past (with me leaning nonchalantly against the brick of the building, trying to look disinterested and interesting all at once – quite a challenge), I could see that Cute Rocker was going to pass just a few feet away from me. Just before he got to me, I looked the other direction, like I was too cool to notice him, the Virginia Slim dangling sexily from my lips, when suddenly it was plucked from my mouth. I gasped in surprise and turned just in time to see Cute Rocker, not take a drag off it himself like most of the boys would have done but instead toss it on the ground and crush it with the toe of his Chuck Taylor high-tops.

"You're too cute to do something dumb like smoke," he said, and kept right on walking. My mouth fell open, and Shelly ran up to me to see what he had said.

I know I stared after him for at least a full minute, before she put

Angela Hoke   A Whisper of Smoke

her hand under my chin and forcibly closed my gaping mouth. I got butterflies in my stomach, and we started giggling like twelve-year-olds. For the rest of the night, I was torn between putting a cigarette in my mouth just to see if he would come over and take it from me again, and not putting one in my mouth to show that I was indeed too smart for smoking, but definitely smart enough for him.

I looked really cute that night, too. My hair flipped just like it was supposed to, and I had on my white lipstick and tall white go-go boots. My plaid jumper was very short and I had on a white mock turtleneck underneath that hugged my curves in just the right way. I was feeling very womanly and magnetic. I had my mojo on.

You would have been jealous.

Or maybe you wouldn't have.

Anyway, the whole cigarette-crushing thing was very upstanding, and I thought immediately that you would approve.

Oh, and one other thing – I found out that his name is Daniel Foster, and he just graduated from Durbin High. I think he's going to college to study something hard, too. He had that smart look about him. I liked him. I'd like to know more about him.

He still doesn't compare to you.

* * *

I paused, not knowing where to go next. My thinking wasn't clear, and my eyelids were drooping. I decided to leave the letter unfinished for now, and surrender to sleep. When I woke tomorrow, it would officially be Christmas morning. I found myself smiling and looking forward to it, to everything, for the first time in a long time.

A Whisper of Smoke   *Angela Hoke*

I turned over and switched off the light, then burrowed into my warm bedding. I drifted to sleep, the ghost of my smile lingering for the angels to see.

Everyone had almost finished opening their gifts, and my family members were sprawled around the room in languid poses. I vaguely noticed that I hadn't gotten many gifts, but I was not upset. I was just glad that Hank and Annabelle were so pleased with their presents. I was content, even before Mother pulled a small box out of the middle of the tree and presented it to me with uncommon glee.

I felt a brief uneasiness, remembering past episodes when Mother had been gleeful for disturbing reasons, then pushed it aside. It *was* Christmas, after all.

Suddenly, everyone's attention was focused on me, even Lorelei's. I was curious, and a little nervous, as I ripped at the paper and removed the top of the box. Inside were wads of tissue paper which I tossed aside to reveal a silk flower lei and an envelope. I picked up the lei slowly, a tentative comprehension dawning. I glanced up at my family, at my parents. They were *beaming* at me. *Can this really be happening?*

I reached down and tried to retrieve the envelope. My fingers were shaking, and I couldn't seem to grasp the corner. Finally, I flipped the box over and the envelope slid out. I picked it up reverently, still not quite believing, and opened it slowly.

Inside was a bundle of cash.

"How?" I screeched, my voice cracking.

"She sold that dumb old broach," Annabelle piped up, and Mother made to reach out and tug her into silence. "She made me go to all these stinky pawn shops until we found one where the man at the counter didn't act like a dirty old codger," Annabelle said and then Mother pinched her hard on the arm and gave her The Look. Annabelle winced, but looked smug that she was able to steal a little of the attention.

My eyes watered and my heart filled up – that crusty old ruby broach was one of the very few family heirlooms Mother had. It had belonged to Mother's grandmother, who had brought it over with her on the boat from Europe.

I was conflicted. I didn't want to feel grateful to Mother for anything. I'd only begun this manipulation because I had no other choice. But now that it was here, I was overwhelmed at her selflessness, particularly since it was completely uncharacteristic. Before I realized what I was doing, I jumped up and hugged her. She stiffened in surprise, then hugged me back, making my eyes spill over. When I hugged Daddy, he chuckled with pleasure into my hair. I was smiling so hugely my face hurt, as everyone started talking at once about the money, what it meant, and why I was going all the way to Hawaii to see Calvin. I was overcome with an indestructible happiness, and was sure that nothing could diminish this moment or the promise it represented.

That is, until Mabel came over and crushed it into dust.

"Susanna!" Mabel exclaimed, bouncing into the house and following me up to my room. We both flopped on the beds, as I waited to hear about Mabel's Christmas morning.

"You'll never guess what Calvin sent Mom for Christmas," she said, her eyes dancing.

My stomach fluttered at the sound of his name. "What?"

"He sent her a ticket to Hawaii! Can you believe it? She was so shocked – I've never seen her speechless like that, ever."

I couldn't help but smile, both at the thought of Mrs. Conner's reaction and Mabel's exuberant recounting. "That's great – is she excited?"

"Well," she said, dramatically, as she changed positions on the bed (she never sat still for long). "At first, she tried to say she couldn't go. I think she was just scared, because she's never been on a plane before. Heck, none of us have!" she declared happily.

"But then, and you're never going to believe this, *Daddy* told her to quit making excuses and get ready to pack her bags. That's when she started getting excited. She was like a kid! I've never seen her look like that before."

I was smiling, swept away by Mabel's contagious excitement.

"Doesn't that just sound so great?" Mabel continued. "I wish I could go too, but we only have enough money for one of us."

"So your mom is traveling all that way by herself?" I asked.

"Christine is going with her, of course. Besides, she is so excited to see Calvin, I think she would go through space if she had to." She sighed. "Can you imagine how romantic it will be when Calvin sees Christine?"

Mabel became absorbed with some romantic fantasy, and she didn't notice that I had doubled over like I'd been punched.

Christine is going! How could I have been so stupid?

Mabel chattered on for several more minutes, not realizing that I was no longer with her, and I was grateful when Mabel finally said she had to go to help make pumpkin pies for dinner. Somehow, I held onto my tears until I heard Mabel telling the rest of my family good-bye

Angela Hoke   *A Whisper of Smoke*

downstairs.

It took me two days of hiding out in misery before I could bring myself to tell Lorelei what had happened. Lorelei quietly told our parents, and pity replaced the euphoric atmosphere that had been so short-lived.

Mother didn't even ask for the money back. But I couldn't keep it – it was way more than my parents had ever spent on any of us, and way more than they could afford. So first I clandestinely searched through Mother's room until I found the pawn ticket, and I called the shop only to find that the broach had been sold already. So two days before I had to return to school for second semester, I offered to take Hank and Annabelle for a drive. To their dismay, I took them to a shoe store and bought them both new shoes – both sneakers and dress shoes. I bought myself some as well. We all needed them badly, and this would spare Mother and Dad from having to come up with the cash to buy them.

Then, I bought my dad some new rabbit ears for the TV. The old ones were always falling over, and half the time he had to sit in a chair by the TV and hold them just so we could get a usable signal. Finally, I bought Mother the handbag she'd been lusting over. It was purely a luxury item, but I knew it was something she'd never buy for herself.

Since the money was virtually my whole Christmas, I did spend some of it to buy some new clothes and some fabric so I could make a few things too. Even after all that, I still had a sizable amount left, and I was determined that Mother and Dad would take it back.

Once I'd repaid them for the Christmas gift, I convinced myself that I was out of their debt, that I no longer had to pretend appreciation. My obligations fulfilled, I grabbed back onto my anger because I still wasn't ready to forgive them. But I found that, this time around, my anger served yet another purpose – it distracted me from the hurt that circled my chest like a drain, hurt that I was determined not to feel again.

As the end of break approached, I tried to get excited about wearing my new outfits to school in a few days, but it felt hollow. I couldn't help thinking about the plane that would be leaving for Hawaii in just over a week, without me on it – and with that Christine in my place. I tried to be smart, and reason my way through the jungle of emotions. Obviously, Calvin wanted Christine there. She wouldn't be going uninvited. I had clearly read too much into his last letter. He was just lonely and vulnerable, and maybe taking me a little too much for granted.

I had to remind myself of what he'd told me the night of his going-away party (or, at least, what I could remember of it). Even though some of it was fuzzy, I couldn't forget the pain I'd felt when he'd rejected me. And his rejection had gone beyond denying my love – he'd also told me we could no longer be friends.

A sick feeling stole through me as fragments of memory stabbed at my brain, but I pushed them back. *There's no sense dwelling on all that stuff again. We're friends again now, and I'm grateful for that.*

Now, here I was alone in my room, facing the unfinished letter that I knew I'd have to complete. *He still needs me – I love him too much to let him down,* I realized, even if he didn't love me back.

So I picked up my pen, and prepared to finish the letter, starting with the last sentence I'd written.

He still doesn't compare to you.

Angela Hoke   *A Whisper of Smoke*

I read the last line, seeing all the meaning behind it, and was overcome with the urge to scratch it out, erase it and the stupid sentiment it represented. I sighed. I couldn't do it. I may not be able to confess everything that I was feeling to him (because, for one, it would be utterly pointless and humiliating), but I would stick to my pledge to be as honest as I could be. I just had to make some serious changes in my life, beginning with somehow forcing myself to stop pining for Calvin. Then, I could write my true feelings and there would be no danger in them.

So I left that last line, and I continued, trying to be strong.

* * *

Christmas is over now, and Mabel tells me that you sent your mom a ticket to come to Hawaii and see you. That is really sweet. According to Mabel, your mom was beside herself with nervous excitement. Even your dad was supportive. I know that was expensive, especially since you'd already sent a ticket to Christine, but you did a good thing, Calvin. You are going to give her memories that she'll never forget.

I really, really hope that your leave is everything that you need it to be. I have to admit that I'm a little jealous, but I look forward to hearing all about it in your next letter.

As always, my sweet friend, please be safe. You are always in my prayers.

Your girl, always,

Susanna

* * *

Before my tears could warp the paper and betray my true feelings, I sealed up the letter and sent it around the world.

Chapter 21: Lava Rocks Have Sharp Edges

February 1969

Dear Susanna,

I'm sorry I haven't written in a while. We've had a lot of action lately. Danger lurks everywhere. The scratchy swish of dry elephant grass haunts my dreams, hiding small dark-haired men with AK-47s bent on my destruction. In one recurring dream, I'm running up this big hill because I think that there is something worth reaching on the other side. Sometimes it's the roar of a waterfall that draws me, promising a spray that shoots off rainbows of refracted light. Other times I imagine that our corn fields are on the other side, and that it is the sound of the corn stalks rustling that I hear instead of the elephant grass. Whatever it is, it is a promise of life and of peace. So I run and run as hard as I can, and I'm panting and my heart is pounding and the sweat is pouring off me. Then, when I get almost to the top, almost to the point where I can see over the precipice to the peaceful landscape that awaits me, I realize that I've climbed to the top of a giant termite mound. Just as this realization sinks in, the top begins to collapse so that I'm slipping and falling towards the gaping hole that marks the entrance into their blind domain.

Then I awake with a heart-racing start, as I land, not on a swarm of crawling termites, but on the pallet covering the hard earth, and my pack that is serving as my pillow. For the first ten seconds or so, I am filled with terror and my

A Whisper of Smoke   *Angela Hoke*

heart tries to escape through my chest.

I'm sure we could analyze my dream and discover meanings both complex and simple. I don't want to analyze it, though. I just want to stop having it. I do not like to feel so afraid.

I've learned over the past weeks new sounds of battle. In the rainy season, it is raining so hard, you can barely tell the gunfire from the sound of the raindrops beating down. Not that it sounds the same, exactly, it is just that there is a sensory overload. There is so much sound that there is no sound.

Now the sounds of the jungle are different. The constant crackle of dry branches makes us all jumpy. Mortars are our thunder. Tracer rounds flick past like strobe lightning. And the only rain is caused by the spray from the grenade that we throw into the river, so that we can have fish with our C Rations for dinner.

The waters in the rice paddies are draining, and the villagers take their water buffalos on the narrow paths as they wade carefully beside them, harvesting. Occasionally, they harvest a land mine instead, thoughtfully buried by the VC, ironically placing it where it will kill villagers but where it is less likely to harm soldiers.

It is hot as hell here. In certain parts, the ground is hard and dusty, exposed to the sun. But under the triple canopy, formed by the dense jungle trees, there is a separate eco-system. It is muggy and the vegetation is green. But it is also incredibly dense. We feel loud as tanks as we cut our way through the bamboo and vine.

We get supplied much more often now because it is so dry. But when we are in a fight, sometimes we use up our stores of water too quickly and so we have to go in search fresh water until we can be resupplied. We use iodine tablets to purify it and carry as much as we can carry in our canteens. Using both official and unofficial means, we get enough to drink. But bathing is another story.

Angela Hoke   A Whisper of Smoke

I'm ashamed to tell you how long it's been since I bathed. You would find me disgusting, I'm sure. But I can't smell myself. We all smell the same, and we are used to it.

One good thing about the dry season is it makes it a little easier to see the bamboo vipers. They can kill you within a minute of biting you, or so they say. I've seen two and they scared the snot out of me both times. Some days I look so hard for them, that every vine seems to be writhing and hissing. Like we need another thing to set our nerves on edge.

The only other good thing about the dry season is that it's not the rainy season.

You would have loved Hawaii. It was just as beautiful as I had imagined it. I am so glad that my mom got to see it. The whole six days, she just kept walking around saying, "Would you look at that? I couldn't even imagine anything like this." It was so sweet. She was like a little kid. And I can't ever recall, in my whole life, ever having been around my mother when she wasn't caring for little ones. At first, she didn't know what to do with herself, and you could tell she was trying hard not to mother me too much. But after about a day and a half, she started going on walks through the surf. She brought back pieces of lava rock and pink conch shells and packed them away in her suitcase like they were treasures. Every morning, the hotel staff put fresh orchids in our room, and Mom would take one and put it into her hair. She glowed like the sunsets, and, except for glimpses of her worry for me, I've never seen her so happy. Someday, if I can afford it (and if I can get my stubborn dad on a plane), I am going to bring my whole family there for a vacation.

You probably know that Christine also met me there. I felt so awkward with her at first – I forgot who I used to be with her, and I was anxious about getting it right. Mom gave us lots of privacy when she went on her exploratory walks. So Christine and I went on walks, too. We walked along the sandy beaches, and when the wind blew up the sand and it pelted our skin, I thought of the dirt blown from the termite hills. When we heard the constant crash of the surf and the waves, I heard instead torrential monsoon rains. When we walked under the shade of coconut palms and banyan trees, I was back under my triple canopy.

Everything was a reminder of my other world, yet I was a foreigner in every sense.

Our conversations were the weirdest I've ever had. Christine was so nervous, that she kept up a constant and inane chatter. She talked about the green birds we saw, the tropical flowers that abounded with waxy green leaves, vinyl-like red petals and an erect yellow pestle that, in combination, looked obscene to my jaded eyes (though I couldn't say that), and the beauty of the sunsets. She wondered at the curious absence of snakes and expressed fear of the indigo waters that, in her mind, hid schools of hungrily waiting sharks. When I didn't provide the appropriate responses (because (a) I literally couldn't reason out the appropriate responses, and (b) I was afraid to talk for fear of accidentally saying 'fuck' (something told me she would not have responded well to that as it would not have fit with her version of Calvin)), she got pouty. She started to become insecure, worrying that I was lusting after the native girls in their grass skirts, with their golden skin and bright white smiles. (Okay, so maybe I did notice them, but I wasn't a cad – I didn't stare or drool). She would then alternate between striking (too) deliberately provocative poses in her demure bathing suit, and dropping her shoulders in an all-out sulk. I was at a total loss.

We'd inevitably end up back at the adjoining rooms, where I had one and Mom and Christine shared the other, her on the verge of tears and me wishing I had a smoke and a beer. Mom would peek out and, reading the tension, would somehow manage to spirit Christine away for some kind of girl

Angela Hoke   A Whisper of Smoke

talk, leaving me free to go to the bar. I'd sit in the back, a bottle of the coldest beer sitting before me, smoking just the one or two cigarettes I could bum off another GI (that's my limit – it's how I keep myself from becoming full-out hooked, or so I tell myself), and listening with relief to the crude conversations of the other soldiers, some on R&R like me and others stationed there (lucky bastards).

Finally, when it seemed somehow as if enough time had passed, I would settle up at the bar and make my way back over to our rooms. I would find Mom and Christine sitting out on the joint veranda, watching the last of the sinking sun.

Mom would smile in her knowing way and then quickly excuse herself, and Christine would smile shyly at me and scoot over to make room for me on the bench swing. We'd sit there quietly for some time, as the night turned from fire to ink, all the time, the noise from the surf was unending, a tidal monsoon.

The only time that I could bring myself to give her the attention she so desperately sought was when the night was at its blackest, and she would snuggle to me in her old way, and I would become overcome with a desire that was animal. I would kiss her with a force we never used to have, and she would shy away and then respond. But I was blind, a rutting stag with no conscience, only instinct. I know she sensed it, because she would tense next to me and in the next instant yield completely. It was I who had to climb up out of the fog and break away, before I promised her something with my body that I didn't mean. That's when I would leave her bewildered on her blanket on the sand, mumbling apologies with no discernible meaning, and go as far from her as I could go. I would strip down under the stars and venture into a habitat owned by sharks and other creatures, animals that understood the primal realm. I'd swim in the cold night surf, and it was thrillingly terrifying. Part of me secretly wished I would get attacked by some sea monster and that the turmoil would be over in a cruel twist of fate, where the headline would read "Soldier Survives Jungle Hell Only to

A Whisper of Smoke   *Angela Hoke*

Perish in a Mirror Paradise."

I have never before felt so out of control. I wanted with a ferociousness that I had suppressed in the jungle so that I would not compromise myself forever by taking advantage of Mai or some other vulnerable.

And I wished, selfishly, that you were there. I think I would have ravished you, and that would have been very unfair to you. But in my delusions, I told myself you would understand it, and me, and it would have been okay. Maybe I could even have convinced myself, in my consuming need, that it was right to surrender to you.

So I'm glad you weren't there. Now that I have my sanity back, I know that I would never be able to forgive myself for using you that way. It would break my heart to break yours. If we were ever together like that, it would be because we were together in every way.

On the last day, we all went to visit Pearl Harbor and read about the U.S.S. Arizona. They both started crying, and I had to pretend like nothing like that could ever happen to me. Mom wept hot, repressed tears, and looked at me like she would swallow me up if she could. Christine cried like her world would never be the same, and that I was largely to blame.

I think the trip was a big disappointment to her – that I was a big disappointment to her. I think she thought that it would be all romantic, that I would lay my head in her lap and she would rub my temples as I shared my innermost, darkest experiences. Except that she didn't really want to hear my experiences. She was as scared of who I have become as I am. And I think she fantasized that I would propose to her. I couldn't do it. I don't recognize either of us right now. It would be like two strangers, committing to each other for a life on shifting sands.

Angela Hoke   *A Whisper of Smoke*

I hope all is wonderful in your life. Please tell me what has been going on in your world. I long to read your words and hear your voice and laughter in my mind.

With love, your Soldier-Man,

Calvin

* * *

How could he do this to me? I had just started to get my head wrapped around the fact that all we would ever be was just friends – very good, dear friends. Now my emotions were all in turmoil again. He'd even driven Daniel from my mind, and our first date had been great.

If there was no explanation as to *how* he could do this to me, maybe the more pertinent question was *why*? On the one hand, I was secretly thrilled that things with Christine hadn't gone all that well. And I was *ecstatic* that he hadn't succumbed to the pressure to *propose* to that... girl. Ugh! The thought of it, alone, was enough to make me nauseous. But why was he torturing me by telling me that he wished he could have, that we could have... made *love* together on the beaches of paradise... And *then* have the gall to insinuate that I would have been *okay* with that?? As if that alone would *ever* be enough?

The disgusting thing was, when I read his words, I got all mushy inside and liquidy in parts that I had been trying to ignore. *Damn it!* Every time I made a little progress, he wrote words that tore through my defenses and made me want him all over again.

I was sitting on my bed, the stupid letter spread out around me, and I pulled my pillow over my face. I pushed it against my nose and mouth, cutting off the flow of oxygen. *Maybe it would be better if I just died,* I thought dramatically. *Then I wouldn't have to keep reliving this stupid pain.* I held my breath behind the pillow for a little over a minute, then pulled it back and sucked in fresh air. I'd always been good at holding my breath, so the pillow thing was not any kind of real attempt. It was just for dramatic effect—making a point to my dolls and stuffed animals that I didn't think I could take this crap anymore. As I looked around at their serious faces, their expressions frozen in concern, I thought they got the picture.

As I lay there, I realized I was fuming. I was mad! At Calvin! That was kind of a strange realization, because I adored him, still. And I knew his life was in grave danger. But how *dare* he reject me in no uncertain terms, over and over, and then play with my feelings like that? Especially since he *knew* very well how I felt about him? And good grief, I had let him know that over and over in the past several months, hadn't I? Like a stupid whipped puppy, coming back for more and more abuse. *I am an idiot!* I thought harshly.

I was in severe need of some clarity. So I called Shelly to get her perspective.

"He's dicking you around," she said immediately, after I had finished reading the letter to her over the phone.

I closed my eyes on my end of the call. I was getting a tension headache behind my eyebrows and in my temples, and I wedged the receiver on my shoulder so I could massage the pressure points.

"What, no reaction? Aren't you going to defend your little Soldier-boy?"

"No," I replied flatly. "I totally agree with you. I feel like a complete fool."

Angela Hoke   *A Whisper of Smoke*

Shelly sighed. "You are not a fool. You just love that boy more than he deserves."

I started to disagree, then stopped myself. Maybe Shelly was right. I would always love Calvin, and he certainly deserved love for many reasons -- for who he was, what he stood for and the way he was serving his country. But did he really deserve my passionate romantic love? Especially when he could not return it?

"I think you ought to go jump Daniel's bones and forget all about Calvin," Shelly suggested.

I laughed despite my despair. "While that's not an unpleasant thought, I don't think Daniel would appreciate that. He's not that kind of guy."

"I swear – you can really pick 'em," Shelly replied in obvious disapproval.

"How do I respond to him?" I asked, my voice desperate.

"How about telling him to go f—"

"No, stop it," I interrupted. "I'm not going to tell him to go take a flying leap or do any four-letter action to himself. You know I can't do that to him. Even if he is, as you so eloquently put it, *dicking* with me, I am still his best friend, and he needs me. I won't upset him – not when it could get him killed."

Shelly sighed with exasperation. "So I guess you are going to write him some sappy love letter, instead?"

"No, I just want to write him like a … best friend would. But what do I say? Do I call him out on the stuff he said? Do I tell him how he's crossing the line, the line that HE drew, by saying that shit to me? Or do I just ignore it, and talk about my stupid life?"

Shelly was quiet for a long while, but I knew it was because she was considering the question. I felt a surge of appreciation for Shelly, my crazy, uninhibited friend who was always loyal, always there for me.

"Okay, here's what I think," she began. "I think that you should ignore the over-the-top stuff in his letter ... no reference to the *ravishing*," she said the last word with a hint of abhorrence in her voice. "You can respond to anything else in his letter. And of course, you should definitely tell him about your date with Daniel."

"Ya think?"

"Oh, yes. Did he not describe to you his make-out sessions with that Christine bitch -- that is when he wasn't talking about taking *you* right there on the beach."

I considered it. "Okay," I said finally. "I guess you're right. I'm going out with Daniel again this weekend. I'll write to him after that. Maybe then I'll have a little better perspective."

"Right. Sounds like a good plan. And how *was* your date with Cute Rocker? You didn't say much about it."

I laughed. "That's because, by your dirty standards, there wasn't much to tell. But we had fun. He's really sweet, and he gave me a very, very nice first kiss at the end."

Shelly sighed. "You are very hard to live vicariously through, I hope you know. I guess I'm just going to have to get my own boyfriend again."

"I guess so," I said, smiling. "Shelly," I added, hesitating, wanting to express my appreciation but knowing that Shelly didn't like mushy talk.

"Yeah, sis?"

"You are the best. I don't know what I'd do without you as my best friend," I said, my voice choking up.

"Yeah, yeah," she said flippantly, blowing off the unusual

sentimentality. "Too bad I'm not queer – we'd make a great couple!"

I burst out laughing in spite of my melancholy mood.

"Okay, gotta go! Call me later if you want," Shelly said quickly, then hung up before any other sappy comments could be slipped into the conversation.

* * *

March 6, 1969

Dear Calvin,

I saw some of the pictures your mother took when you were in Hawaii. You look so grown up! You didn't tell me that you'd grown a mustache. It made you look like a man – it's really weird. And I could tell that your muscles had gotten bigger under your green t-shirt. Don't worry – I'm not going to make any inappropriate comments. It's just an observation. That Christine even looked kind of pretty, with her straight hair all blowy and the orchid behind her ear.

I couldn't tell from your letter whether you got the R&R you needed when you were on leave or not. It sounded kind of tumultuous. I hope that you felt at least a little bit rested, and not just conflicted. I am glad (and I'm not ashamed to admit it) that you didn't propose to Christine. I may have had to go jump off a bridge, or tie a brick around my neck and walk into the middle of our pond if you'd done that. Not to be melodramatic or anything. I just don't think she's the one for you. But I guess it's not up to me, though I'll never understand why you don't turn all your major decisions over to my capable decision-making abilities.

So I've gone out with Daniel (aka Cute Rocker) a few times now.

A Whisper of Smoke   *Angela Hoke*

He is very cute, and sweet. He doesn't even try to take advantage of me – even when I wear my ultra-short miniskirts. He's a gentleman, I guess. I'm not really used to that. I'm used to fighting Chip off constantly – he was always trying to get into my pants, even when we were in a group of people. He was a complete horn-dog.

But Daniel is all sweet and gentlemanly. Like I told you before, I think you'd approve. He just takes me to movies and then for a burger or whatever. He holds the door open for me, and asks my opinion about stuff, and holds my hand in the dark.

Did I tell you that he was in college? He goes to Speed School at UofL. He's going to be an engineer of some sort. He's been helping me with algebra, since you so heartlessly abandoned me by going off to war. He's a good teacher, but not as good as you were. Between the two of you, though, I think I should graduate with a basic understanding.

So he invited me to start going to his "gigs" with him. I'm kind of excited about that. I get to ride with him in his car (a very cool Camaro) to help set up, and then I get to hang around backstage. I guess that makes me a Groupie! How funny.

I hope that you are staying safe. I'll be watching for your next letter, anxious as always to hear from you. But for now, I'd better go. Daniel's coming to get me soon. I've got to get ready, make myself irresistible and all that.

Love,
Susanna

* * *

Angela Hoke   *A Whisper of Smoke*

Okay, yeah, I was trying to make him a little bit jealous. But he deserved it, didn't he? So I mailed it.

Chapter 22: Curse of the War-Time Soldier

March 29, 1968

Daniel was kissing me good-bye, and I was enjoying every second of it. He was a great kisser, and he always left me wanting more. When he pulled back, his eyes flashed at me.

"Until next time, sweet Susanna," he said and smiled. With an exaggerated sigh, I got out of the car.

That's when I heard the cry that would destroy my world.

"Susanna!" Mabel howled, a horrific sound. She was running blindly across the field towards my house, her white shirt glowing in the moonlight. I turned at her voice, hearing the panicked sobs, so incongruous coming out of Mabel's mouth. Daniel put the car back in park, arresting his reverse motion out of the driveway, and got out to see why my face looked the way it did.

I watched Mabel barreling toward me with a shocked detachment. There was no way to make sense of a hysterically crying Mabel – Mabel, a girl who was as tough as she was sweet and funny and who had never cried in front of me in all the years we'd been friends.

It must be Jacob – he's broken her heart.

Mabel rocketed into my arms and blubbered into my shoulder, immediately drenching it.

"Shhh," I said, hugging my friend and patting her back. "It's okay.

Shhh."

"No," Mabel choked.

"Mabel, he's just one boy. There will be others. You are so great, there will be many, many others. He's a damn fool," I said, desperate to get Mabel's attention and calm her down so we could talk through it.

Instead, Mabel just pulled back and looked at me like I'd lost my mind. Mabel's eyes shown in the moonlight like black pools and pain was reflected there that seemed too much.

They must have been a lot more serious than I thought.

I tried to draw Mabel back into a hug, saying, "I know what it's like – when Chip broke my heart, I thought I'd never get over it. But I was really better off." I even believed it, as I looked over Mabel's head at Daniel, who was standing close, coiled tight with an intense desire to help but unsure what to do.

To my surprise, Mabel pushed back again. This time, she took my face in her hands and locked onto my eyes with hers, agony clear in her features.

"Susanna," she croaked, then tried again. "Susanna, it's not Jacob." She said these words very slowly, like she was talking to a small child. I heard them, but my mind still protected its assumptions and resisted any other directions.

"It's not Jacob," Mabel repeated, her eyes filling again. And suddenly I knew.

"It's Calvin," a voice said, and some part of me registered that it was Mabel. "It's Calvin."

Mabel was sobbing again, I realized, but that seemed unimportant now – just a side detail in the nightmare that was engulfing me. I sat down hard on the ground, and Mabel collapsed with me.

"My big brother... Oh, Susanna. My brother's never coming back." Mabel completely broke down. Her words were barely intelligible and her face was a mess of mucus and tears, a mask of despair. I must have looked at her, but then that image swirled away too, losing all meaning in a moment that made no sense but meant everything terrible and wrong.

At the edge of my consciousness, I knew that Daniel was kneeling just behind me, maybe even with a hand on my back. But I didn't feel it—I couldn't feel anything but disbelief. My psyche was suspending belief until things made sense again.

"It's not true, it's not true, it's not true," a voice repeated, sounding wretched. In a disconnected way, I understood the words were coming out of my mouth. I held on to Mabel, whose head was buried in my lap, her fingernails digging into my hips, as if she were trying to rip her reality apart. I wanted her to succeed, wanted all this to be stripped away.

My mind was far away, drifting in a place where everything was fuzzy and indistinct. I heard other sounds trying to break their way in, but I resisted. Someone was repeating my name, annoyingly trying to pull me out of my voluntary exile.

"Do we need to call an ambulance?"

It was Daniel, he sounded scared.

For who? For Calvin? Wasn't it too late for that? They must be wrong! He's not really gone, it's all a terrible mistake!

"Susanna!" someone said, and my head snapped back. I'd been slapped, and Daddy's face was directly in front of me, his hands gripping my shoulders, his face worried. Mabel was in Mother's lap now, and I

Angela Hoke   *A Whisper of Smoke*

vaguely noticed that Mother looked uncomfortable and pained at the same time. But she was stroking Mabel's hair. And then Mr. Conner was there, his face all red, explaining that his wife was too upset to help. He scooped Mabel up and started walking back towards their house. He wasn't much bigger than she was, but he was wiry and strong.

"Come here, baby," Daddy said, and I was pressed against his chest. I fought against him, but he held me tight.

"Should I stay? What can I do?" Daniel sounded so worried.

"No, it's okay. Go on home. We'll call you tomorrow." Then, "Thanks."

Someone kissed my forehead and I recognized Daniel's cologne. Then it was gone, and I heard the loud roar of his engine fading reluctantly away.

I was lifted up as someone carried me into the house. I couldn't see anything, but I wasn't sure if it was because my eyes were closed or if I was suffering from some kind of hysterical blindness.

Then I recognized the feel and smell of my bed. Someone turned the lights off, removed my shoes and tucked me in. I was in my bed, but it didn't feel safe. And I wasn't alone. Hank was sitting beside me, patting my hair.

"Come on, Hank. Let her sleep, if she can."

"I'm not leaving," he said. "What if she needs something? I don't want her to be by herself."

"Alright. You can stay. Tell us if she wakes up," Dad said. "But try to let her sleep. Poor kid. Let her sleep as long as she can."

"I'm awake," I mumbled. Or maybe I just thought it. I tried to come out of the fog, but then terrible things flashed through my brain, things that couldn't be true, and I swam back down into the depths.

A Whisper of Smoke   *Angela Hoke*

I must have cried in my sleep, because I woke up with my eyes swollen shut and my sinuses completely clogged. Hank was asleep beside me, on top of the covers, restricting my movement.

The sunlight was weak, indicating that it was early morning. I wiped at my eyes, trying to see, waking up slowly. Then the horror came rushing back, and my head exploded in fire as tears burned their way out of my swollen eyes, like multiple lava flows, scorching everything in their path. My chest hurt, like a hundred pounds of bricks were pushing down on it. I couldn't breathe, all I could think was *My Calvin, my Calvin. Oh, dear God, don't let it be.*

I barely remembered the funeral. I had wanted to be with Mabel and the other Conners, with the family. I wanted to be in the place of honor, feeling the pain with them, the others that loved him most. To be consoled by people come to pay their last respects, as one who loved him deeply, even though real consolation would be elusive.

But I wasn't family. I wasn't even his girlfriend. Instead, Christine was there, sitting with them and crying. I hated her, but Christine had the right to be there, with them. I was just his friend. His best friend, who'd loved him my whole life. But he'd not loved me like that, and so I remained an outsider.

Instead, I sat in the back somewhere, my family surrounding me, sitting close, trying to absorb my pain. Shelly was wedged in with me, glued to my left side as firmly as Hank was glued to my right. She'd been absorbed into our family, and it felt right.

Angela Hoke   *A Whisper of Smoke*

Daniel was there too, with his parents and his two little sisters, sitting just behind me. He didn't try to insert himself into the ring of protection that Mother, Daddy, Shelly, Hank, Lorelei and Annabelle were providing, but every now and then, when my shoulders started shaking, he would reach up and squeeze them, or give my back a rub.

The funeral was surreal like everything else had been. It couldn't be real. They didn't even have a body to prove it – just some ashes, courtesy of the U.S. Army. What if they'd made a mistake? What if some other boy's family was out there, believing their son was still alive and not realizing that he'd been mistaken for Calvin? I ignored the fact that the dog tags, which were tied around the urn of ashes, had Calvin's name, rank and serial number on them. They could be switched. There could be a mistake.

At the mausoleum, where the ashes would be interred, Mrs. Conner came over to me and put her arms around me. She hugged me tightly, and that's when I started to believe the awful truth. God wouldn't let a mother suffer like this, where the pain leaks from every pore like poison, unless it was true.

For the next several days, I just wanted to be alone.

It was almost two weeks later when the package arrived. It was covered in foreign stamps and the blue and red diagonal stripes that indicated international mail. For a second, my breath caught. But the writing on the package was not Calvin's – it was unfamiliar.

I stood on the front porch holding the package in shaking hands, as cherry blossoms floated dreamily around me. Without realizing it, I was walking through the spring blooms towards the pond. *Our pond.*

When I got there, I sat down and took a deep breath.

I opened the package, and a note fell out in that same unfamiliar hand.

* * *

April 4, 1969

Dear Susanna,

I guess you know by now that Calvin is gone. It's hard for me to believe it, and I was here when it happened. I'm guessing it's pretty much impossible for you to believe it. I want you to know that he died watching my back. He kept me alive, more than once. He was my brother.

Listen, I'm not the good writer that he is – I mean, was. So I won't bore you with a long letter from me. That's not what you want anyway.

Before it happened, he showed me this bundle of letters he saved – they were all from you, and he has carried them around all year. He guarded them like some guys guard their Bible. He also wrote you a final letter – well, more like a damn book. He made me promise to see that you got it, along with all the letters you'd wrote him.

So here they are. After you read them, you'll know how much you meant to him.

Take care Susanna. I also had to promise him not to try to get you into bed when I get home. That was a hard promise to make, but I loved him so I guess I'll stick to it.

Max

Angela Hoke   *A Whisper of Smoke*

* * *

My heart was pounding as it sunk in just exactly what I was holding -- the other half of our correspondence for the past eight months, the other part of our story. And his last words to me. My hands were shaking when I unwrapped the bundle, and opened the thick letter that contained his final good-bye.

* * *

March 1969

My dearest Susanna,

If you are reading this letter, it means I have been killed, presumably in combat. I pray that this is not the first you are learning of it, and that the telegram (surely) has beat this letter back to the States. I know that you will not listen, but try not to grieve too much for me – assuming that your prayer book of penance has worked, then I am in a better place (actually, as I already told you, I was saved long ago – so no worries). And, since I don't believe in purgatory, you can bet that I'm already hanging out with Jesus, and looking down on you.   On second thought, you might pray for me just the same – some sins weigh heavily on my heart, from my time here. It's hard to ask for forgiveness when you don't believe you deserve it... That's the curse of the war-time soldier.

I have written this letter to you, knowing that it will be the last time you hear from me, in this life. Please keep it to yourself, and don't share it indiscriminately. I don't want to hurt anyone by the things I say to you. That's why I have written separate letters to all my loved ones, with separate addresses and stamps. I'm hoping that they will all find their rightful recipients. I am also sending you a package containing all of the wonderful letters that you have written to me since I've been here. Please keep them in the private place between us. I want you to know that I've locked each word away in the depths of my soul, where they are burned indelibly and eternally – I take them with me to heaven, because what heaven would be complete without you in it?

In the stack of letters you sent me, you'll find the first one you wrote. It seems so long ago now. You'll notice how worn and tattered it has become. That's because I have read it a thousand times, then a thousand times more. I read it so often that it came apart at the folds, so that I had to put it together like a delicate puzzle. When I was on leave in Hawaii, I snuck away to buy some Scotch tape just so I could try to repair it. That's how much that letter meant to me.

I don't know if you even remember what you said in that first letter (if not, it is included, in all its battered glory, in the package of letters). I never forgot. I wanted so much to be able to respond to you and express my feelings with as much honesty and openness. But, as you know, I could not betray Christine that way. I loved her, and I was determined to stay true to what we had together.

But now I am gone, and she must mourn me like I know you will do. And you deserve to know how I felt about you, just the same as she did. (It's been good training, by the way, writing to you all these months – I've learned to open up emotionally in ways I never knew I could). So anyway (deep breath), here goes.

I am in love with you, Susanna -- desperately and completely. If only I had known how you felt before I got involved with Christine, well, there's no telling what could have been. I don't think I would have cared that you were dating Chip – I don't think that I would have shown you the same courtesy and respect (barely restrained though it was – ha!) that you have shown towards my relationship with Christine. I think that, if I'd known that I had half a chance, I would have tried to take you from him. I always knew he wasn't worthy of you, and that he would hurt you. If only…

Well, those days are past. And maybe it's for the best. Because I wouldn't want to cause you any more pain and suffering at the news of my death than I may be already. But I will share with you my heart this final time—a heart which has been yours all along. Even when I tried to take it back and protect it, you stole it back from me over these months, one sweet phrase at a time.

When I read your first letter to me, I could not believe the depth of your feelings. Yes, I knew what you had said at my party, but it seemed so unreal. As you suspected, I did try to convince myself that it was the alcohol talking. I couldn't allow myself to believe it, even then, because I knew I would not be able to bear it. But your letter… well, your letter was unbelievable. It took every ounce of self-control not to go AWOL and try to find a way back to you, if only to kiss you one more time. And man, do I want to kiss you – my memory of that first kiss we shared, well, it was incredible. I am filled with longing and affection and a desire that comes from the core of my soul when I remember it, and I'm so thankful that I got to experience it at least once.

But then, what cracks me up is that you don't seem to remember our second kiss. It was the night of my going away party, when you first told me how you feel about me. I don't remember exactly how it happened, but suddenly you were in my arms and I was kissing you in ways that I'd only ever experienced in my secret dreams of you. I've never been so caught up in anything, or anyone, in my life. I wanted to consume you – I ached for you, in every sense of the word. It took every single ounce of self-control that I had, or have ever had, to tear myself away. And then, then I had to break your heart. The look in your eyes has tortured me ever since. My only relief came when I read your first letter to me, *and it seemed like you did not remember it all. I hoped that some of the pain had softened as well.*

My love, my sweet Susanna, you are still the most beautiful girl I've ever seen. Every night, when exhaustion overtakes me, I see your dancing eyes, your long hair blowing in the wind, your adorable, mischievous smile. I remember the way you throw your head back when you laugh, and that the sound of it is infectious. I think about teaching you to ride Franny and Gertrude, your hair just as golden as the palomino's, with you and I sharing the saddle, my arms draped around your tiny adolescent waist. I can see the way you were choked up the first time I saw you with baby Hank and baby Annabelle (hard to think of them as babies now, isn't it?), and what a good little mother you were. I love the way you were always so kind to Mabel, and to the other munchkins in my family, but especially her. She looks up to you so much, and she's really going to need you now. My heart aches for my brothers and sisters – I love them so dearly.

Should I admit to you that I'm blubbering at this point? Not so anyone can hear, but I find myself weeping that painful silent weeping, shedding streams of tears for the life I won't have...

I'm sorry, my darling Susanna. How can I expect you to be strong, when I'm feeling so unbelievably sad? But you have always been stronger than me. I smile when I think of your smart, sassy spirit – you are a force, a solid presence always supporting the ones you love. Just be careful, my darling, not to let those loved ones ever push you down. You are strong, and beautiful, and sweet, and I miss you so very much!

You mentioned the night around the campfire, when we had our first kiss, and how special that was. It was very special to me, too. I can close my eyes right now and be instantly transported to that night – I see your face glowing in the firelight, I feel the thrill that shot through me when your fingers brushed my

Angela Hoke   *A Whisper of Smoke*

chest. I had chills running down my flesh the moment I felt your touch, and when you leaned in and we kissed... I'd never felt a sensation like that before and, with the exception of our second kiss, I have never since experienced anything as special, even to this day. That night, sitting on the hay and looking into your frightened eyes, tasting your sweetness as our lips touched for the very first time and never wanting it to end, that's when I think I first knew that I loved you.

You were beautiful then. Then I flash to you as you are now – and I remember with a rush how unbelievably sexy you've become, and how those last few days at home before I shipped out, you drove me crazy wearing snug little pants and a t-shirt tied at your belly. Did you do that on purpose? Was that your punishment for me, for (barely and painfully) rejecting your advances? Your tan skin looked so smooth and soft, I ached to touch you. Didn't your mother ever tell you that you shouldn't dress that way in front of boys? No, wait. I forgot who your mother was (ha!).

And I must now confess that when I was in Hawaii, trying to be the man that Christine expected me to be, I could only think of you. When I closed my eyes and held her, it was you that I kissed. It was you that I wanted with every part of me. I was repellant to myself, it was so brutally unfair to her. And, conversely, I pitied myself, that it was her there with me and not you.

Even now, as I write these words, giving in at last to all the suppressed feelings that I've had since... well, for a long time, all I want to do is kiss your sweet mouth, tenderly then passionately, and hold you in my arms. I want to touch every part of your body as a physical manifestation of the way I feel about you. I want to whisper in your ear, with a soft breath, that I am in love with you, again and again. And Susanna, I wish I could make love to you, every night for the rest of our lives.

By the way, I'm blushing all the way down my chest – it feels so odd, not *only giving into these thoughts that I've worked so hard to suppress, but also sharing them with you. Oh well – Sin Loi. But in case you misunderstand (and yes, I'm obsessing just a little), let me assure you that I'm not and have never been a guy to be easily overtaken by carnal desire – you know how I cultivate my self-control. I value physical intimacy as an expression of love, even still, after the things I've seen here. I feel the need to explain this to you, even though you know me better than anyone and surely you know this about me already. I just don't want you to think that I am expressing my desire for you lightly. Or that it's just the product of months of loneliness. No, I express it only because, as I write this (and give in, at last, to my heart's desire) I am as overcome with it as I am with my love for you. They are intertwined, as they are meant to be.*

Okay, enough of that. I want to say that Daniel seems like a great guy (I write through gritted teeth). I have to admit that, when you first wrote to me about him, I was insanely jealous. I barked at everyone and Max, my best friend over here, told me if I didn't straighten up, he'd kick my ass. He's a great guy. I hope he makes it home. If you ever want to talk to someone who knows all about my feelings for you, talk to him. I didn't even have to really tell him, he just knew. I think all the guys did. Actually, I think all the guys fell in love with you. I hope you don't mind that I shared some of your letters with them – you were like a dream for us, with your gorgeous picture to boot.

Anyway, I think Daniel, from what you've told me about him, might even be worthy of you. But you take your time to figure that out, do you hear me?? I want you so much to be happy. That's when I knew that I had fallen even harder for you since I've been here – when I knew that I loved you so much that I wanted you to be happy, even if it cannot be with me. And that's after months of denying how very much I wanted you to be with me, so that when I finally acknowledged it, I could barely stand being here, so far away from you.

Angela Hoke   *A Whisper of Smoke*

And yet, I wonder if I would have been smart enough to realize the full extent of my feelings for you if I had never come here. Regularly facing death and living in solitude can make you see things that get lost in the civilized world. I don't know that my code of honor would have ever allowed me to admit that I wanted to be with you for the rest of my life, even to myself, had I not been here. Isn't that sad?

I've asked myself what I would have done had I made it back. Would I have stayed with Christine, out of love and respect for her? Or would I have rationalized that she deserved better than to be with a man who was also in love with someone else? And what about you and Daniel? If I came home to find you happy, and with a man that is worthy of you, would it have been right for me to interfere? I can't honestly answer those questions. I know that, if I came home feeling the way I feel right this second, I would let Christine go and I would be at your feet, begging you for a chance.

I even have this fantasy about how it would go: In my mind, I imagine seeing you behind your house, hanging clothes on the line, not knowing that I was back and watching you. I would come to you and you would turn, sensing my presence. All that has gone unsaid would pass between us, still unspoken, through our locked gazes. Without a word, I would take your hand and pull you into the barn. I would push you up against the wall (firmly, but not roughly) and kiss you in a way that you've never been kissed, my body pressing against yours. I would kiss you until you melted against me in submission (I can't believe I'm admitting this), and I would tell you that I love you with all my heart, and then I would beg you to be with me. Would that have worked? Oh, how I wish I could read your response.

But (and here's what I was afraid of) being back in the civilized world has a strange effect on us returning soldiers – the clarity that we gained in the jungle, from what I hear, fades away pretty fast. If I thought you were honestly happy, well, then I might have decided it was best for you to let you go. I know, I know. You're thinking that it's not up to me to decide what's best for you. You are right. I'm just saying that, well, it would have been complicated. You can't disagree with that, right?

So, right or wrong, I decided to keep my feelings to myself all these months. Because if I had expressed them, and then come home and found that I couldn't leave Christine, well that would have been just cruel to you. So I suffered in silence. I hope you don't find it cruel that I am confessing these things in death.

I guess I'll close now. I apologize for subjecting you to this long, rambling confession. It has taken me two weeks to write it all, and I refused to let myself make any revisions because I was afraid I might lose my nerve (pretty ridiculous to think that I might have lost my nerve to share my feelings, even knowing that I'll be gone). My bigger concern though, as I have been writing this, is that something would happen to me before I had a chance to finish it.

Your friendship to me these past years, and especially these past months, has meant more to me than I could describe in a million heartfelt letters. I would not have made it through my time here were it not for you. I thank you for it with everything that I am. It was a selfless thing to do, being there for me without any hope that I would reciprocate your love. I can only guess, if you felt the words in our letters as intensely as I did, that your feelings grew as mine did. Please don't think me vain, it's just that I fell for you a thousand times over through our letters. If that happened to you as well, it must have been doubly difficult for you to believe that I did not love you back. I'm so sorry for that.

So, as I finally finish this letter and say my last sorrowful good-bye, I want to quote a wonderful writer, "I love you! I love you! Seriously, I love you." I

Angela Hoke   A Whisper of Smoke

wish I could have experienced your way of telling me how amazing you think I am, with kiss after kiss after kiss... I wish I could tell you, and show you, how amazing I think you are... I hope this letter has expressed at least a little of that.

Anyway, good-bye my love. Good-bye. And to borrow the sweet sentiments that sustained me through seven levels of hell, I love you, Susanna. I want you and have always wanted you. And though I can't be there with you anymore, I'll always be here, watching over you from heaven and loving you with the strength of angels.

Your crazy in love Strapping Soldier-boy,
Always and forever, and ever, and ever...
Calvin

* * *

Tears blinded me, falling on the letter like rain. I doubled over, and I sobbed until I could cry no more.

Part III

Chapter 23: Rustling in the Rafters

April 1970

Daniel had been great. It had not been easy, learning to love again, to love someone else. I hadn't even wanted to. I had only wanted to survive somehow, and to try to begin to understand a life without Calvin. But Daniel had been quietly patient and kind and sweet, and exactly what I needed. He never asked for anything except my honesty and for the gift of allowing him to share my pain, and that's how he was able to ease it when no one else could.

He had been there for me every second of my mourning, and had been remarkably tolerant, even knowing that I was mourning for another guy, and even knowing that I had been in love with the one I lost. While he had to have felt some jealousy over the intensity of my feelings for Calvin, he was secure enough in himself that he let me feel it, knowing that I was only trying to say good-bye, understanding somehow that Calvin was gone and that any residual power he may have, any remaining ability to compete for my love and devotion, would only exist if Daniel failed to let me mourn properly.

I asked him once how he could be so tolerant and noble, how he could bear to listen to me tell stories about Calvin and cry for him, again and again. He told me that it was his sincere wish that I would be able to really heal from this terrible loss, and that he believed healing could only happen if I were allowed to fully experience the pain. And he hoped that I might eventually be able to let go and get on with living if I were not forced to horde my memories like secret treasures, only able to examine them when I was alone and sad and when I could convince myself that a love like that would never come again.

What he didn't say was that, with every patient day, every demonstration of kindness and acceptance, he was going to show me that maybe love *could* come again, because he wouldn't say that. He wasn't a man for dramatic proclamations; he was a man of honor and steadfastness. That's the only rational explanation for how he could spend hours and hours with a marginal girlfriend who is crying for someone else, blubbering in dumpy clothes with unwashed hair and no make-up.

So he let me say good-bye, fully, with oceans of tears and a sadness that I carried around like a shroud layered with the heaviest, darkest wool. He was patient though I was often swollen and mussed and utterly unattractive, and though I felt like a shell of a person. He was there, and eventually, the layers of sadness fell away, one at a time, almost without me noticing. Then one day, I felt light again, and the sun was shining, and my heart opened up and let hope in.

These were the reasons that I came to believe that God had sent Daniel to me – a second great gift to help me survive the loss of the first, both of them precious beyond words. I would forever wonder how I could possibly have been deserving of either.

Now that time had slipped by, a year since Calvin's passing, I could look on my relationship with Daniel with a new perspective – a perspective learned through love and earned through loss. My love for

Daniel was different than what I had felt for Calvin. With Calvin, I loved him before I even knew my own mind, before I was even capable of choosing to or not. I was just lucky that Calvin was wonderful, and worthy of great love and adoration. But with Daniel, I had *chosen* to love him, *because* of the wonderful person that he was. He had proven himself worthy, as well, over and over again in the year since Calvin's death. Calvin would approve of him, I knew, and that was the highest honor I could ascribe.

But though I loved Daniel and though I really had said good-bye to Calvin, there were still times when I couldn't help thinking about him. Particularly on a day like today, exactly one year from the date that I received Max's package. I thought of him when something funny happened that I may have told him in a letter, hoping to make him laugh and forget the danger if only for a moment, or when something serious happened and I longed for the intensity and honesty of our friendship. Sometimes it was something tangible, physical, that prompted a remembrance or a longing – like when it recently rained for over twenty-four hours straight, causing gutters to overflow and rivulets to form throughout the yard spilling like waterfalls into the storm drains. My sense of Calvin and the images of him sitting in the rain, holding a poncho awkwardly over his head so he could write me a letter in the saturated rain forest, would come flooding in, taking me by sharp surprise and stealing my breath.

Today as I walked toward the barn through rain of a different sort, of cherry and crabapple blossoms, past the tall grass and the knowledge of the pond hidden just beyond the cattails, I had one of those moments. It was an intense flashback to Calvin pitching hay, shirtless and sweaty, on display for no one, but strong and masculine and unbelievably attractive. For a moment I became so lost in it, I wanted to call out, longed to run to him and throw my arms around his slick torso, and mix my tears with his sweat. And the ache returned as if it had never left.

But time had taught me how to bring the ache under control and to make it dull. I focused on it, and my breathing slowed as the flashback faded. I sighed and thought about how he had been frozen in time, a seventeen-year-old in the vision I'd just had. And I thought how I'd be graduating in just six weeks – I'd be starting the rest of my life, and he would never see nineteen.

My eyes welled up as my flashback returned in a rush, and as my remembered Calvin turned at my approach and grinned his crooked smile, looking mischievous as if he were about to pick me up and toss me in the haystack. The pictures were too painful, so I tried to push them away. That's when my mind committed the ultimate betrayal of my heart, because it resurrected the memory of his last letter, and my body surrendered to a wretched sob.

He had loved me, and I had never known it – not until it was too late.

After the pain tore its way out, I forced back my tears before they could overwhelm me and tried to calm myself. Without realizing it, I had walked the remaining distance to the barn, maybe subconsciously looking for Calvin, expecting to see him around every corner, mucking a stall or harnessing a horse.

But he wasn't there. So I leaned against the wall next to Gertrude, the horse I had once loved and fantasized about before that love and those fantasies turned to her owner. The horse affectionately snorted and nuzzled my arm as those damn unruly tears streamed down my cheeks.

That's when I heard it – sounds coming from the hayloft.

I stood very still to listen. It sounded like rustling and scratching of hay on wood. For a crazy moment, I imagined that it was Calvin's spirit, letting me know that he was still there.

Then I heard the moans. Oh good grief – was someone fooling around up there? I crept silently towards the ladder, my curiosity overtaking me. For the life of me, I could not imagine who might be up there. Maybe Mabel and Rusty? I paused, not sure I wanted to interrupt whatever might be going on between them. But I had thought that Mabel was taking him fishing at the creek today. It was private there, and had a much better breeze – seemed like they could mess around there much more comfortably than they could up in the hot, scratchy hayloft.

I stood uncertainly at the bottom of the ladder, one foot on the bottom rung, not sure whether to proceed. Then I felt the tiniest nudge, urging me on. I whipped my head around, and could have sworn I felt Calvin's presence behind me. Chills ran up and down my spine, but no one was there (at least not visibly).

But now I felt that I needed to go up, so I quietly began ascending the ladder. As I climbed, I tried to mentally prepare for whatever I might see.

"I hope you're not planning to introduce me to Jezzie," I muttered.

But nothing prepared me for what I saw as my head finally emerged from the opening in the floor in the loft.

Hank, my baby brother, was pumping away between the skinny legs of a young girl who, horrifically, turned out to be Calvin's baby sister

Kathleen. She was propped up on a pile of haystacks, her legs spread wide and her back arched as she panted. Her shirt was pulled up, revealing small budding breasts, and she was naked from the waist down. Hank stood gripping her thighs as he pumped his hips between them.

Seeing their pre-pubescent bodies acting out in a supremely adult fashion, I let out an involuntary scream. Hank spun around, and when he saw me, his mouth froze in horror. I barely registered that my brother's pants were on and appeared to be properly fastened before I virtually slid down the ladder and bolted outside, where I stood against the barn, bent over with my hands on my knees as I heaved in breaths of fresh air. I thought I might throw up, or faint, or something.

Oh dear Lord, what had I just seen?

Whatever it was, I wanted to forget all about it. I could pretend it had never happened. I could just march right back to the house, go to my room and take a nap, and when I woke, it will have been like a bad dream. I was so tempted to do that, that I actually took a couple of steps towards the house.

Then I realized – If I ignored the truth, protecting a secret that shouldn't be protected, *I would be no better than Mother* .

I stood still, feeling the tugs of competing emotions, compulsions. There was the nudge again, and a breath against my neck, making the hairs rise up. This time, I was certain it was Calvin, giving me the strength I needed to do what needed to be done. I smiled a small smile and closed my eyes, leaning into his imagined embrace.

After a moment, I opened my eyes, and went back into the barn. Hank and Kathleen were coming down the ladder, and Kathleen was sobbing. Hank's face was red with shame, but he stopped at the foot of the ladder and helped Kathleen down. She took his hand, but could not look at him.

"We weren't doing it," she said between racking sobs. "We were just playing house and making blue-jean babies. That's all, right Hank?" she asked, her eyes beseeching Hank for a moment before returning to the floor.

"We weren't doing it," he confirmed in a mumble. He had let go of her hand.

Kathleen stood there piteously, weeping. "I swear Susanna, we didn't do it!" she wailed.

Calvin, are you here? Good grief, is this what you wanted me to witness, what you wanted me to stop? Then tell me, what in the world do I say?

"Kathleen, go home to your mother, and tell her what's happened," I found myself saying, to which Hank raised his head in alarm. But he didn't protest, he just looked at me, then set his mouth in a line of acceptance, and bowed his head again in shame. Kathleen, however, bent over in hysterics.

"No, no, no," she cried. "I can't tell her, please don't make me." And she collapsed in a pile on the floor, no longer a girl acting as a woman, but just a child – a scared, weeping child.

"I'll take you home. We'll tell her together," I said, with as much kindness as I could muster. I felt that kiss on my neck again, and I silently thought, *You're welcome.*

"Hank," I started, turning towards him. He just stood there with one of the saddest looks I'd ever seen. His eyes were full of anguish and shame and something else resembling grief. "Will you be okay? Don't do anything stupid, we'll deal with this together when I get back."

Angela Hoke   *A Whisper of Smoke*

He only nodded silently, apparently too afraid to speak. Then he turned and walked, then ran towards the woods.

I bent over and lifted the sobbing child. Kathleen was limp in my arms, and I thought, *She doesn't weigh anything.* I put Kathleen's arm around my shoulders and my arm around her waist, and half-carried, half-dragged her to the Conner's house, praying with every step that God would give me the words to say, and that Calvin would sit invisibly beside me as I said them.

When we got to the Conner's back door, Cora came running out, apparently having seen us through the window.

"What's wrong? What happened?" she cried. Kathleen burst into fresh tears.

"She's fine, she's not hurt. Where's your mother?" Something about the look on my face must have communicated *Don't ask questions, just go!* Because that's what she did.

Oh, Lord! This poor family didn't need this. How was I to explain? How could I bear the look that would emerge on Mrs. Conner's already grief-morphed face? I was sitting on the edge of the couch with a limp Kathleen huddled beside me when Cora came back into the room, dragging her mother behind her. Mrs. Conner looked perplexed, then frightened, when she saw the state of Kathleen. Looking from me to Kathleen and back again, Mrs. Conner searched for some kind of silent explanation, but I wasn't about to deliver the news in front of Cora.

"Cora, would you run and get a warm wash cloth and some tissues?" I asked, as Mrs. Conner sat beside her daughter and was at once attacked by a desperate embrace that encircled her waist. Kathleen burrowed her face into her mother's lap and cried, and Mrs. Conner just

A Whisper of Smoke   *Angela Hoke*

looked at me with a bewildered expression, as she stroked Kathleen's silky hair.

"Just a minute," I mouthed, communicating the need for privacy to Mrs. Conner, who just nodded in sad acceptance, all fight gone out of her since Calvin...

Cora came thumping back down the stairs, and dutifully handed the cloth and tissues to me, then plopped herself on the armchair.

"Cora," Mrs. Conner said authoritatively, "Find your brother and go outside. The garden needs weeding, and we need some time to ourselves."

"Sure, Mom," she said, and hollered for Elton. Elton came down the stairs, his hair sticking up and pillow lines demarking his face. He was napping, in the middle of a Saturday afternoon? Mr. Conner would never have allowed Calvin to do that – Calvin would have been working out on the farm somewhere.

Everything was so different.

Elton looked around confused at the three females on the couch, but didn't ask a single question.

"Come on, Mom says it's time to weed the garden," Cora said, grabbing his hand and pulling him towards the back door. I could see the whining teenage complaint on the tip of Elton's tongue, but something about his mother's sad countenance gave him the good sense to hold it in. The two went outside, Cora nearly dying from curiosity but determined to respect her mother's wishes.

When the two were out of sight, I turned to the mother and daughter sitting beside me. Mrs. Conner was stroking her daughter's reddened face with the wash cloth and softly shushing her. Kathleen's hiccoughs were subsiding and her breathing was slowing.

Angela Hoke   *A Whisper of Smoke*

She's falling asleep, I thought, incredulous, then I realized that I was feeling a bit hypnotized myself. Mrs. Conner's eyes were glazed, as if she couldn't bring herself to focus on me and listen to one more terrible thing.

I took a deep breath, and thought briefly about excusing myself, but there was the damn nudge again. *Okay, already.* So I took another deep breath and this time squared my shoulders. Mrs. Conner must have sensed the shift in my demeanor, for she sadly turned to look at me.

For a moment, I held Mrs. Conner's gaze as we both fought tears for our lost one. Then we shared the smallest of smiles, acknowledging each other's continuing grief for the boy who was gone.

But that was not why I was here.

"Mrs. Conner," I began, and Kathleen squeezed her eyes shut tight.

Mrs. Conner just sat quietly, expectantly.

"Mrs. Conner," I began again, "I was in the barn a little while ago, just..." (I paused – what right did I have to be in their barn?) "... visiting Gertrude," I came up with, "and I heard some noises in the hayloft."

Kathleen let out a squeak and buried her face even farther, if it was possible, in her mother's lap. Mrs. Conner just waited patiently for me to continue.

I sensed the presence again, like a finger trailing up my spine, and I shivered a bit. My eyes stung, because I missed him so terribly. But then I felt (or imagined I felt) the equivalent of a spiritual squeeze of encouragement, there was no other way to describe it. So I steeled myself to continue.

"Anyway, I climbed up to the loft to investigate, and I found Kathleen and... Hank. They were fooling around."

A Whisper of Smoke   *Angela Hoke*

Kathleen's shoulders shook, as Mrs. Conner's lap become more and more dampened.

Mrs. Conner said, "Okay," slowly, like she was waiting for the other shoe to drop. Surely there was more to the story than me finding the two kids kissing each other. They were young, yes, but not too young to begin to be interested in kissing and being with the opposite sex.

I sighed and swallowed down my hesitance, then continued, "Well, I thought, at first, that they were... having sex." I blurted the last out and felt the shame in my own face. I sensed that Mrs. Conner's rhythmic stroking had ceased, and even Kathleen had become utterly silent.

"What do you mean that you *thought* they were having sex?" Mrs. Conner asked in the smallest of voices.

"I mean, they appeared to be having sex, until I noticed that Hank's pants were still on and fastened."

Just then, Kathleen raised her snotty face up and cried, "We weren't doing it, Mom! I swear we weren't." Then she was hysterical again, and buried her face in shame.

Mrs. Conner just held my eyes with a steady gaze, silently waiting for me to continue.

"The two have sworn to me that they were not, *have* not done it," I said slowly. "Kathleen said they were making," (ahem) "blue jean babies, which can only mean (I assume) that they were acting like they were having sex with their blue jeans on."

Mrs. Conner looked uncharacteristically flummoxed. It was like her brain could not process a response to these inputs.

"Except," I added reluctantly, "Kathleen's pants were not on."

Angela Hoke   *A Whisper of Smoke*

Kathleen wailed and tried to bolt, but Mrs. Conner gripped her arm with a strength that belied her exterior. Kathleen stopped in her tracks, as shocked as I was at her mother's steely clasp.

"Go to your room," Mrs. Conner said firmly. "I will be up to talk with you in a bit," she said, without the venom in her voice that would have accompanied such words coming from my mother (along with expletives and names like 'slut' and 'whore'). But even without the name-calling and poisonous tone, Mrs. Conner's tone was somehow scary.

It was the disappointment you could hear in it, I realized.

Having delivered the horrendous message, I didn't know what to do or say. So I just sat still for a moment, as we both watched Kathleen trudge up the stairs, shoulders drooped and heaving, as if she were marching to the gallows.

When we heard Kathleen's door close, Mrs. Conner turned back to me.

"I'm so sorry," I gushed. "I... I don't even know what to say for Hank, I can't imagine why..." Again, I found myself fighting tears.

"Susanna," Mrs. Conner said, placing a hand over mine. "It's not your fault," she said, and I hoped that were true.

"Thanks for telling me," Mrs. Conner said. "I know it couldn't have been easy," she added, generously, then gazed through the window towards my home with a flash of judgment in her eyes, then it was gone.

We both sat quietly for a moment, until Mrs. Conner squeezed and released my hand. I took that as my cue to go.

Mrs. Conner started to speak, seemed to be choosing her words carefully, and asked, "Is Hank okay?" Man, she was unbelievably diplomatic. I knew where Calvin had gotten his steady wisdom.

A Whisper of Smoke   *Angela Hoke*

"I don't know," I said honestly. "I've got to go find him now and figure out how to deal with this on our side."

Mrs. Conner looked at her, and I imagined her thinking that that this was a matter for my mother. Then Mrs. Conner's gaze changed almost imperceptibly. She probably realized that, if there was to be kindness and reason in dealing with this, I would have to step in. Mrs. Conner gave a tiny reassuring smile, seeming to let go the momentary concern she might have had for me (as she obviously, and understandably, had no energy left to care for anyone else's children but her own) and then stood up to see me out.

As I walked back towards my house, I tried to put that uncomfortable conversation behind me and focus on the task at hand. First things first, I needed to deal with Hank.

As I walked slowly along the path between the two houses, many options played in my mind. I could ignore it, and pretend like it didn't happen. Tempting though that option was, I had already consciously decided that it was morally unacceptable and would be the worst kind of hypocrisy – plus, who knew what was going to happen when Mr. Conner found out what happened. I thought about telling Mother, but that would be a disaster. Mother's reactions were always inappropriate, virtually without fail. She would have to be told, eventually, but I didn't want Mother's harsh words to be the first ones that Hank heard – at least not until he'd had a chance to offer some kind of explanation. I thought about telling Daddy, but he wouldn't be home for several hours – things were bound to erupt well before then.

So, kind of by default, I decided to talk to Hank, alone, before telling anyone else in my family what had happened. I headed into the woods, walking with increasing dread towards Hank's favorite spot by the creek, where the rope swing hung over a watering hole. All along the trail, trees were budding in their hopeful way, in sharp contrast to my mood. And the birds were chirping and mating frenetically and with a mocking irony.

As I walked along, I hoped that I didn't run into Mabel and Rusty right now. I couldn't face them just yet – I felt the shame of what Hank had been doing with their innocent baby sister, and needed to understand and come to terms with it myself. Even though Kathleen and Hank were both twelve, it still seemed like Hank was the instigator – though maybe that assumption was merely the product of the picture the two of them painted, with him driving away at her submissive body.

I sighed with trepidation as I approached the point in the trail where the rope swing would come into view. There he was, sitting on a rock on the bank, repeatedly swinging the rope across the creek with his hand, catching it and swinging it across again. I stopped and looked at him for a moment. I knew that he was not a little kid anymore, but I could still see the blond curls, round face and big eyes of my precious baby brother. My heart ached for him, and for what he had done.

Calvin, are you still there? I thought, hoping he would be there for me once again.

I can't help you this time – you are on your own, but you can do it, I thought I heard. I shivered again, and then I knew he had gone.

"Hank," I said softly, and he started. He slowly turned his head and, seeing that I was alone, dropped his shoulders in relief. Then he turned back around and resumed his rope swinging. I went over to sit by him, and we sat in silence for a few moments, side-by-side.

"Are you going to yell at me, or what? Let's get it over with," he said, his voice defeated.

A Whisper of Smoke   *Angela Hoke*

I considered him, praying silently for the right words to say.

"I'm not going to yell at you," I began slowly. "But Hank, how could you do that?"

He drew his knees up to his chin and rested upon them, then gave a sad sigh, as if the weight of the world was on his shoulders.

"Because I'm a terrible person," he said, his voice cracking.

"No," I immediately responded. "You are *not* a terrible person. That's why I don't understand this. Have you and Kathleen been fooling around for a long time?"

"No, just a few times before now. And this was the first time she ever let me... get as far as we got."

"Is she your girlfriend?"

He shrugged, and I was confused. "Does she know that?" I asked, feeling defensive of Kathleen.

"I guess she probably thinks that she's my girlfriend," he admitted.

"Do you love her?" I felt silly even suggesting it. How could he possibly love her? He was barely twelve. And then I remembered that I was not quite fourteen when I started dating Chip.

"I don't know!" he said miserably, burying his face in the void between his chest and his knees. "I know I should," he added reluctantly.

"Hank, I need you tell me the truth. Will you do that?" He mumbled something like a yes. "Have you and Kathleen had sex?" I asked, afraid of the answer.

"No, I swear. We haven't," he said emphatically.

Thank God. "Well, do you have any idea what you could do to her reputation? Not to mention messing her up. You guys are too young to be almost having sex!" I tried to be firm without being too harsh, worried that he would shut down on me.

He was silent and miserable.

"Do you know how babies are made?"

"Yes! Of course," he said, blushing.

"Then you realize that she could get pregnant, right?"

"I *know*," he said, his voice petulant, and he sounded very much his age at that moment.

"But..." he began.

"But what?"

"But we *weren't* having sex!" he said in a rush.

"Come on. Maybe you weren't this time, but the way you were going, you would be next time, or the time after that. Right? Surely you can admit that."

He buried his head in his arms again, mortified and ashamed.

I shook my head. "I don't understand this. I don't understand why you are in such a rush to be with a girl."

"No, I guess you don't," he said bitterly, his eyes ablaze. And then it was gone in a flash, and the misery returned.

I was taken aback at the anger in his tone. "Where did *that* come from?"

It was several moments before Hank answered me.

"I'm messed up," he whispered.

"What do you mean?"

"Stuff happened to me, Susanna. You weren't there, and I was all alone. And those parties... stuff happened to me that shouldn't have happened." His voice caught.

I was too stunned to speak.

A Whisper of Smoke   *Angela Hoke*

"And now I am so messed up – I feel like, sometimes, I can't even control myself. I know it's a sin and that I'm probably going to hell," he said, his lip quivering, as his eyes filled up.

My vision darkened with horrific realization of what his words meant – *I left him alone!* I suddenly realized how self-absorbed I'd been, and regret washed over me like acid.

Hank's head was buried again, and his slender shoulders were heaving as he tried to control his emotions. I looked at him and thought how beautiful he was. He was a very good-looking boy, with short, light blond hair, straight, symmetrical features, those big blue eyes, tan skin and an engaging smile. All the girls his age had crushes on him, and for that reason, all of them may be in danger.

Oh, what am I thinking! I was horrified with myself. This was my precious brother Hank – the same little boy that read to me when I was too depressed to drag myself out of bed; the same little boy that was constantly trying to earn Mother's affection and love, and who rarely lost his temper or said a harsh word; and the same little boy that took all the shit that our family dished out, and never complained, never asked for anything!

And then I came to the most devastating realization of all – *I was no better than my mother*. I, not unlike Mother, had failed to protect my innocent brother, a child I loved almost as if he were my own, even though I *knew* there was danger. I didn't even *warn* him! I just left him alone. I might as well have served him up on a golden platter to the damn drunken perverts!

"Dear God, forgive me!" I whispered.

Hank turned to look at me, and his face was a picture of agony.

Angela Hoke   *A Whisper of Smoke*

"Hank," I touched my hand to his soft cheek. "I am so, so sorry," I said, and started to cry.

Anxiety replaced the agony in his eyes. "Susanna, it's okay. Don't cry."

"No. It is most definitely *not* okay. I have let you down in inexcusable ways. And now you... you lost your innocence, because I failed you."

"No, you didn't. You didn't know. It wasn't your fault. It was my fault for not locking my door."

Dear Lord, he was comforting *me*! My fragile composure dissolved once again.

"Please don't cry," he said pitifully, and his adolescent voice cracked. His mouth turned down, and the muscles of his face tensed as he tried to keep control of his emotions. A single tear slipped out and down his cheek, and he wiped it angrily away.

He turned away, and it gave me a moment to regain some semblance of control. I took some deep breaths, and both of us were quiet for a few moments as the sounds of the creek camouflaged our pain.

Once I'd calmed myself enough to speak, I placed my hand on his shoulder. "Hey."

He turned to me, his arms still hugging his knees and his eyes red. With another deep breath, I tried to explain, my voice gentle. "My heart is breaking that you think it was your fault. Nothing that happened to you could have *ever* been your fault."

He just looked at me, his eyes flat, radiating shame.

"I mean it," I said. "Do you understand?"

Maybe it was the quiver in my voice, but Hank nodded, wanting to please me. But the acknowledgement didn't reach his eyes. He cast them down, his blond-tipped eyelashes brushing his cheek like they did when he was a baby. I was overcome with the desire to cover him with my arms and shield him – to hide him in the nook he once fit into so nicely, just under my collarbone, where I could keep him safe from all harm. But I didn't move, for fear of frightening him away.

I cleared my throat, hoping my voice wouldn't fail. "No, I'm serious," I said, dipping my head low until I could catch his eyes. When they locked on mine, I drew his head up with the force of my gaze.

"You were hurt by awful grown-ups, and *none of it was your fault.*"

He started to turn away again as his eyes filled with tears, but I grabbed him in a tight hug instead. He went rigid in my arms at first, then he submitted, his shoulders shaking with silent sobs, as I wept my own silent tears. I gripped him as if I could in fact pull him into me and protect him with my body, but sadly it was way too late for that.

"I don't want to be bad," he cried into my shoulder, his voice a little boy's whisper. "I keep praying that I won't think bad thoughts, but they keep coming anyway," he sobbed. "I don't deserve to live."

An icy dread came over me like a douse of cold water. It brought fear with it – the crippling kind that pulls on your awareness, seeking to shut it down because of the pain it threatens.

"N-no," I stuttered, then steadied my voice. "No."

In that instant, I was awash with a fear like I'd never known. "Please don't ever say that. Please." The ragged sound of my terror hummed like an electric current. He heard it, and he looked at me, his eyes once again full of concern for me. *For me!* God, I loved that boy. At

Angela Hoke   *A Whisper of Smoke*

that moment, I realized I could not love a person more than I loved Hank – the brother that was like my child.

No way – I was *not* going to let him blame himself. "You deserve to live," I told him as firmly as I could. "You were just a child, and we should have protected you. You *deserved* to be kept safe."

He crumpled again, weeping into me and shaking his head under my chin. His hair was still soft, babyish, and smelled of boy sweat and sweetness. The despair radiated from him, and I prayed that I'd reached him. "Please, listen to me," I begged, pulling back to look into his face. "I couldn't stand it if anything happened to you. You are precious to me. Precious!"

He just looked lost, and resigned. But he didn't deny that I had read him correctly. He *was* lost and I was the only one there to save him, and I was not going to let him down. Again.

"Look at me," I demanded sternly, forcing him to focus on me and what I was saying.

"I would *die* if I lost you too. Don't you think I've suffered enough? I don't think I could go on living if I lost one more person that I loved."

The words seemed to slowly sink in with him, and he nodded slightly. I hated to resort to guilt trips, but I was desperate to keep him from doing something awful to himself. I wasn't lying when I said it would kill me.

"I'll help you get through this, I promise."

"How do I stop?" he asked in a quiet voice.

And, for the moment, all I could do was hold him because my voice had fled, chasing away the demons that wanted to destroy him, or the angels that wanted to take him.

A Whisper of Smoke   *Angela Hoke*

How do I stop? he had asked. I knew I had to answer, but I needed divine guidance to determine what in the world to say. The wind shook the trees, and I found myself speaking, as the answers to my silent prayers fed my words.

"Well, first, I think you need to go apologize to Kathleen's family," I said, wincing a little at the look of horror on his face.

"I know it will be hard," I said quickly. "But I think the humiliation might be good for you." *Yes, that seems right,* I realized, recognizing the wisdom in the words and the chance for redemption they represented – maybe the only chance.

He looked at me, uncomprehending.

"I think it might make you think twice about going near Kathleen, at least for a while. And we've got to break your habit – fooling around can become kind of..." I searched for the right word. "Addictive."

He nodded in agreement. "Okay," he sighed, his shoulders slumping. "I'll do anything you say, Susanna, if you think it will make me into a better person."

He gave me a brave smile, and my heart melted.

"Then, I think you should tell Daddy," I said.

His head fell. "I knew there had to be more."

"Maybe Daddy can give you some ideas for ways to..." I wondered how to put it delicately. "Um, satisfy yourself without being with a girl."

He blushed from collar to hairline at that, and we looked away from each other simultaneously.

"Okay," he said again, after a time. "I want to be good."

Angela Hoke   *A Whisper of Smoke*

Then he flung himself at me, giving me a tight hug and catching me by surprise.

"I love you, Sis."

"Oh, I love you, too, sweetie," I said back fiercely. And just as quickly, the moment was over.

"Let's get this over with," he said, standing up, and offering me a hand. "Will you go with me?" he asked, his voice tremulous.

"I will be right here, by your side," I promised. "I won't leave you alone again."

And so we went, and he took his punishment, and punished himself for much longer than anyone would know.

Chapter 24: Day of Reckoning

Spring 1971

Ever since what happened with Hank, I had begun to rethink my harsh judgment of my parents. I had been angry at them for so long, barely even letting them in when Calvin... well, when everything was so awful. I had continually shut them out, and yet they had *still* been there for me. They sat with me in shifts in the beginning, rubbing my hair, resupplying my tissues, bringing me cups of broth and tea. They rallied around me like nesting birds, protecting me, nurturing me, gently nudging me towards healing. My mother created adventures in my room where she explained through fancy my inert state, and where she, Annabelle and Hank would act out a drama that was designed to draw a smile from me. My father sat at the foot of my bed asking me questions about his crossword puzzles, questions he knew the answers to, and brought home books for me from the dime store – romances he knew I once loved, could get lost in. I didn't have the heart to tell him that they were too painful to read anymore. And still I didn't really let them in.

Though I was weary to the core from the effort it took to maintain my anger, it had become my habit. My existence was steeped in it, saturated with it to the point that I was stained a different color. The source of my anger had seemed so very righteous, and justifiable. I had been so sure that my parents had been callously negligent with the safety and security of their children – but now I had to reconsider. They *had* been negligent, yes. But I was no longer sure that it was out of callousness, or even selfishness. I was beginning to think that it was out of ignorance. Or if I were being generous, I might characterize the source of their negligence as gullibility, or even faith and the need to believe in the ones you love.

Even though there were reasons that they should have been on guard, maybe they didn't realize. And even if Mother *may* have known that Uncle George was messed up, she may have never dreamed that he would be a danger to others. Maybe she blamed herself for whatever happened in their childhood, and so thought others would be safe. Or maybe she had blocked it out, like I now realized *I* had done, thinking of the disturbing fragmented memories that sometimes poked at the periphery of my mind.

Mother had been only fifteen when she left home – just a child, not much older than Hank, and much younger than I was now. Is a person even mature enough, at that age, to be able to evaluate a situation, to evaluate dangers? Mother had never been good at reason or logic. Perhaps she didn't have the ability to foresee consequences like some people did. Perhaps, when you leave your childhood behind too early and jump into adulthood, certain parts of you never fully grow up. They just become stunted child parts disguised in a grown-up body.

Maybe Mother had always been young for age, in the same way that I had always been old for mine.

All at once, it was like the whole picture making up my view of reality had scrambled itself into something totally different – all the parts were the same, but the whole was not what I had thought.

Then I thought how I had hated that my mother had been so eager to forgive Uncle George. I had been appalled and even disgusted. Oh, how my perspective had changed now! I thought about my sweet

Hank, and how some terrible person or (*God forbid*) *people* had abused him, robbing him of his innocence and changing him forever. I thought about the urges and thoughts that troubled him now, and how easily they could lead to the same type of reprehensible behavior. I prayed that he could resist, and that, somehow, he could become whole again. But I couldn't deny that he had been damaged, and he was potentially capable of hurting someone.

But even knowing what had happened, and the demons that tortured him, I could not bring myself to abandon him. And I was pretty sure that there was nothing he could do that would make me hate him. No matter what the future might bring, I would always look at him and see the small, sweet boy that I helped raise and that I'd adored since the day he was born.

Whether that was right or wrong, I didn't know. I only knew my own heart, and how he owned a piece of it – a huge, vital piece, without which I would not survive.

No, I would not abandon him. I could only help him be accountable, and pray that God would heal would I could not. I could only spend my life trying to make it up to him for letting him down. I could only love him and treasure him and never abandon him again.

I thought all this, making this a private pledge. And when my thoughts turned involuntarily to Mother, and how Mother would not, could not abandon Uncle George, I realized something that knocked the air from my lungs.

Uncle George was Mother's Hank.

And then came the most disturbing realization of all – *She's not that different from me.*

Angela Hoke   *A Whisper of Smoke*

Just like that, the hard shell in my chest cracked open, and my heart begin to thaw.

When Daniel proposed, I had cried – my emotions had been a jumbled mix of joyful surprise, and the echo of sadness, as I thought about the one that could have been. We'd set the date for June, after his junior finals, and I was ready. I looked down at the small diamond on my left hand, and I felt a surge of love for Daniel. He had rescued me from the darkest of places, and he had loved me in his calm and tolerant way.

Now, I sat in my room, and thought how I wouldn't live in it much longer. Nostalgia overtook me, followed by a surge of sappy sentiment, tinged with guilt. But this new guilt was different, born of my recent revelations and the resultant burst of blinding insight. Once I'd gotten past the worst of the pain from the death of Calvin, during the early days of my engagement, I had been almost cruel to my mother. Every time Mother had reached out and tried to help with the wedding plans, or be included in some way, I had shut her down mercilessly, still consumed as I was by my anger.

Finally, Mother had stopped trying, and we had barely spoken in more than two months. But now I knew that my Mother was not exactly who I had thought, and that neither was I. I had been so judgmental, exacting a punishment without really comprehending. Even when Mother and Dad had stood by me through all of the terrible grief, rallying everyone to support me, I had not softened.

Now I was consumed by a guilt that I never expected – guilt that I had mistreated my parents, particularly my mother. And, sadly, now that so much time had passed, I didn't know how to fix it. I didn't know how to let Mother back in.

We had never been good at communicating our feelings to each other. In fact, Mother had never been good at that, period. Mother's natural inclination was to deflect from her true feelings, using sarcasm or cruelty as her weapons and shields. I wondered if I could break through her defenses and let her know, somehow, that I forgave her. Let her know, without calling attention to the premise that Mother had done anything *to* forgive, that it was time to move forward. It would be a painful process, I was sure. But I was just as sure that I had to try.

Downstairs, there was a commotion as Mother and Annabelle came in the house with groceries. Annabelle was talking loudly, and whatever she said made Mother laugh. Just hearing Mother's laughter, and knowing I had not been the cause of her laughter in so long, filled me with remorse. All at once, I was filled with a need for my Mama.

Mama, I thought ruefully, realizing I hadn't called my mother that in a long, long time. I had not even thought of her as Mama since... before. Before things went wrong, and beloved, familiar family members became hideously unfamiliar, and before best friends and great loves were lost forever. *Mama* – the name I had used for my mother when she still had the power to create magic, to defy reality and make an ordinary state into something desirable, something that made you feel lucky to be a part of.

Does Mama still have that power? I wondered. Or had my loss of belief, my conscious refusal to believe, robbed her of it? And in turn, robbed me of its magic?

I sure could have used some magic after Calvin was lost. Mama would have given me some. Hell, she'd tried. Even without my permission, they'd all hovered around me like sentries, guarding my heart as best they could, for months on end. I knew they were there, I watched them in their efforts and on some level I was comforted by it. But I could never totally let my parents in. I wasn't ready to accept their love, had not been prepared to owe them for anything. So they loved me from the outside, and things were harder than perhaps they needed to be.

Maybe it could be easier now, starting today. I would just have to force myself to quit my habit, let go of my stubborn insistence to be angry. I was not a child anymore, after all. I was an adult, and this was an election that I could choose to make – a choice to receive the freedom that God gives you when you forgive someone else, whether they deserve it or not. Plus, I realized, I would be relieving myself of the burden of judgment, because it wasn't my right anyway – it was never my right. And I had learned that lesson with a drowning dose of humility – humility born of knowing that I had failed Hank in every way that I believed Mama had failed me, failed all of us; humility that had painfully driven home the realization that every human being is capable of terrible transgressions, and exquisite goodness, and that neither has to define a person.

Like Calvin – a person who became the product of the forced contradiction of war. A person who died with the memory of horrific experiences and a depth of guilt that I would never understand, but who would always be one of the most purely good souls I would ever know.

I went downstairs, and stood at the foot, as Mama and Annabelle swirled around me, putting stuff away. Mama and Annabelle went into the kitchen and were chattering pleasantly, in the enviable, comfortable manner that they had always had with each other. They were baking

A Whisper of Smoke   *Angela Hoke*

something. I followed them into the kitchen, but they barely acknowledged me. They were used to me being a part of the background. How long had I been on the outside, without realizing it? Now that I wanted to be on the inside, I had no idea how to break in.

I cleared my throat. "Mama," I said, and she turned to me in surprise. "Can I help?" I asked, my voice tentative.

And it was a beginning.

Chapter 25: Daniel's Charms

Summer 1971

Lorelei was helping me get dressed. It was the most time we'd spent alone together in a long time. I watched as my sister pushed and heaved and buttoned and zipped my body inside the borrowed white gown. There was something I had wanted to ask Lorelei, but had been too nervous to do it – too afraid of her reaction, not sure if I was prepared to hear the response. But I didn't know when I'd get another chance like this one, so I took a deep breath and steeled myself.

"Lorelei, are you disappointed in me?" I asked, my voice tentative. "Am I disgrace to women's lib?" I joked then, hoping to hide my insecurity.

Lorelei's head snapped up.

"What?"

"Are you disappointed with me? With who I've become?" I dropped the glib pretext.

"Don't be silly," Lorelei said, dismissing it as she bent down to straighten out the short train.

"No, really. I… I want to know," I insisted, and Lorelei stood up then, crossing her arms over her generous chest. She waited for me to explain.

"You are so smart – you're about to graduate college and become a nurse, just like you always dreamed. You were always like that – so determined to break away and never look back. You followed your dreams, like Mama always told us to. Whereas me, on the other hand, all I've got is a job as a telephone operator so I can support Daniel through his last year of school, and I'm getting married before I turn twenty. Have I... disappointed you? Did you expect something different, something more from me?"

"Susanna, come here," she said in a stern voice. She pulled my hand and led me to a tattered loveseat. We sat down gingerly, careful not to muss the satin and taffeta.

Lorelei sighed, her mouth set as she considered her words.

"You have a different destiny than I do. You are smart and kind. But you use your gifts to take care of people, to protect them."

I shook my head, thinking of how I'd failed to protect Hank.

"No, listen. That's who you are. You are a natural caretaker – you nurture, by nature," she said and laughed. Then she turned serious again. "I'll force myself to take care of people in my job, but it doesn't come easy to me. I will be a nurse because I love the order, the challenge, and mostly, fixing the immediate injuries, then moving on to the next patient so I don't have to be around for the healing."

I was surprised at Lorelei's words, then I wasn't. I never questioned Lorelei's desire to be a nurse because Lorelei was so fixed in her path. Lorelei's determination gave her decisions an air of confidence, and I had always respected that. But Lorelei had never been as tender-hearted as me. I had attributed that difference to Lorelei's strength, as contrasted with my own self-perceived weaknesses. But now Lorelei was explaining the difference as if my empathetic nature had merit – almost like it was virtuous.

"In many ways, you are a lot smarter than me," Lorelei said, and I was surprised anew.

Angela Hoke   *A Whisper of Smoke*

"What do you mean?"

"I mean, you learn from your experiences. You've learned from *our* experiences. You've picked someone to marry who is whole, who is nothing like what we grew up with. Me, I pick people that are comfortable to me, even if it's not good for me. I repeat the sins of the past. Plus, did it ever occur to you that the way I followed my dreams, that my determination you so admire, was a lot like running away?"

I peered at my sister, thinking about the air of desperation that surrounded Lorelei's single-minded quest to go away to college. The way that she agonized over exams, the way she flipped out when she didn't think she could afford tuition, and then how she worked her ass off to make sure she could. Yes, I could see truth in Lorelei's words. I could even understand what might drive her to escape. I had thought about it from time to time too, but I believed that I lacked the courage, not to mention a legitimate reason for leaving. Even now, I asked myself many times if I was marrying Daniel to get away, but I knew deep down the answer was no. I had stayed because I had to take care of Hank and Annabelle, especially after the bad things happened. And I had stayed because I was part of the family, and leaving was not part of my make-up. No, I wasn't trying to escape. I had less reason, or desire, to escape my home now than I had ever had before. And that's what made me finally free to go.

Lorelei smiled at me.

"You're too young to even know how good your judgment has become," she said, making my pride bristle in a deeply familiar way. "Someday you'll realize. Honestly, I don't know where you get it from – maybe you've got some spirit guiding you. Maybe it's a guardian angel that you have, whispering in your ear and steering you in the right direction."

She was teasing me, I knew, but I a chill raced through me, as I thought of Calvin. And suddenly I was certain I could feel his presence beside me, and that he was chuckling.

"That means a lot to me," I said finally. "You know how much I've always looked up to you, right?"

"Oh, don't look up to me. I'm not perfect."

Then Lorelei looked back at me and smiled. "I'm not good at this, you know. I love you, and all that. Can we talk about something else?"

"Sure. Hey, you're blushing – you're all flushed," I noticed in surprise.

Lorelei got up and walked over to where her bouquet was resting in a vase. She absently arranged the flowers just a bit.

"Lorelei, what? What is it?" I asked, as I tried to heave myself off the loveseat without popping any buttons. It didn't work, and I fell back, defeated.

"Nothing."

"No, tell me. I can tell something is up with you. My protector instincts are kicking in," I joked, trying to lighten the mood, invite a confession.

"It's nothing – don't worry about it. I don't want to take anything away from you today."

"Damn it, tell me!"

She looked at me for a long minute. "You do realize you are in a church, right? You little heathen." I glowered at her.

"Okay," she said finally, sighing. "I'm pregnant."

"What?"

She grinned sheepishly, resting her hand on the slight mound of her stomach.

"Are you… Is it Mark's?"

"Yes!" she replied, a little indignant. "We're getting married in September."

"Do Mom and Dad know?"

"No, not yet. We're going to tell them after your wedding. You don't think Mama can read minds, do you?" asked Lorelei, and I gave a little involuntary shudder. There were many times during our childhood when it seemed like she could.

"But you'll still graduate."

"Yeah, I'll be done in December."

I was a little stunned. My sister was going to be a nurse, a wife and a mother by this time next year.

"Are you happy?"

"Yes, I am," Lorelei said, and she looked like she meant it. "Now – are you disappointed in *me?*" I threw a pillow at her, and Lorelei deflected it with her hand, laughing.

"Help me up off this *darn* couch, will you?" I asked.

Lorelei hauled me up, and I caught her in a quick hug. Then Lorelei pushed me off, chuckling. Mama came in then, to help me with the final touches to my hair and gown.

"I'll go check on everything," Lorelei said quickly, flashing a grin at me before slipping out. "Bye Mother," she said over her shoulder, not willing to risk Mama reading something telling in her face or her body, if not her mind.

Mama looked lovely, but she didn't look like the young woman of my childhood memory any longer. When did that happen? When had she gotten overweight, her breasts over-large and lower than they should be? When had her face erupted in tiny red spider-veins, and gone soft in the jowls?

She was dressed sharply in a purple double-knit suit, her make-up toned down the redness of her cheeks and nose and softened the circles under her eyes. She had on an over-sized faux pearl necklace and matching earrings, and suede pumps died to match her suit. She was wearing one of her best wigs, a formidable up-do with two large muffin-like sections, sitting one on top of the other like two scoops in an ice cream cone, topped with a ring of pin curls like chocolate shavings. It was caramel-colored, and close to Mama's original hair color.

As always, most of Mama's appeal came from some inside place. Whatever that source was, it was still there. Yes, she looked lovely – an attractive middle-aged woman.

"Mother," I said with a welcoming smile. "Mama."

"Susanna," Mama said, pausing like she was trying to work herself up to what was coming next. "You look beautiful."

I looked at her, waiting for the rest, for the backhanded remark that was sure to follow. Mama looked uncomfortable – compliments were usually a one-way street, in her book, and that street generally was directed *towards* her, not from her.

"Thanks," I said, rolling my eyes.

"No, I mean it. You really are beautiful. And smart, and strong."

I blushed, embarrassed by words that made no sense coming out of Mama's mouth. But I looked at my mother, and there was something different there – an intensity in her eyes that was familiar, though not in the context of this face. *Sincerity! That's what it is*, I realized with a shock.

"Mama…"

"Don't say anything – you'll ruin this mother-daughter moment. Besides, you get it all from me."

I grinned. "Of course."

"I like Daniel, even if he is a little too straight-laced for my tastes. But we're pretty convincing. Maybe we can turn him around."

I frowned at her. "*Mother*...."

"Yeah, I know, you don't want him corrupted by us. Your loss."

She fussed over my dress for a moment, smoothing a wrinkle here, tugging on a gathered place there. "In all seriousness though, he suits you," Then she smiled and her eyes sparked like a flint. "And he's not a bad dancer... oh!" She covered her mouth with her gloved hand, her expression one of mock chagrin.

"What?"

"Nothing! Let's not ruin the surprise," she said, her shining eyes big and bright as new quarters – the eyes of her younger self.

A knock came at the door. Shelly was there in her bridesmaid dress, as were Annabelle, Lorelei and Mabel, standing close behind her. My four best girls were gathered, waiting to stand at my side as I took vows with my sweet Daniel.

I turned back to my mother, and the butterflies danced merrily around my stomach.

"Come on, Susie Q," Mama said, bringing my veil down over my face. "It's time." And I gave her a quick hug that made tears spring to my eyes. Then Mama was gone, ready to be escorted to her seat by Hank, who looked so handsome in his light blue tuxedo. Hank flashed a smile at me through the open doorway, and then they disappeared through the double doors to the sanctuary.

"Are you ready?" Shelly asked.

A Whisper of Smoke   *Angela Hoke*

"Yes, go line up. I'll be right out," I replied, flashing them a smile.

I was alone for a moment, and I looked through my veil at the image in the mirror. I waited for my nerves to settle down, taking deep breaths. Then the hair stood up on the back of my neck, the way it does when someone walks over your grave, or there's a ghost in the room.

"Calvin?" I whispered, and my veil fluttered, as a chill raced down my spine. I grasped at the presence, falling into its invisible embrace for just a moment before letting go. It released me as well, but not without first giving me the familiar nudge. *I know he's wonderful, Calvin. You don't have to tell me.*

I fingered the delicate charm bracelet on my wrist, and smiled as I thought back to the night before, when Daniel had given to me.

"Are you happy?" he'd asked, holding me close on my parents' couch after everyone had gone to bed. The rehearsal had gone smoothly, and it had lifted my heart to watch the joy on Daniel's face as he played with his band at the post-rehearsal party. They'd not be playing at the reception, of course, because all the band members were part of the wedding.

Most of the guys had moved on from the days of playing together, either to college or factory jobs at GE. But each of them was also waiting, in some way or another, before really beginning their lives – waiting to see whether their draft numbers would be picked, and whether their destiny would be in their own hands or at the mercy of the army. So this was almost like the last hurrah for the band, and there was sadness behind their smiling faces.

Angela Hoke   *A Whisper of Smoke*

Daniel's band mates expressed their conflicting emotions in a predictable way – by covering Daniel's car in rubbers while we were inside thanking family members for being there. Rubbers were tied to the antenna, the side mirrors, and were coming out of every seam and crevice. Daniel had been embarrassed, mostly because of our parents. Obviously he was still getting to know my family, because my parents thought it was hilarious. I was just grateful they hadn't done it to our honeymoon car.

When we got back to my house and after the rest of my family had gone to bed, we snuggled on the couch together.

"I am very happy," I'd said, closing my eyes and smiling contentedly. He squeezed me and kissed my neck. His breath on my neck aroused me, and I turned to him for a proper kiss. It was deep and warm, his lips tender. But my body became insistent, and I pressed my lips hard against his. He responded, gathering me up, his hands roaming my back, my waist, my hips. Then we were lying down, and I was on top of him, kissing him deeply, pressing my body against the length of his.

I could feel that he wanted me, and my body melted in submission. He pushed my shoulders back and looked into my lidded eyes. Then he grinned, his eyes sparkling. "Can you not wait *one* more night?" he asked, teasing me, as he set me aside and extracted himself from beneath me.

"You are killing me!" I groaned.

"And what exactly do you think you're doing to *me*?" he asked, putting my hand over his pants so I could feel the intensity of his erection. My eyes widened in surprise that he risked letting me touch him like that, even through clothes.

"See?" he said, his eyes dancing. "You are just going to have to wait until you make me an honest man," he teased. "Do you think you can control yourself?"

I sighed, mocking him now. "I guess."

"Hey, now that you've settled down, I have something to give you."

"Really? What?"

"A wedding present," he said, reaching into his jacket pocket.

"Oh, no. I didn't get you one. I didn't know we were supposed to."

"No, no. I don't want a thing from you, except your body and your soul," he replied, kissing me on the nose. "Did I mention that I expect your body?" he teased, and I laughed.

"Quit distracting me," he said then, pretending seriousness.

He handed me a long velvet box.

"What is it?" I asked, and I could feel my eyes blazing in the low light.

"Open it!"

I smiled at him, and slowly opened the box. Inside was a delicate silvery charm bracelet, with two beautiful white gold charms – a circle with an etched cross and a scallop-edged heart.

"Turn them over," he said gently.

I did, and gasped.

Each charm was engraved on the back. The heart had our wedding date on it, and said *Yours forever, Daniel.* The cross had another date on it – *3-29-69*, and the words: *CC, Never forgotten.*

My eyes filled with tears. He held me then, letting me cry with happiness for what was to come, and with sadness for all that had come before.

Angela Hoke   *A Whisper of Smoke*

Now here I was, on the precipice of my new life, and my heart filled with a joyful anticipation that I had not thought possible two years ago, or even a year ago. If Calvin were a different kind of man, I might have worried that he would think me disloyal, even in death, for moving on with my life. But I knew that Calvin wanted me to be happy, and would only be disappointed if I made bad choices or... stopped living.

The push came again. *I know, I'm going. I'm ready. You made me ready for him, and for that I'll always be grateful.*

A warmth stole over me, then it was gone, and the hair on my neck relaxed.

Good-bye, I whispered. Then I went out to become one with the man that would be beside me for the rest of my life, God willing – the man I'd chosen.

Epilogue

Christmas 1978

I was dreaming about him again.

We were standing next to the pond under the largest oak tree, about ten feet apart, looking at each other. The outdoor sounds were all around -- the rhythmic buzz of grasshoppers, the chirping of birds, the rustling in the tree leaves and long grasses, the gentle lapping of water on the bank. I was speaking to him, in a soft voice, and my words were doubtless being carried away in the breeze. But he could hear me with his extraordinary senses.

"I think about your dream sometimes, and I imagine I'm in it. Like your dream, I am drawn to the rustling of the corn stalks and the promise over the hill. And I believe, as I walk through the fields that were our childhood playground, that you are there somewhere – whispering just at the edge of my hearing, beyond the cattails, the flashing white of a secret silver poplar, taunting me like a whisper of smoke in the trees.

"It reminds me that good things are always around me, even though I might not see them, even if it's disguised as something ordinary, something so prolific and normal that there's a danger of taking it for granted. Wonderful things, people, are around us all the time, and sometimes we don't even notice them."

"Like me?" he said, smiling his half-smile.

"Yes, like you," I said, smiling back. "But also like my family – my crazy, messed up, loyal family. All of it, all of you – you're home to me."

Angela Hoke   *A Whisper of Smoke*

He smiled again, his eyes twinkling like I'd figured out some secret.

"It can hide bad things too," I mused aloud, and he frowned a bit as he nodded at me, encouraging.

"The worst thing could be right next to us, visible in one second, then just as quickly swallowed up with a change in the wind. It would be easy to pretend like it wasn't there, like you'd never glimpsed it."

His eyes were kind, sympathetic.

I sighed. "But you can't ignore it, of course. Just because you can't see it anymore, doesn't mean it's not still there, lurking.

"Sometimes," I said, pausing, glad I could look on his face and see his dancing brown eyes and the half-smile I loved, thankful for the primitive comfort it provided. "Sometimes you even have to go looking for it."

He smiled widely then, then turned and started walking away.

"Don't go," I called after him, suddenly sad. "Do you have to go?" Even to my own ears my voice was a little pitiful.

He paused and turned, looking back at me.

"You have all you need," he replied, and smiled again. Then he was gone.

Daniel woke me with a tender kiss, on my cheek, then another on my neck, just under my ear. I shivered and opened my eyes.

"I have all I need," I said, repeating Calvin's last words.

Daniel's face lit up, and he hugged me to him.

"Me too," he said, his warm breath tickling my neck. I could feel the heat of his skin through his pajamas all along the length of my body,

A Whisper of Smoke *Angela Hoke*

and his strong, safe aura surrounded me like a cocoon. I thought I could stay there forever, but my bladder disagreed.

"Be right back," I said, kissing his nose. I rushed to the bathroom, shaking my bottom at him as I walked, just to hear him laugh.

In the bathroom, I looked in the mirror and saw the happiness in my face. I smiled at my reflection – a smile that was all about Daniel and the life we had built. Then I saw the falter, the breath of melancholy that washed across my expression like a sudden spray of water. It transformed and then just as suddenly dissipated, a weakening that coincided with the haunting flash of the Calvin from my dream. For a moment I wanted to hold on to him, to his face, the face of my dreams, with his half-smile and eyes that knew my whole self, but I knew the trap in that and, at the bottom, that terrible ache – the one that would overwhelm any dark comfort I might find. I knew with a practiced heart that there was nothing but pain in clinging too hard to the past, in letting it become more than a memory.

I also knew that it would be a betrayal to my love for Daniel, an unfair diversion of my heart's desires. And that, alone, was reason enough not to indulge.

This was an old internal struggle, and I sighed at the weariness of it, not willing to fall into it again. I liked that Calvin cut a long stretch of bricks in the path of my life, maybe even helping to shape its curvature, even forge its way through the wilderness. But I wouldn't let him become a brick wall barring my way – partly because he would never have wanted that, but mostly because I had learned to go on living. So I let him go again, a tiny decision that had to be made a million times for it to take effect, while at the same time I kept his memory in my heart's treasures. I let him go, and once again Calvin rested in his rightful place

Angela Hoke   *A Whisper of Smoke*

of precious past, a place of prominence but also impotence. I let him go and that's how life resumed for the millionth time, as I bent over to brush my teeth.

I relieved my bladder, put on some deodorant under my gown. Then I opened the door softly, trying to keep it from squeaking so I wouldn't wake the kids. I dashed back to the bed, jumping on it and making Daniel bounce. He laughed. When I was close enough, he grabbed my hand and pulled me to him. He covered me with the blankets, then tucked me back into his safe place. He held me and kissed me, and then he stopped and gazed at me in his intense way, chasing the ghosts back to heaven.

"I love you," he whispered. And he kissed me again, deeply, causing my conscious mind to spin away.

There was a rattling at the door.

"Mommy?" the little voice said. "Why is the door locked? Let us in."

"Coming," I called out, as I wriggled from Daniel's grasp. He chuckled, then jumped up and trotted into the bathroom.

"I'm going to jump in the shower," he called.

"Okay," I replied, as I swung my feet to the floor.

As I searched for my robe, I recollected my dream in object safety, and wondered at the purpose of his visitation. I thought that maybe it was Calvin's way of giving me strength for what I had to do today. He no longer visited like he used to. Not once since I'd been married to Daniel. At first that made me sad – the realization that his last visit, on the day of my wedding, was his last, stoked my waning grief like a dry log. But then again that was classic Calvin. He would never dream of interfering with another man's marriage. That was a moral boundary he would not cross.

But from his place in heaven, if he was still looking down at me, watching over me every now and then, he might find another way to get a message to me. He would encourage me, if he could, to do the scariest things, the things that need most to be done. That was his nature, and it was a comfort.

And he was right. I needed to be reminded why it was worth the trouble, worth the conversation that I had to have. You can't ignore the dangers lurking, hidden in the tall grass, just because they vanished from sight, any more than you should fail to acknowledge the goodness that hides in those same stalks. You can be bitten by the snake you can't see just as easily, more so even, than by the one that you can. It was my job, as a parent, to search these things out, and to be able to discern the difference – to recognize where lurking danger lies and where subtle goodness dwells. It was my job to protect my children and teach them how to discern the difference for themselves.

The pounding sound intensified, shaking my mind from its reverie. Two sets of tiny fists were working on it now. So I opened the door and let my son and daughter in.

We pulled up to the house I grew up in, and the kids were beside themselves with excitement. The snow had been shoveled from the walk, and Dad had decorated the house with lights. It looked warm and inviting.

"Will Grandma give us an adventure?" April had asked on the way. She hadn't stopped chattering the entire drive.

Angela Hoke   *A Whisper of Smoke*

"I don't know, sweetheart. She might be too busy today. But we'll be here all week, so let's ask her."

"Are they good as yours, Mama?" she asked, and I smiled at the unintended compliment.

"Oh, they're better," I assured her, turning around to look at my daughter's face. April's eyes were big with incredulity.

"Really?"

"Yes. Your Grandma is the original adventurer. She taught me everything I know."

Wow, April mouthed, and I turned back around before April could see my amusement and get offended.

But now we had finally arrived, and whatever adventures were in store were about to begin.

"Can we get out yet?" April asked excitedly from the backseat, as we pulled to a stop.

"Yes, you can get out," I said, as I saw my dad open the front door, then my mother behind him.

"Grandma and Gramps!" Jimmy yelled from his seat. April opened the door, and the two children were out, trudging through snow that was up to their knees.

I watched them make their way through the snow – they looked funny, like two little Eskimos on the arctic tundra. Mom and Dad were grinning big, their faces lit up with pleasure, as they came down the stairs of the porch to scoop them up.

My parents hugged my children with undisguised love, and it warmed my heart. Mama looked over Jimmy's small form, which she held sweetly in her arms, and raised an eyebrow. I waved at her, holding up one finger, *One minute.* Mama nodded, and they all went inside.

A Whisper of Smoke   *Angela Hoke*

I sat in silence for a few minutes, taking in the throngs of people I could see through the window, the reason for all the cars in the driveway and along the road. Since Gran and Pappy had passed away, within a year of each other, Mom and Dad had been having family Christmas parties at their house. Mama's relatives were all there – even Uncle Mutt and Uncle Magoo, and of course Uncle George and Cheryl.

"Are you okay?" Daniel asked, reaching over to squeeze my hand. I squeezed back, grateful, and gave him a small smile.

"What you did was hard, I know. But you did the right thing," he said.

"I know," I replied. It *had* been hard, harder than I'd expected, trying to explain to my two babies how some grown-ups can hurt children, touch them in ways they shouldn't. And that they should never be afraid to tell me or their dad if any grown-up ever touched them in one of those ways. That part was hard, yes. But then I had to give the specific warning, the one that had been denied me and my siblings – the one not to ever be alone with Great Uncle George. And it was that warning that brought back the flood of memories, of missed chances to protect, to save someone else from a damage that maybe could have been avoided. It reminded me of the betrayal I had felt each time my parents believed someone else over their own children, or brought dangerous people into our home and then were too drunk to keep an eye on us, or acted as if nothing was wrong or like you weren't supposed to acknowledge it if it was.

Or when they forgave people for unforgivable acts without even explaining why such a thing should be possible, maybe even understandable.

Angela Hoke   *A Whisper of Smoke*

I wasn't angry anymore. I'd used up all that anger years earlier, and the last of it ground to dust when I realized I had failed Hank in many of the same ways. But I was still saddened by it, and by the childhood I could have had. When I imagined a childhood with a mother as creative and magical as mine could be and a father as sweet and hard-working, minus the booze and the really bad things that happened, my heart hurt because *that* was a childhood of fairy tales. But I couldn't change my childhood experiences now any more than I could have ever changed them in the past – no child can shape his or her own childhood. That is the parents' job.

And now it was my job – mine and Daniel's. It was our job to shape our children's childhood, and I wanted to do that by filling it with wonderful memories and positive experiences. But to do only that, without acknowledging the bad things that could happen, well that seemed irresponsible.

"They've gotten too big for us to watch them every second, we had to tell them," I said, as if to convince myself.

"I know, Susanna. You were right. You did the right thing."

"It's just that I don't want to make the same mistakes that..." My voice caught. I wanted to be the magical mother and for Daniel to be the sweet, hard-working father, without the terrible things. Even so, I had been in agony when trying to decide whether to talk with my young children about unmentionable subjects, knowing that it would destroy a little of their precious innocence. And the looks on their sweet faces, expressions of confusion and then fear, were confirmation of this sad consequence.

"Come here," Daniel said, pulling me into his arms. He kissed my temple, my forehead.

A Whisper of Smoke   *Angela Hoke*

"They'll have a different life," he reassured me, and some part of me knew he was right. We were already choosing a different path for our little ones.

"And you don't mind being with them?" I asked, pulling away and gesturing with a nod towards the rowdy, raucous houseful of people. "Even after knowing our secrets? Even knowing how screwed up we can be?" I persisted, still amazed. I loved them, yes. I couldn't help loving them, because they were my family. But how could he learn to love them, knowing what he knew?

Daniel was quiet for a moment, as if he were thinking about the answer, or carefully choosing his words. "I know there's bad stuff, Susanna. Every family has bad stuff." I gave him a look, and he added, "I know your family's demons may be worse than most. And I'm not naïve enough to leave our kids alone with your family." He looked chagrined.

"The point is," he continued, "we can either be bitter about it, or we can learn to look for the good in people and choose to value that."

He reached over and took my hand, squeezing it.

"And if I know one thing from being with your family, it's that they know how to weather the storms and still stand by each other. That's a gift you got from them, even when you haven't always understood it. And that's how you each were able to survive some pretty painful times."

My eyes blurred with unshed tears, as I thought about some of those painful times and remembered the love of my family, and how it saw me through the darkness, the loss of Calvin. I'd never imagined love like that, the way my family came together for me, snatching me from my free-fall with a net built on the strength of their steadfastness, their constancy.

Angela Hoke   A Whisper of Smoke

I paused. I'd always known that Calvin captured a piece of my soul, and that he'd changed me with his goodness. Not because he was perfect, because he wasn't. But he'd taught me with his faults, as well as his virtues. And I'd realized for years that he had readied me for a life with Daniel. But I hadn't realized that he'd also given me another gift – the gift of showing me how much my family really loved me, and how much I loved them. And Daniel, bless his soul, was just the type of man who would recognize it, and make sure I did too.

It had been there all along, my family's love, hidden in plain sight. I just took a best friend and two great loves to get me to stand still long enough to see it.

Discussion Questions

1. Why do you think Lorelei kisses Calvin after Susanna? What does that say about Susanna's and Lorelei's relationship? How does it ultimately fit or not fit with Lorelei's assessment that Susanna is a natural caretaker, and how does that contrast with Lorelei's personality?

2. Why is Susanna so much more protective of Hank than of Annabelle? What/who is she compensating for?

3. Why do you think Mama forgives Uncle George for what he does to Annabelle? What does that say about her?

4. Why do you think Daddy ultimately forgives, or at least tolerates Uncle George? What does that say about him? Why is Susanna so much more devastated by Daddy's actions than Mama's?

5. Do you think Calvin is as honorable as Susanna thinks he is? Why or why not?

6. Is it fair for Calvin to hint that he'd rather have Susanna in Hawaii with him than Christine? What does that say about what Calvin is going through?

7. What do you think about Mama's actions towards trying to help Susanna get to Hawaii? Are those actions redemptive at all?

Angela Hoke   *A Whisper of Smoke*

8. Are Uncle George's steps to stop being an abuser adequate? Is redemption possible for him?

9. Is it fair that Calvin proclaims his love for Susanna in his last letter? Did that cause her more or less pain? If it were up to her, do you think she would have wanted to know?

10. Does Susanna do the right thing when she finds Hank and Kathleen in the hayloft? Does she overreact? Are her steps to make sure that Hank is "held accountable" sufficient to help break the cycle of abuse?

11. Is Daniel a good match for Susanna? Why or why not? Is she getting married too young?

12. Does Susanna do the right thing when she warns her young children about predators? Should she permit her children to be around Uncle George at all? What if prohibiting contact means that she also misses out on spending time with the rest of her family at special times like holidays?

13. Should Susanna also warn her children about Hank? Does the fact that he was abused automatically make him a potential danger? Why do you think it might be difficult for Susanna to view her brother as a potential danger?

Acknowledgements

This book has been a labor of love for ten years. It explores some questions that plague many families, and which I wanted to better understand. I hope it helps you, as the reader, think through some of these complicated questions as well.

A few people helped me early in the process by reading my first draft. I want to thank my mom, Nancy, for giving me her perspective as a person who grew up in Louisville in the 1960s. I want to thank my friend Bill for helping me gain perspective and correct some of the inaccuracies regarding Calvin's deployment and tour in Vietnam. Any remaining mistakes are entirely mine. And I want to thank my friend Beth for evaluating my characters and the story and giving me honest feedback that was critical to the evolution of my book. My second draft also had a great group of readers – namely, my sister-in-law, Kelly, and the members of the Between the Covers Book Club who graciously read my manuscript as its selection one month – thanks to Brenda K., Brenda W., Ann, Michelle, Doreen, Rebecca, Tonia and Lalia (the members at that time). Finally, I want to thank Terri and Shari for reading my book in its near final stage and giving me the encouragement to finish it.

While all of those acknowledgements are important, the most important is to God – I am so thankful for the desire he placed in me as well as whatever amount of talent I may or may not have. I hope that, by using the gifts He gave me, I've brought a blessing to someone's life.

Angela Hoke   *A Whisper of Smoke*

Angela Hoke

About the Author

Angela has worked for nineteen years in accounting, writing in her spare time. She began writing at the age of eight, when she produced a neighborhood newspaper, until an expose written based on sketchy facts shut her down for good. Her short story, *The Ceremony* (inspired by a scene in this book), was a finalist in the 2009 New Millennium writing contest, and she studied craft at the Algonkian Writers' Conference. She lives in Nashville, TN with her son, one tiny dog and a bob-tailed cat.

Made in the USA
San Bernardino, CA
16 January 2014